CW00469327

Night Night Necropolis

Katherine Black

Best Book Editions

BBE Best Book Editions

1 3 5 7 9 10 8 6 4 2

Copyright © Katherine Black, 2023

The right of Katherine Black to be identified as the author of this Work has been asserted by her in accordance with the Copyright, Designs and Patents Act 1988

All rights reserved

First published in 2023 by Best Book Editions, bestbookeditors.com

Paperback ISBN 9798378282982

This publication may not be used, reproduced, stored or transmitted in any way, in whole or in part, without the express written permission of the author. Nor may it be otherwise circulated in any form of binding or cover other than that in which it has been published and without a similar condition imposed on subsequent users or purchasers

All characters in this publication are fictitious, and any similarity to real persons, alive or dead, is coincidental

Cover by Best Book Editions

A CIP catalogue record of this book is available from the British Library

Thank you to Cheryl Jaclin Isaac for reading this through and making me believe it was worthwhile before publication.
And, as always, to Peter Gillespie-Merrigan for all his help and another fantastic cover. You only get one best friend.

Contents

Chapter One

H omicide detective Silas Nash wondered how often he'd opened a task force briefing with the words, 'Listen up, team.' And after forty years on the force, it still gave him a surge of adrenaline.

He had tried out his new title to the amusement of the old man in the mirror. He had the same number of stripes on his dress-uniform lapel and the same letters in front of his name, although he'd still be working in his civies. His promotion wasn't so much a move up as a side shuffle into the branch of policing every green rookie wants to attain. It gave him a better pay grade, but he was sad that Barrow, in the arse-end of England, even needed a homicide task force. They never had before. Twelve years ago, the horrific case of Poppi Worthington rocked a nation. It sickened everybody that a child could be neglected and abused right under the authority's nose. The case had slipped through the cracks until it was too late. It was agreed in the gravitas of the town hall building, built in 1877, that it should never happen again.

Barrow-in-Furness was a town with potential on the southern tip of the picturesque Lake District. Nash's blue-collar ship-building town is surrounded on three sides by the turbulent and often aggressive Atlantic Ocean. Barrow wasn't accustomed to nurturing murderers until the last few years—and now they needed a homicide division.

Tag. DCI Nash is It.

His beat extended as far as the county border in all directions, but even so, they'd never needed it before.

Nash killed the overhead lights and turned the spotlight to face his whiteboard. He had the room's attention.

'Our first official case. Let's nail this fast and earn our stripes.' Nash turned his back on the team and wrote neat capital letters on the whiteboard. His hand moved across the smooth surface as he uploaded the intel from his brain to his fingers, and despite the speed, when he drew lines, they were straight, and his writing was always concise and legible.

He'd separated the board into two-thirds on the left and one on the right. In the right segment, he attached a map and stuck a red-capped magnetic pin over Dane Avenue, just before the T-Junction with Dalton Lane.

'Crime Scene: 98 Dane Avenue. The victim is to be confirmed, but we believe it's Mrs Alma Cullen. Aged 64. Lives alone since her husband passed away after a short illness last year. The probable cause is blunt force trauma, to be confirmed by Bill Robinson at autopsy, but it was pretty conclusive at the scene. The murder weapon is missing but is likely to be the round end of a household claw hammer or similar. No obvious motive.'

Nash pinned several photographs of the victim and heard his team's reaction. Nobody liked to see an old lady who had been brutally attacked and humiliated. There was something tragic and heart-wrenching about an old person with a black eye. It brought out the protector in every good citizen. But Mrs Cullen's black eye extended across her entire body. The fact that the old lady in question was a year younger than Nash stuck in his craw. He turned to face his team. 'Questions?'

'Next of kin, sir?' Bowes said. Bowes and Lawson made up the junior end of the division. They'd worked with Nash before, and although green and prone to speaking out of turn, they were good men. He'd hand-selected his team.

'That's a sensible question. Two daughters: Isabel and Charlotte—they are both married. The younger one, Charlotte lives in Canada and hasn't returned for two years. Missed her father's funeral. She's out of the picture, but I'd like to know why she didn't come home for that.' Nash pointed. 'Isabel lives on Levens Close in the Tantabank area of Dalton. She and her husband are both working and have a couple of kids. No apparent difficulties or alarm bells, but we'll be looking into both girls' relationships with the victim, and we'll have a poke around in their finances.'

Nash noticed DI Molly Brown's sour expression when she'd opened her mouth to get in first, but Bowes had beaten her to the first question. She didn't like that. Nash smiled. He had to work hard at not thinking of Molly like a favourite niece. They'd been through a lot together. His boss, Bronwyn Lewis, was sitting in on the brief, and Nash knew Brown would want to be seen. She made sure she got in next. 'It's a quiet area. Was it a break-in? Burglary gone wrong?'

'It looks that way, yes. A small glass panel in the back door was broken so the perp could get their hand in and unlock the door.' Nash put up a photo of the door on the board. 'The victim was found in her armchair and was attacked from behind. We don't know if he spoke to her before he hit her. Her home help—do they still call them that?—found her when she went in at nine AM to clean the house. At this point, we're making no assumptions about the staging.

'Renshaw, I want you in the office on the donkey run today. All the usual. Do the legals. See what's what. Find out about any probate or Power of Attorney. Get out, meet the victim's solicitor, and see how chatty he is. Apply for a release of records from the court, the same with bank accounts and phone records. Dig out marriage docs and birth certificates. A will would be great if you could pin it down. I'd be surprised if this one died intestate. Then let's find out who Alma Cullen was. Hit the socials and dig around on Facebook. Get a list of friends and check out web pages and hobbies. Any arguments or falling outs, you know the score. By the time we get back, I want to know how she liked her steak cooked, her favourite song—and who wanted to hit her over the head with a blunt instrument.'

'Sir,' Renshaw said. 'I'd prefer to be in the field, sir.' He glared at Molly Brown.

'I'm sure you would, Renshaw. However, I want Brown with me. After looking over the crime scene, I've got a lead on a friend of Mrs Cullen's that we want to talk to. Lady of a certain age, I've got a feeling she might open up better to Brown. That's if we get warm and fluffy Molly, not the Bengali tiger. If she has the interviewee in a headlock in the first three minutes, we've lost our window. So, Brown. In case you didn't catch that. You're with me.'

Brown cast a look at Bronwyn Lewis before replying. 'You can't say things like that anymore. I could put in a formal against you for that, sir.'

4

'What? For saying you're with me?'

'No. For calling me a tiger, sir.'

'Meow,' Bowes said.

'If that's your roar, you'd better keep out of the jungle.'

Bowes went red, and shut his mouth.

Nash said, 'Good to have you keeping me on my twinkle toes, Brown. Now. Are we going to solve a murder, or do you want to have me hauled over the coals for being a misogynistic old bastard, which we've already agreed, I am, and you have to live with that?' He winked at her to win her over.

'Actually, that isn't true, sir. I don't have to live with it. I keep asking that you treat me the same as the men.'

'And I keep trying, but you smell of perfume and all that good stuff. However, in the interests of equality, you're driving, and make sure you get the car with heated seats. Bowes, Lawson, you're with Renshaw.'

'Sir,' said the two officers.

'Thank you, team. Let's kick a killer in the coccyx.' Nash made a sharp exit before Brown could say anything else. He could see she wasn't done. He'd be in for an earful in the car. DI Brown was a strong team member. If he had to admit it, he liked her a lot, but she was a royal pain in the arse. She was strong and ambitious and didn't always look between the cracks of a case. He put a lot of time into teaching her the between-the-lines part of police work that you can't learn on courses, and he liked to tease her and bring her down to earth. But after winding her up, he'd have to spend the rest of the day appeasing her. And by the end of it, he'd wonder if getting a laugh out of his team at her expense was worth it. Molly Brown would have been efficient in the office and would probably have dug more information out of the computer than Sergeant Renshaw and the two PCs put together, but she had a way with people, and that's what he needed today.

Molly Brown wanted his job when he retired, and he didn't have a problem with that. She'd probably get it—and on merit too. She was a fine officer, but, given a choice, he'd still prefer to spend the next eight hours stuck in a car with Renshaw talking about football and cars.

DCS Bronwyn Lewis pulled him to one side before she went back to her office. 'Lay off Brown, Silas. Don't make me have to talk to you in an official capacity.'

Nash laughed. 'She loves it.'

'Seriously?'

'It's the way we banter. How many times has she reported me for misconduct or sexist piggery—or just for being an arsehole?'

'Never.'

'Exactly. But she threatens it twenty times a day. To her, it's like saying, "Do you want a brew?" And me saying, 'Yeah.'

'And what if I find you offensive?'

'You won't.'

'What if I already do?'

'You don't.'

Lewis walked away and shot him a parting remark over her shoulder. 'Bring me back a murderer, Nash.'

'You got it, boss.'

Lewis would attend to her job and leave him to run his unit. She liked to be included in every case's first and last briefing, and he admired that. Not many bosses bothered. They'd worked together for fifteen years, and he'd watched her rise from being a terrible police constable to one of the county's two highest-ranking officers.

The day she'd walked into the station fresh out of training and as shy as an arctic fox, Nash remembered looking at her and wanting to run a book on how many days she'd last before she quit. In the first few weeks, he'd seen her wanting to cry on a daily basis, but she never did. He'd only ever seen her in tears once, and that was the day she'd had her old family dog euthanised and then came to work without saying a word to anybody until she broke down. She was on the town beat that day, and a drunk young upstart had knocked her police cap off.

The word was that she'd thrown him to the pavement and was on the point of breaking his arm before you could blink. He'd only tipped her cap off her head, and her overreaction was phenomenal. The humiliation the idiot boy caused her was the tipping point that opened the floodgates to her grief, but once they opened, she'd cried for an hour. The youth had a grazed face and shouted police brutality until he'd puked, sobered and was mortified by his behaviour and full of apologies. Lewis was raked over the coals, and she'd narrowly avoided an official warning on her record because the lad refused to press charges. The story had a lovely ending when the youth left flowers at the front desk for her the next day after one of the arresting officers let slip that she'd lost her dog. That was the only time he'd seen Lewis cry. As for Brown—that woman was made of steel.

DI Molly Brown was waiting for him in the car. Two cups of coffee were in the dual holders, and she handed him a bacon butty from a paper bag. She'd already eaten hers and started the car. 'Might as well start as we mean to go on, but having the Bob-In Café virtually next door is too convenient.'

'I'll bring you some porridge tomorrow. Much better for you. Keeps you regular.'

'Tell me you didn't just say that. I misheard you, right?'

'Good to be back on the road with you, Brown.'

She grinned, pulled into the flow of traffic, and swore when somebody cut her up. 'What are we looking for?'

'Nothing specific. We're looking for a feeling. The Scenes of Crime team understand hard evidence when they see it. But we're looking for what isn't there as much as what is. Anything that feels wrong or out of place. We're after that item that poses a question or that we can ask questions about.'

'Gotcha.'

'You understand?'

'No. Not in the least. You keep talking in riddles, sir, and, I'll look for our killer.'

Nash laughed. He had a great team and a good rapport with them. He couldn't abide pomp and ceremony. When they were within public earshot, they had to call him sir, but alone in the field or in the office, they often called him Nash. He liked it that way. He invited opinions and ideas. His brain was the oldest on the team, and while he considered it to be as sharp as a hunting blade, he wasn't great with pop culture. The younger members of the team had a lot to offer that he was clueless about. He hoped they'd all say he was a good boss if asked.

They pulled up at the victim's house.

Chapter Two

The constable outside Mrs Cullen's home had done a good job of clearing the rubberneckers. Mrs Cullen had been taken away, and that's the time when the ghouls usually packed up their deck chairs and flasks of tea and went home in time for the news to see if they were in the crowd. The single strand of crime scene tape blowing in the wind seemed superfluous. An old lady had been knocked on the head. So what? The show was over.

It was one of the few houses at this end of the street that wasn't a bungalow. It was neat, with well-kept flowerbeds and a tidy lawn. The double garage doors were painted dark blue, and a small gate beside the garage led to the back of the house. The bolt was closed, but it had no lock. Nash and Brown suited up in white protective clothing and blue caps. They went through the gate and opened the rear door. Bracing themselves, they prepared for what waited inside. Tracing the killer's steps put Nash inside his head.

'It would have been evening. Already dark. He wouldn't risk turning a light on but may have used a torch. There's just enough light from the streetlamp on the corner to stop him from bumping into things. He'd have been able to make out the table and two chairs in the middle of the room. I don't think he intended to kill her, so I doubt he brought the weapon with him. Not many old ladies have a claw hammer lying around in the kitchens, do they, Brown?'

'Probably not.'

With his gloved finger, Nash turned on the light. 'Yes. He used a torch. Our killer heard the television from the other room.' Nash read the scene and spoke his process out loud as he touched the light switch again to ground his thoughts and rubbed his hand along the unit underneath. 'There are no fingerprints in the dusting powder. Did he have gloves on? Possibly not. But he was taking no chances.' Nash dragged the sleeve of his suit over his hand. 'He pulled his sleeve down to turn the light on. A man wouldn't do that. A woman, younger. Blunt force, strength. Maybe, though. Maybe a woman. He wanted to talk, that's all. Somebody she knew. What did you want? Money? No. "I'm going to smash your face in." Anger. A lot of anger. Jealousy. Something to do with a man—or money. More likely to be money. Brown, I think this was a woman.'

'That's a hell of a lot of assumption.'

'No, it's profiling, and at this stage, it's all we've got. Look at that utensil holder. What's missing?'

'Nothing as far as I can see.'

'Exactly. I'd have expected him—we'll stick with him for now, but I'm still leaning towards it being a female—to go for the rolling pin, but it's still there. It's to hand, and he wouldn't have had to risk opening any drawers and making a noise. I know what the murder weapon was. Look around again and tell me what isn't here. It's quite dark, remember.'

'I don't know.'

'Look, Molly. You have to learn to see what there isn't as well as what is. Something's missing from this room. What is it?'

'I don't know. Two more chairs?'

'It's a two-seater table. Look again.'

He watched her impatience. 'Can you stop playing games and just tell me?'

'I can, and I will, but it means that you've learned nothing. You'll tread water if you lean too much on other people to make the calls. You're ambitious, and that makes you efficient—but a machine is efficient. You have to feel the job. That's what you have to learn if you're going to take over from me. Be observant.'

'I don't see it. What am I missing?'

'See the big ceramic honey pot with Kos written on it?'

'Yes?'

'Describe what's next to it.'

Brown huffed and made it clear to Nash that she was fed up with the lesson. 'A white dish.'

'Made of? SOCO's Finished. Go and touch it.'

'I don't have to. I can see from here that it's marble.'

'Touch it. Feel the scene and let it talk to you.'

'God's sake.' Brown picked the dish up and ran her hands over it. 'It's heavy, with much more weight than expected. White marble with a blueish vein running through it.' She put her fingers inside and then held them to her nose. 'There's a powdery residue in the bottom, not much, just a trace, and when you rub it between your fingers, it leaves an oily taint. It smells like an old lady's cupboard.'

'Excellent. Well done. See how much more you gave me than just a dish?'

'You'd think she'd have washed it, wouldn't you?' Brown said.

'Two more questions before we move on. What's the dish's purpose, and what's missing?'

Brown's smile from receiving praise faded. 'One of those things you crush herbs in.'

'When was the last time you made Bolognese?'

She laughed. 'You're messing with me, right? Do I look like Gordon Ramsey?'

Nash shook his head. 'Give me strength. I wonder how you young people survive. Do you know that an egg comes from a hen's arse? It's a pestle and mortar, and the pestle is missing.' He shouted to the SOCO team. 'Has anybody found a pestle?' He already knew the answer.

They left the kitchen and moved into the hall. There were coats and scarves on hooks by the front door. A blue glass vase was on a shelf built into the wall with wilting flowers. 'Brown, throw those flowers out and wash the vase, please.'

'What am I, the hired help?'

'Don't bother. I'll do it myself. The house is being opened to her daughters today. Would a vase of dying flowers be the first thing you'd want to see?' He moved past her with the vase and emptied the flowers into the wheelie bin in the garden. He put the vase by the sink to soak. 'It smells. I hate the smell of old flowers—and honeysuckle. Can't abide the stuff. See? that's something else you need to learn, Brown.' She'd followed him into the kitchen and watched him drying his hands on a sheet of kitchen roll that he pulled from a dispenser on the wall. Brown rolled her eyes and went back to her phone.

'One of the most important things to remember is that you must stop seeing the victim as a body and remember them as a person. Our clients live on in their families, and we have to do what we can to honour that. Our role is to help the loved ones left behind find peace. The perps are just the detritus we're left with.'

'Another lecture?'

'Never touch anything in a scene that hasn't been signed off, but once it's been given clearance, be kind to the dead, Molly.'

'Kind? That's above my pay grade, sir.' She grinned at Nash. 'Hah.' She held her phone out towards him. 'I've been looking at pestles and mortars online, but they're normally smaller than this, aren't they?'

'See what you can find if you look? From the size of the mortar, we can see it's industrial. Do you remember her late husband's occupation? I mentioned it in the briefing.'

'He was a chef.'

'Well remembered. From the size of the mortar, we can deduce that the pestle was a long-handled heavy piece of kit. Now, do you understand about looking for what's missing? We have our murder weapon.'

'Every day's a school day.'

'Make at least one Bolognese before you die, Brown. I dread the thought that you lot are going to be running the country in ten years' time.'

'My lot, sir?'

'Bloody yuppie thirty-something career women.'

'Nobody has used the word yuppy in the last thirty years, Nash.'

'Get over it, Brown. Right. Living room. Prepare yourself. They said there's a lot of blood.'

'Did you hear that Hayley Mooney, that tenant of Max Jones, has signed up for the cleaning crew? When they're done, we could recommend them to the daughters for a deep clean.'

'Good idea. I've got their card. I'll have a word.'

'How are Hayley's family doing?' Brown asked.

'They're fine. The kids are in after-school clubs, and I heard they planted a tree in the garden to commemorate Max. He'd have loved that.

'Anyway, let's get this over with, and we'll go next door and see the neighbour. A good friend, apparently, who often popped in for tea. Lawson gave us the heads up that she likes to talk,' Nash said. He opened the living room door, and they went in. Brown did as Nash had instructed her many times. She used her brain and her eyes before opening her mouth. Nash gave her a minute before speaking. 'Read the room.'

'Pretty much as expected. A large blood stain on the rug and spatter on the wall, indicating that the killer hit her from behind and on the left. There are three distinct arcs. I think the second, third and fourth blows caused these.' She traced the line of the arcs with her finger. 'The first shattered the skull, and from the fifth, the blood didn't spray as much, and that's where we get these lower-level spatters. I'm picturing him hitting her with the pestle.'

'Good. Describe him.' Nash wanted to see if she remembered him saying he thought the murderer was female.

'I can't describe him from a blood stain. Not too tall, and he hit her from the left. I don't know any more than that.'

14

'Draw on what you see and what we already know. Is he right-handed? Look at the wall and go back to the blood patterning. The arterial gushers can't give us anything. That was down to the victims' blood pressure, and the fountains are determined by that. But look at the lower bloodstains. The perp wasn't very tall, five-five, five-seven at the most. He—and I use the word loosely—tired after half a dozen blows, but there was bloodlust and rage, so he carried on hitting her—but without much force. The perp isn't very fit. They're right-handed, and I'd say middle-aged, and I'm going to hang my hat on this one. It's a woman,' Nash said.

'You can tell all that from the blood?'

'We'll know more when the reports are in. SOCO found a fibre on the chair that doesn't belong to the victim and a single cat hair. The victim doesn't have a cat. I'm guessing the fibre will prove to be wool from a coat. It's grey. Probably tweed. Not cheap, and most middle-aged women wear nylon these days. I'm putting our perp in the mid-fifties to sixties bracket and Middle class. Mrs Cullen had tea with somebody before she died. We've yet to establish if that was the lady next door. However, I'm guessing it was our killer. I think they talked, and she did sit down for tea—but she didn't touch it. The full one is still there with milk scud on the top. There are two side plates, but only the victim used hers and left cake crumbs. The rest of the cake was on the coffee table.'

'No DNA on the tea mug, then?'

'No, but the perp wasn't thinking about that. She's watching her weight.'

'You assume a heck of a lot.'

'You start with an idea, then work on proving or disproving it. Always move and adapt. Never be so stuck in your pet theory that you can't come away from it and see something else. Zebra.'

'What?'

'The zebra theory. If you hear hoofbeats outside your window, would you assume it was a zebra?'

'Not beyond the realms of possibility, Confucius. I live half a mile from South Lakes Animal Park, and their beasts are always escaping. The number of times there's been escaped lemurs on Queen Street is ridiculous. And once, Angus, their highland cow, got out, and don't get me started on that poor white rhino they shot on the bypass. So, yes, it could well be a zebra.'

'Okay, smart arse. When you hear hoofs, think horse, not zebra. The phrase still stands, for most of us mere mortals living in urban England, hoofs on the street would belong to a horse and very rarely a zebra.'

Chapter Three

C onnie loved Jeff, but like most men, he liked to be in the know. She went into battle with him because, this time, she knew she was right. 'You're wrong.' But he knew everything about everything, so she'd go in strong and then back down. He'd win. It was a blatant waste of breath.

Jeff said, 'I've just read it on my phone this minute. I'm telling you. Toiletries go in hand luggage.'

And there it was. Ding ding. Two seconds in, and he'd played his winning card right off the deck—bang—his irrefutable proof that he was right because he'd read it. That's what made him so clever. He read a lot of things.

And, by the same token, it's what made Connie dumb. Because her next line should have been, 'Show me so I can read it for myself,' but it wasn't. 'That doesn't make sense. If there's a terrorist attack, the bad guys are going to put stuff in the bottles in hand luggage, aren't they? Not in their cases. They need to whip it out and spread the deadly contagion about. Ergo—therefore,' yes, she really did use the word ergo. Twit. 'Ergo, what you've just said doesn't make any sense whatsoever.'

'I'm telling you, I read it half an hour ago.'

'Okay, whatever. What do I know?'

The big guy in the uniform looked smug but nowhere near as smug as Connie. 'Didn't you read the guidelines, sir? You can't bring that through here. We're going to have to confiscate it.'

'I told you. I bloody told you so. And by the way, did I say I told you?' There was nothing humble about her victory despite losing two expensive bottles of coconut sun lotion, the pump-action stuff for easy application. She'd also lost a bottle of shampoo and conditioner, a new tube of toothpaste, a bottle of shower gel and three deodorants, two female and one male. Her feet floated through the X-ray machine that pinged like a winning slot machine, which meant a female security officer had to pat her down. 'I told him, but he wouldn't listen,' she said to the bored guard who'd heard it all before. She caught the eye of a man a few plastic trays down, and he smiled. Yeah, I bet you stored your bottles in the right place, didn't you, mate? she thought.

She didn't win often, so she was taking this one to the moon. She asked the guard what happened to the confiscated items. Were they given to homeless charities?

'No. We can't do anything with them in case they've been contaminated. They just get thrown away.'

Connie bet they got their pickings, though. She considered voicing it, but it wouldn't do any good. She was angry, but not because their things had been taken. They deserved that. It was the skips full of

18

thousands of pounds worth of products a day, and it didn't stop at toiletries. There were drinks too. It could do so much good for people that couldn't afford a foreign holiday and really needed them.

She pondered her disease. Was it a disease or a condition? She wasn't sure. Jeff would know because he knew everything, but she didn't feel like asking him. She wanted to kill him, but they were going on holiday, so that would have to wait.

Tourette's. Effing Tourette's syndrome. And not the fun kind where you get to call random strangers a wanker and tell them they look like a puppy drowner, either. At fifty years old, Connie had been diagnosed with a boring brain condition Called Trigeminal Neuralgia—TN-type 1—that fit snugly into the Tourette's syndrome family. She didn't swear at people—well, not often, and never unintentionally—but she did have facial tics. It was caused by her trigeminal nerve pressing against the primary blood vessel in her brain. The predominant symptom was a planet load of agony. Without medication, the pain was off the scale, and one NHS source online said it was the most agony a human being could endure.

Wow.

'Beg to differ,' Connie said to nobody in particular at the time. 'I've been through childbirth, and that was way worse.'

The good news was that Connie had tamed the beast with the help of some awful medication. She had the pain under control and some of the worst tic symptoms. Jeff, her partner, eight years younger and a handsome man in his prime, said going out with her in public was like being out with a circus act. She had to take that one. They used humour to get through most of life's bad situations. Like old age and not being able to read the small print.

The worst thing about the medication was that it caused some kind of chemical reaction that stopped food from turning to energy, yada, yada. The result was that people generally put on two stones in the first six months. She was no exception. Here, lady, have a condition. And, have twenty kilos to go with it. She'd cut down on food, used a treadmill and did a bit of yoga to get ready for the holiday, but all it had done was increase her fitness, which was no bad thing. She'd take that, too, but this was a no-bikini holiday. She saw Jeff eyeing up pretty young women in the airport, like any man—every man. She couldn't deny him that pleasure. The jealousy stabbed deep, and a bright overhead light set off her TN. She did a head-twerk dance with her ticking and came across like a complete idiot.

They got through security, did all the official stuff, and while she doubted the wisdom of trusting Jeff with her passport and boarding pass, he talked about getting coffee. But first, he had to find the smoking area. Of course, he did. That was something else she could be smug about. She'd quit ten months earlier.

She found a table and sat with the bags while he went for a smoke. She was the Cosmopolitan traveller as she opened her tablet on the Formica table and read from her Kindle. She'd read a sentence, get distracted, and look at the other travellers around the lounge. She wondered who was on the same flight and going to Kos. Some of them might even be in the same resort. She decided which she'd like to meet by the sun loungers and which would be the Brits from hell.

'Excuse me. Are these yours?'

It was the man from the security queue. She smiled, more because of her absent dopey boyfriend than the man who'd bent to pick up Jeff's glasses. However, despite the wedding ring, this one was a definite yes in sun lounger roulette.

They needed this holiday. It was a celebration of sorts because Jeff had come good on some investments and decided to take time out of work. He owned a furniture company, and he had a good team in place to run it. After six years together, their relationship would do no harm from taking a boot in the romance department.

He came back looking sexy with a cup of coffee in each hand. She always ordered Latte, and he always reminded her it was wrong. She'd tell him she knew which coffee she liked, and she'd remember she preferred cappuccino when the latte came. Damn him.

She wasn't thinking about the temperature when she noticed how hot he looked. He was gorgeous today, and she felt a pang of love for him, making her smile a beamer—not least because he was carrying coffee. This was their first holiday since meeting six years ago, and it would be amazing.

'I'm going to have a look in WH Smiths,' Connie said.

'Hang on. I'll come with you. I want a book.'

'No. Stay with the bags. It saves dragging them with us. You can go when I come back.'

He looked hurt. She didn't know why he did that. Sometimes she wanted five minutes to do her own thing. He saw it as rejection.

She remembered a holiday with a previous boyfriend. They'd arrived at a B&B in Prague at midnight. They were in the middle of nowhere, hadn't eaten much since leaving the house at ten that morning, fourteen hours earlier, and there was nowhere to get anything to eat. It was a miserable start to their holiday.

Connie wanted to pick up sandwiches for later. It was only a tiny thing, but she'd like to surprise him. Ever the pragmatist, she'd been sensible. He'd wanted to go the whole hog and order extra legroom, in-flight meals and headphones. She'd put her foot down and said they'd be a ridiculous price, and they'd get a sandwich once they were through security.

She was making her selection when she saw him beside her. It irritated her.

'What are you doing, Connie?'

'Riding an elephant.'

'Okay, stroppy. But we don't need sandwiches. We're all-inclusive, and we can find something to eat when we get there. Come on, help me choose a book.'

He'd dismissed her good deed. And she wasn't about to go hungry or be controlled. 'I'm buying some food. It's what I want to do, please go and buy your book and I'll see you back at the table.' He flashed that hurt look again. Sod him and the horse he rode in on. The joy had gone out of her shopping.

They got back to the lounge and chose a new table. Theirs, the one that belonged to them, had been taken. She tutted and went to grab their bags from beside somebody's legs. Jeff's bag was tucked well underneath, and the woman was using it as a footstool. Connie's holdall had been on the outside, with *been* being the operative word. She could only see one piece of hand luggage and panicked.

'Excuse me, do you mind if I look under your table, please? Those are our bags.'

'You shouldn't leave them unattended,' the man said.

Connie pulled out Jeff's holdall. She pushed it towards him and went back in to search the floor between the couple's legs. Then the seats next to them.

'I'm sorry, is there another bag, please? Mine's missing.'

'Shouldn't have left it alone,' the man said again. Connie wanted to punch him.

Jeff moved her to the side and went on the attack. 'You must have seen it. I only left them for a moment to see what my wife was doing in Smiths. It was right here.'

'I haven't seen nothing, mate.'

'I don't suppose you passed your English exam either?' Jeff said.

'You shouldn't have left them unattended,' the woman said. They were harping on a theme and seemed to have a shared single-celled brain.

'Has anybody else been near the table while you've been sitting here? In our places, by the way, when you could see the table was taken.'

While he spoke, a security officer appeared beside them. 'Is everything okay here?'

'He says we've nicked his bag,' the man said.

'We haven't even seen it, and said he shouldn't have left it unattended,' the woman backed him up.

'Is this true, sir?'

Connie spoke before Jeff got in first. 'Thank goodness you're here. One of our bags has gone missing. We didn't actually accuse these people of taking it.'

'Good as,' the man said.

'These people? What do you mean, these people? Who're you calling these people? Do you think you're better than me, you snotty cow?' the woman said. Her voice was a screech, and Connie wanted to punch her too.

'Can you come with me, please?' The officer led him away from the heated discussion and dropped Jeff's arm when he saw that he would follow without complaint.

'Yeah, and just watch who you're accusing next time,' the horrible man shouted after them.

'You go with the guard, and I'll have a look around to see if I can see anybody with my bag.' Connie was walking away when the guard stopped her. 'Madam, I need you and your husband to come with me.'

'But if he's in departures, he must still be here. No gates have been opened in the last ten minutes. I can find him.'

'We'll deal with it by following the correct procedure. You shouldn't have left your bag unattended. It's dangerous.' Connie glared at Jeff, who had the good grace to look sheepish but still had to have a dig.

'You should never have gone for that sandwich.'

'I knew this would be my fault.'

The guard led them into a control room with a wall made up of a bank of cameras. There were more monitors on computer desks around the room. 'Davey, zoom in on the food court.' The guard pointed to their table. 'Here, make it bigger, and go back five minutes.'

They crowded around the screen, and Connie squirmed as the camera zoomed in on them, holding hands at the table and looking very much in love. She took her purse out, put her tablet back in her bag, and got up. She trailed a hand over Jeff's shoulder as she walked away. The camera showed her going into Smith's and Jeff watching her.'

Three minutes later, Jeff left the table and followed Connie, and immediately, the couple they'd had the run-in with shuffled into opposite sides of the table. They buried their heads in their phones, and the only movement apart from scrolling thumbs was the man's head going back as he laughed at something on his screen. 'Ignorant bitch,' Connie said as they watched the woman lift her foot and put it on Jeff's bag.

A man walked past the table. Then a family with three children. The middle child was having a tantrum, and the parents were ignoring him. The next people to pass were a group of ten people, four adults and the rest were a rabble of kids ranging from about ten to late teen years. They were in high spirits, and it was clear from their pushing and shoving that they were rowdy. 'This is it. Got them,' Jeff said. They leaned closer to the monitors. Connie's bag was still there. It was on the floor, leaning against the table leg and facing inwards. She was glad she'd taken her purse with her cards and ID. The family were level with the table when somebody passed them on the inside, a woman in her mid to late twenties. She was moving faster than the group. The boys all wore tracksuits, and, with the exception of the youngest child, the girls were indistinguishable from the boys. The little one was female and was wearing a pretty Disney dress with purple ankle boots. Her white jacket offset the smoky melded quartz colour of her skin, and as she walked, ignored by the adults, the child of about six chatted to herself.

The crowd of people on the walkway was condensed, and their view of the table was obscured for a second. Nobody stopped or spoke to the couple, engrossed in their phones, and the social warriors didn't look up or acknowledge them.

And that was all it took, that one second of smoke-screen activity. When the family moved on, Connie's bag was gone.

Chapter Four

'There. Look,' she shouted. They've stolen it. It's one of them.' Connie concentrated on the teenagers in the group, and her gaze raked over their hands before they walked off camera.

'I think not,' said the guard as they watched the large group taking the escalator down to the shop's level. He pressed a couple of buttons on the keyboard and zoomed in on a camera showing the corridor outside the ladies' restroom. During a lull in passenger activity, it was empty.

'There's nobody there.'

'Smoke and mirrors, luv. There will be.' A middle-aged couple came into view, and the lady went into the restroom, leaving the man standing awkwardly outside with their bags.

'We're wasting time, and my tablet and earbuds are in that bag. Let me out to go and look for it, please.'

'Here we are.'

Connie turned back to the monitor. The woman they'd had a brief glimpse of came around the corner, walking fast.

'It's her,' Jeff said, 'and she's got our belongings.' They watched her disappear into the toilet block.' The guard held his hand up for them to wait. And less than two minutes later, the woman came out without Connie's bag. She had her own bulging canvass gym sack thrown over her shoulder.

The guard thumbed his walkie-talkie. 'My guards are already there waiting for her. Target in position. Go. She's just left the Ladies' bathroom.' Two guards appeared from a room along the corridor from the restroom and moved at speed into the block.

He thumbed his device again to alert the rest of the security team. 'All guards, please look for a woman mid to late twenties with brown hair in a ponytail. She's wearing black trousers with white trainers and a long navy-blue jumper. And she's carrying a waxed tan canvas and leather holdall with black writing. The young woman may be travelling with a companion who she'll pass the stolen goods to. Please apprehend all passengers in her party. Over.'

'Is that it? Do we just sit here waiting? Our flight will be called soon,' Jeff said.

'If you hadn't walked away from our things in the first place, we'd be on our second vodka in the bar.'

'Don't start. Christ, I've got the message. Enough people have told me.'

Connie turned to the security manager. 'What if she hasn't hidden my bag somewhere?'

'She won't have. I can guarantee that. I've got a guard bringing most of your things here now. I'll need you to go through them carefully and tell me what's missing.'

'What do you mean she won't have stashed it?'

'I would lay money on your belongings being thrown on the floor in one of the toilet cubicles. I hope, for all our sakes, it was a clean one. We see it every day, and it isn't even an organised crime situation. Logic and common sense could prevent it from happening.'

'I don't understand.'

'Somebody leaves their valuables unattended, despite warnings everywhere asking people not to.' He cast a look at Jeff, who raised his hands in supplication, and the guard gave him a smile. 'It's okay, Mr Pearson, you aren't the first, and you won't be the last—not even today.' He smiled at Jeff. 'Somebody walks past and sees the bag unattended.'

'But there were people at our table when she went past,' Jeff said.

'She'll have been watching. She probably didn't even intend to steal anything today—but to a certain type of person, it's like a beacon calling to them. I'd guess that she's a big friend of long pockets when she goes to the supermarket. She took the bag, but what was she going to do next? She can't walk around with it. What would you do?'

Connie laughed, 'I don't know. I'm not a thief.'

'She takes the bag to the privacy of a lockable toilet cubicle, the one place in the airport where there are no cameras. She has to move fast, so she opens it and discards what she doesn't want on the floor. Anything of value or that she takes a shine to goes into her bag. Sometimes they zip the luggage back up. Most of the time, they don't and leave stuff lying on the toilet floor. Sometimes they have a partner working with them to pass the stuff to, as if that's going to make a difference, and often, it's just an opportune split-second decision that they make acting on impulse. It's a fast job, but these people are stupid because almost every inch of the airport is covered by CCTV. We have eyes everywhere, and they always get caught.'

'There was a tap on the door, and another guard brought in Connie's bag.' He gave her an apologetic smile as he put it in front of her to go through.

''My tablet and phone are both missing. And my earbuds. Bitch, she's taken my Nike Phoenix hoodie. That's a caramel colour. What's this?' Connie pulled out a green fleece. This isn't mine.'

'She made room in her own bag for your things. I presume you want to press charges.'

'Of course, I do. Who the hell does she think she is?'

Footsteps rattled down the corridor, and they heard a woman shouting as they receded. Her anger at being caught turned to sobs that faded as they went into a room somewhere close by. Connie heard the sound of children crying. 'Please, there's been some kind of mistake.' A man's voice faded into muffled pleading as the door slammed behind them.'

'She had children with her?'

'Often the case,' the manager said.

'What will happen?'

'She'll be interviewed and processed, and then it'll be down to the police. I should imagine if she has prior convictions, it'll go to court.'

'Will they be allowed to fly?'

'What, and have you tearing lumps out of each other on the same flight at thirty thousand feet?' He grinned. 'No. The police will deal with her.

'What about the children?'

'Their father's with them.'

'But their holiday?'

'That's not your problem. Is it?'

Somebody else came in and asked about her belongings. Once she had described them in detail, they were returned to her. Connie was relieved. She was terrified that all this would make them miss their flight. 'Can we go now, please?'

Papers were brought for Connie to sign, saying that everything had been returned undamaged, and she was happy to take them away. 'Come on, let's go.' Jeff was already at the door. 'Thank you very much for everything.' Connie was quiet. 'Come on, Connie,' Jeff said. We can still make the flight.'

'Please don't call the police,' Connie said. 'Don't make the children miss their holiday. I won't say anything to her. I promise.'

'Have you gone mad? She stole your luggage. We're throwing the book at the bitch.'

'I'll throw a book at you in a minute, and it'll be War and no Bloody Peace.' She grinned at Jeff and shoulder-bumped him. 'Please just let her go with a warning. I've got my stuff back, and there's no harm done. I just want to get on with our holiday.'

They thanked the security staff again. The manager assured them that the woman and her family would be allowed to fly on the proviso that there'd be no contact between Connie and Jeff, and the other family on the flight. They'd be re-seated in a different section of the plane. Connie said she had no axe to grind and hoped the woman had learned her lesson. Jeff received another lecture before they left the control room and couldn't get out of there fast enough.

Jeff went to the burger stall and came back with a burger for himself and a tray of Tater-tots for her.

'Thank you, but I said I didn't want anything.'

'I thought you'd like them.' She ate some but regretted them five minutes later when she felt sick. Connie struggled with eating too much, too fast.

She struggled with many things. Her knees ached when she climbed the stairs, and she had trouble kneeling. If she got down, she laboured to get back up again. Slut dropping was a thing of the past. Unless she had a rail to hold onto and did it fast. Down, up, fool the body before it has a chance to react, overbalance and throw you on your backside. It was a blessing that slut dropping wasn't something she was prone to. She'd only done it once on a night out. But that was before TN and before menopause and funny knees that were no laughing matter.

Connie and Jeff had only been together for six years. Both of them were starting again. When they met, the partying and sex were off the scale. They were out until three every time they saw each other. Drinking more in one night than Connie had drunk in six months. And then having sex until dawn while the room played helicopters with her.

'You used to want sex all the time. You weren't tired then,' he'd say.

And she'd feel like a piece of worthless shit again. 'It was easy to keep it up, then. We only saw each other three nights a week for the first few months. I could party like a beast and spend the other four days dying. I'd go to work, hit my bed and wouldn't move until I saw you again.'

She was fat, unattractive and worthless. But this holiday was going to cure all that. They had ten days to be together, no work, no responsibility, and no pressure. Just them, like in the old days, in love and together.

This holiday was everything to her. It wasn't a make-or-break situation, nothing dire like that. They were in love and content—but it was ready for a livener. Content wasn't a word she wanted to get too cosy with, and their love life wasn't what it was in those early days before they moved in together. It was going to be okay now, though. Everything would be fine, and she'd get her mojo back and take it home with her.

He loved her. She believed that. But how could she expect him to want her if she couldn't bear to look at herself? The menopause was a bastard and seemed to hit overnight. Something had to be done.

Her thoughts had taken her to a dark place again. They did that a lot. She scanned the room for distraction and looked at Jeff. She wanted to make this work, and so did he. He wore a blue turtleneck with his dogtooth blazer, and although his face was cracked and lived in, and his belly was more rotund than he'd have liked, he looked happy. And that was attractive. He smiled, and she returned it, hoping that he saw something similar in her. He'd dressed for walking through a departures lounge and being seen. She'd put on clothes for comfort. Black leggings, converse, and a blue jersey top that covered her thighs and all manner of sins.

He returned to his book, and she caught the eye of the man from earlier. He was sitting with a pretty lady across the way from them. She didn't mean to stare and looked away. Connie wondered if pretty was a word to describe a lady well into middle age. Handsome was usually the preferred adjective to describe men, but it suited her better than pretty. She was slim—of course, damn her. Her features were angular, and the lady had a make-up-defined contour for every fleshy pouch Connie had. She was dressed in a green trouser suit and heels. Another

33

traveller dressed for walking down the concourse. Her eyebrows were plucked into an expression that made you wonder what the question was. She was attractive with her hair—pleasantly brown with natural grey streaks—pulled into a loose barrette, but if Connie had to describe her in one word, it would have been cold.

'Ray, are you listening to me?' The woman's clipped tone carried across the eight feet of walkway separating them.

'Sorry?'

'You blanked me. Have you any idea how annoying that is?'

'Sorry.'

'I said when we get back, I want you to work with that landscape gardener we used once before. I want him to create some new features on the east lawn. You're better with the creative side and thinking about these things than I am.'

'East lawn? We have an east lawn? Is that the bit of grass at the side or the average-sized lawn in front of the house? And you expect me to do this when we get back? Jesus, we haven't even left yet. Can't we just enjoy our holiday? I won't be around, then. I told you I'm in Singapore for nine days. The Kwan contract.'

'Sing-a-bloody-pore?'

'I don't know it, darling, but if you hum it, I'll try.'

Connie laughed out loud and covered it by pretending her coffee had gone down the wrong way. Jeff had his back to them, but even he had been distracted enough to give up on his book. He grinned at her and pulled a face.

'My mother was right about you, Raymond Farrell,' the woman said.

She went on to tell the poor man exactly what her mother thought of him. Connie was fascinated, and it brought home to her that everybody has problems to deal with. Jeff leaned over the table so that he didn't share his thoughts with the world.

'Have I told you I love you today?'

'Nope. I don't think so.'

'That lady has just made me realise how much I appreciate you. And you were pretty amazing back there. That big heart of yours is lovely.'

'Funny. Because my mother warned me about you.'

'You don't have a mother.'

'Good point. It must have been your mother, then.'

Chapter Five

N ash knocked on the door of the house a few doors up and saw an opaque figure shuffling towards them.

'Wait a minute now, pet. I'll just get the key. Where've I put it?' Even through the front door, they heard the lady's warm Geordie accent. Nash rubbed his hands, and Brown danced from one foot to the other. The weather was turning, and a cruel wind punched Nash in the centre of his lower back.

'Hello. Come in. Don't be standing out there letting the cold in.' They walked into the hall, and a blast of heat hit them with a slight aroma of old lady. Nash had been through the initial house-to-house reports. Margery Hodges was seventy-six, twelve years older than the victim. There was an age gap, but they were good friends.

'Sit yourselves down, and I'll make you a cup of tea. You look as though you could do with it. Tea or coffee?'

Nash answered for them. 'Thank you. Tea for Detective Brown, no sugar. I'll have a coffee, please, with one.'

Brown said, 'Can I give you a hand?'

'I can still just about manage to make a cup of tea on my own, pet. You sit there and thaw out a bit.'

It gave them a chance to have a look around the room while she was gone. Nash read the scene and came up with a profile based on science that couldn't be denied or refuted. It was that there was nothing to see here. It had a typical, floral three-piece suite, a tidy living room with the three-bar electric fire on full power and a dozen photos on the mantlepiece. The room was a shrine to her family. One was of Margery with her late husband on their wedding day, and one had three little boys in a posed photograph, that were likely her grandchildren. When she came back in holding a tray, Nash jumped up to take it from her. She handed them their mugs—not ridiculous cups and saucers, thank God—and settled in the armchair across from them.

'Go on then, lassie. Ask me what you like, and I'll tell you what I can.' Nash knew not to underestimate the old woman who had seen the nod from Nash telling Brown to take the lead on the questioning.

'Lovely tea, Mrs Hodges,' Brown said with a suppressed shudder.

'Call me Margie, pet. You make me feel like my mother. God bless her soul.' She crossed herself and looked at Brown. Catholic.

'That one there, not saying anything. He's your boss, is he, hen? Letting you butter the old girl up.'

Brown laughed. 'Maybe. Something like that.'

'Aye, well, crack on then.'

'I see you're left-handed, Mrs Hodges. And how tall are you?'

'I used to be five-foot-six, but I'm shrinking. Am I a suspect, dearie?'

Nash jumped in to curb Brown's enthusiasm. 'Not at all, Mrs Hodges. Detective Brown just asks too many questions—and usually the wrong ones.'

Brown consulted her mobile device. 'I believe you told my colleague, PC Lawson, that you were at Mrs Cullen's house last night around teatime. Does that sound right?'

'He was a right charmer, that policeman. Had me wrapped around his little finger, he did. Yes. That's right. I did a bit of baking yesterday afternoon and took some scones to have with a cup of coffee. I went at four and came back at half five for my tea.'

'That was going to be my next question.'

'I thought it would be.'

'Am I right in thinking Mrs Cullen hadn't lived here long?'

'That's right. She bought the house two years ago, to be closer to Isabel, you see. And she came over from Chester after her Reggie died.'

'He was a civil servant?'

'No, dear. He worked for the government. Very hush-hush, Alma said. And she was a secretary of some kind, in Chester. It's posh there. "Alma," I'd say. "Alma, you don't plop rose petals, love." She didn't like that.'

'And how did Mrs Cullen seem yesterday? Anything out of the ordinary? Anything at all that seemed different or odd?'

'No. Nothing. Their Callum, that's her grandson, has just got one of those belts in karate, and she was telling me about that. She can be nasty, though. She said it was better than my lad Tommy—that's my grandson—going to ballet classes. He's only six and loves going dancing with his sister. Callum might have got an orange belt, but my Tommy got a gold medal on a ribbon for around his neck last month. 'Beat that,' I told her. To be honest, all of them bairns bouncing around on the stage gave me a proper migraine, but I wasn't letting her put my Tommy down. He's a real boy, not soft like her Callum. And I don't mind if he does grow up and decide to be gay. Like she's got room to talk, but she said it's different with girls. I told her, so long as he's happy, that's all I care about. I'd spit in her scone batter next time if she was still here.' She winked at Brown. 'There was one thing, I suppose, but not yesterday. This was one day in the week. She was complaining about a man selling her electricity. She sent him away with a flea in his ear. I know, Alma. If she had one of those smart meters, she'd watch it all day and would have been too afraid to put her fire on, so not very smart at all. I told her it was cold in her house, but she wouldn't listen. It only struck me as odd because he didn't knock at my place, that's all. Doesn't matter now, does it? She won't be cold no more.' She blessed herself again.

'Tell me about her daughters. What was her relationship with them like?' Brown asked. Nash only had a mild interest in the past to fill in the blanks. Isabel and Charlotte had a tight alibi, as did Isabel's husband. It was good to have a picture, though. They told a thousand words.

'Isabel's a good girl. She could come and see her mum more often, though. I know she's busy, goes to work, has the kids, kids and helps Damien with his business. And they're never here. Always off somewhere for the weekend, but they get on well. Fall out sometimes, but only because Alma always tells her to bring the kids more, and Izzy says she's too busy. She works for a doctor, you know. One of his receptionists.'

'And what about her other daughter, Charlotte?'

'Oh, I do like Char. We haven't seen her for five years. She went off to university and did one of those break years. Something to do with the environment and forestry in Canada. That's where she met her girlfriend, Kelly, and they've only been back once. Another busy one.'

'And yet her dad died not so long ago. Couldn't she get home for that?'

'They had a big fall out, pet. It's sad. They never got over it before he died. They were both as stubborn as each other. Apple of his eye, Char was. He didn't mind that she was one of those lesbians. And before you type that into your little computer as if it's a clue, I think he enjoyed telling people at the bowling green. No, it was when she wanted an artificial baby. He didn't like it and wouldn't lend her the money. Charlotte and Kelly had already had a few goes at it and couldn't afford it anymore. Reggie said that was God telling them that it wasn't right.' Nash was impressed that Brown held her opinions at bay and smiled over her coffee cup without choking.

'And they never made up? How did that affect the relationship between her and Alma?'

'They talked on the Google when Reggie was out shopping. She didn't exactly keep it a secret, but if he ever came in and she was talking to her computer, it'd end in a row. And then Alma asked me if I'd help—with the money. She had a bit put by that she could get past Reggie, and if I could help, it might be enough.'

'Really? That was asking a lot of your friendship.'

'I didn't mind, but I've got my own kids. I have my savings, but if I gave it all to Alma, I'd have nothing left. She called me selfish. And then it was all so confusing, and I didn't know if it was the right thing to do. Artificial babies, I mean.'

'Artificial insemination.'

'Pardon, pet?'

'That's what it's called.'

'Anyway, part of the reason Reggie wouldn't pay was that Char wasn't carrying it. So, he said that it wouldn't be any relation to him. But Char explained that they were taking some of her eggs and then some of Kelly's eggs and putting them into Kelly's belly with the boy's contribution. I think it blew his mind.

'And then the last straw was that they'd put five eggs back in the womb. So, they could have ended up with five babies, some of Kelly's and some of Char's, and they'd never know which was which. That was too much for Reggie. Too many Christmas presents to buy if you ask me.'

'And Charlotte has never been back in the country? Not even to visit her sister?'

'Never been back on British soil. Ah, but here's the funny thing. Kelly's been back. She turned up on the doorstep bold as brass just over a week ago. It was last Monday. No, it was Tuesday. The milkman had been for his money, so it must have been Tuesday afternoon. Now here's a funny story. You'll like this one. Fred, that's the milkman, was going out of business due to the supermarkets and corner shops, so he gives every customer a Mars Bar when he comes for the money on a Monday night. He says that's what's called enterprise. He enters, and I get a surprise. What do you think of that, eh?'

'That's marvellous. But what did Kelly want?'

'She said she was marrying Char and wanted Alma to be there. But she was doing it on the QT, a big surprise for Charlotte.'

'How did Alma take that?'

41

'Kelly wouldn't stay for supper, which upset her. She said she barely sat down long enough for a cup of tea. Alma wanted her to stop over. If she couldn't see her daughter, I suppose her daughter's girlfriend was the next best thing. But she wouldn't. Alma said she'd love to go to the wedding, and Kelly asked her for some money to cover Alma's flights and a hotel. She didn't have that kind of money lying around. Alma said she'd write a cheque, but Kelly said her bank wouldn't like that, what with it being a Canadian bank. She said she'd come round again before she went back home. She just told her about the wedding and left.' Margery burst into tears and took a tissue out of her cardigan sleeve. 'She won't be going now. It's so sad.'

'That's a line of enquiry we can follow up. Did she come back?'

'I don't think so, and Alma tells me everything. I know she went to the bank and drew out a lot of money for the wedding. Three thousand pounds and the bank manager took her into his office because it was so much, and she'd never done that before. Alma was frightened because she thought she was going to get told off. But he gave her the money and put it in a white envelope that she put in her shopping trolley because it wouldn't fit in her handbag. And she was scared all the way home in case she got mugged. She said a strange man sat beside her on the bus, and it was awful, and when she got off, she thought he was following her, so she tried to run, but what with arthritis in her knees, she couldn't. She has terrible knees. Sometimes they swell right up like two watermelons.' Margery used her hands to demonstrate the melons.

'That must have been painful. Did she say what this man looked like? Had she ever seen him before?'

'No, I don't think so. She'd have told me, I'm sure. Creepy. That's what she said he was. Creepy.' Her hand flew to her mouth, and she gasped. 'Do you think it was him that killed her? Will he come back? What if he knocks on my door? I won't know if he's come to kill me or sell me new electricity and put one of those machines in. I don't want that, but sometimes these people can be very hard to say no to. If he comes to my door, I'll hit him over the head with my walking stick.'

Nash wasn't sure if she meant the salesman or the man from the bus. The heat was a welcome joy when they went in, but now it was unbearable and suffocating him. He'd been pulling the knot in his tie for the last half hour. He hated dropped standards, but for the first time, he envied his sergeant, Phil Renshaw, for the jeans and sweatshirts he often wore for work. He'd been watching the witness and wasn't sure how much of her statement he was buying. He wanted to wrap this up and get out of the stifling room. Brown could go back with Renshaw the next day if they had any more questions,.

'Before we leave, Mrs Hodges, I want you to think very hard. Is there anything else you can tell us? It may be vital to our investigation, even if it doesn't seem important.' Brown broke into his leaving gambit with the question, and Nash could have killed her. Now the old bat would go off on a tangent for another half hour.

'I don't think so, hen. Of course, there's always the first Saturday stuff, but I don't think you mean that. No, lass. I think that's everything.'

Nash stood up.

'What about the Saturday stuff?' Brown asked.

43

'Every first Saturday of the month, Alma went to see a friend. Wouldn't tell me who, and when I asked if I could tag along, she bit my head clean off. I never mentioned it again, I can tell you.'

'Where did she meet this friend?'

'I have no idea. Told me to mind my own neb when I asked. But she was always gone for hours. What brings it to mind is that she never looked like she wanted to go. I'd say she was frightened, and her mood would change on a Friday night. No. Not frightened, that's too strong, worried maybe. But she was a daft ha'porth getting herself worked up because she was always happy when she came home. Face on her for days, then bounced in with cakes for tea, and a new coat or jumper for herself every month.'

'That's helpful. But you can't remember anything else about it?'

'Not a thing. As I said, I knew my place where the first Saturday outing was concerned.'

'Just one more question, Mrs Hodges, and then we'll leave you in peace. I'm sure you've got things to do.'

'Oh no, pet. I'm perfectly happy sitting here talking to you. It's been lovely. Poor Alma, though.'

Nash cut in and was determined to bring things to a close this time. 'Quite. Do you happen to know Kelly's surname?'

'I don't think it's ever been mentioned. But she had lovely brown boots on. Does that help? Now, there's a thing. If they get married, what will Char call herself?'

Nash got up. He couldn't stand the heat any longer, or Mrs Hodges.

'Thank you, Mrs Hodges. You've been very helpful,' Brown said.

'Come back if you need anything else. Just pop in for a cup of tea when you're passing, pet. It'd be canny to see you.'

Brown smiled. 'We will, Mrs Hodges. You take care now.'

They waited until they were in the car before speaking.

'No matter what the weather's like, old people always wait on the doorstep and wave you off,' Brown said as they waved out of the window like trained sea lions.

'It's an ancient ritual known in the old world as good manners, Brown. Anyway, what do you think?'

'There's plenty to go at—the salesman, the daughters, one's girlfriend turning up out of the blue. The money and then the man on the bus. And there's the stuff about her disappearing once a month. I'll investigate that as well. It's probably nothing. We'll see what phone records and finance digs up regarding this wedding and the money. I know there were no large sums of cash in the house. So where is the three grand Alma Cullen brought home?'

'Good question. That's our first point for the murder board. Thought I was going to die from the heat in there.'

'I know. Anyway, didn't you ever fancy having an artificial baby, boss?'

'I'd have to find myself an artificial husband first, Brown. I'm not having any luck getting a real one.'

Chapter Six

Their flight was called. She hadn't been on a plane for eight years and couldn't wait. Those Tater-tots hadn't been the best idea. She still felt queasy, and that was before the thrust of taking off. They powerwalked over ten miles of concourse, weaving and dodging through people. The plane was going nowhere until everybody was on it, but Connie was itching to get on. There was still a long queue as the excitement mounted, and they crawled the last leg a step at a time.

The bright girls in white and blue blouses, blue caps and tied neckties smiled as though they were pleased to see them. Fifty people were in front of them, with two hundred and fifty to come. They must have strong jaw muscles. And how sickening to greet every passenger as if they were celebrities, especially the ones that a layperson like Connie could see were going to be trouble. They took that final step from ramp to plane.

'Guess what, Jeff.'

'What, Connie?'

'We're on a plane.'

'I can see that.'

They were in row 19, seats C and D. They bumped, banged, squeezed and said sorry a dozen times until they got to their seats. It was a shame they had the aisle separating them. It was like a bad metaphor when she wanted to be close to him.

'We should have paid to pre-book seats,' Jeff said.

'It's fine, darling.'

Connie plonked into her seat while Jeff stored their carry-on bags in the overhead lockers. She'd have to move again when Mr and Mrs A and B rocked up. She hoped it was Mr and Mrs and not two screaming kids or, worse, part of a hen party. She remembered the Tater-tots and couldn't stomach too many renditions of *I'm Getting Married in the Morning*. There was a commotion and people shouting a few rows behind her. It was some kind of family dispute, and an overbearing barrage of abuse came from an irate child toward his mother.

Connie tried to listen but was distracted by the passengers who had booked the empty seats beside her. They were indeed a couple, and as they got close enough to smell, Connie stood to let them in. They danced, she and they. It was intimate, with far too much of Connie's body touching far too much of theirs, but eventually, the lady was in the window seat, and Connie had no choice but to sit again while the man stored their luggage. There was nowhere else to be. She was overweight, and one of her stock self-deprecating remarks was, 'I'm big, but I don't take up two seats on a plane.' They were three large people, Connie trailing a good couple of stones behind the lady and nowhere near as large as her husband. Her face was level with his stomach, and he thrust his pelvis forward to let somebody pass behind him. His t-shirt rode up. She was horrified as he stretched to the locker. It kept rising until

47

she was confronted with belly and hair and sweat. She turned her head with a nanosecond to spare, and his belly button connected with her cheek rather than kissing her mouth. She may have uttered a disgusted noise because his wife looked at her sharply. She peeled her face off the husband's wet tummy and smiled. He was done and shoehorned himself into the middle seat. Connie would have preferred bumping breasts with his obese wife. He brought his laptop down and opened it to play a noisy game. The game didn't bother her, but Connie knew that when the Fasten Seatbelt sign came on, he'd be told to store it overhead, and they'd go through the rigmarole again. She reached into her handbag and got a wet wipe at the ready.

He wore shorts, and his naked leg touched her from thigh to ankle. She moved onto her left buttock and tried to turn towards the aisle. It did no good. The tenth of an inch it bought her was used up by Sweaty Leg inching over. It was subtle, a slight movement, but it was there. He couldn't help being overweight. It was possibly an illness, and she didn't subscribe to the thought process that all he had to do was stop eating and start exercising. And if it wasn't physical, then it was mental. Nobody chooses to get into his state. However, that didn't stop her from thinking she might just hate him and the pie he rode in on.

The ruckus behind them was gaining momentum. The same kid was still yelling at his mother. 'Shut your damn mouth, our Dale, or I'll shut it for you.' Other voices had joined in during the issue regarding seating. She heard the soothing tones of the hostess trying to control the situation, and Connie knew, that it was the gang of benefit scroungers she'd seen earlier. Connie was ashamed. In two minutes, she'd passed judgement on the overweight couple beside her and now a gang of ten or twelve people. What the hell made her think she was better than them?

Jeff grinned and reached across the aisle for her hand. 'We're ten minutes late taking off now,' he said. And it annoyed Connie. Every second of this holiday was precious. It doesn't matter if you aren't sitting together, she thought. Just get in a seat, let the plane take off, and sort it out when we're airborne, you absolute finger-blasters. They could only link their hands for a second. The extended family from hell were coming closer. A sub-contingent of them had broken off, and the flight attendants guided them up the plane.

'This isn't on. I've paid good money for this holiday, and we can't even sit together? It's a bloody joke.'

'I'm sorry, ma'am, but you didn't pre-book your seats together.'

'I shouldn't have to. It's obvious that if you come on holiday, you want to sit together. It's crazy.'

Connie kept her head down to avoid eye contact as they passed her seat. They blocked the aisle a few rows ahead, and Jeff's seat neighbours, more late arrivals, were trying to get past. Jeff got the skinny minis, but—they had a baby. Connie would never coo over a child. She didn't like babies, and the damned thing was already screaming.

Future Prison Boy said, 'You're all bastards. I don't want to sit here. I want to be back there with our Levi. This is a shit holiday. I wish I'd stayed at home.'

'I'm going to knock your head off in a minute, our Dale. Shut the hell up while I get this sorted. I'm going to need some money back for this cock up.'

Dale was about thirteen and at least fifteen stone. His mouth disappeared into the fleshy mounds of his face, and he had piggy eyes. He was wearing a grey tracksuit and a bad attitude. One of her other sons moved forward. 'Mum, you're making a scene. Dale, come with me, and I'll help you get settled in your seat.'

'Piss off, Levi,'

All three attendants were speaking to the family. 'I'm sorry, madam, but we're running fifteen minutes late now, and the plane can't leave until everybody is seated.'

'I don't see why me and three of my kids have to be separated from everyone else. It's not fair.'

Connie leaned over to Jeff. 'I'm going to offer to move. It might help.'

'Don't you dare.' He lowered his voice. 'They're awful people.'

Levi spoke to the staff, and there wasn't a single swear word. 'I'm sorry, they're just upset. We expected to sit together. If you show me the four seats, I'll help Mum settle the kids.'

The mother wasn't giving up. 'It's not even as if that's four seats together, two are there, and the other two are at the front. What if my kids get kidnapped like that girl that went missing in Portugal?'

'Mum, please stop talking. You're making us look stupid.'

Connie was fascinated that Levi looked about sixteen and had more respect than his mother and brother put together. His clothing left a lot to be desired, but what a lovely young man. The monstrosity he was wearing must have been designer because only something very expensive could be that tasteless. It was another teen in a tracksuit, but this one was white and purple tie-dye. It was awful. His black hair was a cloud of tight twists around his head, and they made a perfect

50

ball shape framing his dark face. He smiled, looked embarrassed, and apologised to a few people who showed their irritation. Connie smiled as he herded his mother and three siblings along the plane. The mother was still ranting, and Dale's voice pierced the static air in the carriage as he complained.

A man stood up, and Connie could just make out the top of his head. 'If it helps the situation, we don't mind moving. That will free up two seats.'

They were a bit ahead now, and Connie had to lean into the aisle to see what was going on. It was the man called Ray. She wasn't surprised he was a gentleman. He looked kind. Not so his wife. 'Raymond, I said no. Sit down. You're making matters worse.'

The fracas was losing momentum, and the unruly family realised they'd better sit down if they wanted to see Greece before it sank into the ocean from global warming. And at last, that bloody baby had stopped screaming, but only because Jeff was making silly noises at it and playing peek-a-boo. He'd be holding the damned thing next and rocking it to sleep.

They were twenty minutes late, and the pilot came on the tannoy to say that although there was a delay, he was confident that they could make the time up and arrive on schedule. A ripple of cheer came in a Mexican wave along the carriage, but it was more of a murmur than a roar. They were moving. Snail-pace, but moving, nonetheless. The taxiing was underway.

A seatbelt sign had come on, and everybody was putting their tables up and fastening their belts. The attendant moved along the aisle, checking that everything was in order, and when they reached Connie's row, they asked the man beside her to store his laptop. Connie had to get out and hover while he put it in the locker.

A voice that Connie recognised all too well bellowed down the plane, 'For Christ's sake, sit down. You're holding the plane up.' It was that awful mother.

Connie and Sweaty Leg sat back down. Everybody had a seat, and the plane was taxiing along the concourse. She couldn't believe it when the man next to Jeff pressed the assistance button. Jesus, what now? The flight attendant came down the plane with her big plastic smile leading the way.

'Yes, sir?'

'Do you have a microwave, please?'

'Sorry? A microwave?'

'Yes, to heat my baby's milk.'

Jeff nearly did his neck an injury when his head turned so fast to see if he was joking. Was this idiot for real? Thanks to Connie's boyfriend, the baby wasn't even bawling.

'Yes, I can do that for you, but would you mind waiting until we're in the air, please? It won't be long now.'

'But what if my baby gets hungry?'

'I'll come as soon as the seatbelt signs go off. I promise.'

The attendant sat in her seat, and the plane picked up speed.

'We're going faster,' Connie said to Jeff.

'I can see that.'

'We'll be in the air in a minute. It's really happening. We're going to Greece.'

And then the wind was taken out of her sails when the plane slowed, and they taxied for another five minutes.

And then it happened. The speed increased. It went stupid fast. With the thrust, Connie was forced into the back of her seat, and she turned to watch the ground disappear out of the window.

'We're in the air.'

'We are.'

'We're flying.'

'I know.'

'Good, isn't it?'

'I've seen less excitement from my kids. And had less commentary. You're like a child.' He laughed at her and looked delighted to see her so happy.

'I know. Brilliant, isn't it? Are we having a drink?'

'I don't see why not.'

The flight attendant came around with the drinks trolley and leaned over Connie to take the order beside her. The man bought six tiny bottles of whiskey and two tiny cans of Coke.

'I'll have two whiskeys, two vodka and two cans of Coke, please,' Jeff said.

Connie wasn't going to be outdone by the couple beside her, and she was still bouncing with excitement. 'Make it three.'

Jeff laughed and amended his order. 'Three whiskeys and three vod-kas, please.'

Connie had never drunk more than one celebratory drink on a plane before. Since being diagnosed with TN she had to be careful about mixing alcohol with her medication. She'd done great and surprised herself with how few facial-tic attacks she'd had throughout the day. However, the double dose of medication she'd taken was wearing off, and she could feel the pressure in her head building. Once she ticked and her head jerked all over the place, she'd take great delight in head-butting Sweaty Leg.

They'd bring the drinks trolley around twice during the flight. 'We'll have another three when they come back,' she said, grinning at Jeff.

'If you like, but that cost us thirty-six pounds. Don't forget we're all-inclusive at the hotel, and alcohol is included.'

'That's scandalous.'

'Honey, you're so out of touch. We've just bought six spirits and two cans of Coke. It's not that bad.'

'Bugger me. We'd better enjoy it, then. I warn you, though, I've never been tipsy on a plane, and might want to sing.'

'Please don't.'

'Charming.'

Chapter Seven

The decorators had gone, leaving the smell of fresh paint. It gave some people a headache, but Nash loved it. It was a clean smell, like bleach, and he appreciated anything clean. His ex-boyfriend Sandy had defaced his house, and it had cost him a fortune to redecorate. He was sad more than bitter or enraged and found a way to be philosophical about it. Sandy was gone, and Nash had been an old fool who got burned. And that, he decided, was the price to pay for love.

He'd adhered to one of Sandy's favourite sayings for the feature wall in his lounge, 'Go loud or go home.' Nash was home but couldn't deny that his choice of wallpaper might not be loud, but it was busy. He preferred the adjective classy. It was a William Morris print from the Arts and Crafts movement. The room wasn't big enough to accommodate rich paper on every wall. It was expensive at eighty pounds a roll, but he'd always loved the classics and enjoyed the story Morris told that he'd been inspired for the *Strawberry Thief* design when he saw blackbirds stealing fruit from his kitchen garden. It set off Nash's art deco marble mantlepiece. He'd chosen the blue phase and had eggshell satin paint on the other three walls, which was enough to take the weight out of the paper.

He'd used paper on the feature wall in the master bedroom too, and it replaced the homophobic slurs with elegance and flair. He'd gone for an airy design that encouraged light into the room. Colefax and Fowler's *Seraphina* in the amethyst colour choice was perfect. It was an oatmeal background with well-spread clusters of hanging Wisteria. He hoped it wouldn't remind him of honeysuckle in the worst night hours when he lay in bed alone. The merest hint of the smell knocked him sick.

Sandy had been gone for three months, and Molly Brown nagged him to get back out there. He'd never been out there in the first place, wherever there was. His first boyfriend had been his high school sweetheart. They'd had ten glorious years together before four thugs killed David in a takeaway after a night out. Neither of them flaunted their homosexuality. Only the brave people did that during the seventies, and with Nash being a young, beat copper, he protected himself and his force with a fierceness that had stayed with him throughout his life. It took Nash years to get over it. His colleagues at the station helped him recover from his flatmate's death, and he threw himself into work. They never knew the true status of their relationship.

The only other partner he'd had apart from Sandy was the man Silas called his husband. Gay marriage was illegal in England until 2014. They thought about it, but they'd been together for twenty-five years by then. It meant everything to Colin to be married, but Nash couldn't get over his prejudice. It felt as if he'd have to give up everything he'd attained to parade himself in the spectacle of marriage. Even though they could have done it quietly and had just Colin, himself and a couple of witnesses, they couldn't reach a compromise. Colin wanted to celebrate their love with a lavish wedding—Nash didn't. Being a copper, he'd hidden who he was all his life. Colin was a practising Catholic, and while it wasn't recognised in his church and he'd been ostracised from one parish for his sexuality, he clung to his religion vehemently. He wanted marriage, even if it was only recognised legally and not by faith. He needed marriage and said Nash could put in for a transfer to a different region. They'd move to a smallholding in the country and raise chickens, goats, an alpaca, and buy a labrador called Cookie. Nash loved their home, but in the spirit of compromise and making the man he loved happy, he'd agreed to it all—apart from the wedding. He couldn't make Colin see that, in his line of work, he couldn't be an openly gay man. Not then. And even now, he was finding it difficult because he'd been locked so deep in the closet all his life. Nobody gave a shit these days except Nash.

Silas had given up work early, had the big golden handshake party, and was awarded an Excellent Service medal. They put the house up for sale and found the perfect small farm that needed some renovation in a little village in north Yorkshire. They were in a chain, and when the buyer for their house fell through, it was the beginning of the end for him and Colin. After twenty-five years, the man he'd thought of as his husband left him. Colin always said Silas was ashamed of him. Worse, he accused him of being ashamed of himself. Silas denied it but couldn't make Col see that a gay copper would never rise through the ranks. The times needed to change, but it didn't happen fast enough for them. Colin gave him the ultimatum of choosing his job or their happiness. Silas refused to choose. They could have both. They always had.

Colin chose for him, and one evening Nash came home to see his lover's suitcases by the front door. He only had a couple of minutes to beg him to stay before the taxi came to take him to the station.

Nash was lost. 'Where's your car?'

'I've sold it.'

It was final. While the taxi sat outside with its engine running, Silas followed him into the drive. Colin lifted the first suitcase into the boot, and when he picked up the second, Nash wrestled it out of his hands.

He dropped onto one knee. 'I'll do it. Please, Colin, I love you. Marry me.'

The taxi driver tactfully got back into his car, and Colin held out his hand to help Nash up. They hugged.

'Please, don't leave me. You're my world.'

'No, Si. Being DCI Nash is your world. I'm just a prop. Don't make this harder than it is.'

He'd never seen Colin look so sad. And then he was gone. They sent Christmas cards. Colin was married now with two boys.

Nash looked at his new wallpaper and remembered the old times. He drank his tea and wanted something stronger but didn't keep alcohol in the house. A bottle of wine at Christmas, maybe. He wondered how to go about getting out there. Brown had told him about Tinder, where you swipe right or left depending on whether you found somebody attractive. From the name of the app to the concept of herding photographs through his phone like cattle, he found the idea repugnant. But Nash was lonely and could only fight Brown's enthusiasm for so long—though he had resisted doing anything about it so far.

Being on the dating scene came with a whole world of problems. One of Cumbria's top police inspectors couldn't display his face on a dating app. Brown swooped in like a dating fairy godmother. Nash was unsure whether her help was a kindness or a curse. After Sandy, he was wary of getting burned again. Approaching strangers wasn't his style anyway, but add in the sensitivity of the job, and it opened him up to more risk. Brown created a profile with a fake name. 'Of course, it's not illegal,' she'd said, laughing at him when he was horrified. 'People do it all the time.' She added a photo from a stock library. She'd spent hours trawling through the images and found a face that looked like his.

Nash thought he was better looking than the picture, so that had to be a bonus if he did ever meet somebody in person. Brown told him not to give out too much information when talking to somebody, and when Nash trusted him, he could tell the truth before any damage was done. Under the circumstances, nobody could be annoyed by the initial deception as long as he was honest as soon as possible. If he ever plucked up the courage to use the app, he wouldn't fish in a home pond and would search for people in Kendal, far enough away to be unlikely to run into them when he was on duty. It sounded like a lot of trouble. But most of all, it just sounded sordid and dirty. He wasn't a false name and fake photo—though apparently, now, thanks to Molly, he was. She was ruthless and trod over his sensitivities like wearing crampons on a frozen pond. 'Nash, get over yourself. Nobody gives a toss who you date. Find a man, get married and give him babies or a sausage dog. Do what you like, whatever makes you happy, but get over your ego because the rest of the world doesn't care.'

Sandy had been his only lover since Colin in his early thirties. Nash was sixty-five years old and didn't want to die alone in this house that was far too big for one. Sandy had been a terrible mistake. He knew that. He thought it was love, but Sandy conned him, and his interest in Nash had been financial. They met in the bar where Sandy worked. It was the usual story of boy meets boy. Sandy was younger—an attractive forty-something man with a leaning towards ferret features that Nash still felt lucky to attract. Sandy was a social butterfly. He was camp and flamboyant, and Nash hated that, but he accepted it for who he was. Men didn't come on to Nash, and Sandy could have had anybody. He chose Silas, and their relationship was based on one of them being flattered while the other was only interested in money.

When the bank of Silas closed its doors, Sandy was vengeful and sold sensitive information about The Florists and their victims to the media. It was one of the worst days of Nash's life that he would regret forever.

Again, he was in a position where he'd had to save his career. Through his forty years on the force, Nash had never put a step out of line. Not once had he done anything wrong or unethical, and he was as straight as a queer cop could be. When Sandy was brought in and questioned, Nash had quashed the case. First, Sandy had used him. And then he'd done something worse. He took his soul and compromised everything Nash identified as. He'd been a straight cop until that day, and now he had to wear the label of being corrupt. Although what he'd done never spilt into the ranks, in his own mind, he had to live with that guilt.

Nash took Sandy's phone out of evidence and wrote his ex-boyfriend up for a caution. For days afterwards, he felt sick, waiting to be found out and for the hammer to fall. Nobody knew that Alexander 'Sandy' Burns was Nash's lover or that Nash had any involvement in the stolen evidence. He and Max Jones had run Sandy out of town. He'd made it go away, and it was too easy. It was gross misconduct and unethical. Being found out would have cost him his career and sent him into retirement, stripped of his rank and pension. He would have been a pariah. He'd used his seniority and position for his own ends and hated himself for it. Nash vowed to serve the rest of his time as the cop he'd always been.

Everybody on the force knew he was gay now. And he'd been the one to tell them. It was nothing. Nobody cared. 'Listen up, team.' He'd gone on that day to deal with the debrief of the case. His hands were sweating, and it was now or never. 'I've worked with most of you for some time now, and I think you know me well enough. However, maybe not as well as you think. There's something that I've been keeping from you all for a long time.' He gave a nervous laugh. 'Hell, I've been hiding this since I was a green rookie standing on my first parade. So, here we go. I'm Silas Nash.' They still laughed at his name. 'Yeah, yeah, settle down. I'm Silas Nash. I'm sixty-five, and I'm gay.'

There was a shocked silence. 'No way,' Bowes said. 'You can't be gay. You're too straight.'

'Thanks for that, Bowes. I think. You, too.' Everybody laughed again, and Nash loved getting a reaction. 'Right, let's move on.'

He saw some looks over the next week, and conversations would stop when he walked into the tea room, but it soon died down, and apart from his share of light-hearted gay jokes, it was a three-day wonder. It would have been a different story thirty years earlier. The police force was an openly homophobic institution back then. In his early career, he'd have been prosecuted for being who he was. He'd have been sacked under a cloud of shame. Even when it was legal to be a gay man walking the streets of society, he'd never have made sergeant, never mind inspector.

Now he did his job, and nobody cared about what he did outside work. He took some gentle ribbing, and the latent homophobia, a throwback to ignorant times, was something the gay community lived with every day.

When a tray of cakes came around for somebody's birthday, one of the team said, 'Would you like the doughnut, sir, or do you prefer a ladyfinger?'

'You know what, Patel, I wouldn't touch your doughnut with Bowes' dirty ladyfinger.' Brown bought him a pink-glittery truncheon for his birthday—and he'd laughed and was a good sport about it. 'It's what birthdays are all about,' Renshaw said when Nash opened it. 'You have to find the most embarrassing gift you can.' He wanted to tell him that there was nothing embarrassing about a pink truncheon, only the person who bought it. It was latent homophobia, but they didn't get it. For Brown's birthday, he'd bought a nice stationary set—because nobody wrote letters anymore, and he thought she might enjoy rekindling the art of letter writing.

If Silas Nash spent every second of the rest of his career making up for that one bad decision when he'd quashed Sandy's conviction, it would never be enough. He'd crossed the line, and while he swore he would never do anything against his badge, he was forever a bent cop.

The next day at work was a busy one. As well as ongoing house-to-house investigations, all the witness statements had to be checked and verified. So far, nothing had come to light about the electricity salesman or the stranger who may or may not have followed Cullens off the bus. No skeletons dropped out of either daughter's closets, no matter how hard they rattled them. And so far, the mystery about where the victim went every first Saturday of the month remained that. The daughters were adamant that there wasn't a new man on the scene. They'd know, apparently.

The first thing to close was the mystery of Alma Cullen's missing three thousand pounds. It saddened Nash to find out that Mrs Cullen's Friend, Marjorie Hodges, had used the spare key to sneak into her house and steal it. The old lady faced an opportunist's first crime rap to lament her elderly years. She was given a fine and had to pay the money back to the family, but the shame stayed with her.

The autopsy findings and final tests were back on Alma Cullen. Bill Robinson, the county coroner, brought the results to Nash's office. Robinson didn't make office visits. He was either at the scene of the crime or was in the morgue cutting calligraphy into post-moribund flesh. So, when he told Nash he had news and was coming over, Nash knew it was big. They'd worked together for years and had gained familiarity and respect for each other. And though Nash didn't really have friends, if asked, he would have classed Bill as one. If he took the time to analyse where an acquaintance ended and a friendship was struck, the line between them blurred. They knew how the other ticked and worked well in synchronicity as old colleagues do. Robinson was the county coroner, but he also acted as the lead pathologist for Barrow-in-Furness and did some of the autopsies himself when he wasn't tied up in court.

'She could have died three times,' Bill said.

'How so?'

'Well, there was the blunt trauma, which we assumed was the cause of death. We've discovered that wasn't what killed her. Then there was the undiagnosed brain tumour. It was huge and was cutting her brain from its oxygen supply. That might have killed her, given another couple of weeks. It would have been sudden, a massive stroke. Who knows, that way might even have been kinder.'

'You said three deaths.' Nash was still reading the report and listening to Robinson at the same time.

'Yes. Look at the second page from the third paragraph. We missed the real killer. If it hadn't been for the tiniest spot of blood on her blouse, we wouldn't have caught it.'

Nash looked up. He'd read the report properly later but wanted to hear what Robinson had to say. 'What was it?'

'A very fine needle puncture in the axilla. A couple of minutes before he bashed her over the head from behind, he lifted her arm up and jabbed her in a vein on the fleshy part of her armpit. There was no sign of a struggle, so she let the killer do it. No defence wounds. She either lifted her arm herself or let the killer lift it for her.'

'What did he or she—I'm still thinking female—drug her with?'

'That's what makes this crime so beautiful. Nothing.'

'Embolism?'

'You got it. Alma Cullen died from a blood clot after she was injected with fresh air directly into her bloodstream.'

'And then the murderer hit her?' Nash said. He lowered the report in surprise.

There was a tap on the door.

'Come in,' Nash said.

Paul Lawson stuck his head in and looked thrown when he saw Bill Robinson with Nash. 'I'm sorry, sir. I didn't realise you were busy.'

'That's okay, young man. I'm just leaving.' Robinson left a copy of the reports and test results with Nash and put the rest of his papers into his briefcase. They shook hands, and Robinson nodded to Lawson on the way out.

'Take a seat, Lawson.'

The young PC looked nervous. He had a tremor in his hands and tried to hide it by sitting on them. Nash smiled. 'Is this about Alma Cullen?'

'No, sir.'

'What can I do for you?'

'It's a personal matter. It's embarrassing.' Nash was intrigued. The staff normally went to the HR department for personal matters and petty grievances, He offered the lad coffee to put him at ease, but he declined.

'It's about my sister, Steph.'

'What's she done this time? I hope she's okay.'

Lawson snorted. 'Hardly. She's gone nuts again and signed herself into Dale View for thirty days.'

'I'm sorry to hear that.'

'She's bipolar, and the thing is, Aiden, my nephew, is only fourteen, and she's left him on his own. Our parents split up years ago, and my mum lives in London with her new bloke. Dad doesn't want to know. He drinks a bit, sir.' Nash was familiar with the problem and had booked Mr Lawson senior several times for drunk-and-disorderly or fighting. He'd always been sensitive to keeping PC Lawson well out of the way and, wherever possible, keeping the connection between them undisclosed.

'I'm all Aiden's got until his mum comes out. I've taken him in.'

'Very commendable, Lawson. Do you need an extended period of annual leave?'

'No, sir. He's a good kid and got a sound head on his shoulders, so he can be left while I work through the day. I just wondered if I could be taken off nights and overtime for a few weeks. If that's okay, sir?'

'Of course it is, Lawson. Thank you for coming to me with this. I'll email HR and ask them to add a note to your rota. If you need any additional support, my door is always open.'

'Thank you, sir.' Lawson stood up to leave.

'And Paul?'

'Yes?'

'I think that's a very responsible thing that you're doing for your family. Don't worry about work. We'll fit in with your needs.'

When Lawson left his office, Nash made a mental note to keep an eye on him. His sister and her ex-husband were well known at the booking desk. It was a difficult family dynamic, and Nash was amazed that Lawson had done as well as he had. Nash had him marked for making detective one day. The lad was hard-working and asked the right questions. He'd hate to lose a good officer for the sake of a lack of support during a family crisis, and he'd seen it happen before.

He emailed HR that Lawson must not be put on the rota for night duty until further notice. He was shutting down the computer when he thought about trying the dating app. He didn't want to go home to an empty house again. He wouldn't dream of searching a gay dating site using the work computer—but maybe Brown was right, and it wouldn't hurt to give it a go when he got home.

Even if he didn't get a date, he might find somebody nice to talk to. The hardest part was getting over his feelings of it being something shameful and logging into the profile Brown had made for him.

He had a nice piece of Lancashire waiting for him in the fridge. He'd have cheese and crackers and at least look at a few profiles to see what it was all about.

Chapter Eight

When the drinks trolley came around again, Jeff asked if she wanted anything. She said she was fine, but they'd have another one later on their balcony, watching the ocean.

The couple next to her had no such constraints and had another six shots between them. The only thing holding Connie back from doing the same was the price—but it didn't stop her from calling them a pair of pissheads in her head. She had them down as dedicated functioning alcoholics and allowed herself a moment to be smug for only having three vodkas on a plane and not six.

Sweaty Leg was hot. It was nearing midnight, and he turned his air conditioning on. Connie's medication had worn off, and the stream of stale air hit her in the face. As a TN sufferer, one of her biggest triggers was anything touching her forehead, cheek and the skin of her right eye. The lighter the touch, the worse the effect. She felt it coming and turned away from him and the air stream. Within seconds her hands came up to her face with an involuntary jolt. The right palm didn't touch her but looked for all the world as though she was a DJ holding her oversized cans to her ear and dancing to a pumping house beat.

The hands clawed, her head jerked, and she had a prolonged ticking fit. Jeff put his hand on her thigh, but she was unaware of it. When the run of tics passed, her body relaxed, and she collapsed into her seat, exhausted. Jeff moved his fingers from her leg to hold her hand.

'Are you okay?'

'Yes, I'm fine, thanks.' She shielded her face from the air conditioning and smiled at him to show that she was okay.

'Excuse me, mate,' Jeff said.

The man either didn't hear or was still in shock and ignoring the lunatic—with emphasis on the tic—in the seat beside him.

'Hey, pal?'

The man turned.

'Can you turn the aircon off, please? Can't you see it's making my wife ill?'

She always wanted to laugh when he called her that. Connie cringed. She wouldn't have complained. The man didn't say a word but made his feelings very clear as he reached up and turned the air off. The damage was done, and Connie was on a roll. She called her condition Sparky. Apart from permanent agony in her head and pressure inside her brain, controlled by medication, one of the primary symptoms was nerve pain. Connie was a curiosity, and she was used to people staring. She'd taken early retirement from her job as a psychotherapist a few years before, so at least she didn't have to face her patients. The condition was caused by a swollen blood vessel pressing against a nerve. Her Trigeminal Neuralgia manifested in the rarest form. Most TN sufferers experience severe nerve pain travelling from their jaw to the centre of their brain, usually on the right-hand side. Connie's pain ricocheted along the nerve connecting her eye to the central cortex of her brain. And once Sparky got out of his cage to play, he liked to make the most of it.

Connie sparked again. Her body tightened, her hands came up and clawed, and she had a run of exhausting tics that lasted a minute. Her body slumped.

'Okay?' Jeff took her hand and squeezed.

Connie nodded.

She loved that Jeff was protective of her. They had rebuilt their lives after emerging very scathed from their respective divorces. And while it suited both of them for her to use his name, Pearson, for everything other than her passport and driving licence, she knew he'd never marry her, but there was something shielding about the way he said, 'My wife.'

The man looked uncomfortable. It wasn't his fault. Sweat rolled down his face, and Connie felt sorry for him. As well as being socially uncomfortable with having to sit next to a woman having some kind of fit, he was physically restless. His leg against hers from thigh to calf kept twitching. He flexed his feet, causing his thigh to rub against her. It was wet and cold through the layers of her clothing. She could feel the sweat displacing with every minuscule movement. It put her in mind of crickets—or cicada, as they were called over Grecian skies—rubbing their hind legs to make their distinctive noise and attract a mate. He disgusted her and gave her the ick, as Jeff's son, Sam, would say. She wanted to apologise or at least smile to make him feel better, but nothing came.

'Not long now,' she said into the plane and at nobody in particular. The words were too bright and too loud. Then she ticked. When

70

she came out of it, the man looked horrified, and his wife gave every appearance of needing to vomit. They were trapped, and it must have been awful for them. But they were British and didn't say a word. She wanted to laugh. You had to admire Sparky's timing.

The man reached for the laptop he'd taken from the locker the second the seatbelt signs went out after take-off. It had meant Connie getting up, standing in the aisle, and being inconvenienced again. She had a failsafe recipe for in-flight travelling. You don't move. Once you're on the plane, you don't leave your seat until it lands. You make sure you've been to the loo before you get on, and that's it until you disembark. The man beside her had forced her out of her seat three times.

He turned his laptop on and went back to his game. It pinged. Connie glanced at his screen and saw somebody walking around a stone temple. The game pinged every two seconds. Just too slow to match her breathing pattern that she'd lowered to calm Sparky. The noise didn't bother her, but she felt Jeff's hand twitching with annoyance. She smiled at him and saw the vein in his temple bouncing.

He put up with it for ten minutes. Nine minutes longer than expected.

'Mate. Hey, mate.'

The man looked.

'Do you mind?'

'I'm sorry?'

'The sound on your computer. It's doing everybody's head in. Can you turn it down?' He didn't say please, and as far as Connie could see, he was the only person bothered by it. The world is split into two factions. Those that complain about poor service or minor annoyances,

71

and those who don't. She never complained publicly. She wasn't one of those people.

Apart from Sparky making an appearance and Sweaty Leg's sweaty leg, she loved the flight. She and Jeff would let everybody else off first. There was no rush. They had to reclaim their baggage before they went anywhere. But Mr and Mrs Sweaty Leg had their belts off and were standing up and wanting out before the sign went off.

'Ladies and Gentlemen, please remain in your seats with your seat belts securely fastened until the plane comes to a stop, the Fasten Seat-belt sign goes off, and you are told you can move. This is for your own safety.'

To hell with that, the Sweaty Legs could smell the Greek blend of whiskey from inside the plane and were chomping at the bit to get off. It was another five minutes before the doors opened, and they stood in the aisle, being impatient. Connie and Jeff got up to let their respective seatmates into the aisle to join the traffic jam, and they sat back down to wait.

And then they were off the plane and charging down the concourse. They'd made it and were on a Grecian island. No plane strikes, terrorist attacks, or pandemics had stopped them. They were invincible. Operation Get the Passion Back was underway. Baggage collection was a breeze, and they were through. The Benefit Gang were reunited and loud. And while Mother shouted to hurry up because she was 'Gasping for a fag,' Our Dale pushed through the people waiting for their luggage to ride on the baggage carousel. 'Look at me, Mam. I'm on it. Look, Mam.' Three of his younger siblings clambered on too, and Connie watched a guard running towards them through the arrivals area. There wasn't one redeeming quality about that child, not one as far as Connie could see. She didn't believe anybody was either very good or very bad. We're all made up of every quality and emotion, but all she saw in that brat was bad breeding. Mother should have been spayed before the little bastard was born.

Our Levi retrieved two suitcases for an elderly couple and helped stack them on a trolley, and Connie wished it had been Our Dale that helped, just to keep the universe balanced.

The bright artificial lighting in the airport set Connie off again. She ticked, and because she was standing up, her equilibrium was knocked to hell. Jeff had to guide her to a seat to stop her from falling over. She was embarrassed for him. That would be it now. She'd be ticking and bumbling around like a very drunk person until she could sit somewhere cool and dark to reset.

There were no seats left in the shuttle bus taking them to the taxi ranks. They had poles and straps coming from the ceiling. Neither was any good to Connie, and it was a logistical nightmare. Jeff managed to guide her into the back of the bus and used his body to keep her safe. She jerked and wobbled and did the hustle, the bump and the funky chicken. Nobody offered her a seat, and in between attacks, she kept her head low to avoid the lighting—and the stares.

When they got to the meeting place, she expected to get another bus with everybody else to take them to their five-star resort. She liked that part. It was like a mini tour seeing all the other hotels, watching who went where, and comparing them to her hotel. However, as a surprise, and because it was so late, Jeff had arranged a private car for them. It was ostentatious and silly, but she loved his thoughtfulness. Sparky's fun and games had wiped her out.

Even though it was one in the morning, the heat hit them like a wall as they stepped out of the airport. It was one of the joys of holidaying abroad, leaving bleak old England and feeling the heat haze as you put your first footsteps outside on foreign soil. They went to their hotel with the driver chatting to Jeff through the privacy hatch while she relaxed and re-set her brain in the muted darkness of the car.

At this hour, there wasn't much to see as they drove through dusty backroads and olive groves. It was barren. They travelled through a mountainous area with a sub-terrain of yellow sandy gravel and gorse bushes. There was only one town on their route, and it was quiet with all the bars closed and nobody around. The driver pointed out that it was Kardamena, and Connie's heart sank. This was billed as the nightlife hot spot of the island. The place to be and be seen—but it was dead.

Their journey from the airport to the resort was twenty minutes, and their hotel was built into the side of a mountain. A pigging mountain, for Christ's sake. They were on an island, and she hadn't seen the ocean once. The Diamond Sunshine Resort and Spa was vast and covered a mile of the twisting road. It was incredible that one hotel complex could be a mile long. However, it was clear that they had started with a single structure at the base of the mountain and added buildings on top of buildings over the decades. She would have been happy with the three-star offering at the base of the mountain, but no, for their special holiday, they had to have the five-star pinnacle in the bloody heavens.

They were tired when they got there. It was one in the morning, and the hotel entrance didn't look as welcoming as she'd hoped. This cost a lot of money, and it was their first holiday together. She zipped a big smile into place and gave Jeff a cuddle. It was going to be fine. A holiday is what you make it.

'Tip the driver,' she whispered.

'I can't. I haven't converted any money yet.'

'Give him some English money. It all spends.'

Jeff pulled a ten-pound note out of his wallet. 'Here you go, mate. Thanks a lot.' They waved as the taxi drove away.

'Ten quid? Are you mad? That could have bought us a drink.'

'Honey, we're all-inclusive.'

'This is so typical of you. You never plan ahead. Why didn't you exchange some money first?'

'Why can't you get off my case?'

Chapter Nine

The first view of the inside of their hotel hit a sour note. As they walked in, their bickering stopped short of being a full-on argument.

The foyer was grand—but she'd stayed in grander. There was no denying that it was beautiful. The designers had created a cool retreat as you withdrew from the blistering sun. However, they'd missed the mark of cool by a smidge, and it teetered over the border into being plain cold.

The theme was typically Mediterranean, with lots of tiling. The walls were crystal white with hand-painted scrolls and swirls in delicate pastels to break the blue and white. It should have worked. It did work, but it could have used a touch more warmth. During the early hours of the morning, that's how Connie felt. She wanted to be elated with her high pricetag hotel, but her heart sank. She picked it up, fixed a smile and wouldn't let Jeff see her disappointment.

The reception desk was against the wall as they walked through the door, and a tired concierge failed to greet them with a smile. They had beaten the bus and were the first ones at the desk, which made for a fast check-in. The manager talked to them in a dull monotone and didn't smile once, unlike the night porter who was waiting to take their bags. He was tip-ready and bustling with anticipation. The manager gave them their key card. 'Room 114. Anast will take you up.'

A lone guest was hovering in the reception area with his family's baggage beside him, and he came up to them with a smile.

'Have a great holiday. 114's a beautiful room. We've just come out of it.'

There was something disconcerting about meeting your predecessor, and Connie would prefer not to have seen the last person who had sex in their bed. They passed a few words as the porter moved restlessly with their heavy suitcases.

He led them up a circular stone staircase that narrowed with every step and was precarious in the upper echelons.

The porter, Anast—he had a name, and that made him human—opened the door, showed them in, and waited. Connie cringed. Not giving good service a gratuity went against the grain. She murmured, 'Thank you.' Wishing she had some money and turned her back on the man to hide her embarrassment, as she made a show of moving her hand luggage. She put it on the chair beside the bed, leaving Jeff to deal with the snub. At that second, she hated herself.

And he was gone, and Connie relaxed.

'He's going to spit in your porridge at breakfast. You know that, don't you?' she said. 'And we're going to go to hell in a handcart. We'll make sure we tip him double when we leave,' Connie said.

'Absolutely, I planned to do that anyway.'

Jeff flung the French doors open, and they had their first eyeful of the ocean. It took their breath away.

The balcony was large, with a table and two chairs. The barrier was unobtrusive, with a small gate in the centre leading to their personal hot tub.

The view was infinite.

Clever architecture was such that there was nothing to see from there but the ocean and the twinkling lights of the shoreline, Kardamena, and beyond that, Kos town in the distance.

Her medication affected her mood and made her emotional, something she was unaccustomed to. Before Sparky, she rarely cried about anything. The only thing that ever reduced her to tears was the loss of a pet. Crying always seemed like such a useless waste of time. But the drug she was on was a known depressant. The number of suicides among Type-1 TN sufferers is high, usually from people who can't tolerate the pain. Or from those whose life, as they knew it, changed when the debilitating attacks from their condition struck them down

This was her first attack—the period of time you are ill between remissions— and she'd had no mood swings or moments of depression. The first two months were bad, and then it got better as the doctor prescribed the correct dosage to manage her pain. What it had done, though, was heightened her emotional state. It made her teary which was a new experience for her. When it happened, she was embarrassed because she saw it as a terrible sign of weakness. But Jeff said it was adorable and made him love her more. He told her it was very sweet to see her so raw and vulnerable. It brought out his protective nature.

She looked at the black sea with the beautiful laddered reflection of the light, and she wanted to cry at the beauty of it. This was what she'd dreamed of, that sound, the whoosh and rush of the waves brushing against the shore. Not hard and stormy, not soft and delicate, a solid breaker of sound that put her where she wanted to be and with the man she loved.

It was perfect.

'Drink on the balcony, madam?'

'That would be delightful, Chuffers.'

'Right away, madam, and am I right to assume there will be no gratuity from madam?'

'That is correct, Chuffers.'

'Very good, madam.'

While Jeff went to their mini-bar and poured them drinks, vodka and Diet Coke for her and an ice-cold beer for him, she had to see the bathroom. She wasn't disappointed. The room was furnished in cream marble with veins of golden colouring. It was exquisite.

'There's a bath. Jeff, we've got a bath and a shower, and it's beautiful. However, until we can get to a shop for sunscreen, we'll have to use their body lotion to at least soften our skin, even if we can't protect it.'

'Are you still whingeing about our bottles being confiscated?'

'Not at all, darling. Just saying. That's all. The bath's big enough for two.'

'What, now?'

'Not a chance in hell, Jeff. I'm coming for that drink.'

The night carried a stiff breeze to them as they sat with their first drink on the balcony. It was just as Connie had imagined it. The hotel provided thick white robes and slippers—and throws for sitting outside in the evening chill. Jeff brought two but only shook one out and wrapped it around both of them as she nestled into the crook of his arm. She put the second one over their knees.

That sound. She closed her eyes and listened, smelled, and loved.

Connie had always doubted herself. She'd never felt good enough for the world. And, as was often the case, she wondered if she'd done the right thing by taking early retirement. She'd been a faithful stalwart of lucrative private therapy but had the first two years of her training in the days when starched matrons ran hospital wards like a fascist regime. She'd done her time for twenty years as a hospital psychotherapist and then opted for a back seat and quieter life in a village working at a private practice. Her standards had always been high, but she'd never been able to attain the level of competency set by her own demands. She had to be the best, strongest, kindest, most proficient and, above all, most caring.

Privatisation had been talked about in government for a long time, but the change seemed to happen overnight. Connie and her colleagues were working too hard at the time to see it as anything but a gradual shifting of the sand. In the first couple of months of the nineties, the Conservatives opened the door to privatisation—and from that moment on, care was a commodity and equated to money. Everything was about time and motion, and every second had a pound sign attached to it. A litigious society was born. Where there's blame, there's a claim. Health professionals were retrained in the streamlined art of automation. The patients trundled along a conveyor belt, their symptoms were treated, and there was no time to care about the cause. The aim was to get them in, get them out as soon as possible and try your best not to kill them in the process. Which was just enough to get you your Christmas bonus.

She had always loved her job, but she would have traded every working directive on the planet for a single starched matron on the wards. She thought things would be better in private practice, but the principle was the same. There was never enough time to talk to anybody to get to the underlying causes and problems anymore—and if not that—what was her job about? She spent her career doing the best she could for her patients, but there was always another complaint, the next dissatisfied customer in the waiting room. And that's where the rot set in. They weren't patients anymore. They were customers. She missed her career and felt that her life was worthless. She defined her personality and ego by the work she had done, and without it, she felt like a non-entity. It seemed like a beacon guiding her into retirement when an aged auntie died and left her a sizeable sum of money. Enough to see them through the rest of their lives.

'Earth to Connie. Are you receiving?'

'What? Sorry.'

'Are you hungry? They serve food twenty-four hours a day. We could get some supper?'

They'd had their sandwiches on the plane and crisps and sweets. She wasn't hungry and was so exhausted that she wanted to fall into bed, but as a dedicated foodie, she was dying to see what the restaurant was like. It was too tempting to resist.

They came down the stairs and went through the main entrance hall by a seating area dotted with card tables and board games. A place for quiet time. The green baize covering some of the tables in the card room elevated the tone. The ambience greeted them with imposing double doors carved with rich, swirling designs. They went in, and it was the first of many dining rooms and restaurants, and the main one they'd be using. A man with skin as dark as the sea outside greeted them with a huge smile.

'Welcome. Come in, take a seat, and I'll bring you a drink. My name is Tasos, and I am your friend here. And please help yourself to the buffet.'

They ordered soft drinks and then went to get some food. The choice was out of this world. The bus had arrived, the guests checked in, and all the main players were assembled. Half of the benefits clan surrounded two tables pushed together, leaving an adult—Our Levi's dad—with the younger children. The adults were drunk and loud, and the teenagers were just loud. Mr and Mrs Sweaty Leg had distanced themselves as far as possible from the raucous family and sat alone, devouring a fan of watermelon and a plate of sticky-looking desserts. The couple with the baby wasn't in, and neither were Ray and Lisa. Connie was disappointed at that. They nodded and smiled at a few people they'd seen at various points between England and Greece. Dotted around the tables were established guests whose length of stay could be determined by the colour of their skin. They ranged from white to lobster red, to a golden brown, to the shade of burnished coal.

The food was to die for and was served in the traditional silver chafing dishes. Each of the huge containers for keeping food warm had a slide-back lid, hiding its secrets inside. A huge soup pot emitted a delicious aroma when the lid was lifted. This was the weirdest thing at two in the morning. Connie went no further. It was an easy choice. A ladle of soup and a small slice of the hard white bread that's served with Tzatziki at every Greek taverna. The soup was over-seasoned and over-salted for her taste, but she tempered it with a crack of black pepper, and it was delicious, roasted red pepper and spicy tomato. Jeff had a small dish of chicken curry and rice but couldn't resist a side plate with a piece of smoked fish as well.

It was a fabulous way to end the day. After their light supper, they wanted to explore their surroundings but were too damned tired. They didn't bother unpacking and took out only what they needed to wash themselves that night. Everything else could wait until morning. Both sets of French doors were flung open so she could listen to the ocean. And they stripped out of their clothes and fell into the cold sheets.

The bed was big and too firm, and the pillows weren't filled with feathers in case of allergens, but she was too tired to care and was asleep as soon as her head touched the pillow.

Chapter Ten

Nash wrapped up his final field interview, and as he walked into the station, the desk Sergeant got his attention and pointed to a man sitting on a plastic chair in the waiting area. Two other people sat opposite.

'Somebody to see you, sir.'

'Thanks, Bryce. What's it about?'

'Wouldn't say, but he's been there well over an hour. He said it has to be you. Something about your case.'

Nash had walked into the building and was hoping for five minutes to grab a cup of tea before dealing with members of the public. 'Can I help you?'

'Snow.'

'Sorry?'

'Conrad Snow. You were wondering who I am. And you are Inspector Nash.'

'Yes. I believe you've been waiting for me. Would you mind just giving me a couple of minutes while I find a vacant room?'

'Not a problem. Interview Room Three is available. Thank you for seeing me without an appointment.'

'You know my interview room is free?'

'Yes, Inspector and your four o'clock has been cancelled.'

They were odd things to say, and Nash was confused. He had used the few words with his visitor to appraise him. The man was mid-thirties with blonde hair. He wore a long fringe that fell over one eye, and Nash could tell from his speech and the reaction to his words that he was intelligent. Conrad Snow was nervous, though. Every few seconds, he smoothed his hand over his coat. Apprehension cloaked him.

'Thank you, Mr Snow. I'll be out shortly, and I'm interested to hear what you have to say.' He gave him what he hoped was a reassuring smile to put him at ease. The guy was on edge. Nash went to his office, hung his coat up and locked his briefcase in the cupboard. Interview Room Three was indeed free, and he took a pen and pad with him to make notes. Until he knew what it was about, it was classed as informal information given voluntarily. The interview wouldn't need to be recorded, and there was no need for another officer to be present.

'Mr Snow. I'm sorry to keep you waiting. Would you like to come with me?' He led him in and indicated a seat. 'Can I get you a cup of tea? I could do with one.'

'No. I'm fine, thank you.'

'Sure? Do you mind if I do? It's been a bit of a day.' Nash could have buzzed the duty officer to bring him a cup of tea, but he wanted to give Snow a couple of minutes to work out what he was going to say. He had no idea what the man wanted. Nash stepped into the adjoining room and watched the visitor through the two-way mirror for clues. He wasn't fidgeting now, and a calm resignation had settled over him. He started talking to himself and gesticulating with his hands. Nash hadn't turned the sound on and regretted it. He sighed. The man had seemed competent, but it was the crazy hour again. Nash came back with a steaming mug of tea and smiled. 'Good. Now then, what can I do for you, Mr Snow?'

'This is difficult, and I know you'll be dismissive.'

'If you have any information regarding Alma Cullen, I assure you, you have my full attention, and I'll listen to whatever you've got to say.'

'I have information.'

'I'm listening.'

He was hesitant to continue, and it was like pulling teeth.

'Are you a relative?'

'No.'

'What can you tell me about her?'

The next sentence released a flood, and once he started, words poured out of the interviewee like water.

'I'm just going to get it out. I ask, Inspector, that you let me finish before you interrupt. Please, I ask you to keep an open mind until I've finished. I've done some digging, and I know your reputation regarding information like mine.'

Nash had a feeling where this was going. Not another bloody neurotic crawling out of the gutter. He'd had enough of that nonsense with The Florist case, and that fruitcake got herself killed for it. He'd give him two minutes and then get him the hell out of his station. He tried to keep his expression neutral, though even as an experienced interviewer, with this rubbish, his face had a mind of its own. He waved his hand for Snow to continue.

'I'm here with Max Jones.'

'I should imagine that would be very difficult, considering Mr Jones is dead.'

'You bawled like a baby when he died, and he's insisting that I call you a,' he hesitated, 'a namby bitch.'

'Quite.'

'He's telling me you sat by his bedside every day. He's glad you were with him at the end. He says to tell you he still prefers girls, though.'

Nash was exasperated, so it surprised him when he felt his mouth betraying him with a smile. 'Cute words, Mr Snow, but it doesn't make him any less dead.'

'He's been following me around my house, insisting I came to see you. He said you would give me a hard time, but he wouldn't leave me alone until I agreed to come. Inspector, he sang the doo-doo-doo bits of *Tom's Diner* at me day and night until I cracked up. He wouldn't let me sleep and sat beside me in my car singing Tom's sodding Diner as I came here today. You have to believe me. He's driving me insane. The man won't let up until I do what he wants.'

Nash smiled as he imagined a ghostly Jones waving his hands like a conductor as he sang. 'Let me stop you there, Mr Snow. If you've done your homework, you'll know I hold no truck with this spiritual nonsense. But that's by the by because we, as a force, don't bring in people like you as part of our investigations. It's not our policy. So, I'm afraid you've had a wasted journey.'

'I have to call you a name.'

'You wouldn't be the first, Mr Snow.'

'He's calling you Nasher.' Nash had been doodling on his pad when his hand stopped, and his body tensed.

'I can see that means something to you. He says to tell you he's your Sven and that you'll know who Sven is.' Nash snorted as he remembered Amanda Keys' spirit guide. 'He wants to know how little Isla and William are doing. And he says you're stubborn, and even those random names that nobody will remember won't be enough for you. Sometimes I worked with Amanda Keys, Inspector. She died trying to help, and after everything she did, you still don't have any faith in our ability.'

'What happened to Ms Keys was a tragedy and confirms my opinion that psychics should stick to what they do privately and shouldn't get involved in police work. I'm sorry, but we're done here. Thank you for coming in, but I'm afraid we won't be calling on your services.'

Nash stood up, and Conrad Snow was left with no choice but to leave. Nash opened the door for him, and as Mr Snow was walking through it, he stopped and put his hands to his head. Nash shut the door fast so the other officers wouldn't see this spectacle. Snow's face contorted as if he was in pain.

'Stop it. For God's sake, stop it. I can't do any more. Please, I did as you asked. Leave me alone.'

'*Tom's Diner*?'

'He's screaming it at me on a loop. Please, Inspector.' When Snow straightened up, he looked as though he was in physical pain. 'Okay. I'll try again but stop screaming at me.'

'I take it he promised,' Nash said.

'Yes. He makes a lot of promises.'

Nash clapped his hands. 'An excellent performance, Mr Snow. Please let me know when you're on at The Forum, and I'll buy a ticket, but in the meantime, I'm asking you to leave the building.'

'He's changed it. There's another song now. He wants me to sing it to you, but I've never heard of it.'

'Enough, Mr Snow.'

'Two black Cadillacs driving in a slow parade.' He spoke the lyrics and was about to continue, but Nash sat in his chair. He looked at his hand and saw it was shaking. Nash watched Snow grow confident as he broke through to the detective. 'Max says stop being so stubborn and listen. He says you're your own worst enemy.'

'Okay. I'll give you one shot, but you answer my direct questions and none of your bullshit. Got it?'

'He says you'd better have plenty of fish if you want him to act like a performing seal.'

'What was the name of his dog?'

'Mia.'

'How long did he own her?'

'One night.' Snow looked surprised at his answer, and Nash drew in a sharp breath.

'What were the last words he ever said.'

'He says, "Too easy. Pick something harder." And he's asking if you spat in his sandwich that day in Morecambe.'

'If you think you're for real, tell me his last words, or get out of my office, dickhead.' Nash felt tears stinging his eyes as he replayed Max Jones' last few minutes on this earth.

'It doesn't hurt. That was the last thing he said,' Snow told him.

Nash coughed. This was utter rubbish, but it hit him in the chest. He stood up with his back to Snow and stared through the nothingness of the frosted-glass window to compose himself.

'Is there anything you'd like to say to Max?'

'No.'

'He says, "Typical."'

Nash snorted.

'It's okay, Nasher. Take a minute,' Snow said, but Nash recognised Max's voice.

He shook his head to clear his thoughts, and wiped away a traitorous tear that rolled down his cheek, and even though Snow couldn't see his face, he felt like a complete idiot. He'd never been so unprofessional. His career was built on holding his emotions in check, yet he was on the point of sobbing in front of a member of the public. He'd have told the young WPC's off for less. He pulled himself together, gave another gruff cough and turned back to his seat with his emotions in check. His tone was brusque and business-like. 'I'm not saying I believe in any of this, but you have got my attention, and I'm prepared to listen.'

'Thank you. Inspector. I'll take my window and cut to the chase. There's going to be another murder any day now by the same person that killed Alma Cullen.'

'When?' Nash had his pen poised, ready to write.

'I don't know, but soon.'

'You're not so good when it comes to being helpful, are you?' It was a cheap undercut, but he couldn't help himself. This guy got under his skin. Everything he'd said was correct, but now Nash wanted specifics about the case. Like every psychic before him, he was vague and non-committal. It was frustrating.

'Go on then,' Nash said. 'Tell me. I'm getting an F—does the killer's name begin with F? And maybe he was an infantry soldier in the First World War?' Nash said.

'You're being very frustrating, Inspector. I can only give you what I get as it comes through to me. Max said you'd be exactly like this, so it's not as if I wasn't forewarned.'

'I've heard the excuses before, Mr Snow. Have you got any new material? You expect me to believe that all this is coming from Max?'

'Partly, but when it's about the murders, I mostly see images.'

'Convenient. Carry on. Entertain me.' It was the same claptrap that Amanda told him, and he didn't know if the consistency strengthened Snow's conviction or proved they were all nuts.

'I can see water. An aeroplane. You're going far away across the sea, Inspector.'

Nash laughed, but it was hard and derisory. He'd taken enough of this fiasco. 'Have you heard yourself? You should be performing in a kiosk on Morecambe seafront for a piece of silver. I've had enough of this. I haven't been abroad for years and have no intentions of going overseas any time soon. I guess Max never told you about my camper van.'

'The Good Lady Diana, he's telling me now. Max is killing himself laughing. He says you'll never change and to stop being a dick. He says to use the same intuition as with black Cadillacs, whatever that means. All I know is there's going to be another murder. And you're going on a plane with a woman. That's all I can tell you for now.'

'I'll dig out my budgie smugglers. Thank you for your information, Mr Snow.'

'Euros.'

'What?'

'You were going to ask in a sneer if you should change some money. Certainly, you should. You'll need Euros.'

'I have everything I need. I'll be in touch should we require Max's further assistance,' he said in a derisory tone.

When Snow left, Nash went back to his office and sat alone for a long time. He went over the meeting and couldn't understand how Snow had been so right about Max. He couldn't have known the dying man's final words. It was impossible—but he did. And nobody knew about *Two Black Cadillacs* except Nash and Max. Two bitter women had masterminded the deaths in his last case, and the song by Carrie Underwood was about two women who killed a man for cheating on them. The killers subliminally reminded him of the song, and he hummed it for days before apprehending them. His mind made the connection long before he caught on. According to Snow, Max told him to open his mind and listen to that intuition again during this case.

He swivelled in his chair and laughed. He had an image of Maxwell Jones in spirit form hounding the poor sod until he got his own way. That was Jones, to a tee. Nash slammed his briefcase closed. It was time to go home. His cat, Lola, needed feeding. He grabbed his jacket and smiled as he locked his office door.

'*I am sitting in the morning at the diner on the corner.*' He laughed. 'Thanks for that, Maxwell sodding Jones. You bastard.'

Chapter Eleven

N ash stopped between his mug and the waste bin with a teabag slouching over the sides of his teaspoon. It dripped on his wooden floor, and he'd never be so slovenly as to allow it to happen as a rule, but one word had stopped him in his tracks.

Kos.

He wasn't paying attention to the news as he prepared to leave for work, but the word Kos jumped from the TV. He'd heard something about Kos in the last couple of days. What the hell was it? Or maybe he'd seen something. Through his police training, he'd learned to use his recall ability to read people and places. He visualised the word, Kos. It appeared as an image in blue letters in his mind's eye. Next, he saw a white mortar without a pestle. A honey jar. It was the ceramic piece of pottery, a souvenir from Kos in Alma Cullen's kitchen.

It was such a tenuous thing, but it caught his attention enough that he listened closely to the news report. A British boy had been found dead in a hotel swimming pool on the outskirts of Kardamena on the Grecian Island of Kos.

Evidence indicated that foul play was suspected. Dale Butcher, aged thirteen, was found face down in an outdoor swimming pool, presumed drowned by resort guests as they rushed to get the pick of the sun loungers early that morning. On investigation, it was discovered that the cause of death was an embolism. The report went on to say that his parents were devastated.'

The words of Conrad Snow came back to him. 'You're going on a plane with a woman.' Snow was a kook, and Nash wasn't about to get involved in a Greek tragedy on his say-so. Going abroad to conduct an investigation with the island police would involve a ridiculous amount of negotiation with the Greek authorities. He couldn't believe he was even contemplating reacting on the strength of a honey pot, two unrelated people dying from freak embolism and the words of a crank psychic.

When he got to the station, he knocked on Bronwyn Lewis' door. She smiled at him and motioned for him to sit down. 'I'm glad you're here. We've got intel on a Greek incident. It may be linked to the Cullen case.'

'I saw it this morning.'

They discussed the ramifications of both cases, and although she was willing to give him her backing, Lewis wasn't convinced that the link was enough at this stage. However, she said she'd fail in her duty if she ignored the intel.

'I want to go in undercover, and I want Brown,' Nash said.

'Why?'

'Why what? Brown or the covert op?'

'Both,' Bronwyn said. 'It'll be a massive drama, just getting you out there, never mind undercover.'

They discussed the operation and how it would work. Nash saw from her nodding that Lewis was coming on board with the idea.

'It's a lot of red tape,' Bronwyn said.

'I know, but it could be worth it if it means nabbing Alma Cullen's killer.'

Bronwyn Lewis would have to approach the Greek embassy on his behalf. It would involve collaboration between England and the chief commissioner on Kos.

Nash filled Lewis in on what he needed from her. She sat for a minute without saying a word and twiddled a Biro between her fingers. Nash watched as the ridges of the pen's cartridge travelled over her fingertips.

'You'll authorise it, then?'

'On the say-so of a crank, I must be mad. What's got into you, Nash? This isn't like you.'

'It's not because of Snow. The fact that this kid and Alma Cullen were both the victims of freak attacks but, in fact, died from embolisms is too coincidental. My instinct is telling me I'm right. I promise you. The same person committed those two murders.'

'You want me to send you across the bloody ocean on one of your hunches?'

'I suppose, but when have I ever been wrong? I don't jump unless I'm sure. You know that.'

'Let me run through the logistics of this. You want a jolly that'll cost this department thousands of pounds, and you're taking Brown with you? And not a week, either. You want to book into this fancy 5-star resort for two weeks with a fake moustache, a bowler hat and Brown acting as your daughter.'

'That's pretty much the size of it, minus the hat. You won't have to pay for the resort. The negative press of unsolved murders on their patch will kill tourism. And they can't put a Greek officer undercover in the resort because he'd stand out like a sore thumb. They'll throw room and board at us to sort it for them. If not, the embassy will pull rank and cover the cost, so at best, it'll be a couple of flights and some spending money.'

'What? You're taking the piss.'

'I'm kidding. It'll just be the flights. If we get it cracked in a couple of days, we'll cut it short and come back.'

'Seriously, though, you might have no chance of getting in. The Greek authorities aren't going to want British coppers stomping all over their murder scene.'

'That's why I'm trusting you to use your charm to sell it to them, and if that fails, bully the hell out of them to get it authorised. We'll be undercover, just two more holidaymakers doing our thing. Do you want another piece of my gut with nothing to back it up?'

'Shoot.'

'Tell them if they don't sign off on this, there will be more deaths before the week's out. Make them believe it, and they'll beg us to get out there and catch the perp.'

'You can't know that.'

'I don't, but I can feel it. This person is ruthless. They're getting the taste for this, and they aren't going to stop at two deaths.'

'There's no MO. A pensioner in Barrow and a child in Greece, we have to connect them and make it sound convincing.'

'Tell them to get onto the coroner and make them look for a small needle stick, probably under the armpit. There's a needle mark somewhere on that kid. I guarantee it. And if there isn't, then I'm wrong on all counts, and I'll put my sunscreen back in the cupboard.'

Lewis sat back and pen-twiddled some more. 'Okay, here's the deal. I'll push for them to look for this needle prick during the autopsy, and if it's there, I'll move heaven and earth to get you on the case. That's the best I can do.'

'I'll take it, but please, time is everything. At least look at flights. I need to be out there with Brown today.'

'Don't push your luck, Nash. Now get out of my office. I planned my day, and it didn't involve getting in the middle of a foreign case. I promise you this. They'll be locked down tight. They won't want us interfering. Would you let them in to crawl all over your case?'

'If it saved somebody's life? In a heartbeat, ma'am.'

He went to his office and couldn't settle into anything until he got the go-ahead from Lewis. Getting him on the Kos side of the case wouldn't be easy, but if anybody could get a foot in the door, it was Bronwyn. Hell, he didn't even know if there was a Greek side of the case.

His phone rang, and the desk officer said he had a call on the line from Conrad Snow. When his vocal cords worked without permission, he was about to ask PC Patel to fob him off. 'Thanks, Patel. You can put him through.' Shit. He tried to convince himself that he had no idea why he said that, but he knew only too well.

There were two reasons, and the first was personal. He'd never admit it to anybody, but he wanted those messages from Max Jones. He missed him, and although his brain told him it was hogwash, his heart wanted contact with Max in spirit. At least that reason made some kind of emotional sense. The other one made Nash wonder if he was losing his edge, not to mention his mind. He opened to the possibility that Snow could help in the case. If it hadn't been for his message about flying, he wouldn't even consider going to Greece later today.

'Snow.'

'Hello, Inspector Nash. I want to help you. I'll do anything I can, but you've got to get this nutter out of my head. He's driving me mad. I refused to call you. Does he ever stop talking?'

Nash was aware of a huge grin spreading across his face. 'You have another message from Max?'

He says, "He's always been a good lad. He's family, so go easy on him." He disappeared once I agreed to ring you, so I have no idea what it means.'

'Who is he talking about?'

'Told you, I don't know.'

'That's it?'

'I'm not a personal answering machine, Inspector. He wanted me to pass it on, and I've done as asked. He broke into my last reading and caused mayhem. It's not on.'

'Of course.' The line went quiet, and Nash thought Snow had hung up on him until he heard his steady breathing. 'Are you still there?'

'I've just had a vision. I'm seeing a number. It's a flashing visual, and it's repeating in my head. 114. Does it mean anything to you?'

'No. What else?'

'That's it. Just the number 114. I think it's to do with your current case. Watch out for it, and you'll know you're on the right track. My guide's telling me it's a pointer so that when it comes, you'll know you're right. Goodbye, Inspector. And good luck.'

After they'd said goodbye and Snow hung up, Nash didn't have time to ponder what had been said. There was a knock at the door as he put the phone down, and the duty sergeant stuck his head around. 'Can I come in?'

'Yes, Patel. What can I do for you?'

'We've got a young lad cooling his temper in the cells, boss. Nothing to do with the current case, but I thought you'd want to be informed about this one.'

'Really? Why's that?'

'It's taking without consent and possession, sir. Do you remember the young Whitehouse lad? He nicked his dad's car to joyride around the streets and had a bag of weed on him when we nabbed him. Given your involvement last year, I thought you'd want to know before we spoke to him.'

'Who?'

'Sebastian Whitehouse, sir.'

'Am I supposed to know who that is? You're going to have to give me a clue.'

'Sebastian Whitehouse. Some relation to Max Jones?'

He's always been a good lad. He's family, so go easy on him.

Nash grinned. Okay, Max, I get it, he thought. I've got you. 'Of course. The nephew. We spoke to him along with everybody else involved in The Florist case. Belligerent little shit.'

99

'That's the one. Got him to a tee. His dad's in the waiting room.'

'Who's interviewing?'

'Mason and Renshaw. Phil's leading.'

'Ask Greg Mason to step down. I'll take it with Renshaw. Thanks, Patel. Good call.'

Sebastian Jones-Whitehouse was a typical example of entitled youth if ever he'd seen one. Nash didn't make friends easily, but he lost one of the best friends he'd ever had a couple of months after the last case. Max would laugh if he heard him saying that now. They were an unlikely combination, thrust together when The Florist case went crazy. They'd despised each other, and Nash grinned as he remembered Max giving him the run-around. He couldn't pinpoint when their mutual dislike had pivoted. But he knew that the world lost a good man when Max died of a brain tumour. Nash missed him.

He was a man of science. If he couldn't see, touch, or understand it, he didn't believe it. But he imagined Max, being the most annoying ghost to take up haunting and singing at Conrad Snow for four solid hours. He wondered if Max had sent his nephew to him just to rain crap on his day. 'Get a grip, Nash,' he said out loud and then shook his head because, in real life, people rarely speak to themselves.

He straightened his tie and went into the interview room. 'Mr Jones-Whitehouse, we meet again.'

'So? What of it?'

'You're a charmer, aren't you?'

'And if you're going to interview me, at least get my name right. It's just Whitehouse.'

'Not according to your driving licence.'

He sneered. 'My mum loved having the double-barrelled name, said it elevated her in Barrow society. As if this dead-end town even knows how to spell society. The posh name backfired on her when Max was the prime suspect in a load of murders, though. She dropped the Jones faster than she dropped her knickers as a kid.'

'That's your mother. Don't talk about her like that. You'd struggle to carry a better name than Jones.'

'What do you know? She was supposed to love Max, but it didn't stop her from hiring some awful bedroom author with a penchant for adverbs and exclamation marks to ghostwrite a biography about it. She reckons she's going to get it published when it's done. Max would piss himself.'

Nash had to agree. 'Your uncle was a fine man.'

'Whatever. Anyway, you can't keep me here. I wasn't driving the car, and the gear wasn't mine.'

'So how did your dad's car get from Barrow to Dalton? Did it get there by osmosis?'

'For that, the car must be comprised of a collection of water molecules. That's not the case. If you're going to use intellect as a tool to prove your superiority to me, at least make it scientifically accurate. Otherwise, the delivery makes you sound like a dick.'

'It's apparent that while your parents' money was wasted on your private education, some of it went in. But, young Sebastian, you aren't as smart as you think. Half a dozen cameras picked you up while you were joyriding around on your own like a sad sack. What's the matter, Mr Whitehouse? Got no playmates?' He remembered Snow's words. *He's a good lad. Go easy on him.* 'We could prove you were driving. If we zoomed in far enough, we'd be able to print off a souvenir photo of you smoking a joint. Your parents would be so proud.'

'Get stuffed. I want a lawyer.'

'A lawyer, is it? What do you think this is, *Miami Vice*?'

'It's my right.'

'You know what, boy? I can't be arsed with you. You're a fruit fly in my vanilla ice cream.'

'Eh?'

'An itch between my shoulder blades.'

'You've got an itch?'

'I can't be bothered with you. Driving without a licence will kill you, and smoking weed won't do those zits any favours—and guess what?'

'Go on. You're obviously dying to enlighten me about something.'

'It makes you impotent. Some of my coppers have kids at your school. I can get the word around that you're a shit lay.'

'For that, you would have to assume that I have any interest at all in sex with a partner. I can fulfil all my needs in that department from a screen and in the privacy of my bedroom. If that's the best threat you've got, can I go now?'

'Dealing with you is like cutting your nails, then finding out you have new keys to put on your keyring. You're an annoying little sod. Go on, get out of here. Your dad's too soft and didn't want to press charges. He's outside waiting to take you home, but I bet you're up to your eyes in trouble, mate.'

Sebastian laughed. 'He can't do anything. He's wetter than dog piss.'

Nash let Whitehouse get up before he spoke again. 'A word to the wise, lad. I have the power to take this to court. Unlikely on a first offence, but who knows, it might have even bought you a little stretch in the Big House. Guess what that means?'

'What?'

'I can make life difficult for you, Whitehouse. You owe me. From now on, you're in my debt.'

'Get lost. Are you bent?'

Renshaw snorted and covered his face.

'Excuse me?' Nash said.

'Corrupt, Inspector. Are you a corrupt copper?'

'I am not. But I'll be watching you. You'd better clean up your act. And I can call in a favour from you anytime I want.'

'I doubt it.'

'I'll be seeing you soon, Whitehouse.'

'Not if I see you first.'

'I'm going away on business for a few days, but there's somebody I want you to meet. I'll set it up. The nephew of one of my team is having a hard time and could use a friend. He's a couple of years younger than you, and you could be a good role model for him—or a bloody nightmare, in which case I'll need my head testing for suggesting you befriend him.'

'Are you mad? Do I look like a bloody social worker?'

'It's not too late to take a conviction all the way, Whitehouse. I'd think very carefully about your answer—and about how you treat this lad.'

'You're blackmailing me. That's illegal.'

'What is it you said earlier? So what? Well, back at you. So what?'

'How much time are we talking, and what do I have to do?'

'Just what you can spare, a couple of hours a week, maybe. And what you do is up to you. Play computer games or kick a ball around. You could go to the cinema, maybe. If you hated each other on sight, no problem, meet him, and then you're off the hook—but I have a good feeling about you two being friends. For a start, it wouldn't hurt you to spend a couple of hours volunteering at the refuge centre where your Uncle Max gave his time. It did him no harm.'

'He'd better not be a dickhead.'

'I have more concern about you in that respect.' Nash winked. 'And I'll be watching you to see that you don't lead a good lad astray. The idea is that you sort your head out, not that you teach him how to steal cars and smoke weed.'

'Just when it sounded like fun.'

'Get out, Whitehouse,' Nash said, but he was smiling. Seb wasn't a bad kid. He just needed direction. He was at a crossroads where he could take a right or wrong lane. Nash was willing to take a punt on putting two troubled kids together in the hope they'd come good.

The next few hours were endless. He had several meetings with Lewis and spoke to the Greek embassy and the Chief of Police on Kos. Initially, they weren't happy about having British interference.

Until the next body turned up.

Chapter Twelve

Despite it being late when they went to sleep, Connie woke early and slid out of bed. She hadn't slept much and had woken for an hour at five. But even though she'd hardly had any sleep, she felt great. Jeff slept like the dead. It would take a hurricane to wake him. She'd insisted on sleeping with the French doors open to listen to the ocean. That, coupled with Jeff's snoring, was the first thing she heard.

The blue and white tiles were cool beneath her feet, and she pulled on the robe provided by the resort as she went onto the balcony. The ocean was magnificent. She sat on one of the two chairs and watched the waves crashing onto the shore for five minutes. It was only eight o'clock, but the sun was already high.

A month before, she hadn't been able to stand the sunlight. Her Trigeminal Neuralgia had come in hard and relentless. She'd spent three months wearing dark glasses indoors and out. Natural light stung and burned her face, and the lightest breeze hitting her cheek triggered a tic attack. She had the beast subdued with hard medication, and while it smudged every edge of her being so that nothing was as stark or sharp, it meant she could enjoy the sun again. Artificial lighting still hurt and caused her to tic when Sparky roared and pulled against his manacles.

However, she couldn't have everything and feeling the sun on her face meant the world.

She made tea to take her morning tablets with, took one over for Jeff and kissed him. He reached up, pulled her into bed, and they made love before going into the bathroom. They could have fit three families into the shower with them. It was so big, and the needles from the power jets stung their backs and shoulders. It was bliss.

'Are we swimming this morning?' Connie asked.

'Maybe. I thought we'd explore first, though. Get our bearings.'

'Is that a yes or no?'

'It's a maybe.'

'I need to know whether to put my swimming costume on under my dress.'

'No, don't bother. We might go for a swim this afternoon.'

'Perfect.'

She wore a blue maxi dress with a sports bra and thong that she regretted later, but at the time, she felt good. Her brown hair was long, and she left it to dry naturally so they could get to the restaurant for breakfast. She was impatient, and Jeff took ages getting dressed, but she bit her tongue and went onto the balcony to wait for him.

Something was happening on the sun terrace. She looked over the balcony, but there was nothing to see except staff buzzing around and guests complaining about being herded from their loungers into the hotel.

'Something's happening out here.'

'It'll be couples' yoga, morning Agadoo, or something equally energetic and horrendous.'

'No. Something's definitely happening. It doesn't look good.'

Somewhere below, a woman screamed.

'Come on, Jeff, let's go, or I'll meet you there. Whatever's happened has caused a panic.'

'Right, come on. Let's go.'

Connie had to take it easy on the first few narrow stone steps, then managed the twisting spiral staircase in her flip-flops as it widened out. The reception area, open bars, and chillout spaces were full of people being herded inside. A woman was still screaming and sobbing, and now she could hear other people crying as well. While the crowd was coming in through one door, Connie dragged Jeff further down the room and slipped out of another, leading to the balcony overlooking the pool. It was their first glimpse of any of the swimming pools, and it was magnificent. But she barely registered the splendour.

They were fixated on the body of a young male in a grey tracksuit floating face down in the water.

'Madam, please. This is not a spectacle. Return inside.'

A staff member blocked her view with his body and ushered them to the end of the queue while the door they'd slipped out of was slammed and locked behind them.

The scene was captured like a still photograph in her mind. The boy lying in the pool, and the family standing around, everybody in somebody else's arms. Only a dark-skinned little girl stood apart and a few feet away from two cuddling women. Connie looked at the child. Its brown eyes were as large as planets. She tried to smile at the child, who looked frightened and confused. It was all so sad. She was in a thin nightie with sparkling gold sandals on her feet. They were unfastened and could trip her up. She was holding a brown ragdoll with black woollen hair in plaits.

'We stayed up drinking,' one of the two men from the family said. 'We thought he was behind us when we went to bed.'

'And what time was that, sir?' a policeman asked in broken English.

'A little after three, I suppose. The manager came out and told us to keep the noise down. People complained, and our Gemma was sick in a plant pot. So, we thought we'd better call it a night.'

Connie didn't hear anymore. With the commotion and people gathered in the bar areas, they didn't have to queue for the breakfast buffet. She looked over her shoulder at all the sorrow and went into the dining room.

She was worried about how Jeff would cope with the mass-produced food and the cattle market of three hundred people being fed at every sitting, but if breakfast was anything to go by, she needn't have bothered. He loved cooking and eating. He made all their meals and never missed an episode of Master Chef.

During their time away, they could book six tables at the various a la carte restaurants in the complex, and they intended to take advantage of every one of them. However, most of their meals would be taken in the buffet restaurant. The food was excellent.

Connie was mesmerised by the grandness of it. Five-star dining was a step up from the three-star all-you-can-eat buffets she was used to on holiday. Jeff chose eggs benedict with smoked salmon for his first meal and commented that the bechamel was cooked to perfection.

Connie found the food too salty, but that was the only thing she could complain about. Everything was amazing. She had fresh bread and butter, a slice of cheese and some fruit salad. She couldn't believe there was a full dessert table at breakfast and tried to resist the slice of lemon torte with her morning coffee—but it won. They sat on the outdoor terrace, on the opposite side of the hotel from the pool, and the sun baked down on them.

Jeff's smile was beaming, and she tried to remember when she'd been so relaxed and happy.

'Excuse me, love,' Jeff called to a waitress as she passed the table. 'Would there be any chance of another coffee, please?'

'You wait, yeah. I bring.'

'That would be great, thank you. Just when you're ready.'

'I ready. Okay? What? I no look ready? I bring. Jeez.'

'You rattled her cage. You can tell it's the end of a long season. I bet she was skipping through the terrace the first week,' Connie said, and they laughed.

'Coffee. You want one, now?' she asked Connie.

'No. I'm good. Thank you, though.'

'I don't suppose I could have some milk, could I please?' Jeff asked.

'You want milk, now? Why you no say? I bring. Jeez.'

She was delightful. The sassy waitress was in her twenties and reached a height of four feet at best with an overbite like a deformed Yorkshire Terrier. Connie thought she was brilliant in her impatience and wasn't afraid to put Jeff in his place.

'Yeah, why you no say, Jeez,' Connie laughed. 'She's brilliant. Can we take her home?'

'I'll buy you a bad-tempered Pekinese before having her around. Jeez.'

Whispers about the body in the pool were rife at every table on the terrace, and snippets of conversations floated over them.

'They only arrived last night.'

'What a shame.'

'He was just a kid.'

'Had his whole life ahead of him.'

'Some holiday this is turning out to be.'

'Parents were drunk, apparently.'

'Terrible.'

'Will the pool be cleaned before this afternoon?'

Everybody was talking about it. 'Come on,' Jeff said. 'Let's get out of here.'

They thanked the surly waitress on the way out and smiled at the frazzled-looking restaurant manager, a tiny man with a bald head and high standards.

There was a buzz of doom and excitement in the communal areas, and the doors leading down to the outside pool were locked. The only way out was through the front entrance or by taking the three lifts to the beach a mile below. They joined the short queue. Most guests didn't go to the beach and were more interested in hanging around the bar drinking morning cocktails and coffee to await news of the drowned boy.

They were crammed in the lift with six people. One was a child with a giant inflatable flamingo. The sign read *Lift to the Beach*.

'Isn't it awful about that boy?' an overweight woman in a polka dot costume said.

'His family must be going through hell.'

'The couple in the room three doors down from us found them. Terrible shock. You don't expect it when you go on holiday, do you? They should ask for a refund.'

'I saw them when we were brought inside. They're a rough-looking lot.'

One of the gossips lowered her voice to a whisper. 'And two of their kids are black. Can you imagine?'

Connie wanted to ask, 'Imagine what?' but she kept her mouth shut. It wasn't her fight. Jeff gave her hand a squeeze as she tensed. He knew how good she was being and how hard it was not to voice her opinion and stick up for the people who weren't there to defend themselves.

When they got out, a policeman was waiting to escort them to the next lift, so they weren't tempted to veer off to the cordoned-off pool and crime scene. They were on the same level as the police investigation, and the last thing they needed was more rubberneckers. The policeman had a gun on his hip. When Connie looked up, she saw that most of the balconies overlooking that pool had people hanging on them, watching as the body was brought out of the water. Most of the guests were recording the action on their phones.

'Is that a real gun?' the flamingo boy asked.

'Yes.'

'Can I hold it?'

'No.'

The policeman pressed the button to summon the lift and repeated it every few seconds. When it came, Connie held Jeff back as the other guests went in, and she spoke to the policeman. 'We'll wait for the next one, thank you. I don't want to breathe the same air as a pack of bigots and racists or be trapped in a confined space with them.'

'Well, really,' one of the women said.

The policeman didn't understand and had his foot in the door to hold it open. 'You go in.'

'No, thank you. We'll wait.'

'Connie, he has to go to the first lift for the next load of people. You're holding everybody up. Just get in,' Jeff said. He nudged her, and Connie held her head high and looked at the other adults until they lowered their gaze and stared at the mirrored glass in the lift. It didn't take them long to see their own shame. Nobody spoke again until the doors opened, and the bigots couldn't get out fast enough.

They were below the level of the drowning, and there were no restrictions on this floor. 'We'll take the steps from here,' Connie said. There were hundreds of them cut into stages in the rockface of the mountainside. There were bars and spas, restaurants, shops and chill-out areas to explore on every level.

The beach went from the resort village at the far end of the bay to Kardamena, four miles away. 'Do you fancy a walk into town?' Jeff asked.

She did not. The three hundred steps down to the beach had caused her thighs to chafe, and the heat was crippling. 'Maybe. Let's go in that direction, and we'll see how we get on. I'm not bothered about doing too much today, though, Jeff. Can't we just look at the ocean? Isn't it beautiful?'

The beach had a boardwalk from where they left the steps to the borderline of the resort village. Connie stepped off the boards onto the stony beach when somebody wanted to get past, and her flip-flops sank into horrible sharp pebbles. Nobody thanked her. Jeff did what everybody else did and barged past people coming the other way. Connie stepped off when a boy walked past with a drink in his hand.

'Why do you do that?'

'It's good manners.'

'No. It's that ultra-martyrdom ever-so-subservient thing you do. How many adults do you know that would step off the board for a child?'

'Stop nagging me. Look, there's a beach bar. Let's get a drink and take it to the sun loungers.' Every few yards, there was a beach hut. Some sold trips and water sports activities, and Jeff said he wouldn't mind chartering a sailing boat to take around the bay. He'd done some sailing in his youth. 'I doubt anybody will let you hire a boat to go off in it.'

'Connie, I'm probably a more experienced sailor than any of these jerks. Why do you have to criticise me?' She hadn't, but she pacified him and said it would be nice.

Most of the huts were bars and food concessions. They'd passed a pizza and a doner kebab hut, and there were ice cream shacks and crepe makers, fresh doughnuts and even one offering swordfish and tzatziki with salad in a baked pitta. Jeff said he was dying to try one.

He had a beer, and Connie chose a mojito slushy. The cup of ice was so full of cheap alcohol that any flavour was bleached from it. It was foul but cold, and after all those steps, she was grateful. The heat got to her. They were exposed, and it made her irritable, an emotion that she swallowed and kept from Jeff. She wanted to avoid walking on the pebble beach as much as possible. The stones were deep. With every footfall, you sank to your ankles, and walking was agony. Her thighs were rubbed raw, her feet cut to ribbons, and the sun was too hot. Connie and Jeff sank onto sun loungers, and she was happy to stay there for an hour reading the book on her Kindle.

She got ten minutes. 'Come on, drink up. We've got loads of exploring to do.'

Her heart sank. But she smiled, got up and battled the stones of agony to get back to the boardwalk. A girl by the boards was screaming her head off. It struck Connie as odd that she was wearing a pink swimming costume with a little frill attached and a big blue coral pendant that looked too bulky and mature for a child of about six to wear. It was the same kid that had been bawling in the next room all night and again this morning. Connie saw that she had a disability and walked with a jerky gait. She seemed to be in constant pain.

'Where's your Mummy, darling?' Connie asked. A woman appeared and grabbed the girl's hand, dragging her down the beach. The stones didn't seem to bother her. She shouted at the child, and the girl screamed until they were out of earshot.

The ocean was one of the most beautiful things Connie had ever seen, but she'd had enough of the beach. It wasn't ten in the morning yet, and the sun was blistering. As they'd had their sun creams confiscated, finding a shop to buy more was paramount. Connie felt her face and shoulders burning.

'Should we have a walk to the room through the other three hotels?'

One word stood out in that sentence. Room. Jesus, yes, please. 'Okay. That'd be nice.'

The village was one hotel, but it had been split into four residencies as it climbed the mountain. Each was more lavish and luxurious as it rose. The first level was a huge complex built with families in mind. It had a vast water park, and Connie and Jeff had access to all of the facilities across the complex. 'Fancy a swim? Those water slides look fantastic,' Jeff said.

They did, and she'd have loved a swim. 'I haven't got my costume.'

'That was silly. Why not?'

'Because you told me not to put it on. You said we weren't swimming this morning. You go if you like. I'll read.'

'No, I'm not going in without you. I'll do without, and you can make it up to me when we get back to the room.' There was that blame game again. He had a knack for making things her fault. Something she hadn't done, or should have done, or did do that she shouldn't have.

They went through the first hotel and avoided being run over by a million children screaming their heads off. The parents, as a group, didn't look happy, and Connie counted four impending divorces by the time they'd run the gauntlet to the bars. It was like their hotel, but louder, less lavish, and with more little people.

They found the gift shop, but they didn't have any sun lotion, so they left by the back entrance and through the water park to get to the steps leading to the next part of the complex.

It was a mountain, and Connie's thighs screamed at her. It didn't matter how often she put the material of her dress between them, it slipped out, and her skin rubbed. She felt sick with the heat. A thousand swords had cut her feet. Now, she was out of breath and struggling to climb the steps under the relentless sun. She'd had enough, and they were only a quarter of the way up. She persuaded him to stop for a drink at the next hotel. This one had nightclubs and was geared towards the stags and hens. They had all-day running beach parties, and one was already in full swing. A rep welcomed them onto the terrace and squirted them with a foam cannon. Connie loved it and laughed, but they declined the offer to join in the poolside games. There was only one couple of a similar age, and they smiled at each other over bonded dotage.

Everybody else was younger than twenty-five, and there was so much flesh that Connie didn't know where to look. Nearly everybody was topless, and it was a bouncing-booby bonanza. She might get to have her drink in peace with the scenery being to a man's liking. After the awful mojito, she didn't want alcohol again and opted for a Coke while Jeff had a beer. They were told the gift shop on this level had just closed but would open again at four if they wanted to try later.

And back to climbing. The third building was breathtaking, and Connie thought it was even more stunning than theirs on the top level. It wasn't as classy, but it was beautiful. The design was based along the lines of Gaugin's architecture. From the top balcony, a single swimming pool ran from the sky down to the second-level complex. It was clever because it was a man-made pool split into twenty-one components for all levels of swimming and aesthetics. It dropped by a series of waterfalls and stepped drops. There were manmade caves built with seating behind the waterfalls and pool bars connected by bridges over the many lagoons. Each drop had private areas, loungers around the pool, bars, restaurants, palm trees and fairy lights. It was like being in a Bounty advert.

'Last leg. Are you up for it?' Jeff asked.

She was on her last leg and wanted to lie in one of the sweet cabanas and die. But she was determined not to moan. This was a no-whinge holiday. 'You bet.' She was glad of the maxi dress covering her John Wayne stance as she walked with her legs akimbo so that her thighs didn't touch. As they left, she saw Mr and Mrs Sweaty Legs sitting at the bar. They were pissed, and Connie envied them.

They walked past them and were almost out of earshot when they saw Sweaty Legs lean into his wife. 'Did you see that? It was that woman from the plane. The one that had a fit on me. I thought she was going to throw up all over my lap. They shouldn't have put her on a flight with normal people.'

Connie tore her hand out of Jeff's grip. She returned to the bar, picked up the man's pint and poured it over his head. Actions speak louder than words. He was soaked, and as she went back to Jeff feeling much better, Mrs Sweaty Legs swivelled on her bar stool and stared after them, mimicking a fat fish with her popping mouth.

The mountain wasn't going to beat Connie as they walked the twisting road that meandered up the side of the rock face. She hoped she wouldn't have a heart attack before she got to the top.

'Hey,' she said. 'How do you get a fat bird up a mountain?'

'Go on.'

'One step at a time.'

'How do you get a fat bird down a mountain?' he asked.

'I don't know.'

'A good push should do it.' They laughed. And walked and laughed some more because life was great. When they rounded the last bend, and that cold, austere door awaited them, Connie felt that she'd been returned to the lap of the gods. She knew cool blue tiles greeted them inside. And something fruity with lots of ice.

She smiled at Jeff and felt good. She could have insisted on taking the three lifts back up the mountain. Or they could have waited for one of the buses to come. But she'd done it. She'd walked a mile up a near vertical hill, and she'd done it in under three weeks. Her feet hurt, and her thighs stung, but she was on top of the world.

Chapter Thirteen

C onnie was disappointed. They'd been in the blazing sun all morning, and it was too hot for Jeff. She wanted to sit on the terrace to eat, but he was uncomfortable and insisted on being inside. Her face was crestfallen as he led her away from the sea.

The quiche was too salty but delicious, and the salad was so fresh it was growing. Jeff was a protein man and had a plate of meat, fish and vegetables. He was blown away by the standard and said the quality was excellent.

Full and happy, they had coffee in one of the bars to let their food digest. The talk around them was still about the boy that drowned.

'I heard the chambermaids talking in the corridor outside my room,' a woman said to a couple at the next table, and Connie angled her body towards them to hear better. 'Her son's brother-in-law's cousin is one of the policemen on the case. You'll never guess what.'

'What?' the couple answered.

The woman leaned in closer and rested her bosom on the table. 'They're saying it was murder.'

'No,' the woman said.

'Shush.'

'They think it was the father.'

'Shut the front door.'

'That's what the chambermaid said. Murder. They've got him down at the station.' The blonde woman with the story nodded her head like an exclamation mark. 'Yes.' She was the dictionary definition of smug.

'Did you say Murder?' Connie asked. Butting into the conversation. 'Wow.' Jeff nudged her to shut up while the woman looked around to see if anybody had heard.

'That's what everybody's saying.' She turned back to the woman called Jane. 'Anyway, toots. I'd better go and round his lordship up. I left him getting changed in the room. I bet he's fallen asleep, the lazy bugger. Don't say anything, will you, Jane?' The lady gathered her bag, an enormous straw sunhat and her sunglasses while Jane and her husband assured her that they wouldn't.

When she'd gone, the couple talked about it between themselves, and Connie and Jeff were included in the conversation because Connie had poked her nose in. It was enough to make her one of the gang. 'Terrible business,' Connie said. 'You don't expect it when you come away for a quiet break.'

A man carried the little girl with a disability and the blue necklace through the seating area, and her mother trailed behind them. The child was having another tantrum and thrashed in her father's arms. 'Overtired,' the man said as he passed by a table of people that stopped playing cards to stare. The mother looked ready for suicide. A few minutes later, a family joined the table with the gossiping couple, and three men in their twenties sat opposite Connie and Jeff.

'Can we play in the games room?' One of the kids asked.

'No. I don't want you anywhere near that swimming pool.'

'But it's not the one where the boy drowned.'

'I don't care. It's near enough.'

'Tell her, Paul,' the boy said to the man. They weren't married then. Stepfather, but he seemed to have a lot of affection for the kids. And why wouldn't he? Connie thought.

'Let them go, Ness. They're only going to play air hockey. They'll be fine. And besides, all the other pools have lifeguards now.'

'Have they?'

'Right up to ten o'clock, and then they turn the floodlights on all night. People are complaining that they won't sleep,' Paul said.

'Hey.' Jane moved forward in her seat to talk to Paul and Ness. 'Have you heard?'

'No, what?' Paul said.

Jane beckoned them closer with her hand. 'It was murder.' She needed a collaborator and turned to Connie for backup, 'Wasn't it?'

'That's what people are saying,' Connie said.

Jeff glared at her for being a party to idle gossip. 'You don't know that at all.'

'Murder?' Ness said. Connie was amused because the men sitting opposite weren't talking—but they were listening to the gossip. One was peeling the label off his beer bottle. Another had his phone open but wasn't looking at it. And the third was craning his neck to hear what was being said. He turned in his seat at the word murder.

Jane looked around, and when she saw the man listening as well, she included him in the conversation. It was a free-for-all to anybody with an opinion. 'The father drugged him and then drowned him in cold blood.'

'How do you know this?' The sexually frustrated man who'd been label-picking asked. He turned around, and the third man perched on the arm of the blue chesterfield to get closer to the action.

'My chambermaid's son is a policeman, and he arrested the father this morning. And all the kids have gone, so they must have been taken into care.'

Somebody else came over. 'What's up?'

'Hey, man. You know that kid that drowned?'

'Yeah?'

'It was only his dad. He was carted off this morning, and all the kids are in care. Have you seen the size of him? I bet he put up a fight,' Label Picker said.

Before Connie and Jeff went back to their room, the gossips added that it had taken ten policemen in riot gear to bring the kid's father down, and he'd been high on drugs and alcohol. As they were walking away, they heard Jane say, 'I heard he beats his poor wife, as well.'

'More likely the other way around,' Jeff whispered to Connie as he put his arm around her, and they went upstairs. 'Remember how she kicked off on the plane? Maybe she's the murderer.'

'And killed her own son?'

'I'd murder him. He was a little shit.'

The sun had exhausted them, and rather than go for a swim, they spent a couple of hours in bed until the gift shop opened.

They made love and then dozed over their books while the ocean and the sound of people having fun sang to them. Connie was woken with a start. A child in the next room was screaming its head off. She'd heard it twice before, and she would have laid money on it being the kid with the blue necklace. 'God, does that girl never shut up?'

Jeff opened an eye, 'You don't know it's her.' He was asleep again within ten seconds.

She lay for a while longer, but the screaming and snoring were driving her mad. She poked Jeff in the ribs. 'I'm going for a shower, and the shop should be opening soon. I'll get sunscreen. Are you coming?'

'Yeah.' He went back to sleep.

Connie had an amazing shower, nothing like the one at home, before dressing in her second outfit of the day. She went for a black sundress with a halter neck and flip-flops. She brushed her hair, leaving it to dry in the sun and smothered her sore shoulders and face with hand lotion courtesy of the hotel. Jeff was asleep when she left the room.

When she got back, he was in the hot tub. She opened the balcony doors that had blown shut in the breeze.

'Come in if you're sexy,' he said.

She went out to sit on a chair and talk to him.

'No. When I said come in, I meant come in.' He motioned to the tub.

'Hang on one second.' She went inside and took two ice-cold beers out of the minibar. As an afterthought, she went back and got the complimentary bottle of white wine. 'Let's have a party.'

'That's my girl. Did you get sun lotion?'

'I did.'

'Nice one. You were gone a while.'

'I had to wait for the shop to open, so I wandered around the hotel.'

123

'Did you hear all that commotion a bit ago?'

'No. What?'

'Sounds as though somebody's lost their kid. Joy. Up and down the corridor shouting for her, and then the staff got involved. Don't know what happened after that. Did you see anything downstairs?'

'No, nothing.'

The next day followed similar lines as the one before. They walked around the village. They ate and made love. It was wicked having sex in the hot tub as Connie sat on Jeff's knee facing him. The risk of their neighbours coming onto their balcony added to the excitement. Afterwards, they lay in the hot tub, enjoying the hot water and bubbles. Turkey was to their right, Kos town to the left and right in front of them, a couple of miles out to sea, was a verdant island. Other than that, the ocean extended forever.

Connie was in love, and she was happy.

They didn't hear the knock at the door, and they were only aware of it when a hotel manager and two policemen tapped on the balcony door.

'I'm sorry to bother you, sir and madam. We didn't know you were in.'

'But you came in anyway. What's this about?' Jeff said.

Connie felt uncomfortable being in a hot tub with three men in their room. She was naked.

'I'm sorry, madam, we are searching the hotel for a missing child. And we're speaking to all the guests to ask if they've seen anything.' One of the policemen made a show of averting his face and flashing his badge.

'Oh no. I'm sorry to hear that. Can you come back in a few minutes? Let us get dressed, and we'll do anything we can.'

Jeff had moved in front of Connie to hide her from view. 'Please, gentlemen. two minutes and we'll get some clothes on.' He stood without embarrassment and stepped out of the tub, wrapping a towel around his waist. Connie thought everybody concerned was glad when he walked them to the corridor. 'Would you prefer to come back here, officers, or would you like us to meet you downstairs?'

'We'll wait outside, sir. It's crazy downstairs, and we're clearing the communal areas and asking everybody to see us in their rooms where it's more organised, and we can make sure we don't miss anybody.'

'Thank you. And your name?'

'Ballas. Captain Ballas. And this is PC Katrou. We'll be outside.'

Connie waited until she heard the door lock behind them, and then she got out of the tub. She picked up her dress from the floor and pulled it over her head.

'My God. It sounds serious. The poor kid and her parents. She'll be okay, won't she, Jeff?'

'It's a massive complex. She's probably wandered off and lost her bearings. Aren't you putting any underwear on?'

'I wasn't planning to. Do I need to? I'm covered.'

Jeff had taken the towel from around his waist and rubbed his hair. She noticed his penis stiffening as he looked at her. 'Damn, there's something really dirty about us being interviewed by the police while you're not wearing underwear.'

'For God's sake, Jeff. A little girl's missing.'

He pulled his shorts on and picked up his T-shirt. 'Honey, stop worrying. She'll be fine. I bet they've found her by now.'

'What about all those pools? If she's got as far as the next hotel down, there are caves and waterfalls.'

'Stop it. The swimming pools are the first places they'll look. Kiddies must wander off here all the time. I bet they've got a Lost and Found office just for missing children.'

Connie had tears in her eyes, and Jeff put his arm around her and kissed the top of her head.

'What if it's that poor little girl that's always crying? Little mite. They said the other boy was murdered.'

'And you're listening to twenty-fifth-hand gossip. Behave.'

'What if it's not safe for us here, Jeff?'

'I'll always keep you safe.'

When they were dressed, Jeff opened the door.

'Have you found her?' Connie asked.

'I'm afraid not, madam. Not yet.' A look passed between the police officers, and Ballas smiled at her. 'We only have a few questions, please.'

'Of course.' She pointed at the sofa.

'We are fine standing, thank you.'

'At least let me get you a drink. You must be thirsty, talking to all the guests.'

'We're fine, but as you say, we have a lot to get through, so we'll keep this brief. We need to map where everybody was when the little girl went missing. Who they were with and who they talked to. Mostly we want to know if anybody saw her so that we can track her movements.'

PC Katrou had a handheld device for taking down notes. He turned it on to record the interview.

'Of course, Captain. Ask away.' Jeff took a drink of his coffee and smiled at the officers.

'Can you give us your movements from one o'clock this afternoon?' He consulted his guestlist. 'Mr Pearson? Is that correct? And Ms Swift?'

'Yes, that's right. After lunch, we sat in the seating area by the main bar for half an hour. There was a lot of talk about the young lad who drowned last night.'

'Do you know who was there with you?'

'I couldn't tell you. We only got here in the early hours of the morning the other day. But the entertainment terrace on the other side of the bar and those seating areas are where people congregate. There were a few couples, some children and a gang of four men, probably a stag party. I'm sorry that's not very helpful.'

'No, it's fine.'

'There was a woman called Ness and another one called Jane, and I think Ness was married to Paul,' Connie said.

'No. She wasn't. She was the other woman. Remember?'

'I'm not sure.'

'No problem. That area has good CCTV coverage. We can put faces to names when we do the jigsaw later,' Ballas said.

'Hopefully, that won't be necessary, Captain. She's probably back with her mum as we speak.' Jeff was always optimistic and looked for

127

the upside of everything, but there was that look between the police again. They knew more than they were letting on.

Connie asked, 'Is she okay? She will be, won't she?'

'We're doing everything we can. Now, you say you stayed around the bar for about half an hour, so that would take you to half one?'

'Probably closer to two. And then we came up here, had a sleep, had sex and hit the hot tub where you found us,' Jeff said, and Connie blushed.

'That's both of you? And you were in this room.'

'Yes. Just us. I wasn't having sex with anybody else.'

'No. I wasn't here all afternoon. I went to the shop to buy sunscreen.' Connie's eyes filled with tears. 'I hope it isn't the girl next door. She's a sweet little thing. I'm sorry. I got up, had a shower and went to the shop. I left Jeff sleeping. We needed sunscreen.'

'And what time was that?'

'I knew you were going to ask me that. I don't know—holiday rules. We don't keep track of the time. I suppose it must have been soon after four. No. Before four, because the shop wasn't open when I got there, so I wandered around for ten minutes. When I got back to the shop, it was open. I bought sun lotion and then came up to the room.'

'Where did you go when you were walking?'

'I left by the poolside door. Went down in the lift and took the walkways to the tennis courts. I was going to go a little way along the mountain for the view, but the path ran out after a couple of hundred yards. I didn't even try. There must be cameras. You'll see me on them, won't you?'

'And did you see anybody?'

'Not much around the side of the hotel. Maybe two or three couples playing tennis, that was all. I noticed the doors to the laundry room were open as I walked past, and the washing machines were on. I remember passing a member of the housekeeping staff on the path and said good afternoon.'

'Were you wearing a black dress at the time?'

'Yes. Why?'

'That member of staff has testified to seeing you. Thank you.'

'I could see the beach, and there were hundreds of people down there. At the infinity pools, all the best loungers were taken. I passed some people walking up the steps, but I had no idea who. I didn't pay any attention and couldn't describe them. Women mainly, I think, and a few children. And then I bought the lotion and came upstairs. If I'd seen a child looking lost, of course, I'd have noticed that as unusual and would have tried to help. I'm sorry, I can't tell you more.'

'You have been most helpful. Thank you.'

'If there's a search or anything, let us know. If she's not back with her parents by this evening, I bet there'll be a candlelit vigil for her,' Jeff said.

'I can't imagine what her parents must be going through,' Connie added.

'Please stay in your room. We will release one floor at a time to go to the restaurant this evening. All of the other eateries are closed, and if you've booked tables for tonight, they'll be carried over until tomorrow. Entertainment will be laid on for everybody on the main terrace, but all outside areas will be out of bounds. We're sorry for any inconvenience, and, of course, reimbursements will be made in due course,' the hotel manager assured them.

'Oh goodness, don't worry about that. We don't want anything back. It's not the hotel's fault,' Connie said. 'What's her name, by the way? You didn't say.'

'I'm sorry we can't divulge that information. Thank you for your time, and have a good evening.'

When they'd gone, Connie got a vodka and a tiny can of Coke out of the fridge and passed Jeff a beer. The wine had been left by the hot tub and was undrinkable. 'That was awful,' Connie said. 'Why did you tell them I didn't leave the room?'

'I didn't.'

'You didn't tell them that I did.'

'I forgot.'

'How can you forget?'

'You went to get lotion. It didn't seem important.'

'Something bad has happened to that kiddie, Jeff. I think she's dead.'

'Don't be ridiculous.'

'I'm telling you. She's either dead, or she's been taken. The police know something.'

'And you, my darling, are fanciful.'

Chapter Fourteen

N ash spent the morning talking to his team and bringing everybody up to speed on the case while battling the bureaucracy
involved in getting to Greece with Lewis. Brown knew the score, but
Nash hadn't dropped the news that she'd been chosen as his second.
The gang were in high spirits, and he had to take some ribbing about
his brush with the renowned psychic Conrad Snow.

That afternoon, Brown came in and shut the door behind her. 'You
wanted to see me, sir?'

'Yes, come in, Brown, but don't get settled. The red tape has been
cut, and we have clearance. How do you fancy a few days in Greece?'

'Me?'

'I don't see anybody else here.'

'Are you propositioning me, Inspector Nash? Because you know
that's inappropriate.' She winked at him.

'The plane leaves in four hours. We have clearance, and we'll walk
straight on. That buys us a bit of time. But go home, pack and be ready
in an hour.'

'You don't know women at all, do you? I can't shave my legs in an
hour.'

'Wear tights. This isn't a jolly, Brown.'

'What, not even a little bit? You can't stop that glorious Greek sunshine from pouring down on me while we work.'

'Don't bank on it. I can station you in the basement. Here's the deal. You'll play the role of my daughter. We're there for a fortnight, and the idea is to spend at least the first few days mingling and seeing what we can ferret out of people. There's been another murder out there.'

'What? Who?'

'Another kid.'

'How can you be sure it's our guy? Cullen was sixty-four, and the kid in the pool was only twelve. Now you say there's another one. Much as I want that holiday in the sun, I think you're barking up the wrong tree, Guv. I've been looking at the Cullen autopsy this morning. You can't think it has anything to do with a tiny island in Greece. We're looking for somebody locally.'

'Cullen was killed, had a brain tumour and was dying anyway. She was beaten, but it was an induced embolism that killed her.'

'Okay.'

'Dale Butcher, aged twelve, was found in a swimming pool supposedly drowned. Morbidly obese, the autopsy showed that if he didn't do something about it and lose weight, his heart would have given out on him in a couple of years at best.'

'Yes, but our killer couldn't know that.'

'You could see how unhealthy he was just by looking at him. Method of death was an embolism, just like Alma Cullen.'

'That feels tenuous.'

'Wait for it. Joy Neal—seven years old. Found in a skip four hours ago. Get this. She had a rare muscle-wasting disease that would kill her before she reached adulthood. All three had conditions that would have killed them very soon. When the Greek guys looked for the pinprick, it was there. Tiny, almost invisible, but there. Do you still think it's a coincidence?'

'I guess not, but how does he go from killing an old lady in England to two kids on the same day in Greece? It feels like too wide an MO.'

'That's what we're going to find out.'

'I still don't see how the killer could know that all three of them had life-threatening conditions.'

'If they knew Cullen and saw the state of Dale Butcher, that only leaves the Neal girl, and she had a visible condition—more so than Dale Butcher.'

'True. It does seem to make it credible.'

'Eliminate the impossible, and only the truth remains, Brown. Don't you read Sherlock?'

'Apparently not, but I've seen Benedict Cumberbatch on TV.'

'You're wasting packing time. Fifty-five minutes, Brown.'

The next morning, Nash knocked on Brown's door, so they could go to breakfast together. He was irritated when she wasn't up, and she opened the door in her dressing gown, looking dishevelled.

'For goodness sake. I said, oh, eight hundred sharp.'

Brown dropped her voice to a whisper, 'Are you my dad or a detective? I know it's a while since you did undercover, but oh, eight hundred? Really?'

'Just remember why we're here. I'll see you in the dining room when you're dressed.'

Nash tucked the newspaper he'd had delivered to his room under his arm and took his sunglasses off, looping them over the breast pocket of his Hawaiian shirt so that he didn't fall down the stairs. Given his age, they'd asked him if he required a ground-floor room, and he replied, 'Absolutely not. I'd like a room with a veranda, please.' He got a room with a balcony like everybody else on the first floor.

His preference was to sit inside at a table away from the sun. He wanted to be in a far corner of the dining room but tucked himself into a table for two in the middle of the crowded masses. The predominant buzz of conversation floated around his head like a flock of hummingbirds, and all anybody wanted to talk about were the murders of the two children.

'Can I go and get some more bacon, please?' A boy asked his mum.

'No, your dad will take you in a minute.'

'But it's just over there. You can see me.'

'I said no.'

A waitress who looked tired came to the table and spoke very slowly, 'Would you like a drink, sir?'

'Yes, please. I'll have an Earl Grey tea with lemon and two slices of toast with a soft-boiled egg. And please ensure that the egg is cooked properly. Soft without any loose albumen.'

'Sorry. I'm not sure I can do that. I'll ask my manager for you.'

Another waitress came past in a swirl of starched efficiency but the same tired look. She pushed the younger girl out of the way. 'Drinks we bring. Food, you go on your legs and get yourself. Jeez.'

Nash smothered his embarrassment at being told off as he went to the buffet, and he enjoyed making his choices from the vast array of food on offer. Kedgeree, followed by two fresh figs for breakfast, made a change from his usual bowl of porridge. He was pleased with himself when Brown breezed into the dining room.

She dropped a huge beach bag on the floor beside them, and he kissed her on the cheek. 'Tilly, darling. I trust you slept well?'

'Like a log. The size of that bed, it's big enough for ten people.'

'I hope you slept alone and not with a football team?'

She was wearing a sundress and sandals. Her chestnut hair was loose and shiny in the sun as it fell to her mid-back. Nash had never seen it out of a bun or ponytail.

'You look beautiful,' he said and meant it. Feminine Tilly was going to take some getting used to.

'How are you getting on, Dad?'

Nash lowered his voice. 'I'm enjoying playing the part of the rogue gentleman abroad. And I've been telling anybody that will listen about you, my poor daughter. Cheated on by your cad of an ex-boyfriend and brought away by your dear old dad to mend your not-so-broken heart.'

'You haven't.'

'No. I haven't spoken to anybody. And maybe not so hammed up, but that will be the gist of our story.'

'Whatever. I'm going for food.'

She came back with a plate piled with a cooked breakfast and a side plate with fruit and cake. 'Have I ever told you how much I love my job?' she said around a mouthful of watermelon.

'Stay in character. We never come out of character from now on unless we're behind closed doors and sure nobody is listening.'

'Dad.'

Nash grinned.

Later that morning, they had a meeting with the chief of police. He came from Kos town to meet them at the police station in Kardamena, where an incident room had been set up. Brown suggested getting a taxi from the hotel, but Nash insisted they take the bus in the blistering heat like most other guests.

When they got there, they were taken into a boardroom and given a cup of *camomila*, a sweet, earthy tea. Vasil Ballas, the Hellenic chief of police, introduced them to Sergeant PetroDeppas, and PC Leonard Katrou. 'After our meeting, we will take you to the incident room, and you will have access to our evidence.' Nash knew from his tone that he wasn't happy about sharing his information. 'Given that you are incognito, and we want this locked down, you can have unrestricted access. However, I'll need one of my men in the evidence room with you at all times.'

His English was excellent, and Nash had to strain his ears to pick up the hint of a Greek accent. Nash noticed that he wore a gold Oxford University signet ring on the little finger of his left hand. It had the full coat of arms crest. Nash had never climbed higher than police college.

'Thank you, Captain Ballas, we appreciate that,' Nash said. 'I'd like to take this opportunity to thank you for being such gracious hosts and allowing us to come in with you on this case.'

'It is our good fortune and honour to welcome you here, Detective Chief Inspector Nash. And we look forward to building close working relations between Greece and Great Britain. Please, anything at all that you need, don't hesitate to ask.'

He was charming, but Nash noticed that after the initial greeting, he never looked at Brown once. It was as though she'd been dismissed.

'Should we get down to business, Captain?'

'Of course.' He pulled a manilla file towards him and opened it. 'We are waiting for the official autopsy reports, but working on an almost certain deduction, we have three bodies. Including,' he lifted a piece of paper and skimmed it, 'Your Mrs Cullen.' He handed the sheet to Nash to read. It was an overview summary of the evidence on the British side of the case. Nash read it and passed it to Brown. He noticed the scowl that Ballas gave.

'In Britain, the classification for having a serial killer is a body count of three. We will keep the Grecian murders under wraps for now, and we suggest you do the same. There's nothing like the words "serial killer" to spark panic. I've seen the fevered levels of excitement at the resort this morning, and we need to keep the situation as low-key as possible,' Nash said.

'They are indeed terrible words. In Greek, we say κατά συρροή δολοφόνος, meaning evil killer. It is only thanks to your tip-off that we looked for the needle marks straight away and linked the killings.

I believe that people with children are abandoning their holidays and leaving early.'

'I'm not surprised.'

'Is there anything at all to go on?'

'Other than the probable cause of death, nothing.'

'Witnesses?'

'Nobody saw a thing,' Nash said.

'A busy resort, one murder committed in the early hours of the morning and the other in broad daylight in the afternoon of the same day. It's madness.'

'Bold.'

'The likelihood of waste being brought out to those skips during food service is immense. It was a heck of a risk to take. We do have one thing,' Ballas said.

'Go on.'

'There's no time of death yet, but we can pinpoint the time of disposal to within ten minutes.'

Nash winced at Ballas using the word disposal when referring to Joy Neal. 'Very accurate. CCTV?'

'Nothing as solid as that, I'm afraid. The bins are kept at the back of the hotel in an area cordoned off from the public. After a spate of food thefts by staff, they installed cameras at the beginning of the season, but they didn't last long before they were disarmed. We have two statements here,' Ballas said. 'One from a kitchen porter called Kleanthis Papadimitriou. He has signed and dated it. He took waste to the bins at 16:15 when he went on his ten-minute cigarette break. He was only out there for five or six minutes. At 16:25, Mina Gialbi, a member of the kitchen staff, took out another bin of table scraps. She discovered the little girl.'

'That must have been tough on her.'

'She was sent home in a taxi, and the doctor went to her house to administer a sedative. It meant that we were delayed in getting her statement. One of the things that upset her most was that the body was tipped into the top of the skip, and she'd already emptied the waste onto her. She said it was only when she saw her red sandal sticking out of the food debris that she realised somebody was in there. She thought a child had fallen in while they were playing. Mina was very brave and dragged the little girl out, but unfortunately, she disturbed any evidence in the process.'

'I suppose what we have to determine first is if the killer was a Greek Nationalist who went to England, killed and returned home. If so, are there other bodies to be found in England that haven't come to light yet? Or is it a holidaymaker who originated in England and then came out to Greece? My money's on the latter.'

'I have to agree with you, Inspector. Most people here are simple folk. The island is supported by tourism, which provides the majority of employment. Not many people have much in the way of medical knowledge. Though at this stage, we have next to nothing and are not ruling anything out.'

'What provisions have been put in place for the two families?' Brown asked, speaking for the first time.

Ballas answered her question but addressed his response to Nash as though Brown wasn't there. 'Dale Butcher's parents and one brother have been taken out of the hotel and given one of several villas in the complex away from the main buildings. Same with the Neals. Some of the Butcher family were taken home on a private flight this afternoon. Most of the dead boy's siblings are to stay with an aunt in England.' He handed over several pieces of paper.

Nash made a point of scanning them and then passing them to Brown. 'Here you are, Brown. It says halfway down the page that Mrs Neal's sister is coming out to be with her and Peter, the girl's father. Keep your ears to the ground and pick up on the gossip flying around in the ladies' bathrooms. The female guests will talk more freely when there are no men around to disapprove.'

Ballas looked uncomfortable, and Nash wanted to put any potential problems to bed before they became an issue. 'Captain Ballas, may I speak freely, please?'

Ballas glanced at Brown. 'In front of your staff?'

'Detective Inspector Brown is a high-ranking officer in my department. I hand-picked her to come with me because she will be good cover and can go places a male officer can't, but also because she is the closest member of my team to me in both rank and ability. If ever there's a gun pointed in my direction, this is the officer that I want to have my back. You can speak as freely in front of DI Brown as you can to me.'

'Forgive me, DI Brown. I did not mean to be rude.' He inclined his head to Brown in a nod. 'In Greece also, women officers account for a small percentage of the force. Again, I must blame the island. We are a small piece of land in the middle of the ocean, and I'm used to dealing with men—they stink of tzatziki and break wind a lot —I admit, I let my Greek prejudice overcome my intellect. My sincere apologies.'

Brown gave him a simpering smile, but Nash knew her well enough to see it was tight. Ballas was being ingratiating and Brown was having none of it. Nash and Brown had enough history that she'd accepted his misogynistic ways, but even he never got away with it.

There would be repercussions.

Chapter Fifteen

onnie didn't bathe before dinner. After an hour in the hot tub, she felt so prune-like that she was frightened of being put on the morning buffet to keep the old men regular. She did, however, get Jeff to slather her body in coconut-scented sunscreen—the aroma of holidays—which could have caused a sexual delay in dressing for dinner, but Connie was worried about being disturbed again by the activity in the hotel.

However, the vim was rising as their holiday hotted up. She straightened her hair at the huge dressing table and applied her makeup. She'd intended to wear her sexy scarlet jumpsuit with black stilettos, and to hell with the twisty staircase. But with one child dead, and another missing, it would be inappropriate, so she went with her black skirt and a shirt but kept the heels.

She heard the knock on every door along the corridor as this floor was let out to visit the dining room. The management were staggering the guest traffic so that they could keep track of everybody's whereabouts on the CCTV cameras.

The sun hung lower in the sky, and while it was still hot, Jeff agreed that it would be pleasant to eat outside on the dining room terrace.

Every table had been given a bottle of good prosecco. Nice touch. The five-star service was highlighted in so many ways through the fine detail, and it showed.

They were led through the communal areas and into the dining room. The ushers had done their best to shield the guests from the unfolding drama, but it was impossible not to pick up on the vibe and at least get the rudiments of what had happened.

People around the couches were crying. Guests were comforted by their partners. And women clutched babies to breasts. Some of the men looked angry. There was a queue forming at the reception desk, and three members of staff were trying to deal with the fallout.

'Get me a flight,' a man shouted, and he banged his fist on the desk for emphasis. 'Now.'

Voices floated over Connie as she was marched to the dining room.

'Poor little mite. I can't believe she's dead. Two dead children on the same day. It's awful.'

'Our children are being picked off like flies.'

'What are they going to do about it? That's what I want to know.'

'They'll have to lay on extra flights. Everybody wants to get away from here.'

'I heard it's the boy's father.'

Jeff grabbed Connie's hand and pulled her away from the shocking commotion. They chose a table overlooking the ocean.

'I knew they'd already found her,' Connie said.

'No, you didn't.'

'It was written all over those policemen's faces.'

'We don't know she's dead.'

'Of course, she is.'

'Enough, Connie. There's nothing we can do about it even if she is.'

'You heard what all those people said.'

'We're on holiday.'

'Two children have been murdered.'

'I know, love. But I don't want to be that person that gets involved in the drama and makes things worse. The police will have a hard enough job on their hands without everybody adding to the hysteria.'

'I want to help.'

'How? The best thing you can do right now is eat your dinner. We keep out of the way, and we mind our own business. We'll hear if there's anything the guests can do—but for now, we'll do as we're told,' Jeff said.

'I suppose.'

The waitress, Resting Bitchface, came over to the table with her tablet. Even out here, it had replaced the good old pen. 'You want drinks?'

'Jeez,' said Connie. 'Yes, please. I'd love a pina colada. Thank you.'

Jeff covered a grin, and their waitress pulled a face. Really? Drinking at this time in the evening? It was like pulling down a roller blind. One second, her expression was smooth. The next, her right eyebrow had disappeared into her hairline, and if her frown had been any deeper, you could have planted a crop of potatoes in the furrows.

'Red wine. Let's have a Bordeaux, please,' Jeff said.

They laughed when Resting Bitchface walked away, and Connie was disappointed when her parting shot wasn't the word Jeez.

This was their third meal of the day, and it didn't let them down. The chafing dishes were abundant, and the food was hot and delicious. Connie chose tiny amounts of several hot dishes and ate them with fresh salad and one of the many dressings. Jeff had a plate of meat and fish. They were in heaven, and the pina colada was the icing on the cake. It had a garden of fruit and vegetation that made up the garnish. The glass was filled with crushed ice, and a large chocolate disk was like a dessert in itself. Connie was quiet as she ate. Their holiday was important, but, she told Jeff, so were their lives. She was mulling over a conversation she needed to have with him about leaving early and going home.

She finished her meal with a slice of chocolate torte and a portion of honey-soaked baklava. Delicious. Some of the desserts were entire cakes you cut yourself. You could take a slice or half the cake—that was between the diner and their God. Jeff had a selection of four desserts, but they were tiny.

An announcement was repeated at dinner that the management were appealing for the cooperation of the guests. A man in an expensive-looking suit came into the dining hall with a microphone.

'Ladies and gentlemen, allow me to introduce myself. My name is Sentreas Filis, and I am your hotel manager. There are a great many rumours going around, and I would like to set the record straight for you this evening. It is with great sadness and regret that I have to tell you two children have sadly passed away in our luxury hotel.'

Everybody in the dining room already knew. They'd have to be deaf and blind not to, but an audible gasp filled the air. It was one thing hearing guests' opinions, but another matter hearing it being confirmed in an official capacity. Before he went on, Connie whispered across the table to Jeff. 'I want to go home, love.'

He didn't get the chance to respond because the manager was talking again.

'This is a terrible time for the parents, and they have been removed to our private villas. We ask that if you see them in the complex, you give them the space and privacy they deserve. We will keep you updated with information as we have it, but at this time, all we have to say on the matter is that we are treating it as two unrelated tragic incidents.'

A man stood up and threw his linen serviette on the table. 'Bullshit. My wife and I were being herded from the tennis courts when she was found. That little girl didn't throw her own broken body into a rubbish skip.'

Another gasp swirled around the room, and where it had been quiet, a wall of sound rippled across the tables.

'She was murdered,' the man said. He threw himself back into his chair.

Filis made a gesture for calm. 'We cannot make an official statement at this time. What we will say is that the hotel will make every endeavour to ensure your stay is happy, memorable—and, above all, safe. I repeat. You are safe, and there is no need for panic or for you to cut short your holiday.'

'It's certainly bloody memorable,' somebody shouted.

'There is no reason for anybody to abandon their stay with us.'

'It would cost the company thousands,' Jeff muttered.

'This evening, we respectfully request that guests adjourn to their rooms where complimentary twenty-four-hour room service is available during these difficult times. We have lifted the restrictions on sports and entertainment channels for your viewing pleasure. The Diamond Sunshine Resort and Spa values your custom, and as a mark of our appreciation, we'd like to offer a fifteen per cent voucher off your next stay with us.' He lowered his voice, moved his mouth further away from the microphone, and added, 'Valid for the next six months.'

'They're trying to do everything they can to make people comfortable,' Connie said. 'Hat's off to them.'

'For those of you that prefer to stay downstairs, we ask that you keep to the main areas on the ground floor. This evening, all pools, games rooms and other public spaces are closed and out of bounds. We are sorry for any inconvenience this causes. We will be bringing in extra staff so that every area can be manned and opened from tomorrow morning. Entertainment will be starting on the main terrace this evening until midnight, after which a curfew is in place, and I've been told that anybody found wandering the hotel after this time will be brought in for questioning by Captain Ballas and his officers. The all-night buffet will be closed.

A rumble of disapproval rippled through the room. Two children were dead, but God forbid the entitled guests should miss out on a three-course meal at four in the morning.

The manager raised his hand. 'However, the kitchen staff will be making up assorted plates of food to distribute to guests that want them. Please use the room service number. The Diamond Sunshine Resort and Spa apologises for any upset and inconvenience this may cause to your stay—but we are doing everything in our power to ensure your continued safety and comfort.'

'That's put me on a downer,' Jeff said.

'I know how you feel. It's horrible.'

'Should we just go back to the room and watch TV?'

Connie considered her answer. She said she'd been thinking about it throughout the meal and didn't want to stay there after all this. But it was their first holiday, and she'd waited so long for it. She got over her wobble. She twisted the white linen serviette through her fingers. 'What happened to those children is awful. I can only imagine what the parents are going through. My heart goes out to them. I was going to suggest leaving, but us moping isn't going to bring them back. We need this holiday, Jeff. We've waited so long for it. Let's carry on and not let these horrible tragedies spoil it for us. I care—but this is our time. Let's have a drink in the bar before we go up and then see how we feel about leaving.'

'Okay, at least the killer's only targeting people under three and a half foot.'

'We're old enough to drink alcohol. I think we're okay.'

'You're right. We're here. Let's make what we can of it. Music and maybe a dance?'

Connie smiled. 'Yes, please.'

They went to the main terrace. After two glasses with dinner, Jeff stuck with red wine, and Connie had another pina. 'There'll be hardly any alcohol in that, you know. They're making hundreds of them every day,' Jeff said.

'I don't care. It's delicious.'

'Excuse me, are these seats taken?'

Connie felt a light touch on her shoulder, and when she looked up, the man she'd heard being called Ray was standing at their table. She nearly choked on her drink and was sure she blushed.

'No. Feel free to join us. Under the circumstances, we're glad of the company.' Jeff stood up and shook Ray's hand as he introduced them.

'I'm Lisa,' The woman said before her husband could open his mouth. 'And this is my husband, Ray.' Ray was going to sit down. 'No. Not there, Ray. I want to sit next to the railing close to the sea.' He moved to give her the seat. 'Though, I'd rather we weren't sitting with our backs to the entertainment.'

This woman was a piece of work. Jeff had been sitting next to Connie with his arm around her shoulder. She was enjoying cuddling him, like the lovers they were in the early days. Jeff stood up.

'Here, have my seat, Lisa. You girls can sit together.'

'Can I get you a drink?' Ray asked. 'My round.' They all groaned at the standard all-inclusive package joke, and the ice was broken.

When Ray went to the bar for drinks and Lisa took the opportunity to go to the ladies, Connie aired the grievance she'd been sitting on.

'Why the hell did you give that awful woman your seat? Don't you want to sit next to me?'

'There are two contentious questions there, and no matter how I answer either of them, I'm going to be in the wrong. I gave up my seat because it was the polite thing to do, and yes, of course, I want to sit next to you.'

'She's pretty. Do you fancy her?'

'Here we go. No, I don't fancy her.'

'But you can't deny that she's a lot more your type than I am with her slim figure and designer clothes.'

'And she's a bloody nagging nightmare. She hasn't said one intelligent thing yet, and your intellect is astounding. I don't see you as a body. You're the whole package, Connie. I love being with you, so pack it in.'

She didn't get the chance to say anything else because Lisa came back and purred some idiotic remark to Jeff.

The fact that they wore wedding rings annoyed her. Jeff wouldn't marry Connie, and she was jealous of their marital status. It would be nice to be Mrs Pearson for real.

'Now I know who you remind me of? It's that bloke on *Most Haunted*,' Lisa was still fawning over Jeff.

Connie laughed. 'What, Derek Akorah?'

'No, the other one. The good-looking one with grey hair.'

'Thank God for that,' Jeff said.

Ray came back with a tray of drinks and passed them around. The music was stilted, but the guy on the sax was good. 'I defy anybody, male, female or next door's aged uncle, to not look sexy behind a saxophone. It can't be done,' Connie said.

Lisa laughed and agreed, then changed her mind. 'No. There was this band, and the woman saxophonist looked ready to slit her throat. God, she was miserable.'

'Was it one of those awful punk bands?' Connie asked.

'You mean emo. I like you already. No, I think she was just sodding miserable.'

'We need a toast,' Jeff said when the drinks came.

'To happy saxophonists,' said Lisa.

'And awful punks,' Jeff added.

The band sang popular British songs in broken English. They bonded as they played *Guess the Song*. They were covers that they all knew, but sometimes it took a verse, a chorus and half of the next verse before it was recognisable. Lisa didn't seem so bad once Connie was chatting with her.

Inevitably, as alcohol loosened their tongues, the conversation turned to the dead children. Ray had been to the men's room and said one of the policemen was in there washing his hands.

'Did he have blood on them?' Lisa asked, and there was a shocked silence.

'Lisa,' Ray said.

Including the one she'd had at dinner, Connie was four cocktails in and laughed, but it was one of those embarrassed, gallows-humour laughs.

'What? It's a perfectly reasonable question. We don't know what happened, do we? Just that her body was found in a skip.'

'Do you honestly think it was murder?' Jeff asked.

'It looks that way, doesn't it?' Ray reached for one of the three chocolate discs Connie had been stockpiling from the garnish on her cocktails. 'Do you mind?'

'Fill your boots.' He bit it. She thought it was endearing that he nibbled around the circumference of the chocolate like she did.

It drove Jeff mad that she couldn't eat a chocolate bar straight. Twix had to be deconstructed by the layer and KitKat nibbled around the edge. She had to remind herself that she was in love with the man she lived with, and this stupid infatuation for Ray had to stop. Who gave a shit how he ate chocolate?

A pregnant waitress passed their table, and Connie realised that she'd seen her at breakfast that morning. Jeff ordered another round of drinks from her.

'That poor girl's been on her feet all day. It's not right,' Connie said. The waitress was called Anias. She told them she still had six weeks to go. 'Make sure you get enough rest, won't you love?' Connie said.

'I like to keep busy.'

'Even so, it's not good for you working such long hours.'

'The season will close soon. My husband and I arranged this little one to come after the season so that I can get straight back to work when we open again.'

Connie was horrified. 'No, that's awful for you.'

Anias laughed. 'I'm teasing you, madam.' They all laughed. 'He'll come when he's ready and not before. Our ways are not so different to those in England, and most women here have to work to help support their families. So, what are you having to drink this time? Same again? The bar will be closing soon.'

'Last one, then?' Ray said.

Connie had barely looked at him all evening. She couldn't. She was pleased to see he gave as good as he got against Lisa's nagging. He wasn't a wimp under those amazing biceps. She liked good arms in a man. She was fascinated by the tattoo of a wolf on his shoulder, and she wondered if it had significance other than a pretty picture. She had a fox on her back.

Jeff hated tattoos.

With a clatter, the shutters came down on the main bar, and Lisa jumped. Connie didn't react and seemed to have misplaced all her reflexes. There was a fuzziness where her fight or flight instinct used to be.

'Should we go back to our room and have a nightcap,' she suggested.

'I'm not sure we're allowed,' Jeff said.

'And we should get to bed,' Ray smiled at her, damn him. 'We're going on a boat trip tomorrow.'

She tried to focus on his blue eyes. Were they blue? Green? Yellow? God, she was drunk. 'Rubbish. It's only midnight. Come on. Let's go and party. Have you got a hot tub on your balcony?'

'No,' Ray said.

Jeff stood up, laughing at her. 'What is this? Do we drop our keys in a bowl before getting in the tub? I think you might be giving the wrong impression there, honey.' He kissed her on the side of her temple. 'It's bedtime. Let's go.'

'Let's all jump in the tub with all our clothes on and drink wine,' Connie said. Ray took it in good spirits and was laughing as well.

But Lisa wasn't. Her attitude had changed. She'd been fine all night, but the alcohol seemed to have hit her all of a sudden. She stood up, swayed and knocked into the chair. Ray put her cardigan around her shoulders, leaving his arm free to steady her. Connie felt a stab of good-natured jealousy. Lucky cow.

Jeff helped Connie up, and she took a couple of deep breaths to compose herself for the walk across the main floor. 'You lied to me. You said there was hardly any alcohol in those drinks. She giggled, and Jeff kissed her. 'No hot tub? Are you sure?' She used her pointer finger to poke his chin.

'No hot tub,' he laughed.

They said their goodnights, and Lisa and Ray walked away.

'Do you have to flirt with every woman you see?' They heard Lisa shouting at him.

'I wasn't flirting. I was just being nice.'

Lisa slipped on the tiled floor and fell onto her knees, and Ray bent down to help her up.

'Get off me. Don't touch me, you bloody arsehole.'

She lost her balance and sprawled on the floor. Connie stepped forward to help, but Jeff held her back. 'Don't. She won't thank you for it.' Several people ran over to help Ray, and somebody handed her bag to him.

Lisa turned to her husband, and in the middle of the foyer, she slapped him hard across the face. Everybody stopped what they were doing to look. Connie turned away, pretending she hadn't seen to spare their embarrassment. Lisa blamed Ray for the fact that she'd had too much to drink and had fallen over. The floor was slippy in the wrong shoes. Connie whispered that slice of wisdom to Jeff.

'Come on. Enough excitement for one day.'

'No hot tub?'

'Bed,' he laughed.

Chapter Sixteen

Molly Brown was perplexed. The next day was pandemonium. After their daily meeting, they slipped into character and zipped themselves into their undercover names of George and Tilly Shan. There were extra staff members in all communal areas of the resort. The pools and games room were open and manned. Corridors had staff stationed at the ends, and extra security details with rifles on their backs patrolled the complex in pairs. Brown thought the latter was unnecessary—or at least the weapons were. Who wants to look up from a lounger and see a great big gun in their periphery? They were hardly conducive to the ideal of white inflatable hippos and cheeky mojito cocktails.

'Get to work. Work the room, get into conversation, make friends and take notes,' Nash said.

'I'm all over it. Business in a sundress.' She raised her voice enough to be heard. 'I'm going onto the sun terrace with my book for an hour, Dad. What are you doing?'

'Mad dogs and Englishmen. It's still too hot for me at this time of day. I'll sit indoors by the coffee bar and wait for the delicious cakes to be wheeled out at afternoon tea. Be careful. I know you're all grown up, but you're still my only child, and I haven't got a spare.' The idea was to make friends and be the guests that people singled out to talk to and confide in. They didn't have long, and that level of trust took time to build.

'Dad, it's a sun terrace, not the slums of New York in the seventies. I'm fine. Stop worrying.' She kissed him on the top of his head.

'It's my job to worry.'

'I'll be back when the cakes are out.'

Brown found a table in the middle of the sun terrace and settled. Whereas the place had been packed when they went to the police station, now there were fewer people and more free tables.

She read the room, making a mental note of the people so that she'd remember them and their family dynamics going forward. Brown caught the eye of a man sitting with his wife. 'It's quiet out here today. Where is everyone?' she asked.

The man smiled, and his wife answered. 'The guests are scared—especially the ones with children. Early flights home have been laid on, and a bus took a load from this part of the complex an hour ago. The families that are left are spending as much time in town and away from the complex as they can.'

'Sounds heavy. Do you think that level of panic is valid?'

Asking questions to draw people out was her opening gambit. Once she'd broken through the trust barrier, she could tailor her questions so they required more than a yes or no answer. To keep the conversation flowing, she had to make sure she gave just the right amount of her own input. There was a course for everything in the police force these days, even one on how to wash your hands. Brown remembered her most recent training on communications and how to draw people out to get the best results.

'Of course, it's valid. Especially if you're a parent here,' the man said.

'It's a terrible thing to happen. Why did it have to be on our week?'

The three laughed as strangers do at a weak joke. The throwaway comment meant that the couple had to come back with something or appear rude.

'How long have you been here?' the woman asked, ending an awkward silence that Brown let run, but without breaking eye contact to let them go back to their business.

'We got here yesterday. And walked into this craziness. When did you get here, and what do you make of it all?'

'We've been here since Thursday. They say the father of the first boy is the murderer, but I don't know. Why would he go on to kill somebody else? It doesn't make sense,' the woman said.

'Maybe the little girl saw things she shouldn't have. I'm Tilly, by the way. It's so beautiful here. It could be that there's a witness in the resort, but they're too scared to come forward.'

'Maybe. The place is crawling with police, and all those guns would put me off wanting to approach them with information. I'm Daphne, and this is Ed.'

'Nice talking to you. We haven't really got to know anybody yet. I'm here with my dad, so it's good to have somebody to talk to. I'd love to meet up again for coffee.'

'Yes, maybe. We'd better get on. We're getting the bus into town. Come on, Ed. Let's freshen up. Nice meeting you, Tilly.'

Damn, she'd gone in too hard and sounded like a lonely freak. Her idea was to get people talking to each other so they'd chat about the murders. People were ghouls and liked nothing better than to gossip. She'd gather people in one place to watch them.

'See you later. My round.' She laughed and waved to her new friends.

Shit.

While she waited for somebody else to talk to, a man took a seat alone at the bar. He wasn't looking at anybody and seemed to have no interest in his surroundings. A woman came onto the main terrace, and her step faltered when she saw him. They were way too unlikely to be husband and wife, and they didn't acknowledge each other, but as she passed, the woman shot the obese man a look of unbridled hatred. The venom in her expression could have seared the air.

Brown closed the eBook on her tablet and opened her Notes app. She typed the meat of the incident and clicked a picture of him on her phone. He was oblivious to everything, including the other woman's dislike of him. It was good fortune that the middle-aged woman took a seat by the railing overlooking the ocean because Brown managed to take a selfie with her in the background.

'Stunning isn't it,' Brown said.

'Wonderful,' the woman replied.

'Tilly.'

'Pardon?'

'I'm Tilly. We got here last night. Cure all for a broken heart.' She laughed.

'Connie.' The woman held up her tablet. '*How to Kill Your Family* by Bella Mackie.'

Brown didn't know what to say to that.

'It's the book I'm reading. So, if you don't mind.' The woman dismissed her.

That was rude. Over the next forty minutes, she spoke to a few guests but didn't get anything better than a rude woman reading books on killing people. She went to find Nash.

'There are some unpleasant people in this hotel,' she said as she sat down. But she was stopped from saying more because of a commotion in front of them. A man was struggling across the tiled floor with a huge suitcase that looked packed to the point of exploding.

'You're being stupid, Lisa,' he said. 'There's no need for any of this.'

'There's every need. You're an arsehole. My taxi will be here any minute.'

'How many times do I have to tell you? I haven't been unfaithful. Not ever.'

'You're a liar. And another thing.'

'What?'

'I want a divorce.'

While Brown made frantic notes, the woman, Lisa, took her suitcase and stalked out of the door.

Her husband looked devastated. His hands dropped to his side, and his head drooped until he realised people were looking at him. He gave an apologetic smile and didn't seem to know what to do with himself. He looked at the door, and they could see the cogs turning as he tried to decide if it was worth going after her. And then he gave up. The man sat at the furthest empty table from other people and ordered a beer.

'I'll go and talk to him,' Brown said.

Nash put his hand on her arm. 'I think the man deserves to be alone.'

'If he knows something, he'll be more susceptible to talking while he's in this state.'

'I said leave him. Time's getting on, and we need to go upstairs where we can talk. We have another meeting in less than an hour.' As they walked through reception, Nash smiled and nodded his head at the acquaintances he'd met and spoken to.

They went to the top of the hotel, where Brown had been given a room, and Nash was in a suite with a separate seating area and a small conference room.

***

Forty-five minutes later, they'd compared notes. Somebody Nash spoke to said he and his wife had seen a middle-aged woman walking alone minutes before the girl's body was found in the skip. She was walking fast and seemed to be in a hurry to get away from the public walkways leading from the back of the hotel to the beach. People were already looking for the child by this point, and there was a lot of noise and shouting. The man said the lady looked frightened. He'd assumed it was because children were going missing, and everybody should look for the girl—but now he realised the lady looked as though somebody was after her.

Only a few people, including the man Nash spoke to and his wife, were around that part of the hotel when the child's body was found. They'd been playing tennis and had a tight alibi, along with two other couples who were on the courts at the time. They were among the first to know, and their discretion was requested until the family had been told and the hotel locked down.

Nash had passed a few words with the bar staff, and one of the young ladies behind the bar said she'd seen somebody shifty hanging around that afternoon. Somebody else said they'd seen a lad walking around as though he was in a daze. They asked him if he was all right, but he walked past them with his head low. They were all things that needed to be checked and followed up. CCTV would be cross-referenced to see if these three people could be eliminated. Brown told him what she had for what it was worth.

Captain Ballas and Sergeant Petro Deppas were on time and had come to Nash's suite with Sentreas Filis, the hotel manager. After introductions had been made and the waitresses had brought coffee and pastries, Ballas called them to order. 'Shall we make a start? We have a lot to get through.'

'Certainly, Captain.' Nash was happy to let his host take the lead. They didn't expect to be incognito for the whole investigation. Once he and Brown had gathered what intel they could, they'd be free to investigate openly as equal officers to the local police force. Until then, the captain was in the hot seat.

Ballas put several piles of paperwork on the table. He handed Nash and Brown copies of the three autopsy reports. Nash was impressed with his efficiency. The two most recent findings were there, but he'd also made photocopies of Alma Cullen's paperwork that Nash had given him the day before. He handed them to Nash, Brown and Deppas but not to Filis. The hotel manager had been sworn to secrecy and was told that he must not divulge what was said within their meetings to any third party, including his family. They had his solemn promise, and Nash thought he looked sullen and shifty but could probably be trusted if his job was on the line. He didn't want to discuss the case in his presence but couldn't deny that it bought them vital time when he was included in meetings. It saved them from giving him filtered accounts later. He was the eyes on the ground and had better knowledge of the hotel and his staff and guests than anybody else.

'First, to clarify and state it in cold words for the record. It has been confirmed that we have three linked murders. Remarkably, the brutal killing of Mrs Cullen in England and the murders of Dale Butcher and Joy Neal were certainly committed by the same person. When the killer disposed of the girl, he stepped in the dirt near the waste disposal skip. The sandy soil is too soft to leave any impression, and there was nothing to make comparisons with hotel guests. However, a few grains of soil were found at the site. We sent them away for biometric testing, and the results show that they have come from England. We've further tested the sample—some was traced to the border of North Wales, but some, no more than a few grains traced back to Cumbria. They have a slightly elevated radiation number than Grecian soil, which is why they stayed in the tread of the sole for several days after Cullens murder.

'That's not surprising. We live in one of the most beautiful counties in England, but it's a nuclear triangle with Sellafield, Heysham power station, and Barrow shipyard all surrounding us in Cumbria. One nuke, and we're all fried eggs,' Nash said.

Ballas readied his next sheaf of papers. 'It makes me very grateful for the air we breathe here. It was invented by Hippocrates himself. Now. We've checked flights coming onto the island in the week leading up to the murder of the swimming pool boy.'

'Dale Butcher,' Nash opened his mouth to say it, but Brown got in first. She was learning. They weren't bodies. They were deceased family members and still owned their names.

'Yes. We have also established that all three of the victims had underlying conditions that could have killed them. The weak link in that hypothesis is the boy. The old lady had a matter of weeks—that could have been common knowledge. And the little girl had Spinal Muscular Atrophy.'

'Would that be obvious from looking at her?' Nash asked.

'Yes, I'm afraid so. She was living her final weeks. There was a paper trail, and if this was premeditated, it wouldn't have been difficult to find out about her. She came with her parents on a final holiday from the Make-A-Wish Foundation. That information could have been obtained with little effort.'

'That puts a new slant on the investigation. What you're saying is these three deaths were strategized and planned. It means we have a different kind of killer. Do you believe that, Captain Ballas?'

'This is where we have a problem.' He passed more papers to them. 'Dale Butcher was as close to death as the other two victims and had a silent killer at work inside him. Nobody will have known at that point, but he had a hole in his heart, and the vessels surrounding it were engorged and on the point of rupture. If—when—that happened, our experts confirm that he would've had minutes. There's very little chance they'd get medical help to him in time.'

'That's incredible. How could the killer have known?'

'That's just it, Inspector. They couldn't. We've interviewed the boy's family at length. The mother knew nothing about it. She was defensive when we brought up the boy's condition and called it dog fat.'

'You mean puppy fat,' Brown said.

Ballas consulted his notes. 'Forgive me, yes. That was stupid. Puppy fat. The point is that the boy hadn't been near a doctor for years. She's adamant about that. We can get orders to check his medical records, but this is where you come in and it is one of the reasons it's good to have you on board. We'd have to apply through the British Embassy to have medical records released, whereas you can go in and get them.'

'Not a problem. We'll get on it straight away.'

'Thank you. I've never seen anything like this. We have three deaths, all killed possibly within days of them dying anyway. Why? They suffered brutality at the hands of their murderer. But they'd already been injected with air into the bloodstream to cause an embolism. The secondary—or even third cause—violence was something for the killer to do while he waited for death to come for them. The beating, the drowning and the strangulation all happened simultaneously as the seizures and loss of consciousness took effect,' Ballas said.

'It's left us with a lot of questions. Not least of them, how did the killer know these people were dying? More to the point, did they know?' Nash said.

'Surely, we aren't in any doubt about that. We're not talking ninety-year-old ladies in a nursing home. Alma Cullen was older, but the other two were just children. One, or even any two of the murders could be coincidental—but surely not three?'

'I tend to agree. However, I still don't see how they can be premeditated. They kill Cullen in England, and then his other two victims, conveniently, go to the same resort at the same time, days before the sand in their egg-timer runs out? I'm not buying it. It doesn't feel right.'

Nash heard Max Jones' voice, channelled through Conrad Snow, telling him to listen to his gut and go with his intuition. The timeline didn't fit. Max would have said, 'If it meows like a cat and looks like a cat, it isn't going to be a feline-killing mouse in a Myers mask.' Nash grinned at the thought. And yet statistics said the level of coincidence was too great to be one. 'We'll pull the medical record of all three victims and scour them for any connecting names and coinciding appointments, that kind of thing. I don't see how anybody could arrange for those two unconnected families to be on the same flight.'

'Unless they did know each other,' Brown said. 'I don't like working on coincidence. I agree. It's too far-fetched that they were on the same flight by chance. I'll look into it. If those people were connected in any way, I'll turn over every rock until I find it. I'm thinking maybe some kind of medical appointment put them in the wrong place at the wrong time. Perhaps it's true that they never met. But something connects them. Bloodwork going to the same path lab for testing, or they're all distant relatives of the same bloody travel agent. There has to be a connection.'

'Great, but it's still fitting too many pennies into too many slots and making it look right. It's crazy. DI Brown, you went through the guests' statements. Are they all logged now?'

'We finished the last ones this morning. There are only five outstanding statements from off-duty staff. We haven't managed to catch them at home yet. We'll get those today.'

'Okay. I'll need the details of passengers coming in from Cumbria for the last week, Ballas. And we'll try to get close to them. We don't need two copies. One will do.'

Ballas went through his papers and made a point of handing the single sheet of paper to Brown with a smile. 'There are only three Cumbrian parties. None from Barrow-in-Furness, as it happens. We have two women, a couple from Penrith, twenty-eight-year-olds Shelby Ford and Lana Murillo. Then there's Gary and Rosie Mendoza from Carlisle in their late thirties with their teenagers Brianna and Bendito. And last, we have a married older couple, Judy and Elmo Stanton, from a place called Grange-over-Sands.'

'Do any of them look suspicious?'

'Not yet. When the boy was killed, they were all in their rooms. And with the girl, they check out on initial interviews. Murillo and Ford were on the beach. The Stanton's were by the pool, and the Mendoza family were in Kos for the day.'

'One of these groups is still our best bet because of their Cumbrian connection. How closely have we looked at them?'

'Only surface scratches so far. The Mendozas seem cast iron. We've checked with the bus company, and dashcam footage shows them getting on the 09:18 bus and returning at 18:28.'

Filis interrupted. 'We have them on camera getting on and off the bus outside the hotel.'

'So, unless one of them returned through the day and then went back to Kos to establish an alibi, they're clean.'

'It looks that way,' Ballas said. 'Of course, that wouldn't be impossible. One of them could have got on the bus, and then jumped off further down the hill at one of the other venues. He could have killed the girl and got back on to join his family later.'

'Okay, that needs looking into,' Nash said.

'And we need to timeline all three parties.'

'Good. We'll see what we can find out on the grapevine, too. The next thing is to go through every first interview and check for ailments, conditions and diseases. Was every parent and guardian given the questionnaire, Captain?'

'Everything from a broken toe to measles is listed.'

'Good. Let's see if we can head him off at the pass before anybody else gets hurt,' Nash said.

'We're conducting second interviews from this afternoon, where more detailed timelines will be built and cross-referenced against CCTV and other guest timelines. We're also running all the background checks on staff and external companies, such as taxi services and bus drivers. We have a lot of alibis to check and cross reference.'

'Okay, people. I don't think there's much more we can do for now. May I suggest we meet again tomorrow with as much updated information as we have?'

'Certainly, Inspector Nash. And Godspeed to you,' Ballas said.

Chapter Seventeen

Connie and Jeff were having coffee after their breakfast and planning their day. They were going to get the bus into Kardamena, have a walk around town and hire a car for the rest of their stay. They would keep the car and leave it at the airport on their way home.

Murder was still a hot topic, and escaping the craziness in the hotel for the day would be good. They were ready to get the bus outside the main entrance when Ray and Lisa came through reception. Ray looked worn down and was dragging a huge suitcase, and Lisa's head was bobbing as she gave him another public dressing down, culminating in her demand for a divorce.

When she stormed out to wait for her taxi and Ray sat at the empty table in the corner with a beer, Connie wanted to comfort him, but Jeff wouldn't let her. 'He wants to be alone. He can see we're here. Let him come to us if he wants to.'

'The poor man. He must be devastated.'

'I'm sure he is, but it's none of our business. Let him lick his wounds in private.'

'What are we going to do today, Brain?' Connie said.

'The same thing we do every day, Pinky. Try to take over the world.' He put his arm around her. 'I thought we'd have a look around the shops. They say the town is very quaint. We'll wander about until the heat gets too much, and we'll have a sit outside a bar for a while and then maybe have dinner in a restaurant on the harbour. What do you reckon?'

'That sounds perfect.' She fancied getting the car and heading further afield to find some beautiful scenery in the desolation of the island. But Jeff had been going on about Kardamena, and with it being the closest town to them, she saw little point in arguing. She grabbed his hand and gave it a squeeze.

Ray emptied his glass, looked lost, saw them and went over. 'Morning, you two. I suppose you saw the floor show?'

'I'm afraid so,' Jeff said.

'And last night?'

'How's the face?'

'I'll live. I've had worse.'

'Ouch. It sounds like a lucky escape, mate. Nobody deserves that.' He indicated a seat, and Ray sat next to Jeff. He smiled at Connie, but it didn't reach his eyes. He looked tired.

'I'm sorry for your trouble,' she said. 'Maybe Lisa will come around once you get home.'

'No. This has been coming for a long time. We've been clinging to the wreckage for months. It used to be good, but recently, not so much.'

Connie and Jeff exchanged a look. There but for the grace, she thought. But even though she and Jeff were going through the same thing, they were nowhere near even thinking about splitting up. She loved him. But her head had been turned by Ray, and she couldn't deny an attraction. She was glad when he said there was no chance of a reconciliation between him and Lisa, even though she had no intention of wanting to see if his grass was greener.

Jeff excused himself to grab a new pack of tobacco from their room, leaving Ray and Connie alone. She felt a thrill travel up her spine when he indicated her glass and asked if she wanted another drink. She opted for a tropical slushy, and he called the waitress and ordered three drinks for them.

'It's nice to sit with a lady who doesn't have to have an alcoholic drink at ten in the morning,' he said.

'Somewhat hypocritical.' She indicated his beer but smiled to disarm the sting.

'Come on. We're on holiday. It's allowed.'

'Does Lisa get like that at home?'

'It never used to be this way. She was great at first. We had so much fun. But then the spark went, and the anger dripped in.'

Connie was going to ask more because she was intrigued, but she felt a breeze hit the side of her face, and there was nothing she could do to stop it. This was no big deal for most people, but it was one of the major triggers for her brain condition.

She tried to shield her face, but it came and brought its mates along for the ride. She went into a full-blown tic attack. When the door was closed and the gentle wind shut out, the ticking continued. She knew it was coming with the first draft, and then she was aware of nothing else until it was over, and she slumped into her chair. While she was spaced out, she was aware of Ray putting his arm around her. She heard him calling her name. It was a bad attack, and she didn't want to open her eyes, so she nestled there for a minute, smelling cologne that was very different to Jeff's. It confused her.

'It's okay, Connie. I've got you. Just breathe. That's it. Breathe. Nice and slow.' She heard him tapping his phone. 'Ambulance, please.'

She lifted her head and pushed away from him. 'No ambulance. I'm fine.'

'Connie, you've had some kind of fit. You need to be checked out.'

She raised her voice, repeated that she didn't need an ambulance, and told him to hang up.

Jeff came back and took over. The relief she felt when she saw him brought tears to her eyes. She was safe now. He sat beside her, and she snuggled into him and closed her eyes for a minute to reset. Ray was lovely. After holding her in the chair, he'd put himself on the floor on his knees in front of her and pulled her into him. It was nice, but the wrong thing to do. He was making too much fuss, and it drew more attention to her. The panic in his voice scared her, and she needed calm rationale from Jeff. Hotel staff were buzzing around her now. More talk of ambulances and somebody pushing water into her hand. She had a ring of people staring at her. Jeff cleared them away and told them all to give her space, and said she was okay. 'Show's over, folks.'

'Is she drunk?'

'Don't think so.'

'Maybe she's been poisoned by the murderer.'

'She had a fit.'

'Gross.'

Jeff was handling it, so she stayed where she was with her eyes closed until they all went away. Being in Ray's arms was lovely. The newness of it was exciting, but Jeff was her rock. They'd only had months to come to terms with the TN, but he was very good.

He'd shield her from curious eyes where he could, but for the most part, he ignored it until it passed. His lack of panic was perfect. He'd make sure she couldn't fall and leave her to come out of it in her own time. Not many attacks were as bad as this one.

'It's a brain condition called TN,' Jeff explained so that Connie didn't have to. She pulled herself upright, apologised, and smiled her thanks at Ray.

'You scared me there.'

'It looks worse than it is.'

Once she'd had a run of ticks, she tended to have more. And she went into another round of Sparky does Mambo. When it was done, Jeff wasn't even looking at her, which was great because the rest of the room was.

'You okay to move, hun, or do you need a bit longer? Let's get out of here. You're the star attraction until there's another murder.'

'Jeff,' Connie said. But Jeff and Ray were laughing.

'I think I'm good, thanks. It's passed.'

'Nicely timed, Sparky, my old mucker, because there's a bus due in five minutes. Drink up. Why don't you come with us, Ray? Walk around the town, a couple of beers and a meal?' Jeff said.

'Are you sure? I'm at a loose end without Lisa. That'd be great, thanks. Will she be all right?' Ray asked Jeff.

Connie said, 'She's fine, thank you, and she can answer for herself.'

The bus ride down the hill was interesting, but they'd seen all the other hotels in the complex already. Once they turned onto the dusty road into town, the world was barren. Everything was brown, and the only thing breaking the skyline was a castle built on a hill a few miles into the scrubland. Connie suggested a trip to the ruin one afternoon for something to do. They both loved history and culture, and she smiled when Ray joined in with her suggestion and said he'd like that too. She felt Jeff tense beside her.

Kardamena was charming. After leaving the bus stop—they called it a depot—the town was a grid of streets woven together like the warp and weft of loomed tweed. Every vertical street led you to the harbour, and the horizontal ones held the town in place and stopped it from falling into the sea. The roads were tiny, cobbled and narrow. There was a bar or restaurant beside every few shops, and many of them were named after bands. They passed bars called *The Red-Hot Chilies*, *The Stone Roses* and *The Jam*.

Every narrow street was lined on both sides with stalls. T-shirts, dresses you would never be seen dead in, tacky kaftans, stalls dedicated to chessboards and some with pottery, postcards, keyrings, hats and sandals. Walk, look, repeat. Once they'd been down the first street, they'd seen it all. Everything else was more of the same. But it was charming, and Connie loved it. They wandered around for an hour and then stopped at a corner bar on the harbour. It was opposite the themed pirate ship that took people out on three-island trips.

'There's that boy,' Jeff said. 'The one from the hotel that lost his brother. And where's the rest of the brood? What's he doing in town on his own?'

'He's doing something he shouldn't be. I've never seen somebody look more guilty,' Ray said.

Connie wasn't in the least interested, but she looked up to see the teenager in the garish tracksuit making a terrible job of not being seen.

'He'll be like most young blokes experimenting in a new country. I bet it's drugs,' Ray said. He'll be going to score.'

'How the hell would he know where to get them in this backwater?'

'The internet. And the clubs will be full of them. I bet if you typed into your phone, "Where can I get some drugs on Kos," you'd get an answer. And Google would even be kind enough to draw you a personal map with a big red arrow saying, "Stavros The Dealer, lives here."'

'On the other hand, he could just be looking for another kid to kill. The last boy was his brother, wasn't it?'

'True. That's always another possibility.'

'We could liven this dreary afternoon up by following him,' Jeff said. 'If we find anything, we can turn him over to the police.'

'Could be fun.'

Connie was horrified, 'Not in this lifetime. I'm not trudging after some kid in this heat. Get me another drink, please.'

She was even more appalled when, ten minutes later, the couple she'd named the Sweaty Legs turned up drunk. He was red-faced and glistening, and she could barely walk.

'Hello there. I thought it was you,' Sweaty Leg said. 'I want to apologise for the other day. No hard feelings, eh? I'm an ass sometimes. It's a bad do with all these murders, isn't it? Mind if we join you?'

'We were just leaving,' Connie said, draining her drink and standing up. 'Sorry to run out on you, but we're on our way to the museum before it shuts. Enjoy the rest of your day.'

Sweaty Leg looked at this watch with a puzzled expression as they waved and left.

'Honey. The museum is in Kos, you idiot. Not here in Kardamena.'

They found the gorgeous town square and sat for a few minutes soaking in the beauty and Greekness of it. The sun was baking, and while Connie loved it, Jeff needed to get out of the heat. There were two things to do in this town, walk around or sit in a pub. Their fate was sealed, and the rest of the afternoon was spent in good company doing a pub crawl with Connie as the sober designated driver, even though she should have declared her condition to both the holiday insurance company and the car hire people. She suggested they wait outside while she hired the car. Turning up with two drunk men wouldn't be good. Kardamena was lovely, the harbour and ocean stunning, but there wasn't much to do.

With the possibility of a TN attack, she should never have been driving, but she picked up their Nissan Almera without any problems. On the drive back, Connie pointed to the left as they rounded a corner. 'There we go. Spot the one piece of scenery on Kos. We're surrounded by ocean, and have you any idea how hard it is to find a body of water?' They passed a tiny pond, and it looked plonked in the middle of nowhere by the side of the road. It had one lone duck swimming on it and a lighthouse ornament in the middle by a Japanese-style bridge.

When she let Jeff and Ray out of the car at the hotel entrance, the Sweaty Legs were tumbling out of a taxi. They seemed happy and were giggling with each other as they staggered into the hotel. 'They've had a few,' Ray said, laughing. The men went for a game of pool while Connie parked the car and then took the lifts down for a walk around the resort before bathing for dinner. The sea was still full of people swimming, and two-thirds of the loungers had sun-worshippers on them, though some families had already left to prepare for their evening.

When she got back, Mrs Sweaty Leg was blundering around and looked frantic. She was upset and lurched over to the reception desk without waiting for anybody to come to her.

'Have you seen my husband? I've had a letter from the killer. It says he deserves to die.' She collapsed on the hard-tiled floor in front of the desk.

Chapter Eighteen

After the heat of Kardamena, Connie and Jeff used the tub and watched the ocean play with its white horses. 'Connie, look.' Jeff was excited and pointed out to the sea, and they were in time to see a pod of dolphins jumping. 'I knew we'd see them eventually.'

'I think they're porpoises. But it's still amazing.' She reached for her phone and took a photo. Jeff posed in the foreground, and she was lucky enough to capture the obliging animals in mid-jump behind him. They couldn't believe how close they were to the shore.

It was a spectacular photo—one of her lucky shots. 'Now our holiday is complete,' she said. They made love in the hot tub before finishing their glass of chilled wine. And while they got ready for their evening, Jeff danced around the room singing.

She straightened her hair and gained another three inches of length from losing her natural curls. After adding a dab of serum, her honey-blonde hair shone like burnished gold. Tonight, she wore her red jumpsuit with no sentimental messing about. When her makeup was applied, she felt fabulous, and Jeff told her she looked beautiful.

That couldn't be further from the truth, but judging beauty on a scale with the lower end being her usual at-home slobbery, she'd take it. He came behind her as she applied a final coat of lip gloss, and he copped a feel. She felt his sap rising and slapped his hand away with a laugh.

It was noisy downstairs. They heard Mrs Sweaty Leg crying before they saw her. She was surrounded by the commotion, holding a brandy snifter and sobbing in great gasping bellows. Jeff whispered that she sounded like a warthog calling her young to the watering hole.

'I've lost my husband. Where's Mervyn?' A cackle of women surrounded her, telling her it would be all right. Connie and Jeff had been upstairs, had a brew, and the unfortunate woman was still crying. Talk about milking it.

'But where is he?'

Time was critical. Guests were grouped together into search teams and dispatched to different zones of the complex. Forgetting all the tiny concessions offering food, the five-star hotel on the top level had three restaurants as well as the main dining court. They had twenty-one bars, eleven swimming pools, and the best rooms had balcony hot tubs. That was without going near the other three buildings, the beach and the ocean. 'The sea's claimed him. He'll dissolve to form the breakers, salt and pockets of oxygen,' Connie said.

'Thanks. That's put me off our swim tomorrow morning. All that dissolving flesh turning to salted mush. Cheers, love.'

'No problem. I think it's a romantic concept.'

There were a lot of hiding places on the resort for a man who might not want to be found. He didn't look like the type to slope off to the bars for an hour of rampant sex, so Connie guessed he'd dropped dead in a sweaty, clammy heart attack somewhere and would be found—alive or dead, soon. But Jeff had heard more of the gossip at the bar. Sweaty Leg's wife had found a note pushed under their door—from the killer!

'It's in hand, Connie. They don't need us.'

She looked at her high heels and was grateful they weren't joining the search. They'd ignored their growling stomachs and offered to join in, but the policeman said the search parties would be gone by the time they got changed. Connie kissed Jeff and grabbed his hand to lead him to the dining room. It was hours since lunch, and she was starving. Jeff had a starter of oysters and octopus, and despite the dare thrown down with a gauntlet, Connie declined the unbridled delight of sliding something that looked like congealed mucus down her throat. She was too old to accept dares. 'Do you want me to throw up in the middle of a room full of diners?'

Though calling it full was exaggerated, most people were out looking for the missing man. Jeff said he'd have something to eat and then find one of the groups to join in the search.

His good intentions were there, but he soon forgot about them.

After dinner, they went to the terrace, where a Grecian duo provided entertainment.

'I need a drink,' Jeff said. He brought the cocktail menu over. 'There's too much sadness around us. I say we start at the top and work our way down. Are you up for it?' She surprised herself when she said she was.

'Let's go.'

Ray appeared beside them and plonked himself down at the table without waiting for an invitation. On holiday, friendships formed fast but were forgotten before the plane tucked its wheels in. 'Hi, you two.

Get the drinks in. I've been searching for that missing man, and I'm gasping.'

Connie knew from Jeff's face that he wasn't happy. It would be nice to have an evening for just the two of them, but Connie liked the company, too. 'Actually, Ray, Jeff just laid down a challenge to do the cocktail list, top to bottom. Are you in?'

He glanced over the list and pulled a couple of faces at the options. 'Yeah, why not?'

The first drink they tried was a Mai Tai. It was disgusting. They followed it with a daiquiri, which was better but still awful. A whiskey sour was next, and then something with spiced rum. By this point, Connie regretted agreeing to the challenge, and they weren't even a quarter of the way down the list. She didn't feel drunk. She just loathed the taste of the drinks.

'Do you mind if we join you?' The room had filled up, and two women stood next to their table.

'Of course, ladies,' Ray said, playing host. 'The more, the merrier.' Jeff looked even more unhappy at having their night hijacked. The new couple introduced themselves as Juliet and Mercedes, a mother and daughter. They were fun, and Connie laughed at Mercedes' humour. She drank with her pinkie out and told them she was a broker in the city. The noise level rose as the conversation ran away with itself. Both ladies scanned the men in the room. Mercedes was a big girl, and while outwardly confident, Connie saw it was career related. When it came to speaking to people away from a working environment, her lively persona was a coat she wore—just like Connie did—and hung up behind the door when she got home. She had never lived away from her mother.

Juliet was an attractive blonde in her late sixties. Her husband was unfaithful to her thirty years earlier when Mercedes was four, she said. Juliet had given up on love. She'd never even been on a date since her husband left them and was devoted to her daughter like a patient attached to an iron lung.

It was sad. She was a good-looking woman with great chat and presence. 'I admit men come onto me, but I've perfected a pathetic ice maiden act to protect myself. I'm a hopeless romantic, and I'm addicted to bodice-ripper novels. I let the characters risk life and love while I live vicariously through them and let them be the ones to suffer my heartbreak.'

Half a dozen cocktails in—the espresso martini was the best so far—and under the influence of Sparky and his enhanced emotional reactor, Connie found Juliet's story very sad and looked at the ocean to get her emotions in check, so she didn't start crying. Jesus Christ. Why did these damned tablets make her so emotional? She felt sorry for the well-to-do lady who lived without love in her life. What an awful way to survive.

The band played the opening bars of *Havana*, and Jeff stood up. 'Excuse us ladies, but this is our song. Would you do me the honour?' Connie took his hand, and they moved to the middle of the terrace. They had plenty of room to move with each other, and the spins and turns came fast. Connie couldn't take her eyes off him—and he was locked into hers. When Sparky first arrived, she worried that they'd never dance again. Her balance and equilibrium were affected, and some days, every time she stood up, she fell over. Some were better than others—and tonight was perfect.

She remembered the night they met. They'd danced for hours and, during the very first song, they fell into a rhythm with each other. Later, they went to one salsa class and never went back because Jeff said it was too rigid. He wanted to be free to express himself. Since then, they'd added a few moves—no lifts, though. He'd never get her off the ground, and she wouldn't want to put him in traction.

They moved and twirled and twined in the hold and out of it. In the days before Sparky, just six months earlier, they finished *Havana* with him twisting her through eight spins.

'Go for it,' she whispered now. 'Spin me.'

'You sure?'

'Yep, just be ready to steady me.'

They finished the song to a round of applause. People had stood up to watch, and the waitresses stopped serving drinks until the song ended. They were old people dancing—and had hit that point in life where they could never be good dancers—just old people who knew a few moves and could dance fast. Ten years before, when she was forty, she could do the splits. Now, if she got on the floor at all, she had to use furniture to pull herself up.

It was awful being old.

'Wow,' Ray said when they sat down. 'You hid that light under a bushel.'

'Dancing brought us together. We danced, and I knew she was the woman for me,' Jeff said.

They got the waitress's attention and ordered more drinks. Resting Bitchface had been on the lunch pass, and Connie was sure she'd seen her doing room service trays that morning. She'd been on duty all day and must have been dead on her feet.

Because they were busy, Jeff asked for the next two drinks on the cocktail list for him and Ray and a pina colada for Connie, who had given up on their stupid game. Juliet and Mercedes said they'd sit that round out.

'You want two drinks. Two? Jeez,' Resting Bitchface said.

'Yes, please.' Connie smiled at her. 'It'll save you coming back so soon.'

'No. You have one drink each. One.'

'That told us,' Jeff said.

She went away and came back with a face like thunder and a tray containing three drinks. She slammed it on the table.

'I'm so sorry. I asked for a pina colada,' Connie said. She wanted something sweet after the bitterness of the awful last cocktail.

'Nah. You want a Harvey wallbanger. He said, three wallbanger.'

'No. It was two wallbanger and one pina colada.'

Resting Bitchface looked tired enough to drop, and Connie felt guilty. 'It doesn't matter. This is fine. Thank you.' She smiled again, and Resting Bitchface glared at her.

'Nah, I change drink. Jeez.' She turned away, and Connie heard her mutter, 'Bitch,' under her breath.

'Excuse me?'

'What?'

'What did you say?'

183

'I say, I get your drink.' When she came back, she banged it in front of Connie and stalked off without a word.

'You pissed her off,' Ray said.

'She's scary,' Connie was embarrassed from the public dressing down.

'Maybe she's the murderer.'

They all laughed. She was tiny but fierce, and they agreed you got on the wrong side of her at your peril.

Jeff got up and joined a circle of guests doing the Greek Zorbas dance. He looked more like Eric Morecambe than Zorba the Greek, but the cocktails made him brilliant in his ineptitude. By a third of the way through, Connie and half of the hotel were up with him, and the terrace was full of people doing the iconic dance. When she sat down, she was exhausted but happy.

'You're in love, aren't you?' Juliet asked.

'Madly.'

'We can tell. We saw you two the other day, and I said to Mercedes that I could tell how in love you are. Some couples don't look happy together—or right. But you do.'

Connie wanted to cry. They were okay, she supposed, but they weren't that happy, and this holiday was a plaster over a wound. It remained to be seen if the cut was healed when the plaster was ripped off at home. They'd lost their joy. She could have told Juliet and Mercedes that it wasn't all roses and that they'd been tested lately, but they were beaming at her and Jeff, so she squeezed his arm and let them hold onto the fantasy of their perfect relationship.

They'd had a great night. They never reached the end of the cocktail list, which was a good thing. Connie noticed that despite being a firm single lady, Juliet had a twinkle in her eye for Jeff, and as the wine loosened her inhibitions, she didn't hide it and made eyes at him across the table. If this was her perfected ice-maiden, Connie would hate to see her femme fatale. Juliet was older than Connie, better looking and had a slimmer figure, but she didn't feel threatened by her. A woman knows when she has to worry. Mercedes tried to call time on the night. They usually only had two glasses of wine, and tonight they'd had four.

The ladies were booked to go on a boat trip the next morning. The last time Connie and Jeff had stayed up drinking with a couple—they never made their trip—Lisa and Ray split up that night, and Lisa left the next day. At least that couldn't happen this time. But she had her doubts about whether they'd make the boat and worried about the condition they'd be in if they did.

'Come on you. Bedtime.' Jeff held his hand out to help her from the seat. She was unsteady but happy. They went to bed in a haze of cocktail fugue. 'I'm going to ask Ray to back off and give us some peace,' he said as they got into bed.

'You can't do that. He's lonely. Imagine how you'd feel if you were alone in a foreign country and had been dumped by your wife.'

'I wouldn't cling to another couple like a limpet.'

'Don't be unkind, Jeff. He's no bother. I like him.'

'I like him too, but don't you think it's a bit weird?'

'No.'

'We don't know anything about him. What if he's the murderer?'

Connie laughed. 'Based on what—his dad sandals?'

185

'Nothing specific, just a feeling, that's all. The thing with Lisa and her leaving early was odd.'

'That hardly makes him a crazed serial killer. You're drunk. Go to sleep, darling.'

She turned to kiss him goodnight, but he'd already passed out.

It didn't take long for the snoring to start, and Connie couldn't sleep. Things churned in her mind without resolution. She'd been an admired therapist before her burnout and early retirement, and now she was at home all day. Was that enough? Maybe she wanted more.

He rolled onto his back, and the noises coming from him would give Dr Richter a run for his money. She flung the sheets back and got out of bed.

Damn him.

Chapter Nineteen

N ash heard his phone ping while he brought the morning meeting with Ballas and the hotel manager to a close. It was a message from Snow.

Zoom call 11 A.M.

'Does he mean eleven his time or ours?' Brown asked.

'There is only one passage of time, Brown, and that's the one we live in.'

'That makes no sense at all, but if you say so. I bet he means his time.'

They sat by Nash's computer at eleven, waiting for Conrad Snow to come online.

'Told you,' Brown said at ten past.

Nash gave her a withering look and fired off an angry message, explaining the time difference and saying that while it was inconvenient, they'd reconvene in two hours. He used more words than most people would in a text and grumbled that those silly pictures of vegetables drove him mad.

'And how many people have sent you aubergines?'

'Aubergines, that's random. None. Because anybody I converse with knows better. If I need a recipe, I'll use one of my cookbooks. I don't need to see pictures of people's dinner.'

Brown grinned, and they turned the laptop on at one o'clock to wait for Snow. When he came online, Nash muttered, 'Idiot.' If Snow heard, he gave no indication.

'Snow.'

'Good morning, Inspector. You're looking very dapper.'

'Excuse me?'

'Okay, then. Sun-kissed, if you prefer.'

Nash's gaydar gave a jolt and then settled when he realised it had been broken since birth. And while he could spot a criminal at a hundred paces, any attempt to determine the attractions of people on a personal level eluded him. It was fancy to imagine a man twenty years his junior could be remotely interested in him. And look where it got him the last time he'd run down that rabbit hole.

'Mr Snow, what can I do for you?'

'I have information. Possible next victim, but I see you aren't alone, Inspector.'

'Hi.' Brown raised her hand.

'Hi yourself.' Snow smiled, and Nash noticed his teeth were perfect. The insufferable oaf was flirting with Brown now.

'Yes. I forgot. DI Molly Brown, Conrad Snow.'

'Hi, Molly. You've got a beautiful smile.'

'That's DI Brown to you, Snow,' Nash said.

She did that thing women do and patted her hair on the side before answering. 'Hi, Conrad.'

'Of course, Inspector.' He winked at Brown, and the glare Nash gave her chased the blush from her cheeks.

'Name,' Nash barked.

'Conrad Snow.'

'Not you. Fool. The next victim.'

'Inspector, you're barking at me. Might I suggest a Pepto Bismol? It seems the food there doesn't agree with you. The name I've been given is Ruby Vang. V.A.N.G.'

'Is that a foreign name?'

'I have no idea, and I'm not even sure it's the next victim. I just said it might be, but she is alive and well as of now because I saw you talking to her.'

Nash had a good memory—near eidetic—for names, and he was sure he hadn't spoken to a Vang or a Ruby. If Snow was to be believed—and the jury was still out—it must be in the future. 'Description?'

'I only saw her hand across the table. The image was situated on you.'

'Bloody hell. Why can't you be more specific?'

'Why can't you be more agreeable? I'm trying to help you here with nothing in it for me. I'd thank you to remember that, Inspector Nash. It could have meant anything if the image had shown her without you. At least we know it relates to your case and isn't one of my other clients. We take what we're given with gratitude and thank our spirit guides.'

Nash's face was expressive, and Brown had to intervene. 'Thank you, Conrad. We understand. Please just do your best. We're thankful for whatever you've got for us.'

'Indeed. She had painted nails.'

'What colour?'

'Something pale, cream or silver. Muted. A very pale blue, maybe.'

'Was it blue, or was it cream?' Nash said. 'They are hardly next to each other on a colour wheel?' The man wound him up. The nature of Snow's job irritated him to the point of inherent sarcasm. He realised he wasn't helping, and his attitude could actually harm the case, so he sat back and let Brown come forward.

'Thank you.' Brown said. 'Unfortunately, a lot of women have their nails done to come on holiday, and many will have them done while they're here. Did you notice anything else?'

'Nothing. I'm sorry. I wish I could be more helpful.'

'A name is a brilliant place to start. It's amazing that you can get that in its entirety. Thank you, Mr Snow.'

'You're welcome, guys. I trust you have a good day over there, topping up your tans. Oh shit.'

'What?'

'Nash. A young man's going to jump. He's still at the resort, but you haven't got long. They're showing me a clock. Tick tock, tick tock. You need to stop him. Tiny building. A blue door that says *Helios* on the nameplate. Go.'

Nash remembered the villas on the complex had Greek names. It was a good place to start. He slammed the laptop shut without saying goodbye and grabbed his jacket.

'The bereaved families have been put in villas,' Brown said.

'I'm on my way. You get the guest lists and check for guests or staff called Ruby Vang.'

'Okay. Just go.'

Nash didn't have time to queue and take lifts down two of the three levels of the complex. He was grateful for his years in the gym back home as he ran but hadn't factored in the crippling midday heat. He stopped at the bottom of the steps to catch his breath.

'Are you all right?' A couple rounded the corner and ran up. The lady had her hand across his shoulders. He was lost in a haze of strong perfume and coconut lotion that stole and replaced the air he was breathing. The man was trying to manhandle him to the floor as he gasped for breath. 'Get an ambulance.' The man turned to more people as they approached. 'Stand back. This old man's having a heart attack. Give him some air.'

'Get off me, you bloody fools.' He launched himself away from the wall and carried on running. If Snow was wrong, he'd kill him for this. When he got to the row of villas, he scanned the name plaques. They had far too grandiose a title. They were even too small to be called cottages. They reminded him of quaint fisherman's shacks against a harbour buttress in a chocolate-box coastal town—but these were finished in Grecian tourist style with traditional whitewashed walls, blue tiles and hanging bougainvillaea. The world didn't change much when tourism was paying the piper.

Helios. The nameplate was there, just as Snow said. It was the only villa with the door open. He hung back, hiding behind the corner to avoid being seen. He had no problem hearing, though. There were two women's voices. They were loud and screaming over each other. He risked a look.

'Don't go. Please, son. Just come back in.'

'Come on, our Levi. Let's talk about it,' the other woman said.

He peered around the corner and saw the first woman holding onto the sleeve of a young man's hideous tie-dyed tracksuit in gaudy yellow and blue. He could guide ships with that clothing. The boy was pulling away from her and clutched a gift shop bag to his chest.

'Let me go. You can't stop me.'

'I can. I'm your mother. Now get in that house and do as you're told.'

The boy had tears running down his cheeks. All three of them were distressed, but the young man seemed on the point of collapse.

'I've got to do this, Mam. I'm doing it for our Dale.'

'Please, son. Don't hand yourself in. Your dad wouldn't want that.'

'I'm going to make this right, Mam.'

He pulled away from his mother and ran down the hill. She fell into the smaller woman's arms and sobbed. Nash retreated and heard her say, 'I can't take any more. I can't lose another one.'

The door closed, leaving him free to come out of hiding and follow the distraught young man.

When he got to the gift shop, Levi stopped and took an envelope out of his bag. He posted it in the post box.

Nash shook his head. I see—you silly boy.

The lad went to the infinity pool where his brother's body was found four days earlier. He stood in the shadows by the cold-water showers. It was as though it had never happened. Every lounger around the pool had somebody on it. Guests worked on their tans, reading the latest over-written novel penned by authors thinking they were Avant Garde for writing dirty words. Every lounger had a table with ice-cold cocktails twinkling condensation down the sides of the glasses in the sunlight.

There was a low drone of conversation and, above that, the excited noise of children in the pool. Two kids jumped from the side into an inflatable toy and missed. Somebody was trying to do lengths, but this pool didn't have lanes roped off for that purpose. Nash wondered why the man in red Speedos hadn't walked another hundred yards to use the sports pool around the corner. A couple of pretty things in bikinis sat on the edge with their feet in the water, attracting other pretty things of the opposite sex. A woman in her thirties with rich auburn hair and no cellulite was in the pool up to her thighs, inching in with her hands spread on the surface as though she could stop it from rising up the warm parts of her body. And a couple were making foreplay and splashing each other in the corner. Tray-carrying waiters sidestepped people and wore fake smiles.

The only thing out of place in the typical summer-holiday scene was the boy with the tragic eyes. Nobody saw him. He was a ghost. Invisible.

Nash had never seen anybody as lost and out of place as the boy on the periphery of so much fun. He thought about approaching him now and taking him for a quiet chat. He might get through to him, but chances were, the kid would clam up and refuse to speak. It wouldn't stop the inevitable play-out of what needed to happen. It could only delay his actions, and Nash might not be around next time. He didn't want to interrupt the lad if Snow's warning was rubbish.

Levi Butcher took something out of his bag. Nash didn't know what it was but sensed the boy's frustration. He put himself inside Levi's mind to read what he'd do in the boy's situation. Whatever was in his hand was hard. Levi looked at it with reverence. It was something symbolic. He wanted to get closer to the pool. It looked as though he needed to put the object on the water—to float it. His idea was to lay it in the water—like his brother had, face down, floating. Nash felt the anger surge through his body as it did through Levi Butcher. There were too many people. Nash saw Levi feeling that he couldn't even do this right for his brother. He was a failure.

He watched the young lad bend down. Nash's thoughts were all supposition, and he could have been way off track, but he doubted it.

Levi put the object at the base of a flowering tamarisk bush in one of the flower beds. He arranged things around it, lit a tea light, put it inside the ornament and then stood up and looked to check that he wasn't being watched. He walked away.

Nash watched him leave before following him to the skip where Joy Neal was found. There were some wilted flowers on the ground and leaning against the container. Half a dozen bunches. It had been three days, but with the heat, they were dead. Some of them were trodden into the dirt as the staff used the waste disposal area again. The crime scene had been cleared, and everything the police needed to do had been done. The staff had a hotel to run, and they were too busy to have kids dying all over the place.

Levi picked up the trodden flowers and moved them out of the way, standing them against the wall of the skip on the unused side to prevent further damage. He looked around to see that nobody was coming, and Nash shrank into the shadows.

Levi took more care this time. Again, Nash felt his frustration. This one wasn't as important as the first, but a lack of privacy had hampered him. Levi wanted to honour Joy Neal, but his brother was the one he really wanted to say goodbye to. He grieved Joy through the association of her with Dale and by the belief that his father had murdered them. His grief for Dale came through the weight of love. He lingered here. It was the wrong way around. This should have been the drop-and-go site, and Levi wanted to spend more time where his brother had been found. Nash felt it.

The boy was easy for Nash to read. His emotions were open, and his thoughts were as transparent to the experienced detective as sliding one page to the next on a tablet. Levi kept glancing at the kitchen door, waiting for it to open. With a kitchen as busy as this one, and the staff smoking area at the side of the skips, it wouldn't be long before somebody came out. He knelt on the ground. Taking something out of his rucksack in a paper bag, he emptied it and screwed it up, forcing it into the tiny pocket of his tracksuit. He was beside a large industrial waste unit where all he had to do was lift the lid and put the bag inside. The boy wouldn't even have to look, but he couldn't do that. It's where she'd been, and there was a smell. He would die rather than release that awful smell of rotting food—and things thrown to waste. There was nothing psychic about Nash's thoughts. He was just a copper making a cold reading as his training had taught him. He was closer this time and could see better. The boy's torment touched him with the thought he'd put into his purchases.

Nash realised the young man who was seen sneaking around Kardamena the day before looking guilty enough for guests to report it to Ballas was Levi. He went into town alone in the aftermath of his brother's death.

That journey would have been excruciating for him, and he'd try to make himself small. The stares and the gossip around him would get into his brain. Everybody was talking about his brother, his family, and his dad. Nash wondered if the relatives had noticed him missing in the madness during those hours. Had anybody spoken to him about his grief, or were they too immersed in their own? Levi had put ornaments that are replicas of shrines called iconostases or kandilakia at the murder sites.

Nash imagined the family. They were on the bus being driven to the resort from the airport in the early hours of the morning. It was the start of their holiday, and they were filled with hope and excitement. The tour guide will have tapped an antiquated silver-ball microphone that crackled with static as she went into her spiel. She'd have told them about the shrines, and that every stall in the markets sold the miniatures as souvenirs. And Levi was probably the only one who was listening. It's not the sort of thing you could make a point of buying without knowing about its significance. The plastic or stone and metal shrines were found throughout Greece on the roadsides. Tributes and memories of loved ones killed in traffic accidents on dangerous island roads with high mortality rates. Like murder stones in England, Nash thought, but less gruesome. These weren't a reminder of death but hope for the protection of the fallen person's soul in heaven.

The light-up shrines were shaped to resemble churches, with tiny glass doors that opened onto tea lights illuminating the lantern. Nash and Brown had been through the same spiel. He could see that Levi took everything in, the type of kid that absorbed learning like a sponge.

Levi opened the door and lit the candle to make the lamp burn. He took the top off a bottle of scented oil and sprinkled a few drops over the shrine. Taking his tacky image of a saint in a white plastic filigree frame that resembled a doily, he placed it with devotion against the little church and made the sign of the Cross. Levi took a newspaper cutting with the little girl's face and smoothed the creases out. He put it by the scene and secured it with pebbles. The last thing he did was drape a necklace made from blue seashells over the shrine because it had been reported that Joy was found wearing a blue necklace.

Nash wasn't a religious man, but it was fitting that he lowered his head in respect, too, as Levi said a prayer over his offering.

Levi seemed calmer and not as devastated when he left. He scrubbed his dirty face with the back of his hand and wiped it on his trouser leg. His posture straightened, and he walked away faster. Nash had seen the same demeanour change in people before when their jobs were complete, and they'd made peace with what had to be done. Levi was oblivious to everybody and everything as he took the steps down to the level of the ocean. He went up the walkway to the far end of the beach and was lost in contemplation. He didn't slow for the people in front of him or stop and let them pass. Nash was free to follow him in plain sight.

The sweeping concrete path that was interspersed with flights of steps as they climbed the side of the mountain led them away from the condensed areas of the complex. The long bend took them out of sight of all the people. It was vast and brought them from the south to the east side of the mountain. Here there was only rock and ocean. The concrete path came to an abrupt halt once the veneer of being in the public eye was unnecessary. Nobody came this far off the track. Levi didn't look behind.

He picked over the loose shale, limping but unaware of the tiny stones intruding between his feet and the Sliders he wore. Nash saw the dark stain of perspiration that turned the back of his tracksuit from blue and yellow to indigo and gold. Nash didn't think this boy wanted to die, but he sensed that Levi felt there was no other way out.

He stood on the rock looking out as far as Turkey. Nash shuddered as he saw the waves breaking onto the sharp rocks a hundred and fifty feet below. Levi raised his arms, and it looked as though he was wondering what it felt like to fly. Nash wanted to copy his stance as the boy made a cross out of his body with his arms extended.

Nash drew from his training. This desperate kid still had the surface of his feet on the rock. He hadn't taken the final step, so his toes were ahead of his body in free air. That was the moment when the deliberations were over, and the goodbyes had been said. Nash knew the difference between somebody who was thinking about taking his life and could back out and a man in his final moments of life.

And while he hadn't taken the last step before plunging, Levi was that desperate man. There was no going back, and he was jumping. Nash had a minute.

Less.

This boy was going to die.

Chapter Twenty

Nash had to get Levi's attention without startling him. Despite the loose shingle, he hadn't disturbed the boy from his thoughts. He cleared his throat, and Levi jumped and turned around. He wobbled as if he was closer to the edge than he thought. It was still close enough to be fatal if he'd fallen forward, but self-preservation stopped that, and his brain had righted his body so that he looked at Nash with an expression of confusion and anger at the intrusion of his privacy.

Nash risked another step so that he was level with the boy but not close enough to invade his place on the rock. They were on separate ends of the same piece of stone five feet apart. Nash took the last stride to the step between safety and freefalling. His toes were in the air. With nothing to stop him from falling, he was terrified and forced himself to look down. His natural instinct was to stare at the horizon to keep himself in place. Perfect posture, one slip, and it was game over. Levi came closer. He was within touching distance. If Nash was wrong, and this boy was the murderer, he could push Nash over the edge.

If he wanted to.

'Isn't it magnificent?' Nash said. 'There's worse places to do it, son.'

He spread his arms to gesture to the expanse of ocean and horizon with Turkey to their left and a tiny island, too small to name, rising like a mirage from the sea mist in front of them. He closed his eyes for a fraction of a second, steadied his balance and was careful not to show his fear. Levi stared at Nash, and the detective read between the lines. The young man must be wondering how this shift in balance happened. He was in control and in charge. He'd laid it out to this mother and his aunt, and while they didn't know about his final gambit and suicide plan, he'd told them how it was going to play out. With his dad in custody, he was the head of the family. It was down to him to put things back as close to the way they were—before—as he could. It was his duty and his right. He'd sort his family out and get his dad back so his mum might stop crying. He could do it all except life in prison. He couldn't do that. He had it under control. His Dad didn't mean to kill Dale. It was a horrible accident. He was the best man ever. Levi was taking the fall for his dad.

When he hesitated at the post box, Nash deduced that it was his written confession to the murders, and they were addressed to the island police so that his father would be released. But Levi couldn't face prison. Only this old dude was beside him, and the stupid bastard might fall. The old man was here to kill himself too. The world had gone mad. Levi had made his decision. He was ready. And now, this. He was in an agony of indecision and confusion. The boy didn't reply.

'Yes. Magnificent. This. Nature. Look at us, standing here, contemplating our mortality. You and me. And what are we?'

Levi stared at him.

'What are we? We're nothing, boy. Nothing. You, me. This. None of it matters. See that wave there?' He pointed. 'No. It's gone—this one. Here we go. Watch this one. Nope, that's gone too. Do you see what I'm getting at? The inevitability of everything? Nothing matters. Like the wave, it's there one second, gone the next. Irrelevant.'

'My brother wasn't irrelevant.'

'Your brother?'

'Dale. The boy. You know.'

'Oh, him? Yes. An obnoxious little shit, by all accounts.'

'What the hell?'

'You disagree? You don't think he was destined for drugs, jail, or a life on the dole, living the existence of a useless parasite? And what about you, Levi? What did your future hold before this?'

'You don't know us. You can't judge us like that. Who are you?'

'I'm nobody. People look at me and see an old man. Had my day, blight on society. That's me. Nothing left to offer. Might as well call it a day.'

'Wait. Stop.'

He'd only moved a fraction of an inch, but that was all it took. Levi read the intention in the minor muscle shift. He grabbed Nash and pulled him away from the edge. Nash thought his heart was going to burst with fear and needed a second to recover. They stumbled to safety together, and Nash motioned to a grassy knoll away from the edge. They sat.

'That's a bugger. You shouldn't have stopped me. We'll have to start again and get our balls back to go through with it. How do you want to do it? Should we do it together? Do you want to go first? Should I? Show you how easy it is?' Nash let a note of bitterness into his tone.

'No, man. It can't be that bad. What about your wife? She'll be waiting for you at the hotel?'

'My daughter. I'm here with her. She's young. She has her own life.'

'She must love you. Think what it'll do to her.'

Levi put his hand on Nash's shoulder. He took a second while they contemplated their time on the edge. This kid was something else. In a heartbeat, he'd put away his own feelings to make Nash feel better. They sat without words.

'What about you, kid? What's brought you to this beautiful cliff on this glorious day?'

Levi released his grief, and his tears fell. 'I did it.'

'What?'

'I'm the killer. I killed Dale and that little girl.'

Nash nodded his head and let go of Levi's shoulder. The boy looked at Nash.

'Did you hear what I said? I'm the murderer.'

'I heard you, son. But hearing something and knowing it are two different things.'

'What do you mean?'

'I guess I ought to be scared for my life up here with a cold-blooded murderer.'

'No. You've got it all wrong. I'm not going to hurt you.'

'I know. Did you need to take her clothes off?'

Levi hung his head and looked ashamed. The shame was real, but it wasn't his to take. He was reduced to mumbling. 'I suppose.'

'And was she face up or face down when you put her in the skip?'

Levi paused, and Nash watched him pick the girl up, lift the lid and drop her inside. He felt Levi wince. 'She was kind of face down, I suppose.'

'Joy Neal was fully clothed when her body was found. You're not even a good liar, son. Let alone a killer. When the police get your confession tomorrow, they're going to wipe the floor with your statement in two seconds. They will bring you in for questioning, you know. They'll have to.'

'How do you know about that?'

Nash ignored the question. 'It'll take them about as long as it took me to know you're not the killer. But you know, you should have more faith in your dad. It's not him, either. They'll know that soon enough and let him go, and then you can all get on with your lives and heal. Your family needs you. If you'd gone through with this, you wouldn't have saved your mother today—you'd have destroyed her.'

Levi looked confused. 'Are you an angel? How do you know all this stuff? Everybody thinks it's my dad. Even the police.'

Nash laughed. 'No. I'm just an ordinary old man here on holiday. You've listened to a flock of sheep. Open your heart and look inside it. Is your dad a murderer?'

'No.'

'How do you know?'

'Because he's a good man. I'm sorry. I shouldn't have doubted him,' Levi said.

'No.'

'What do I do?'

Nash looked at his watch. 'High tea on the terrace would be a good start.'

The drama was done, all bar the wailing mother. They walked back to the villa, and Levi grinned when the door burst open, and his mum came out like a tidal wave of fury. They probably heard her across the water in Bodrum.

'Where the hell have you been, you little sod? Have you any idea how worried I've been? Don't you think I've got enough on my plate with your dad banged up, without this, and you going AWOL on me? Get in that house.'

Nash hoped to speak to Levi again before they left.

When he got to the hotel, he saw Brown with a crowd of people in the lounge, but he didn't want to get into the conversation. Damn, it was hot. With all the tragedy, he'd forgotten his discomfort. He fancied a swim and then a lie down before he had to get back to work. Whatever Brown had dredged up could wait.

Chapter Twenty-One

B rown had spent all morning going over statements, building timelines and mapping people's whereabouts. Now, she sipped her cocktail—and they call this a career. She'd isolated the names of the three parties in the hotel that had any geographical connection to Alma Cullen, the woman who started all this. She was pleased with herself for corralling two of the couples. With the donkey work of the morning done, she was sitting at a table on the terrace with Shelby and Lana and an older husband and wife, Elmo and Judy. However, there was no stopping the image of a puppet coming to mind whenever somebody mentioned Elmo's name.

The third family came from Carlisle and had no interest in sitting around the bars and terraces. She'd managed to get into the queue for pizza behind the mother, Rosie, earlier and tried to engage her. Other than a cool 'Hello,' Rosie made it clear she wasn't interested in chatting while their stone-baked pizzas cooked. She had pink nail varnish, unlike the pastel tone of the person that Snow mentioned on their Zoom call. Rosie's polish wasn't garish, but a woman would never call it soft. It was too bright for that. An hour after she'd finished breakfast and an hour before the restaurant opened for lunch, Brown was left with the smallest pizza on offer, a child's six-inch Hawaiian, that she didn't want. She forced it down for the team.

Lana and Shelby were lively. She liked them. Judy had a few stories to tell, but Brown hadn't extracted much from them so far. Neither of the girls had their nails painted, and Judy's looked as though they'd been polished and given a coat of clear varnish, but she couldn't be sure. So far, her morning was a washout as far as intel gathering went. She discovered the girls met at Leeds University and hated each other on sight. They'd laughed at that and stared at each other, with love shining between them like a laser. Lana played the cello, and Shelby loved rock music. Judy had her intrigue as well. She'd had a brief affair with a legendary drummer from one of the top 70's glam rock bands who lives in Ulverston.

A woman in espadrilles and the most hideous creation of a dress in pink chiffon plonked a handbag the size of a small town on the empty chair at the end of the table and took off a pair of white cotton gloves. She did it like the Queen, pulling an inch from each finger before degloving her delicate hand. She was about sixty but far from old and was beautifully manicured in deep coral. She sat down, foregoing the manners to ask, and clicked her fingers for a waitress without looking to see if one was available.

'Oh God, I'm completely and utterly knackered. Why do these God-awful countries have to be so bloody hot?'

This one looked as though she might be a talker. 'Join us,' Brown said.

The woman took out a slender black cigarette holder and put her lighter on the table. She attached a cigarette to the ridiculous tapering rod of plastic. A silver case was engraved with initials, and she put it beside her while a waitress appeared from nowhere to light her cigarette. They had clearly been ordered to stand on ceremony, ready to come forward, when the rude woman waved her holder. 'And who the hell are you? The bloody hula girl? Do I get a lei around my neck? Jesus. Spare me.'

'Actually, we were in the middle of a conversation, so the same could be asked. Who the hell are you?' Brown asked.

The woman pulled her sunglasses to the end of her nose and peered over them at Brown. 'You've got spunk. I like you. I, my dear, am Lady Claudia Glamis, countess and cousin of the late Queen. One is thirty-sixth in line to the British throne and second cousin to the King of England.'

She might be, but Brown noticed her cigarette case had the initials BW in the top right-hand corner. Connie had this bitch sized up. She wanted to be noticed and made sure everybody knew who she was. Why did she have somebody else's cigarette case? Surely a woman of her heritage would have her own initials and the bloody royal crest above them. She probably had her title emblazoned in a diamond vagazzle.

'I should be addressed as My Lady, and you should rise and curtsey on my approach. But, to hell with all that, just get me a drink and rub my aching feet, and I'm happy.'

There was a shocked silence, and it was as though a Martian had walked onto the terrace. The countess let out a laugh that sounded like a barn owl on the hunt. She howled in her seat.

'Your faces. I'm joking—about the feet, at least. The rest is all laboriously true. One has been sent to this ghastly necropolis for what they call a rest. It's tiresome.' She did the air quotes on the word rest. 'In plain English, what the old bastards mean is, "You drink too much, Claudia, and it's been decreed—again—that you are embarrassing The Crown." Not one of them has the guts to say it to my face.'

'I hope you don't expect us to curtsey.' Lana said, 'It's not happening, mate. I'm not a royalist. Never have been.'

'You're not a countess,' Shelby laughed.

'Indeed I am. I know all the palace secrets, and they hate it when I speak out of turn. I'm what's called a loose cannon, my dear.'

'Blimey,' Brown said.

'And as for that used tampon calling himself a king, my cousin, Queen Elizabeth, wiped the floor with him in her heyday. She was formidable, you know?' She took the stub out of her holder and replaced it with a fresh cigarette. A tilt of her head was the signal for the waitress to move forward and light it.

'So, what do you do?' Judy asked.

'Ma'am.'

'What do you do, ma'am?'

Brown was dying to point out that she could also command the title of ma'am if she chose to. While others were talking, her job was to take mental notes and write her report later.

'I don't do anything. I have an apartment at Kensington Palace and a villa in the Seychelles. I party and make a nuisance of myself. One drives one's neighbours mad. I often play the piano when I can't sleep, and I'm prone to delicious rages of melancholy where I smash a lot of expensive glassware. They've removed all the good stuff. Though I did once paint makeup on the Grand old Duke of Wellington—apparently, the stuffy old portrait was priceless and cost thousands to restore.

'Andrew comes to stay in his apartment at Kensington, you know—he's a twat like the rest of them.' She jiggled the ice in her whiskey for a refill and replaced her cigarette. The waitress took the glass and lit her Embassy Regal. The bar manager was watching like a hawk and catapulted the girl in when countess Claudia raised her glass. A second waiter was sent to wipe the table, and Claudia grabbed his chin and turned his face towards her.

'You're pretty. Do you make house calls?'

The kid was young and blonde and as out of his depth as it was possible to be. Claudia scribbled her room number on a napkin and stuffed it in his belt. She waited for him to leave and kicked off her sandals. 'They told me to stay in my room—and not drink. Can you believe that? I've never heard of anything so preposterous. I'm bored and want some company if I've got to spend another ten days in this hell hole. I believe there is gossip abounding.'

'The murders you mean, Miss?' Judy said.

'For God's sake, woman. Just call me Claud. The murders, how delicious. One feels it's just like being at home. Of course, it's not my first suspicious drowning. There was a scandal at my villa a few years ago. Identical to this, but it turned out to be a bore with all their endless questions.'

Brown didn't have to ask for details. Lana was in like a shot and did it for her.

'It was very much like this. We'd had a fabulous party, and the next morning a teenage boy was found floating in the swimming pool. One thought he'd climbed over the fence to frolic—but the policeman said foul play was involved. It was even suggested by *The Sunday Times* that several young men had been purchased, like the ice sculpture and the extra crystal. Quite ridiculous, of course. One does not have to pay to have people attend one's parties. I like young people. That isn't a crime. One likes to have young men around. They are such fun—and good in bed.'

'What happened?' Brown asked. There was no way she was adding any titles, and that was understood between them.

'The Firm took care of it, and it went away. The simpering, doe-eyed one got pregnant again, and that took the front page away from me. And the day after that, the American one made the simpering one cry over a dress or some such nonsense—and life went on. Officers of the law questioned one for hours. At first, it was all a hoot, but it did get a little sordid even by my standards—and I don't have many. Standards that is.'

She saw Shelby reach for Lana's hand and swooped on them like an eagle on a desert rat. 'You're lesbians—what fun. My first husband was a friend of Dorothy, you know. All terribly hush-hush back in the day. Lilibet was quite furious with me. Well. It was hardly my fault, was it? I didn't make him gay. But in the end, they sided with him. Of course, I had lovers. Why wouldn't I? Indiscrete, they called it. I was told not to draw attention to myself. I'm the soul of discretion.'

'I can't imagine why they'd think otherwise,' Lana said, eyeing the yards of pink chiffon.

'Well. At least I knew which side I liked my bread buttered on, and I stuck to it. Though there was that one night when a lady dancer kissed me in her dressing room. Anyway, it was all a load of hoo-ha, and they bought him a place to stop him from bleating. Elton and David were regulars. I was green with jealousy and injustice. He was nothing until he met me. The next scandal was smothered before it ever leaked to the press. Of course, Lucien killed himself. Although they questioned me for weeks, any other suggestion was just preposterous. Lilibet made it go away. She was good at that, though I would have liked to be the one to push the big fairy off the palace wall to his death.'

'What have you got?' Nash asked.

Nash and Brown were in his suite. They were sitting at his table with papers arranged in neat piles in order of importance. Brown had brought a selection of cake and pastries in with her and ate three with coffee while they discussed her findings.

'Plenty. I'm not sure where to start.'

'So I see. You're half blotto.'

'Only half and not enough to blunt my intellect,' Brown said. 'All that listening is thirsty work.' She pushed piles of papers across the desk to him. 'I spent the morning with a consultant from the hospital on this pile. 'He kept going on about having a woman with a hysterectomy waiting on a slab for him.'

'Was she dead?'

'I don't think so. Operation, I think. Maybe he said, gurney. Anyway, we have seventy-three people with conditions and twenty-eight with serious, or what we'd define as life-threatening ailments. I've collated them youngest first. There's one disabled kid on the bottom level of the hotel. Other than that, it's all minor stuff. A bit of infant onset asthma and the like,' she slurred over the pronunciation.

'Would you like to try that one again?'

'Infant onset asthma.' She laughed and opened her notepad, pointing to a couple of hand-written pages. 'These are my observations about nail polish and who is wearing what. And this,' she tapped the largest pile of typewritten pages, 'is a list of cross-matched timelines of who was where at each murder—and around the disappearance of Mr Gould. A photocopy of the note threatening him is in there. This one relates to staff—and this to the guests.'

'Anything else?'

'Nothing more to report on Mr Gould's disappearance. No new evidence has come to light. It's as though he vanished into thin air. The police search is ongoing, and the aerial search is underway.'

'And the murdered kids?'

'One of the Butcher boys has a gap in his timeline that can't be accounted for, but two of the other kids say he was playing football with them. It can't be substantiated. But, get this,' She referred to her notes, 'some guests in Kardamena said they saw Levi Butcher in town that afternoon when he was supposed to be playing footie. He was acting suspiciously enough in light of events for them to hunt Ballas down on their return to report it.'

'Good work. Levi Butcher. I know about that, and it's been sorted. The kid's been cleared. Anything else?'

'Are you sure? It sounded suspect to me.'

'Nothing there. Move on.'

'Okay. A couple of staff members weren't where they were supposed to be. A waiter didn't show up for his shift on the day of the two kids' deaths, leaving the dining room short-staffed. The manager said it was out of character for him. Ballas is checking it out. And the only other thing is that we're living among royalty.'

'Really?'

'Apparently so. She's a Countess. Lady Claudia Gamis. The King's second cousin, she says. Odd about the initials, though. She uses a different name—I suppose it's a royalty thing. She lives in one of the palaces and has been sent here to dry out. I asked why they didn't send her to the Priory, and she said she'd been kicked out of three of them. I've only just started my research, but from what I can gather, she comes down the late queen mother's line from the Bowes-Lyon lot. Most of that generation had a recessive gene and were locked in an asylum for forty years—five of them, apparently. All girls. And the Queen Mother just left them there to rot, saving the royals from the stigma of instability in the mental health of the bloodline.'

'What's that got to do with this?'

'Maybe nothing, but this one's as mad as a box of frogs. She's racist, homophobic and expects mere mortals to bow and scrape to her. I was giving you the background first. Like you taught me to.'

'It's interesting, and I am familiar with the Bowes-Lyon scandal. The Queen Mother said the five relatives were all dead, knowing they were alive. Nerissa Bowes-Lyon and Katherine were first cousins of Queen Elizabeth, and the other three were second cousins. They were incarcerated in the Royal Earlswood Asylum for Mental Defectives in 1941 and were forgotten about. The state paid for them. Tragic and a sign of how corrupt and ruthless our royal institution can be. But has it got any bearing on the case, or were you just feeding your need for gossip?'

'If you let me get a word in. You have to know everything about everything, don't you? Why did you have to know about the defective children? I wanted to educate you for a change.'

'I read a lot of books while you're in the bars and gin joints of Barrow.'

'Do you want to hear this, Nash?'

'If I must.'

'She told us an identical story to the one about Dale Butcher drowning. A teenage boy drowned in her personal swimming pool after one of their posh parties.'

'Okay.'

'Okay? Is that all you've got to say? It's the same. MO accounting. And that's not all. She was accused of bunking her husband off, as well.'

'Excellent work. I'll look into it. However, water and alcohol don't always match well. Drink more coffee, get some sleep and come back ready for work. I need you on your game. Sober up and report for duty.'

'Yes, sir.'

Chapter Twenty-Two

J eff looked at his lobster-red face in the mirror. 'This bloody sun. I'd better not peel.'

'I'll still love you if you look like a leper by the end of the day. Are you sure you want to go into Kos?'

'God, yes. Let's get out of this infernal resort. It's feeling more like a death camp every day. Whose idea was it to go on holiday again?'

'Ours, darling, it was our idea. I tell you, if Resting Bitch Face is rude to me again this morning, I won't be responsible for my actions.'

'I know. I've never known such a surly waitress.'

'Jeez,' they said together and laughed. Jeff pulled her onto the bed, and they toppled with an almighty crash.

'Oh hell, have we broken the bed?'

'Doesn't look like it. Good sturdy oak, just like you, my love,' Jeff said.

'Can't I be a beautiful blossoming cherry just once?'

'With a trunk like that, you're kidding, aren't you?' Before she could come back at him with a hurt look or a retort, he kissed her, and she suspected it was to shut her up. However, landing hard on the bed jarred

215

her head and set off a tic attack. Jeff stood up with a sigh waiting for her to come out of it.

'Sorry,' she said.

'It's okay.'

'Do you want to come back?'

'No, that killed the mood. Let's get going. Just one thing, though.'

'Yes?'

'Can we have one day where it's just us without Ray tagging along?'

'Of course. I told him last night it was a romantic date for two. Jeff Pearson, if I didn't know better, I'd say you were jealous.'

'Get out, you. The day's wasting. I forgot to ask, did you message my mother to see how the dog is while you were in the library yesterday?'

'I said I would, didn't I?'

'And?'

'And what?'

'And how is the bloody dog?'

'He's fine, but your mother's sprained her wrist.'

'Damn, I'll give her a ring later to see how she is. But for now, come on, or the car will be too hot to drive.'

The old Kos town was scorching, dusty and beautiful. At last, they found the history and culture that was missing from the barren wastes of their resort. There were gardens, with statues of fallen heroes, for sitting and reflection. The architecture was Grecian and beautiful. They wandered the streets, letting each cobbled stone carry them into the tourist quarter. To go anywhere else would have taken a concerted effort to turn back on themselves and force the break between meandering towards the vendors and landing in the sub-culture no-man's-land of poverty and shacks.

They would both prefer to see the real town but were content to follow the backs of people in front of them until they hit a larger version of Kardamena. The streets were narrow and identical, with stalls lining both sides. The wares were the same as in Kardamena but repeated on a grander scale. The town was built on a familiar grid with all horizontal streets flowing down to the harbour. It was impressive, and while Kardamena Harbour had tourist pirate ships for trips and quaint fishing boats, The Kos version was home to yachts and grand sailing boats belonging to the rich and famous.

They found a pavement café and ordered frappe coffee to sit with and watch life go by. At that second, Connie didn't have a worry in the world and felt a serenity, the like of which she only felt in a hot foreign country. Life and its woes lifted, and she was truly happy. She gave Jeff a smile and saw his face turn from a look of love to an intense annoyance.

'Fancy bumping into you two here.'

'Ray,' Jeff said.

'Hi, guys. When you said you were coming today, I thought I'd hop on the bus and see what all the fuss was about. I never thought for a second that I'd run into you. Small world, eh?'

'So it would seem.' Jeff didn't hide the resentment in his voice.

Connie squeezed his knee to indicate that she was annoyed, too. 'You're here now. You might as well sit down,' she said, to break the awkwardness of Ray just standing there and Jeff looking murderous and as though he wanted to drown him.

'To be honest, when I saw you here all loved up, I thought of turning around and slipping down one of the side streets before you saw me, but that'd be silly. I'd have to spend the rest of the day looking around corners to check if you were there before moving.' He laughed at his own joke. 'However, if you'd prefer to be alone, I can vamoose.'

'No. Not at all. As I said, you're here now. And you're welcome to join us.' Connie was ever the peacemaker, and Jeff kicked her under the table.

Jeff was sullen, but if Ray was aware of it, it didn't show as he kept up a run of lively conversation, and Connie tried not to burn from the heat of Jeff's anger as his arm pressed against her.

They left the pavement café sooner than Connie and Jeff would have done had they been alone and free to talk. The midday sun was vicious, and they'd saved the museum until now to have somewhere to escape it for a couple of hours.

Ray stopped to look at a stall selling bamboo sunglasses, and while he talked to the stallholder about their benefits and sustainability, Jeff pulled Connie aside.

'Get rid of him,' he hissed in her ear.

'I can't.'

'If you don't, I will. And you won't like it.'

'Behave. He's not doing any harm.'

'He's breathing. That's harm enough. He's getting on my nerves, and if he doesn't back off, he's going to be sorry.'

'What do you think?' Ray pivoted to them in a pair of John Lennon glasses made from light bamboo.

'Beautiful,' Connie said.

'Beautiful,' Jeff mimicked, and Connie jabbed him in the ribs.

Jeff was quiet as they walked, and Connie felt him fuming across the gulf between them.

The museum of Kos was a square building against the far side of a large town square. It was dominated by a restaurant with two orange domes and a tall tower. The pavement cafés were hung with cooling ferns to shade their visitors from the sun, and the scene was idyllic. But they were grateful to get out of the heat and into the cool entrance hall of the museum.

While Jeff bought their tickets, Connie went to an information plaque telling visitors about the museum, exhibits and ancient relics. She put her bag on the plinth in front of her and read, devouring every word. From that second, she was lost in history and oblivious to the world around her. Every letter was a time machine that took her back to the era of the great gods.

One of the lady curators came over and spoke to her in rapid Greek. Connie pulled away from the story of Hermes' birth, still immersed in a different time. She had no idea what the woman was saying to her.

The curator took her bag, walked through a door with it and put it on a public bench.

'What? I can't take my bag with me. Is that what you're saying?'

The woman babbled at her some more. 'Here, Madam. Put bag here.'

'But I can't leave it there. Don't you have a place behind the counter or something?' To her later shame and humiliation, Connie went to the original wall plaque and put it back on the stone table underneath.

The woman followed her and picked it up again. She was shouting at Connie now and gestured to the table at knee level.

Ray came over and put his arm around Connie's shoulder, leading her way. 'Honey, she's not saying you can't take your bag in with you. She's saying you keep putting it on one of the original standing stones dating back thousands of years to when this guy with the tiny penis was just a bairn.'

Jeff had moved away to look at other things. He was even more keen on ancient history and culture than Connie and only turned to them when he saw Ray with his arm around her. 'What's going on?'

Ray told him the story, and they laughed at Connie, who was mortified. 'She put her bag on one of the original relics and then argued with the curator about it, mate.'

'I never once looked down to see what my bag was on. I just put it there. I feel so guilty.' The men bonded over her ineptitude and made jokes about the wrath of the god Hermes for the next half hour.

The museum was fascinating, though it wasn't built to house the artefacts. The main temple was never moved. They simply built the museum building over it. Connie blocked out the other tourists and was transported back in time. She saw herself walking down the same street they'd come through to enter the museum.

When the earthquake of 1933 destroyed Kos, something was unearthed. The ruins of the ancient city of Kos were hidden beneath its modern buildings. This very temple, with its four corner pillars of white alabaster, made up the centrepiece and the spectacular mosaic, in its entirety, covered the floorspace within the pillars. Among the ruins, other significant floors were found, embellishing courtyards and walls in their elegant and impressive beauty. The *Arrival of Hippokrates* was the most amazing mosaic that covered the entire courtyard floor of the Museum. And Connie stood at the edge of its majesty and history with a statue of the man himself overlooking it.

They wandered around the museum looking at the statues with missing arms, legs and faces. They saw the weaponry and artefacts found from the archaeological digs. They displayed tiny vases, jewellery and currency of ancient times, but Connie couldn't shake the melancholy that had come over her.

She left the others looking at spears and debating the wars of Ancient Greece and found a stone bench in a cool corner of the uppermost floor. She checked it was a public bench before sitting down. Connie was horrified when she felt the tears coming. She tried, but there was no stopping them. She thought about all the football hooligans abroad and the bad name British tourists had earned over recent decades due to loutish behaviour in guest countries. The lady shouting at her was awful, and she'd put her bag on the ancient relic, not once, but twice as though disregarding what the lady was saying, and she felt guilty for the way that curator perceived her. She cared about respect and would never insult another country or its culture. She should have paid attention to what she was doing.

That morning she'd taken her tablets as usual and couldn't predict how they might affect her. Today, Sparky was going straight for her emotions. Six months earlier, she would have laughed off the incident after feeling silly. Now, it was the most important thing in the world. She dabbed her eyes and had to make it right.

Connie went to the ground floor and spoke to the curator. 'I'm sorry about putting my bag down. It was an accident, but so disrespectful.' She had no idea how much the lady understood, but she seemed to get the gist and touched the back of Connie's hand in a gesture of kindness that set her off again. She ran up the stairs two at a time and scuttled back to her bench in the cool quiet out of the way. She hadn't even been missed, and the men were still at the far side of the room, pointing at one of the covered display cases.

Connie assessed her emotions. She'd been a practising therapist for years. Through her work, she'd seen suffering first-hand and had never been unprofessional or let her mask of calm compassion slip. Old Connie would never descend into histrionics and weeping. She didn't recognise this fool who had possessed her very sensible body.

Her reaction to what the men were already calling Bag-gate was over the top, but she couldn't get beyond the minutiae of how the curator felt about her and what had gone through the middle-aged woman's mind when a Brit disrespected her culture. She'd sorted it and had put it right, but the melancholy wouldn't lift. The tears came again, and she cursed them.

Ray came over, and Connie turned her face away.

'Hey. What's the matter?' He put his arm around her and pulled her face into his chest. The floodgates that were only half open until now parted and poured. She sobbed against him.

'I feel terrible. What must that poor woman have thought of me? I can't believe I was so stupid and disrespectful.'

He stroked her hair, smoothing it down and holding her tight. He was more supportive when she was upset than Jeff. 'Connie, don't worry about it, sweetheart. It was nothing. She's probably forgotten about it. Do you think you're the first person to put something on that altar? I bet they do it every day. The floor there will be worn out from her asking people to move their bags. I don't know why they haven't just moved the thousands-year-old artefact from its rightful place—it would be far easier.'

'Every time I come around a corner, you are cuddling my wife.' Jeff didn't hide his anger.

'Bit weepy,' Ray whispered over her head. 'Bag-gate.'

'I'm not deaf, you know.'

'Connie, come on, stop being silly. It was nothing. Let it go now. You're overreacting,' Jeff said.

'I went to see the lady and apologised.'

'Really? Christ, I can't leave you on your own for a second. There was no need to do that. You're making a huge thing about nothing. Come here, you idiot.' He opened his arms, and she left the warmth of Ray's tight embrace for the aloof hold of her man. Jeff gave her a quick hug and kissed her cheek.

'Ugh, snotty. Come on. I need a drink.'

When they got to the street, Jeff waited for his opportunity. Connie had stopped to stroke a dog, and he pulled hard on Ray's arm. The other man swung around to face him. Connie stood in time to see the threat in Jeff's eyes and thought he was going to hit him.

'I reckon it's time you laid off my missus, mate.'

Chapter
Twenty-Three

They found a different street corner with a different bar and ordered drinks. Beer for the men and Coke for Connie, who was the designated driver. The tension between Jeff and Ray was palpable, but Ray didn't take the hint and leave them to their day.

Somebody was shouting, and a man came into sight chasing two ladies down the street. They turned to watch, astonished. The man was waving a walking stick at them and shouting in a mixture of Greek and broken English. The only words Connie made out were, 'English swine.'

Again, she had smoothed the waters between Jeff and Ray, and an uncomfortable truce had settled between them. They watched the man give up and saw him talking to a pair of stallholders and gesturing down the street.

Connie was shocked to see it was Juliet and Mercedes being chased. 'Hi, guys. Can you believe that? The man back there was going to call the police on me. I've never heard anything like it,' Juliet said as they came around the corner and out of the man's view.

'Mummy, sit down, and I'll get you a nice drink.'

Connie smiled and gestured to the empty seats. They must have been caught shoplifting, but they'd struck Connie as being so upper-class and strait-laced. They were such elegant people, and the last guests Connie would have pegged as thieves. Mercedes was distressed. She was hot, sweating and wasn't far from tears. The hair had fallen out of her topknot and hung in lank tendrils around her face. She'd lapsed into childish talk and called her mother, Mummy. It was sweet and disturbing at the same time, coming from a woman nearing her thirties. She raised her eyes to Connie, Jeff and Ray, imploring them to look after her mother while she went for drinks, and she still looked traumatised as she went to the bar.

'You look like you've run a Marathon,' Connie said.

Juliet ignored her and turned her baby blues on Jeff in a play of flirtation. 'I'm so glad you're here. I've had a terrible experience.' Connie watched as the woman laid her hand on his forearm and couldn't decide whether she was pissed off or amused. She wasn't jealous. She knew when her man had eyes for a particular lady, and she had nothing to worry about where Juliet was concerned. She might have been concerned about Mercedes, but she wasn't his type either, even though she was pretty and young. Jeff had been prone to having his head turned, but as far as Connie was aware, he'd never played away. Mercedes had too much junk in the trunk for his liking, and the mother-and-daughter pairing was a weird dynamic.

They were intermingled and co-dependent. Connie liked them because they were interesting, particularly Mercedes, who she thought was a breath of fresh air, but there was no straying from the fact that they were oddballs.

When she came back with soft drinks, Mercedes sat beside her mum. She went into Juliet's handbag and took out a box of tablets. She tried to be discrete about it, but Connie craned her head to see what they were. As a retired mental-health practitioner, it was a habit, and she had a Pavlovian response to seeing a pill box. She had to know what they were and what they were for. Juliet was taking Clozapine, a strong antipsychotic often used in the treatment of schizophrenia.

Before she zipped up the bag, Connie saw another box. This one was Risperidone. Another antipsychotic used to dull the senses and reduce hallucinations, amongst other things. She wasn't surprised. She'd seen the fire casting shadows in the woman's pupils. Connie had treated enough mental illness to spot when something was off.

'Here, Mummy. Take this,' Mercedes said.

Without any warning, a murderous look cast a shadow over Juliet's face, and she raised her arm to strike her daughter. There was a collective gasp. But Mercedes was ready for her and looked as though she'd dealt with this a thousand times before. Her reflexes were fast, and she grabbed her mum's hand and brought it back to her lap before it made contact. She spoke to Juliet with a sad softness.

'Don't do that.'

Juliet screamed and fought against her.

'Don't do that.'

Her mother battled to hit her and flung her head around, trying to headbutt her daughter. In between screaming, she lapsed into unhinged mumbling.

'Do you mind?' Mercedes asked Ray, who was sitting next to her.

'No, of course.' He looked awkward and didn't say anything as he grabbed Juliet's other arm and held her down. She lowered her head to bite Ray, and Jeff jumped out of his seat and held her back.

'She'll stop in a minute,' Mercedes said. 'But be careful. She's strong.' It took a few minutes of Juliet writhing and struggling against them before she calmed. She was screaming and mouthing crude swearwords in her rage. When she stopped, it was similar to Connie coming out of a tic attack. It was exhausting having your brain fighting that level of agitation, and while the conditions were vastly different, she thought she knew how Juliet felt. Mercedes handed her the glass of orangeade and let her realign with the world while she took a drink, and then she offered her the pill again. 'Here, Mummy, take this tablet for me.' This time, Juliet took it like a child from a parent.

She didn't look embarrassed, and it was as though she had no memory of the psychotic episode. 'Mercedes and I thought we might go to church tomorrow. Didn't we, dear?'

'Yes, Mum. We'll see.'

An uncomfortable silence fell over the table. Mercedes smiled her thanks and an apology without saying a word, and after the shocked silence had drawn out too long, they all spoke at once to bridge the nothingness. Juliet ranted about religion, was animated, and spoke too fervently about God and how He would punish the sinners that didn't worship at his altar. 'Being on holiday is no excuse for not going to mass. Evil will get in through your pores if you don't worship the Lord our God in his house. The ones that don't worship God will lapse into sickness, and it's a sign that they will be smite with his wrath.'

Mercedes made a point of changing the subject, and Connie realised that she'd done it several times the night they'd had drinks together. It was adroit and seamless and went unnoticed. 'We might see the porpoise on our way to church tomorrow, Mum. We saw your pod this morning, Connie. Didn't we, Mum?'

'Oh yes, dear. Four big ones and a tiny baby. Jeff, you must come to our balcony this evening, and we'll watch for them under the moonlight. You too, Connie.' But it was clear from her expression that the tag-on invitation was given grudgingly.

They chatted, and Juliet returned to normal as her medication took effect. Connie sneezed and had a tic attack of her own, and she wanted to make a joke about them providing enough entertainment between them that they should sell tickets—but she didn't.

'That must be awful for you, dear,' Juliet said, and Connie choked on her drink. She laughed and covered it with the cough that made her tic again. Juliet made a show of looking around and seeming embarrassed, and after what she'd just done, Connie appreciated the beautiful irony of it.

A police car pulled up to the kerb, and two policemen got out of the front. They opened the rear doors, and a woman climbed out carrying a child of about six. He was old enough to stand, but the mother wasn't letting go. The old shopkeeper with his walking stick got out of the other side.

The woman said something in Greek and pointed at Juliet. Although they didn't know for sure what was said, it was clear enough. 'That's her.'

The police didn't speak any English. They ran up, screaming at Juliet in Greek. One of them knocked a chair over, and Connie thought it was unnecessary. They used incredible force to drag Juliet from her seat and pushed her over the table to cuff her hands behind her back. The police officers shouted at her the whole time, and the old man ranted beside them. He jumped around shouting, 'Kidnap.' Ray and Jeff had to hold him back to stop him from beating Juliet with his stick. Again, the implication behind the angry Greek words was obvious, even if the crime wasn't.

Mercedes screamed, 'Please don't do this. We're very sorry. My mother hasn't been well. It was a terrible mistake. She was confused. Mum isn't a bad person. Please let her go.' She tried to get the policeman off her Mum, and he thrust her aside so that she fell to the ground between two tables.

'Hey. There's no need for that,' Ray shouted at the policemen as Jeff and Connie helped Mercedes up. After that, everything happened fast. People were shouting, some in Greek and others in English, as Juliet was dragged to the police car.

'I didn't hurt her. I'd never hurt my little girl. I would never do anything like that.' They saw her tear-stained face pressed against the window as they drove away, leaving them standing on the pavement. Juliet looked terrified, and Mercedes was shocked. They helped her into a chair.

'I need to go to her,' Mercedes said.

'We'll find out which station she's been taken to and get over there. It might be an idea to ring the British Embassy. I don't know if they can help, but I think that's what they're there for.'

The barman came to them to see if he could do anything. He was kind and spoke enough English to give them directions to the police station, and with a common cause to fight for, the tension between Ray and Jeff was put to one side.

Chapter
Twenty-Four

The police station at Kos was a single-storey whitewashed building with excellent air conditioning. A woman, Juliet Milton-Barr, was arrested and questioned in relation to the two murders in Greece. In addition to this, she was interviewed about the disappearance of Mr Mervyn Gould, with an order pending for an arrest through the British system for Alma Cullen. Jumping on the fact that she'd tried to kidnap a little boy in broad daylight, the Grecian police were lumping all the recent crimes on the unbalanced woman for an easy win.

Nash and Brown had pulled up in a taxi outside the police station.

'It's the countess, isn't it? I knew it was her,' Brown said when she heard a woman had been arrested.

'No, it's somebody else. Vaguely similar type, well-to-do, on holiday with her daughter. She has some mental health issues and took a funny turn in a bar yesterday. They brought her in for the attempted kidnap of a boy, seven years old.'

'They've got the killer, then?'

'Looks that way, but we have no information yet. Let's not jump to conclusions. But that's not all. Later that night, when the guests were back at the hotel, six officers stormed the dining room and dragged the daughter out to a waiting police car. The mother has fingered her as being up to her neck in it, so they've got both of them. So far, though, they're only going for the mother.'

'That's some heavy shit. What are your thoughts? Did they do it?'

'Too early to tell, but I'm concerned for their wellbeing. Suspects don't have the same rights as in England, and I'm worried about how long they'll be interviewed without a break. We'll see how the land lies when we get in there.'

'I was sure it was that countess. Can you imagine the scandal back home with the royal family up to their eyes in trouble again? It would make a whole series of *The Crown*.'

Nash grinned as they waited to go into the first interview with Mercedes Milton.

'What?' Brown said.

'Nothing.'

'Don't give me that, boss. What do you know about the royals?'

'Did you do any research on our Countess last night?'

'No. I was knackered and went straight to bed after pouring over reports all evening.'

'Pissed, you mean.'

'Come on. What have you got on her? She's as shady as hell, isn't she? I know she's hiding something. Wrap sheet?'

The light above the interview room door had changed from red to green. 'It seems we can go in.'

'Tell me about the countess, sir.'

'No time. Come on.' He tapped on the closed door and waited to be let in.

They went into a stark interview room. A long desk and chairs were the only items in the room except for a camera with the recording light flashing in the corner of the ceiling.

Introductions were made, and it was explained that the session was being recorded. The suspect, Mercedes Milton, sat on one side of the table with an interpreter beside her. She had no legal representation, and Ballas explained for the tape that it had been offered and declined and that the British Embassy had been informed regarding the situation and the two arrests. Nash had a meeting later that day with the embassy when more information had been released.

Mercedes was distraught. She had deep sweat stains under her armpits, and her makeup had run over her face. It was clear she'd been crying, but at this point, she was exhausted, and there were no tears. Ballas and his sergeant Petro Deppas interrogated her. The affable island detectives that Nash had got on with very well were gone, and from what Nash could see, in their place, there were two shouting bullies.

Nash and Brown's cover could be blown if either mother or daughter were later freed to return to the hotel.

Ballas was confident of conviction and told them that wouldn't happen. He was frustrated by several changes to the mother's story, though he had a confession from both parties on the attempted kidnapping of the Greek boy.

Ballas explained to Nash in front of Ms Milton that her mother had been taken to a medical facility and had been sedated after a violent episode during her interview. Deppas touched the ugly scratch on his cheek, setting the daughter off crying again.

'Please let me be with my mother. She needs me. She'll be so frightened and won't understand what's happening to her. Please, I've answered all your questions a hundred times, and there's nothing else I can tell you.'

Nash said, 'Ms Milton, we are detectives from Britain, and we're here to assist Detective Ballas in a number of related cases. As British citizens, we will do what we can to have you and your mother transferred to England for further investigation if you are formally charged.'

'That is not going to happen, Inspector,' Ballas said. 'And to tell the suspect it is so will only cloud the waters. This is our investigation, and the ladies are our suspects. You are here as our guests.'

'Of course, Captain Ballas. However, we will do what we can to have this lady and her mother taken home.'

'Thank you. Please can you help my mum? I don't know where she is. Can I see her?'

'We'll do what we can, Ms Milton.' Nash turned to Ballas. 'How long has she been locked in here, Captain?'

'Since we picked her up at eight-fifteen last night. And I must inform you, Inspector, that we will not be releasing Ms Milton, or her mother, Mrs Milton-Barr, into your care. Should she be charged, and I believe she will, the crimes in question were committed on Greek soil and, as such, will be tried here.'

'In the interim. I respectfully ask that Ms Milton is given refreshment and something to eat and is allowed to rest while we look at the case against her and her mother.'

'We are not yet finished with the interview, Inspector Nash.'
'I believe we are, Captain Ballas.'

They had a busy morning. Nash was at loggerheads with the Greek police force and tried to pull rank over what he said were barbaric policing procedures. In the interests of international cordiality, Ballas consented and agreed that Ms Milton be taken to a cell to rest. It was the best he could do for her, and he promised to return after an eight-hour respite for the next interview. Ballas huffed and said if they lost the momentum of the interrogation and the suspect clammed up because of the insipid British interviewing techniques, he would hold Nash responsible and would be submitting a report to that effect. Nash told him to eat his report and choke on it.

They were locked in heated debate for two hours as they trawled through the evidence against Ms Milton and Mrs Milton-Barr. After reviewing endless papers and reports, Nash was of the opinion that the daughter was innocent of the crimes but couldn't confidently say that she didn't know something and was protecting her mother. As he listened to sections of the interview tapes, the daughter was level-headed at times and clear, but then she'd be highly strung and seemed to lose her grip on reality. She'd never lived apart from her mother or stepped out from under her wing. Mercedes' personality seemed to morph in and out of being her own person, but sometimes was a second embodiment of her parent. By the same token, the mother needed the daughter as a nursemaid due to her schizophrenia and mental condition. They did everything together, and it was difficult to determine where one started and the other finished. They could be in it together. Nash listened to all the evidence against them with an open mind. The link between the mother's story and the murders was tenuous at best. Assuming she—or they—were hardened killers was a long reach. But there was no denying that with both parties having some unusual mental-health issues and their strange interwoven dependency on each other, there could be something to it.

Like most hotel guests during the night of the drowning, they claimed to be in their room asleep. Their alibi was each other, and Ms Milton swore that Juliet Milton-Barr couldn't have gone out in the dead of night murdering teenage boys because she'd had enough Temazepam to drop an elephant. She took two 30mg capsules before bed. Otherwise, she would be up all night, and the agitation and unrest it caused invariably led to a psychotic episode.

Ballas had asked. 'How can you be sure your mother took her medication that night?'

'Because I stood over her and watched, Captain Ballas.'

'Do you take any night-time medication to help you sleep?'

'No. I need to be alert in case Mother wakes. My sleep is light.'

'So, you would know if your mother got up and left the room through the night?'

'I would. I took the bed closest to the door for that reason. I wake at the slightest movement.'

She was convincing, and Nash believed her. When Joy Neal was murdered, they were in their room again, this time sitting in their hot tub before getting ready for their first evening at the resort. Choosing not to eat in the dining room, they'd opted for one of their pre-booked meals at the La Scala restaurant, one building down. Mercedes said her mother was sleeping when Mr Gould went missing. Mrs Milton-Barr had suffered a headache that afternoon, and Ms Milton was reading. On all three occasions, they claimed to be in their room, and CCTV footage around the hotel accounted for some of their comings and goings. There were some gaps that couldn't be accounted for when either of the ladies could have left their quarters.

When Nash and Brown met Ballas at the private institution where Mrs Milton-Barr was being held, Nash was sickened. The lady was awake and distressed. She was shackled to the bed at ankle and wrist and was confused and sedated.

'Is this necessary?'

'We believe it is most necessary, Inspector. These suspects may have killed four people that we know of. Would you have her set free to cause havoc around my island?' Ballas said.

'Of course not, but I don't think tying a small lady down is conducive to her human rights. Surely a guard posted at the door is enough?'

'I will not risk the lives of my people—or yours, Nash. All precautions will be taken.'

'Please. Let me go. I'm not a monster.' Mrs Milton-Barr thrashed on the bed, and her skin at all four sites was abrased under the harsh leather manacles. Nash sat beside her and put his hand on her shoulder to calm her.

'Where's my daughter? Where's Juliet?'

'She's safe. And I'm doing everything I can to get to the bottom of this.'

'What's happening to me?'

'You've been arrested for trying to take a little boy away from his mother and grandfather. Do you remember?'

'Yes. I think so.'

'Can you tell me what happened?'

'I've told them so many times. It was an accident.'

'Please could you tell me? Just once more, so that I have it in your own words as you remember it.'

She sighed and flopped back against the pillows, exhausted. The medication made her groggy, and she'd used the last of her energy struggling. Her eyelids were drooping.

'I'll let you rest in a minute, but can you try and tell me what happened, please?'

'I don't know. Not now. It's all so hazy. I was confused, and Mercedes was sitting on the stool in the shop. She was being such a good girl and didn't ask me for anything, so I said I'd take her for an ice cream.'

'But it wasn't Mercedes. Was it Juliet?'

'I thought it was.'

'It was the little boy from the shop. Wasn't it?'

'They tell me so, but I was sure it was my Mercedes.'

'I see.'

'I wouldn't hurt her. I just wanted to take her for a treat.'

'But do you understand that it was a little boy? You took him by the hand and tried to drag him out of the shop. And when he wouldn't go with you, you picked him up and ran with him.'

'She's so naughty sometimes. She'd been good, but she was making a scene. So, I picked her up and carried her. Any mother would.'

'Mercedes is a woman now,' Nash said. 'She's grown up and is old enough to have children of her own. His mother was very frightened, you know.'

'Yes.'

'The thing is, Juliet. For your defence, I need to know whether you understand what happened.'

'No. Not really.' Her eyes gave up, and she fell asleep.

At dinner, Nash speared a forkful of excellent swordfish and looked at Brown in amusement.

'What?' Brown said.

'You're about as subtle as a sledgehammer. You think I didn't notice the flyer you left with the papers you brought me before dinner.'

'The one for the gay club in town, you mean? And?'

'And what?'

'And it would be perfect. We could have a look. You might meet somebody nice to talk to, and if it goes no further than that, then we've had a pleasant night.'

'No way, Brown. Besides, do you think I could relax with you gawping at me like Cilla bloody Black?'

'Who?'

'Exactly. That's a young man's game, and I'm not interested in a casual holiday fling with some pretty young man hoping for a boost to his wages.'

'But you might meet somebody perfect.'

'Forget it.'

'Okay, your loss. Completely changing the subject before it becomes intolerably awkward for both of us.' She lowered her voice and moved in closer to Nash. 'Let's get out of here to discuss what we've got.'

They finished their meal and went upstairs, where Brown made a coffee.

She said, 'Let's go through them one at a time. Levi Butcher?'

'They questioned him after getting his written confession, kept him overnight and grilled him hard by all accounts. I have the transcripts and will be going over them later to advise Mr Butcher on his best course of action for recompense. The investigation regarding him is closed. They released him this morning, and he went home. He was flown back to Britain with the rest of his family this afternoon. Dale's body was released and went with them.'

'It wasn't them, then? Any of them?'

'No. Clean.'

'They've gone. Dad as well? The lot of them?'

'There was nothing else they could tell us. No charges stuck on either Levi or his dad, and there was no reason to keep the body any longer. They are a family in crisis and should be left to heal and grieve their son. I spoke to Levi briefly before he left. He's a young man with a lot of promise. He even spoke about a career in the force.'

'And I bet you said you'd put in a good word for him. You can't fix the whole world, you know. Okay, then. What about today's craziness? Those are two unpredictable ladies.'

'Maybe, but one in four people have mental health issues. It doesn't make them killers—or kidnappers.'

'You can't be sure.'

'They live in their own time, and it's a little bubble just big enough for the two of them. They didn't kill anybody, and I believe the mother about the kidnapping. In the end, despite Ballas' best efforts, nothing stuck.'

Later when they went downstairs for supper, Brown said, 'Damn, I'm going to get fat eating so many times a day.' Then she lowered her voice and whispered, 'We've come full circle, right back to the countess. She admitted it herself. With what I gave you, Ballas must be ready to arrest.'

Nash grinned.

'Why have you got that ridiculous smile on your face again?'

'Because I've been looking forward to this.'

'What?'

They waited until the angry-looking waitress had swooped past and refilled their coffee cups without being asked. She tripped over the handle of Brown's bag and glared at her.

'Jeez.'

'That's you in trouble again.'

'She hates me. How can a waitress have so much damned attitude? She's like a bulldog and snarls at everybody.'

'Damned efficient, though. I bet she'd be great at filing and getting on top of our backlogged paperwork. It's filling up in here. Let's take our coffees to the terrace, and I'll tell you about our royal relative.'

Chapter Twenty-Five

Instead of going to the terrace, they found a quiet area in the card room where they could talk but checked regularly for people hovering. Brown's phone pinged and she looked at it, frowned, and put it face down on the table. When they had a coffee in front of them, Nash nudged Brown. 'There she is.'

The countess flounced in, wearing a lime green sundress that looked as if it had cost the earth.

'Charity shop,' Nash said.

'What?'

'I'd lay my career on it that her wardrobe came from charity shops. The silver case with somebody else's initials gave it away.'

'No way. She told me she gets an allowance from the King. A hundred and fifty thousand a year, just to behave herself and not cause any scandal—and she has the apartment at Kensington Palace rent-free.'

'Royalty—my eye. Nice work if you can get it.'

'I'll say.'

They listened, and her cut-glass accent was easy to pick out and isolate from the low hum of voices around her.

'I said to Richard, "Darling. When you send that spaceship into orbit, I need a seat in first class." He said, "There would be no party on the moon or anywhere else without you, Claudia." Richard and I are very good friends. Bublé was in love with me, you know. Before he met his darling wife, of course, but at that time, I was in the middle of a frantic affair with a Middle Eastern tycoon, so I had to turn him down.'

'Are you buying all this?' Nash said to Brown. Her phone had pinged again, and she was answering whoever it was. She didn't say anything to Nash, and he didn't pry.

'She's so over the top, isn't she?'

The countess was still talking to anybody that would listen. 'It's the initiation of every debutante entering society. At least one affair with a tycoon—two at the same time to really make a splash. If things turned nasty with one of them, let's just say a nod to my Royal mafia contact, and the waters of the Thames are cold, darling. He was never heard from again. That's the kind of influence I have.'

Brown was ready to tackle the elderly lady to the ground. 'Bodies in the Thames. A full admission in front of witnesses. This is so out there it could be real. We've got to act on it now, boss.'

Nash put a hand on her arm. He did that often to still her exuberance. 'Sorry to burst your bubble, Brown. Meet Doreen Irwin. Aged sixty-two. She's a retired school dinner lady from Bolton. This is her first time out of the country, apart from a honeymoon in Corfu thirty years ago. She's never met the King or the Queen before him. Though she possibly has a tea towel with her face on it from a visit to London in 1998.'

'So much for being the King's cousin.'

'If she is, I'm the Grand Old Duke of York. She was having you on. Total fantasist—but completely harmless. She's been diagnosed with a pathological lying disorder.'

'What about the kid drowning in her private pool?'

'Fairy stories. One in four, remember.'

'But she had waiters following her around and lighting cigarettes for her.'

'Brown. We are staying in an exclusive five-star resort. If you ask them to hover behind you and wipe your backside after you've used the bathroom, that's the level of services the guests are paying for.'

'She sounded convincing.'

'That's part of her condition. She talks until she believes it herself. While you were messing about with your makeup last night, I pulled her passport, legals, medical history and financial records. She was married and divorced years ago, and then she shacked up with a plasterer in Westhoughton. I got Renshaw to tap up the Bolton police to send out a PC to talk to her fella and the neighbours. She wanted to go on holiday. He didn't. So she took a strop, bought a ticket on his credit card and swanned off with a note telling him she'd be back in two weeks and his dinner was in the dog.'

'She's incredible.'

'Her partner says he's never known her to lie to this extent before, but she does like telling tall tales. And she's part of the local am-dram group. End of story.'

'She's not our killer?'

'I'm keeping tabs on her, but I highly doubt it. She's just an eccentric woman having some fun at everybody else's expense. It's a good job it's all-inclusive, or she'd have everybody buying her drinks.'

'Every time we get somebody in our sights, it comes to nothing.'

'Better that than locking up an innocent person.'

'True, but it's frustrating.'

'We must come up with something soon to justify being here.' Nash said. 'Apart from anything else, after today, the two ladies know we're police.'

A woman walked through reception with a fractious baby sitting on her hip. She went downstairs to the main indoor pool. Nash commented that she looked angry, but Brown disagreed and said that was an expression of worry.

The lady came back five minutes later and went to the reception desk. 'Is that policeman still here? I've lost my husband.'

'Here we go again,' Nash said.

'I asked him to get nappies for the baby, but he didn't come back to the room. That was three hours ago. I've been looking for him everywhere,' the woman said while the baby screamed and she jiggled it.

'I'm sure there's no need to panic, madam. I'll ring for Captain Ballas, and we'll find your husband in no time.'

'Not another one.' Brown said in a low voice. 'Women are getting very careless with their husbands around here. Makes me glad I haven't got one.'

'Indeed.' Nash said. 'I notice your phone keeps pinging, though. Am I to assume the affair with a certain person is back on? You know my feelings on the matter.'

'No, I promised you. It's over with Renshaw. He's just not getting the message.'

'Don't let it get messy, Molly.'

Before she could answer, a woman a couple of tables away screamed. Everybody in the room looked at her. The middle-aged lady took the glass she was drinking away from her face with a horrified expression. Her lips and chin were covered in blood. She held a white linen serviette to her mouth and made a series of mewling noises but seemed incapable of movement. She gestured to her face.

'What is it, Connie?' the man beside her jumped up and fussed around her. Along with everybody else, Nash and Brown left their seats and moved closer to see what was happening.

The woman felt inside her mouth and pulled out a shard of broken glass. It looked as though there was a lot of blood, but when the man looked properly, he said it looked worse than it was. The bar manager checked her glass. It was intact, which seemed to absolve him of any blame. He ordered a brandy to calm her nerves and offered to call an ambulance. The middle-aged lady refused both. The bleeding had stopped, but she looked very shaken.

'It's a warning,' she said, feeling the outside of her mouth.

'What the hell are you talking about?' her husband asked. Nash and Brown had managed to get to their table.

'Can we do anything to help?' Nash asked.

The man ignored him, 'What are you talking about, darling?'

'I was going to tell you later and ask for an interview with the police. I didn't want to spoil our night and thought it could wait.' She rummaged in her handbag, brought out a piece of paper, and handed it to her husband. Nash craned his neck to see and was dying to tell them not to handle it so that he could get it bagged.

'Watch out. You're next,' the husband read aloud. 'What the hell, Connie? When did you get this?'

'Perhaps you might put the paper down until the police get here,' Nash said. 'This could be important, and you don't want to contaminate it.' The man didn't answer, but he adjusted his hold on the sheet so that he was only touching one corner.

'I'm sorry, Jeff. It was slipped under our door this evening when we were getting ready to come down. I just wanted us to be normal before I said anything. I should have told you sooner,'

'Damn right you should.' He turned to the bar manager. 'Call the police.'

'They are already here, sir. This is Captain Ballas and Sergeant Deppas.'

The police rushed over. Nash nudged Ballas and motioned to the man holding the note. Ballas reached over and took the sheet of paper from the hotel guest in his handkerchief. He spoke to the bar manager, 'Please get a clean plastic bag to put this evidence in and another one for the lady's wine glass.'

The woman with the screaming baby was shouting. 'What about my husband?'

Nash took her arm and guided her into a seat. 'They'll do everything they can,' he said.

The baby was dirty. The woman called Connie pulled a ten Euro note out of her purse and called one of the bar staff over. 'Please go to the shop and get some nappies for the baby.'

'Nap?'

'Nappies. Diapers. Go.'

Nash put his wine glass down. The merlot didn't seem so inviting now that a guest had found some broken glass in her drink. Without moving, he shrank into the shadows and sat at an empty table in the gloom. Brown was still in the middle of the fray. Nash could make himself invisible in a crowded room. Taking care not to draw attention to himself, he took a pen and paper and wrote down the room as he remembered it when the commotion started. He listed names he'd heard of people in the rest areas at the time and pinpointed where they were positioned. Then he added other guests with a brief description. They were all on camera, and he could pull their records from the descriptions. Next, he added the few people that had drifted in after the event to see what was going on.

He considered some initial questions for the police. Most notably, he wanted to know who served the woman called Connie with her drink. Did she get it at one of the three bars in the room or bring it through from the dining room with her? The angry waitress, who seemed so irritated with the British guests, was hovering at the periphery of all the drama.

Nash admired the way the police got on top of the two coinciding incidents.

'Everybody stay where you are. Nobody leave's the room until you have been interviewed and cleared,' Ballas said.

He spoke to the manager about shutting the complex down. But in the interim, he called in every available officer to open the search for the young father. PC Patrou was on site, and he put him in charge of the search. As the young and fit completed their interviews, Ballas and Deppas asked them if they would go to their rooms, change out of their dinner clothes and join the search.

The guests that were already upstairs would be interviewed on a room-by-room basis by the officers. Nash couldn't be tied to sitting around for hours with the rest of the corralled cattle. He had things to do. He whispered to Brown to keep an eye on things. 'Take photos on your phone of anything you note and try and get recordings of anything relevant.'

'Isn't that illegal?'

'Covert recording is illegal in Britain, but the law isn't as rigid in Greece. It's not illegal to record a conversation. It's only an offence to use it afterwards.' Nash wanted to know what was being said around the room. 'Use the restroom cubicles. People are loose-lipped when they don't believe there's anybody else around.'

Nash was the first to be interviewed so he could get away from the crowd. He said he felt nauseous, and Deppas offered to escort him to his room to see him in safely, but they slid into the hotel offices. Nash made photocopies of his hurried initial notes. Deppas put him in a side office next to the one set up for interviews. Because Nash had clearance, he logged him into the police department's database so he could pull records and dig into the private lives of the guests at the scene.

Two things played on his mind. It was good of Connie Pearson to buy nappies for the distressed baby when she'd suffered immediate trauma herself. However, a kind lady could also be a busybody. She may have seen something she was unaware of that made her a target. And the waitress with the abundance of attitude was a concern. He wanted to know more about the man who was missing. Did he have a medical condition like all the other victims? There was nothing on his record. Had he and his wife fought that evening? He could have escaped a nagging woman in one of the many bars, but Nash didn't believe that. They had to investigate every possibility. But that wasn't his immediate thought when Mervyn Gould, a morbidly obese man in his fifties, went missing, and this time, it was only something else to eliminate. Every stone had to be turned over. The note and Connie Pearson's glass needed testing, but anything of use could have been obliterated by the time it got to the lab. And the biggest flag of all—it was common knowlege that Ms Pearson had a brain injury.

In the room next door, he heard the murmur of voices, but he couldn't tell what was being said in the interviews. He longed for a proper interview room and a two-way mirror. At first, it had served their purpose for them to come in undercover and use the guise of George Shan and his daughter, Tilly. But they'd hit the point where it was proving more of a hindrance. He wanted to be in on the interview process so he could ask the right questions.

Chapter Twenty-Six

Connie opened the door of her room. The security guard was sitting on a plastic chair outside her door. It was seven thirty AM, and he was still asleep as he'd been three hours earlier when she'd looked out. She didn't think he'd slept all night in that awful chair, but he looked comfortable enough now. She closed the door and went for her shower.

The cut in her mouth was tender and would make eating difficult. Some would say she'd been lucky. She was a woman with a target over her head, and the police wanted to know why she'd been singled out. She knew the day would be filled with the Greek police firing questions at her in their pidgin English and misinterpreting her answers.

To be fair, the one in charge was okay. He had impeccable diction but was a bully and tended to shout. She was the victim and was scared enough about being interviewed without the police tearing her inside out.

She let the hot water flow over her body and thought about Ray. He'd been so attentive to her. Far more than Jeff, who was calm and sensible. Jeff looked after her. He was the one with his arm around her and who guided her to their room. But it was Ray that showed actual concern. He expressed anger at the killer coming for her, and he was the one who'd asked how she was feeling without assuming to know.

She made coffee and went onto the balcony to drink it while Jeff slept. The morning was peaceful, and she needed those few minutes to face the day. She topped up her coffee, made one for Jeff and took it to him. He stirred, and they had wake-up sex. Jeff was first in the bathroom afterwards, and he saw the note by their door. Jeff flung it open, but there was no guard sitting outside their room. He tore open the second note.

I'm going to get you. Had any more of your weird fits lately? I'm coming to fix them for you. Bitch.

They spent the morning in their room with detectives and went over recent events. The police wanted to keep them contained because it would be safer for them than going to the interview room. That would mean walking them through reception when at least one of them had a target over their heads.

'Because the killer's hitting people with illnesses, it's possible that he has something wrong with him, as well,' Ballas said. And Connie assured him she'd avoid guests with obvious limps and ailments.

At lunchtime, Ballas suggested they take room service on their balcony and spend the afternoon in quiet pursuits like reading and watching the TV with a guard posted outside their door.

'Are we under arrest, Captain?'

'No. Of course not, but we're concerned for your safety and must know where you are at all times. Don't underestimate the seriousness of these threats.'

'I understand them all too well, and you have no idea how frightened I am. However, if we aren't on room arrest, this is still supposed to be our bloody holiday. At least let us go to the restaurant for lunch where we can pretend to have fun.'

'I urge against it, but if you insist, we will have a guard accompany you and sit at a respectable distance. But please come back to your room afterwards.'

'No guards, thank you. Not while we eat lunch in a crowded room,' Jeff said.

'I understand this is inconvenient for you. However, you were in a packed room last night when you were targeted with broken glass. I must insist that you are accompanied to your luncheon. It isn't up for discussion. Have a pleasant day.'

Jeff laughed when Ballas left. 'You got railroaded there. I wouldn't dare stand up to you like that,' he said.

'Go and boil your head.'

'Oh hell, Resting Bitchface is working again,' Connie said as they took their usual table in the dining room. Despite insisting she wouldn't be minded, Connie noticed two officers sitting three tables down. 'I suppose it's a deterrent,' she said to Jeff.

Resting Bitchface came to take their drinks order. 'What you want?'

'Iced tea for me, please,' Jeff said, smiling at her.

'And cola for me, though I should have brought my own glass this time.' Connie didn't smile. 'Where's the pregnant girl today?'

'It's her day off, madam.'

'I'd prefer to have her.'

'And I'd prefer to be off tonight. Jeez.'

Jeff laughed, and Connie seethed. 'Don't laugh. You'll encourage her.'

'I like her, darling. She's funny, and she's got the measure of you. Don't have the salad, by the way.'

'I was going to try the soup and a slice of bread. But why not?'

'If he's watching you, he'll know you always go to the salad bar, but the soup's even worse. He could drop anything in there.'

'You're paranoid. But thanks for putting me off my food. Does the pasta dish meet with sir's approval?'

'I suppose so, but only take some after somebody else has ladled it and make sure you rake through it.'

'Bloody hell, why don't I just wait for them to bring out a new dish from the kitchen? Then I know it hasn't been tampered with.'

'Good God, no. If it's one of the kitchen staff, you're a sitting duck.'

'They're communal dishes.'

'This is a mad psychopath. Do you think he'd worry about taking half a dozen people out, as long as he got you?'

'And has it occurred to you that you might be the target, not me? Neither of the notes had my name on it.'

'But he did call you a bitch, darling. Far more suited to your character than mine. Wouldn't you say?'

She wanted to sock him but settled for a withering look as she went to the buffet tables. One of the police officers followed her to each service as she made her selections. 'Are you my King's taster, mate?' she asked.

She came back with a banana and a yogurt. 'You've put me off eating anything. At least these are sealed and haven't been tampered with.'

'They could have injected the banana skin with something. She put the banana to one side, checked the yogurt pot for pinpricks, and ate it, watching as Jeff tucked into his plate of fresh fish, meat, vegetables and potatoes.

When he had his dessert, Jeff persuaded her to try some. Connie was a slow eater anyway, but with her mouth cut and sore, it took her longer than usual. Three times she put her spoon down, and Resting Bitchface swept in to take her plate. The first time, Connie smiled at her. 'I'm sorry. I've only just started eating it.'

The second time, Jeff said, 'Do you mind? The lady is still eating.'

It was a power struggle. Connie held onto her spoon between mouthfuls and didn't put it down. When it felt ridiculous, and she dropped it onto her plate for a second, Resting Bitchface was there, swooping on it like a raven. The waitress took the dessert dish before Connie could lower her serviette from her mouth.

'For goodness sake. This is ridiculous. Will you please put my wife's plate back? She has not finished with it. Just back off and let her enjoy her meal.' This time Jeff's voice had risen, and he shouted at the waitress, drawing the attention of every diner in the restaurant. 'This is the third time you've tried to take her food away from her.'

Connie was embarrassed. 'It's okay, Jeff. I've finished. Take it away.'

Resting Bitchface cleared Connie's side of the table, leaving her to watch Jeff eat again. He turned in his seat to get the attention of the restaurant manager.

'I'm not having this. It's terrible service.'

'Leave it, please, love. Don't make a scene. There's enough drama around here without us adding to it. I'm going for a swim before we go back to the room.'

'You've just eaten. You should leave it at least an hour.'

'I've had a single mouthful of yogurt. I'm fine.'

'They told us to go straight back upstairs.'

'I'm sure Pinkie and Perky will be around to watch me.'

'Hang on. I'll come with you.'

'No,' she demanded. 'I want to be on my own for five damn minutes.'

When she got back to the room half an hour later, Ballas and Deppas were standing with Jeff by the bed. The covers had been pulled back.

'Somebody put three mousetraps in your side of the bed.'

It was worse than that. Connie stared at the three mice that were crushed in the traps. She gagged and turned away.

'It's a warning. A message saying he can get to you any time he wants. It's no laughing matter, and we are treating it very seriously,' Deppas said.

Jeff put his hand out and touched Connie's head. 'Your hair's dry. I've just told the police you went for a swim.'

'There are hair dryers by the pool, you know. Anyway, it was full of kids, so I watched for a while instead.'

'You watched kids swimming? You hate kids.'

'I needed some space. I got lost in all the noise. It calmed me. Jesus. It's bad enough having this lot interrogating me without you starting.'

'We are concerned about you and want to keep you safe, Ms Pearson,' Ballas said.

'I get that. Thank you, Captain, but I'm terrified and feel like a trapped bird waiting to be picked off. I don't mean to be difficult.'

'Please try to stay in your room as much as possible. And tell us immediately if you hear anything.'

'Actually, Captain,' Connie said. 'I wanted to draw your attention to somebody. I'm sure it's nothing, but I've seen a woman watching me. She's an attractive young woman, and she's here with her father. They're always whispering together, and I see them talking to a lot of people. The man's suspicious too, but he hides it well. I've been watching them, and they might just be nosey people, but they take a lot of interest in what's happening. And then there's one of the waitresses. She hates me.'

'Thank you, madam. We'll be sure to look into it.'

Jeff was sleeping late that afternoon, and Connie was bored. She looked outside the door, and the guard was in his seat and awake for once. No chance of slipping past him.

She heard the couple next door leaving their room, and a plan hatched. Every balcony had a gate leading to the hot tubs, which were on a walkway the length of the corridor. She'd never paid attention because there was no need to, but there was a fire escape at the far end of the row. None of the hot tubs was currently in use at this time of day, but if she dared use the walkway, it meant hoping that nobody was using their balcony either. And then, of course, if she didn't want to be found out, she had to get back the same way. She put her black leggings on with her converse trainers and a loose-fitting top. Jeff didn't wake up.

There was something delicious about being able to get one over on the guards. She was confident Jeff would sleep until she woke him to get dressed for dinner that night. The man could sleep for England. Nobody would ever know she'd left the room—unless there were cameras above the fire escape. She had to take a punt on there not being.

She went out of the gate at the end of their balcony to their hot tub and looked over the divider into the same space next door. It was empty, and there was room to squeeze past the end of the divider to the next hot tub area. There were hundreds of people below her on the sunbeds, in the pools, and on the terraces and bars. The beach was packed, and it seemed the world was enjoying the late afternoon sunshine. Why should she be left out? She wasn't having it. They had no right to keep her locked up. She needed to get out of that bloody room. And getting away with escaping was exciting. Maybe Ray would be in the bar.

She moved past three rooms without any trouble but heard voices in the fourth. Connie had two choices. She could go back or risk moving on.

She slipped through the divider and into their space. She kept her body low as she ran past the open door, hoping she wouldn't cast a shadow into the room. There were no other people to see her along the row. It crossed her mind that she could go in and out of every room freely and help herself to anything in there because she had a cast iron alibi with a sleeping man beside her and a policeman posted outside her room. She might escape, but she would never steal.

When she got to ground level, she made for the back of the hotel to freedom.

She walked into the open but pulled back and hid behind a corner when she heard somebody shouting. As she peeped around the wall, she saw Resting Bitchface in a fierce argument with a young man.

'I need some money, Maria.'

'I've told you. I don't have any. Jeez.'

'Get me some. Today.'

The man was in his twenties, dressed in black jeans and a hoodie, like most of the local kids. His voice was menacing, and his manner aggressive.

Connie slipped away from them without being seen.

'Aren't you ever getting up?' she said, shaking Jeff. 'I've run you a bath.'

'Are you making a brew? I wonder who has been murdered or gone missing tonight. It's like Ten Little Indians in this place.'

'It'll be me tied to the totem pole.'

'How can you even joke about it? Especially when it's your head on the block.'

'Gallows humour. I'm terrified and don't know how else to deal with it.'

'If we're going to the dining room for dinner, just make sure you stay beside me at all times.'

When they went downstairs where the familiar buzz of drama circulated in the rest areas, though no loved ones were wailing.

'What's happened?' Jeff asked a lady who was gossiping on one of the sofas.

'One of the waitresses hasn't turned in for her shift.'

'That can't be unusual in a hotel, surely?'

'They say it's out of character for her, and she was going to the orchard to pick lemons for evening service. She never left the resort after her lunchtime shift, and her basket was found abandoned.'

'Is it Resting Bitchface? I can't see her.'

Connie could have spoken up about the argument she'd seen. It was the right thing to do. But it would have meant confessing that she'd sneaked out. She kept quiet. If it was relevant to the police enquiries, she could come forward later.

'What about the man who went missing last night? Has he come back?' she asked.

'He's still missing, and his wife's distraught, apparently. And then there's a woman in the hotel who had her throat cut last night on the glass, and she's been getting death threats.'

'Had her throat cut?' Jeff asked. He squeezed Connie's hand.

'She's in the hospital, apparently, and in a coma.'

'Crikey.' Jeff looked at Connie and said, 'Fancy sleeping through your holiday like that.'

'I wouldn't be seen dead sleeping in a coma ward,' Connie said.

Jeff turned back to the woman. 'Well, thanks a lot. Stay safe.'

Connie waited until they were out of earshot. 'Stay safe? What the hell.'

'It's what you say in a crisis.'

'I can't believe it's gone around that I had my throat cut, and I'm in a coma. The gossip mill in this place is incredible.'

'Considering nobody knew anybody else a few days ago, they're all very friendly now. God forbid that there's a murderer in their midst.'

Connie said, 'Let's eat and get the hell out of here. I want to go into town and dance. Bozo, the Policeman, can come with us if he must, but let's try to give him the slip,' Connie said. Jeff wasn't upset by the constant police presence, but it was driving her mad. She felt suffocated and needed to get away.

Another escape plan was called for.

Chapter
Twenty-Seven

C onnie enjoyed playing with the police officers, and to pacify Jeff, she promised to stay close to him all night. She was walking to the car when he stopped her. 'No. Somebody might have done something to the car. I'm not risking it on these hills. We'll get the bus, and if necessary, we can jump into a taxi on the way back. And, my love, there's a method in my madness because it means you can have a drink, too. Let's have some fun tonight.'

'Christ, I'm up for that after the last few days.'

The bus had to park further away from the stop as a crowd of guests piled their luggage into a row of waiting taxis. Panic was rife. Connie and Jeff got on the bus with half a dozen other guests from the hotel and went to the back seats like a pair of kids. They'd already pulled away and were nearing the first bend when PC Katrou ran out of the hotel at full pelt and chased the bus. It was a hoot. They couldn't resist waving at him until they were out of sight.

Kardamena was only a small town. They were wearing their glad rags, and getting the bus made it obvious that a night out was on the cards. Connie said it was like a game of dodgeball, and they would have to elude cops and killers all night.

She grinned at him, high on the joy of the night. 'It isn't you, is it?'

'You got me. But instead of murdering you in the comfort of our home, I splashed out six grand on a holiday to strangle you on the rocks overlooking the far shores of Turkey.'

'I like your style, psycho boy.'

Jeff's face changed as they pulled into the stop at the next hotel level down.

'I don't believe it.'

Ray got on the bus, and his face lit up when he saw them. 'Hi, you two. I thought you were on house arrest, so as I'd lost my playmates for the night, I wanted to see what the bright lights of Kardamena has to offer a Billy no-hoper.'

'You mean Billy no-mates,' Jeff said.

'Nah, mate, no-hoper. I've been married to Lisa so long that I wouldn't have a clue what to do with a woman if I caught one. I'd probably tickle its gills and throw it back.'

Connie felt Jeff tense on the seat beside her. They didn't know they were coming into town themselves, so unless Ray had psychic abilities or was following them, there was no way he could have known. Yet here he was.

'You don't say,' Jeff said.

'Without being too coarse about it, mate, I shaved my crack and sac, had a swim and a lovely massage. No happy ending, though. She was about fifty and had arms like a rugby player. That kept my beast at bay. After that, I had a full pamper session. Sauna, steam and facial shave ready for the ladies. That's why I was on this level when I got on the bus. I spent the afternoon in the spa. I recommend it if you haven't tried it yet.'

At the mention of the word beast, Connie felt Jeff's tension again. She tried to work out if Ray had been following them, would he have had time to drop a level and be at the bus stop in time for the bus getting there? The lift would be too slow. But he was fit and said he worked out. Perhaps he'd have had time to run down the steps, but he wasn't even out of breath. It was possible, but she didn't want to think about the significance of something that creepy.

Jeff wouldn't think Ray was the killer. He just moaned that it would be nice to have some time to themselves. Tonight wasn't that night. Connie didn't mind and felt that the evening had jumped up a notch. She liked having Ray around and pacified Jeff by telling him it would be another pair of eyes on her if he went to the bar.

'Just keep your paws off my woman, eh, mate? I won't be as nice about it if it happens again,' Jeff said.

Ray held his palms up in an offer of supplication, and the men shook hands.

They crawled the bars of Kardamena and were having a great time. Jeff loosened up, and she saw the resignation on his face. There were three of them in this relationship tonight, and he had to learn how to share.

He was glued to Connie's side until he needed to pee, and then he insisted that Ray didn't let her out of his sight. They filled Ray in about what had happened. He knew Connie was being targeted, and they were under police protection. Ray carried on with his story about the spa, which was a hotbed of gossip. He'd picked up loads of information and had spent an hour in the company of the King's second cousin. 'Man, she could have drunk me under the table if I'd let her.'

Ray also said that Juliet and Mercedes had been released and deported.

'Surely it wasn't as serious as that?' Jeff said.

'Well, deported or not, Ballas couldn't wait to get them out of the country and out of his hair. And now this waitress has gone missing.'

'Do we know who? Not the pregnant girl,' Connie said.

'No, they're saying it was the bad-tempered one.'

'Jeez,' they all said together.

'Right, drink up, Connie, you're lagging. Onwards and upwards,' Jeff said.

They partied through the evening, and the next place they stopped at was their last bar. If they'd carried on drinking at the rate they were, they'd have been unconscious before midnight.

The Radiohead bar had a huge façade that was open to the pavement with a deep awning. It had a tropical theme and was strung with fairy lights. The bar was still quiet when they got there, but the DJ assured them it would be bouncing later—it wasn't, but that didn't matter. It was a feel-good place.

Gioti, the DJ, made a fuss of them and insisted on giving them their first shot. They didn't argue, and whatever firewater it was hit the spot. Malvina, the barmaid, was a sweetheart.

There were three parties of customers, and another British couple came in a few minutes after them and sat on the high stools at the bar. They'd been making the tills of Kardamena sing, and the girl, in particular, was loud and friendly. She was called Gabby, and her boyfriend, a recent acquisition, she said, was Rich. He seemed sweet. She was full of herself but fun—to begin with.

'I'm a professional singer. I'll sing for you on the karaoke. What do you want me to sing?' she asked them.

Jeff got a round in.

'You want shots with that?' Malvina asked, picking up a shot paddle with a dozen holes for glasses in it.

'Hell, no. The last one was like petrol.'

'I'll have a shot,' Gabby shouted. 'I'm a wedding singer, and we always have shots. Don't we, Rich?'

'Why not?' Ray said. 'I'll get these. What other shots have you got? Something a bit gentler.'

'You English can't handle your drink. I have slippery nipples,' Malvina said.

'I bet. That would be lovely,' Ray said. 'Go on, line them up.'

'I'm a singer, and I was doing this wedding, and Rich was one of the guests. When he heard me sing, he fell in love with me at first sight. Didn't you, Rich?'

More shots appeared in front of them even though they hadn't asked for them, and Jeff coughed up. Three shots and two drinks in, and the party was underway. Connie said she'd have to slow down, and the two factions separated on the rounds to set their own pace. Gabby and Rich were drinking twice as fast, and with every drink, Rich got quieter, and Gabby was louder.

DJ Gioti owned the bar. He took a shine to Gabby, who was young and blonde. While she was chunkier than a slender filly, Connie observed that Gioti was taken with her at first. They talked about Gobby—as Connie named her—going back next year to work as a singer and host in the bar. He soon retracted that offer.

After begging people to beg her to sing another six times, she took the bull by the horns. 'I'm a professional singer, and I don't normally sing unless I'm getting paid for it, but because you've asked, I'm going to sing you a song.'

Nobody had.

Not content with making sure that Jeff, Connie and Ray were impressed by the gift she was giving them, she went to the other couples and told them she was singing for them.

She told Gioti to put *Proud Mary* on. Connie noticed the first double take from Gioti when she didn't use any manners and issued her command as an order.

The song choice was mediocre and sung by every female karaoke singer the length and breadth of England, but Jeff was charitable and said it was a crowd pleaser and probably why she'd chosen it.

After her bragging, they expected her to be brilliant. She wasn't very good. She was loud and a shouter more than a singer. She screamed and reached for notes that weren't kept on a particularly high shelf.

'If I'd paid for her at my wedding, I'd be asking for a refund,' Ray said. 'Jesus, she looks like a drag act.'

268

When she finished, there was a smattering of polite applause, and Connie gave a half-hearted cheer.

Gobby kept bowing and looked as though she was trying to be sick. She straightened, raising both of her hands to signify that she deserved greater applause. 'Come on, more, more. Yes, go on then, if you insist. I'll sing for you again, but I'm a professional wedding singer, and I normally get paid for doing this, you lucky people.' She pointed at Gioti and ordered him to put on another song.

Connie cringed.

After the first verse, Gobby went to the bar, necked another shot, and spoke into the microphone. 'That's my boyfriend, right? And even though I'm a professional wedding singer, he's never seen me dance. So, ladies and gentlemen, tonight, I'm going to show him that I can dance, too.'

She pranced about like a pony learning dressage. Connie had to admit the girl was entertaining, but for all the wrong reasons. It wasn't any dancing that she'd ever seen in human form. She gavotted five paces forward as she sang. And then she trotted five paces back again. And that was it—on repeat. Jeff and Ray started laughing, and Connie felt sorry for Rich, who was dying a million deaths.

But Gobby wasn't done. Gioti egged her on. He put on, *You Can Keep Your Hat On* and then took her hand. He helped her onto the high bar with a chrome pole at both ends. Malvina threw her a black bowler hat from behind the bar. Connie felt her blood pressure rising and was concerned about whether the bar had accident insurance. Gioti turned the music up loud and watched her go.

Gobby was wearing high wedges and a tiny denim miniskirt. She performed her dressage up and down the bar. She hadn't seen the poles, and Malvina had to point one out to her. She got the idea and wound herself around it, falling in a heap onto the bar. Connie saw the sweaty red welt the pole had left along her thigh. 'That's going to be sore tomorrow.'

Gobby lurched upright, showing more backside cheek and lady tulip than anybody needed to see. She went back to her pony dance.

Connie stood up. 'This is stupid. She's going to get hurt.' She wanted to encourage her down, but Jeff pulled her back.

'Leave her. She's having fun.'

'Until she falls and breaks her neck.'

Gobby undid the buttons on her top, and her lacy bra was on show. 'None of our business. Come on, let's move away from the bar and get some comfy seats.'

By the end of the song, Gobby had her top in one hand, her bra in the other, and she yelled, 'Ta-da,' as she bounced her ample boobs like all she was missing was a pair of tassels, much to Jeff and Ray's delight. If she hadn't been helped off the bar by Gioti, she would have ended up with her breasts in traction.

Jeff sang and knocked Gobby's performance into a cocked hat. The applause for Jeff was greater than Gobby had.

Later, he got Connie up to dance. They twisted and spun with more grace than Gobby would ever muster with her pony gavotte. She was furious at being upstaged twice and marched to the DJ booth before the first chorus finished. 'I want to sing again. Put on *Wrecking Ball*.'

'Sure, after this song,' Gioti said.

She picked up the mic from his booth. 'No. Put it on now.'

'When this song has finished, it's your turn.'

She stormed over to Rich, grabbed her drink and sat at the table farthest away from theirs.

'Somebody isn't happy,' Jeff said.

They couldn't see Gobby, but they felt her fury.

Gobby and Rich left without saying goodnight. She stalked out in front, and Rich followed, carrying her bag and shoes. 'They can go to hell,' Connie heard her say as she stomped down the street. She felt sorry for Rich and hoped, for his sake, that the relationship didn't last long.

More people came in, and the atmosphere was lighter after she'd gone. The place was never full, but it turned into a cracking night. Ray danced with a couple of ladies, and Connie was jealous. She wanted to be the one in his arms. She told herself she was stupid for being attracted to another man.

'Are we going to make a move? It's getting late, and I don't know if you've noticed, but PC Katrou's lurking at the end of the bar,' Jeff said, laughing.

'I'm just going to the ladies before we set off. Won't be long.' Connie left Jeff and Ray talking about women.

She couldn't walk back into the bar. She'd stumbled out of the restroom and into the corridor leading to the room but fell and had to crawl the rest of the way on her stomach.

A lady at one of the tables in the back was the first to see her, and she screamed. Jeff knew it was to do with Connie. She was lying on the floor, barely conscious, with a crowd around her. Within seconds, Katrou was beside them, and he called for an ambulance.

Blood ran from a deep wound on Connie's temple, and her cheekbone was bruised and already swelling. Her right eye was closing. Jeff tried to manhandle her into the recovery position, but she fought against him to sit up.

The men helped her into a seat, where she rested with her good eye closed. Gioti brought her some Brandy, but Ray waved it away. 'Water, please.' Connie didn't speak until she'd rested.

'Did you fall?' Gioti asked.

She shook her head and took a few more breaths before speaking. 'I came out of the toilet cubicle, and somebody jumped me from behind and hit me over the head.'

There was a gasp around the room.

'It was that Gabby girl.'

'But she left ages ago,' Jeff said.

'She's gone,' Gioti agreed.

'I'm telling you. It was her.'

'How do you know, madam? Did you get a good look at her?' Katrou asked.

'No officer, I smelt her. And a woman knows another woman's perfume. It's her. She's been stalking me all this time. I remember now. They came in behind us when we got here.'

PC Katrou went with Malvina to check the toilets, and when they returned, he looked worried.

'There's nobody there now, madam. You're quite secure. You shouldn't have gone off like that. We can't keep you safe if we don't know where you are.'

'I'm sorry, officer. Will you find her?'

'I'm sure we'll pick her up for questioning either tonight or tomorrow morning. We'll find out which Taxi she used so that we can build a timeline. Don't worry. Nobody is going to bother you again tonight.'

'Officer, please. You must see she's shaken. Can't this wait?' Jeff asked.

'I'm afraid not, sir. Not when a serious attack has occurred. Are you well enough to answer a couple more questions, Ms Pearson?'

She nodded.

'The ambulance will be here very soon. It's on the way from Kos Town.'

'Thank you.' She relaxed into Jeff's shoulder and let him hold an ice pack against her cheek.

'Do you have an injury to the back of your head, madam?'

'It's very tender.'

'May I?' The policeman felt the back of her head, bringing his hands around to the side, and Connie wondered if there was a breach of protocol there. If she had a haematoma, he could be causing greater damage. In England, a police officer wouldn't have done that. It shocked her and took her by surprise.

'And the attacker only hit you once?'

'No. Twice. First, she hit me on the back of the head with something heavy like a rock. And then, as I fell forward, she followed it with another blow to the side of my face.'

'Were you anywhere near the window at the time?'

'No.'

'We found a smear of blood on the windowsill, but it's at the other end of the room.'

'That's it. Don't you see? She climbed in through the window, which is why nobody saw her return. She must have caught herself on the windowsill,' Connie said.

'We'll take samples and have the evidence sent for testing. It's a terrible thing that happened to you Ms Pearson. After this attack, we are even more concerned for your safety. However, you should never have left the safety of the hotel.'

'As if that place is any safer,' Jeff said.

Chapter
Twenty-Eight

C onnie was checked at the hospital and kept for two hours of observation before being released. She was shocked. They would have kept her overnight in England.

Later that morning, there was a sharp knock at the hotel room door.

'Jeff, wake up. Answer the door, will you?'

'Come in.' Jeff was still half asleep.

'I didn't mean like that. I'm naked, you idiot.' Connie pulled the light sheet, which was the only coverage she had to hand, up to her neck.

Jeff went to the door. Ballas and Katrou came in and averted their eyes. 'Forgive me, madam. We have gathered information and need to ask further questions about last night.'

'Would you mind waiting outside for a few minutes while I put on some clothes?' She blushed and, with moving, the pain in her face throbbed like the fires of hell. Her cheekbone wasn't broken, but it was very badly bruised, and her eye had blackened and closed.

'I was about to suggest the same thing. Please don't rush. We'll come back later.'

Ballas gave a bow, and they left seconds before the swelling in her eye caused an attack.

'Do you think they've got her?' She asked as Jeff passed her medication and a glass of water. It was as if there'd been no break in proceedings.

'I hope so, love. I really do.'

When Ballas came back, he was on his own. They shook hands, and Jeff indicated a chair for him to sit on.

Ballas was watching them and seemed reluctant to get to the point.

'You said you had some new information for us?' Jeff's voice held a tinge of impatience, and Connie put her hand over his in a calming gesture.

'We have, sir.'

'Did you get that Gabby woman and bring her in?' Connie asked.

'I'm afraid not. However, we have located the resort she was staying at. Her name is Gabrielle Rice. They left the Radiohead Bar at 12:48 last night. Does this fit with your recollection of the timeline?'

'Pretty much, I think. Though we'd had quite a bit to drink, so don't pin us to exact times,' Jeff said.

'They went to The Club Zone in the next street where they were well remembered, especially Miss Rice, who was very loud and quite drunk. At 01:03, her partner, Mr Horne, excused himself to go to the men's room. He's seen on the CCTV footage at the bar, giving us an exact time marker.' Ballas paused.

Connie gripped Jeff's hand. 'Go on.'

'Mr Horne doesn't remember if Miss Rice was still there when he came out of the lavatory or while he was at the bar. She was gone when he returned to their seats with fresh drinks.'

'Gone where?'

'We don't know, but she never returned to the hotel and hasn't been seen since.'

'The clever cow. That makes sense. She'll be lying low. Won't she?'

'We don't believe so. I don't wish to alarm you, Ms Pearson, but we believe she's been taken, probably by the person stalking you.'

Connie pulled her hand out of Jeff's and covered her face. She shook her head, aggravating the wound on her cheek, and winced. It launched a tic attack, and the policeman looked uncomfortable and cleared his throat. He fiddled with a pen until Connie came out of the twitching.

'No,' she said. 'I don't believe that.'

'Mr Horne is distraught, and another search has been arranged.'

'It's a daily occurrence around here,' Jeff said.

Tears escaped from Connie's eyes. 'She hasn't gone missing. Don't you see? This is her plan. She's hiding and waiting to get me while everybody thinks she's been kidnapped.'

'This is a line of enquiry we will be following, but, at this stage, we believe a third party is involved in her disappearance. Her shoe was found in an alley between the two venues. You were seen in the couple's company, and it could be that in the dark, the killer thought she was you. We urge you to take extra care, Ms Pearson. You must listen to us and stop treating this like a game. It's impossible for us to protect you when we don't know where you are. Considering the detailed information you gave us about your attacks, Miss Rice is still a person of interest, but this has put a new perspective on it that needs serious investigation. I can't stress how dangerous we believe this is, Ms Pearson, and urge you to take the utmost care.'

'Of course, Captain.'

'The *Dolofónos* is at large, madam, and we urge vigilance. You must tell us immediately if anything else happens.'

'Sorry, Dolofono?'

'Forgive me, killer, the murderer. *Dolofónos,* A very bad man.'

'Or woman.'

After Ballas left, Jeff wanted to order food in their room. They had long since missed breakfast, and the dining room was open for lunch. Connie only had a yogurt and a spoonful of dessert the day before, but her mouth was less tender, and she was both hungover and starving.

'How can you face eating a proper meal with a hangover?' Jeff asked.

'How can you not? Some people get beer munchies, and I get hangover munchies. Come on, let's go downstairs. I don't want to eat here. I've got to get out of this room. It's like a prison. We won't be alone, so I'll be safe.' She motioned to the door as though she could see the guard through it.

'I want to keep you safe, Connie. Anyway, I didn't have a shower this morning, so give me half an hour.'

'For God's sake, I'm hungry now. You get your shower, and I'll see you down there. I'll get a table in the shade.'

'No. You can wait for me.'

'Excuse me?'

'You're not going down there on your own. You can wait until I'm ready.'

'And is that a request or an order? You know I eat slowly, but with a sore mouth, I'm even worse. If I go now and make a start on lunch, I might get to eat it today without having my plate taken away. With Resting Bitchface gone, my food might be safe. I'll see you in a bit.'

'Connie, that's a horrible thing to say.'

'True, though. And you rush me, too. Because you can eat a meal in five minutes, you finish yours and then let your impatience show waiting for me. I can't enjoy my food and give up on it.'

'I don't rush you.'

'You always do.'

'That's unfair, but anyway, I'm not letting you go down there by yourself. I won't be long. Read a book or something.'

'Jesus Christ. You're so controlling.'

'I'm what? Is it wrong to care about you? I want to eat lunch with my partner. I don't want to walk into a restaurant on my own. I want you on my arm and to know that you're safe.'

'And I want to choose my own food without you advising me on what to eat. You're stifling.'

'What do you mean?'

'Suffocating. Being with you is like being smothered with a pillow. I'll see you down there.'

'I can't believe you've just said that when all I want to do is look after you.'

'Look, Jeff, I need some space. This is doing my head in. You're too much. I need to be on my own for a while. Okay?'

'Yes, message received loud and clear. Don't worry. I'll get out of your hair. I'll tell the guards, you won't let me look after you, though. You can't stop me from caring about you.'

'Leave me alone.' Connie grabbed her bag. She checked that her tablet was in it so she could read while she waited, and then she stormed out of their room, slamming the door behind her.

She was halfway down the corridor and nearly at the stairs before the guard jumped out of his chair. He followed her discretely, but by now, the jungle drums had gone three times around the hotel. Everybody knew she was being stalked and was under armed guard. And they stared at her as though she'd grown two heads. As if her tics weren't enough to draw attention, now she had this to contend with. All the Greek police carried guns in a holster at their hip, and it was like being followed around by the Godfather. The difference was that gangster victims had a horse head put in their beds—Connie had the three blind mice.

She let her anger carry her around the food choices, opting for a piece of quiche and her usual fresh salad. They were tiny offerings but so good that she had to have a second square. She felt sorry for the guard leaving his seat to follow her every time she moved.

She had finished her second piece of quiche when her anger gave way to guilt. Jeff looked sad when she said those horrible things to him. He could be opinionated, and he liked things his own way—and even he'd admit he could be controlling. He said the fact that he didn't get away with it was what made them work. He once told her he'd walk all over a weaker woman, and the day he said that Connie had felt strong and his equal. She let him have his way most of the time because it suited her. She would only let him control her as much as she wanted to be controlled. When it mattered, she made a stand. And on those occasions, she always got her way. He wore the trousers, but only because Connie was wearing the jeans.

She thought about how good they were together as she drank her cappuccino. They weren't perfect, but they rarely fought. It was hard and vicious for a few minutes when they did, but Jeff made decisions, and Connie agreed with them. They'd only got into a real screaming humdinger twice. They went head-to-head in open warfare, with Connie winning both times.

This time she was sorry. It was too harsh. She was hungry and wanted to be able to eat a meal without feeling under pressure to leave it. Don't make me angry, she thought. You won't like me when I'm angry.

When Jeff came down, he'd already been to the buffet and sat without acknowledging her. The ice coming off him could have filled a thousand cocktails.

'Are you okay?' she asked.

'Fine.'

'I'm sorry. I didn't mean a word of that.'

'Didn't you?'

'No, of course not.'

'The way you dismissed my concern for you was disgusting. I won't be treated like that. You don't need me? Fine. I get it. You can have all the damned space you need. I've booked myself on a two-day sailing trip.'

'You've what?'

'You heard. I'd hate to suffocate you any longer.'

'Stop it, Jeff. I've said I'm sorry. What about me?'

'What about you?'

'What am I going to do?'

'I haven't the faintest idea, and I wouldn't dare suggest anything for fear of being called controlling.'

'I'm coming with you.'

'No. You're not. Maybe you aren't the only one who needs some space. I'm evaluating our relationship. I'd hate to hold a woman back or make her feel controlled. Perhaps I'm not the man for you—and you aren't the woman, I thought. I leave in an hour, and we get back at sundown tomorrow night. If I were you, though, God forbid that I dare make a suggestion for your safety. I'd stay close to your guards and do as you're told. I hate that you've pushed me into leaving you like this.'

'Jeff.'

She shouted after him, but he swallowed his first mouthful of food, left the rest of his meal on his plate and stalked out of the dining room without looking back.

'Jeff,' she called again, leaving her salad and scraping her chair on the floor. People were looking, and the guard kept a close eye on her without even trying to be discrete.

Jeff must have ordered a glass of red wine because the pregnant waitress came over with it—but he hadn't ordered anything for Connie.

'I'm sorry. He's gone. I'm afraid he's in a mood with me,' she said.

The hold-up over the wine was enough for Jeff to have left the hotel. As Connie got to the door with the guard behind her, she was in time to see him setting off with a guide in one of the hotel's tuk-tuks.

'If that's the way you want it. Sod you, then,' she shouted after him.

Connie didn't know what to do and felt a hand on her elbow. She jumped. 'Allow me to escort you back to your room, madam,' the guard said.

'Not a cat in hell's chance, mate. I'm going to get drunk.' She went to the bar and saw Ray in conversation with the countess. He'd formed a friendship with her, and by all accounts she was fun.

'Mind if I join you?'

'Connie, hi. Of course not. Come and sit down. Where's Jeff?'

'Don't even go there.'

'Ah, like that, is it? Do you know the countess?'

'Nice to meet you,' Connie said, holding back from telling her to get lost.

'Likewise.' The woman was anything but pleased to meet Connie and looked as though she'd like to scratch her eyes out. Connie wanted to laugh. The woman was like a cartoon caricature. Connie ordered a pina colada and a whiskey chaser. To hell with the hangover—and to hell with Jeff.

They chatted, but the countess didn't stay long. 'Oh, look, there's the Barton-Smythes, lovely couple. I must go and ask them how their trip to Bodrum went.'

'Something I said?' Connie laughed.

'More like something you did. Breathing, maybe.'

'She wants to get into your pants.'

'I know. Fun, isn't it? So come on, sour puss, what gives with you and Jeff?'

As she told him about their argument, she alternated between fury and guilt.

'You need cheering up. Do you reckon you can lose your bodyguard one last time?'

'I shouldn't. I've been read the riot act after last night.'

'Four people have gone missing from this island. One of two things have happened to them, either they've got off it—or they're still on it. And I think we should get the hell out of Dodge for a few hours. I have an idea. You extract yourself and meet me at your car in five minutes. And given the state of you, I'm driving.'

Chapter
Twenty-Nine

Brown angled her head to get a better look at the photographs. 'It's like a gallery of mugshots. What a bunch of misfits. But he looks interesting.'

'Let me see.' Nash pushed Brown out of the way so he could get his head in front of the phone screen. 'He looks a bit lived in.'

'That's weathered.' She read his profile and paraphrased for Nash. 'Dave, forty-eight, a local groundsman, so loves anything outdoorsy and connected to nature. He has his own cottage on the grounds where he works and loves to entertain. Says he's not a bad cook.'

'I like eating. That's a start, I suppose. He's far too young for me, though. Brown.'

'You look younger, and he looks way older than he is, so it's all good. And you could do with somebody to get you out walking in the fresh air. You said you didn't want a bar fly, and he doesn't look as though he does bars much—or flies. It says here that he likes dogs and is the dad to two black labs. That's cute.'

'Lola won't be impressed.'

'She's going to have to learn to share. She'll hate whoever you're with. Lola, the cock-block cat. Message him. I dare you.'

'Not a chance. We're as far removed as the two poles. What have I got in common with a poacher?'

'Pole dancing? And he's not a poacher. He's a groundsman. That's like asking what you've got in common with a criminal.'

'Not interested.'

'You so are. Message him. I dare you.'

'What are you? Five?'

The dating app had a function where members could find out who's been checking them out. They'd been on the same profile for several minutes when Nash's inbox pinged.

'No. I've got a message. Turn it off. Quick.'

Brown looked at him as though he was deranged and snatched the phone on her way to the minibar in Nash's room. She passed a beer to him and a clean glass.

'What does it say?'

'Hang on, give me a chance.' They waited a few seconds for the page to load. 'I like him. Pheasant Plucker says, "Saw you looking." He's flirty. I like that, Nash.' Brown clicked on reply, and her fingers moved over the keys like lightning.

'What are you doing? No. Stop. You can't reply.'

'Too late.'

'Damn. What have you said to him?'

'Saw you watching. I could do with a gamekeeper to help me with a grouse problem.'

'You can't say that. He's going to think I'm an idiot.'

'Trust me. I've done this a million times. If they've got any intelligence, a pun gets them every time.' A new message came through. 'Bingo. We've got his attention. He says, "Grouse are my speciality. How can I help?"'

'I have a famous one, but it's too much to manage by myself.'

'Molly, you've as good as thrown me at him. I don't want to drink whiskey with him or anything else for that matter.'

'Hang on. He's typing. He says, "Should I bring my gun?"'

'Is that a euphemism for a sex thing?'

'Well done, granddad, getting the innuendo. I think so. Don't worry. I'll put him in his box. "No, that won't be necessary, just some intelligent conversation and a rain check until I get to know you better." He's typing back. He says, "Thank God for that. I thought you were one of those who wanted a one-nighter. That's not my scene." This is sounding promising, boss.'

'How can you call me boss when you're arranging my love life?'

'As it happens, I'm going to shoot off. It's getting late, and I've got some stuff to do before I turn in. I'll leave you and lover boy to get acquainted.'

'You can't leave me.'

'You'll be fine. Just be yourself. He'll love you.'

Before he could stop her, she'd hopped off his bed and left.

The next morning, Nash had an enjoyable breakfast with Brown posing as Tilly. The waitress, Maria Karali, was still missing, and Nash said the restaurant was less efficient without her. She may have been brusque, but she was good at her job. Any hope of finding her alive was fading, and she left behind a mother and three young sisters. On investigation, Ballas told him that her life expectancy was short because she had a serious heart condition. Surgery had bought her some time, but it was temporary. Her heart was a ticking time bomb that could have gone off at any moment. Despite her condition, Maria had no choice but to work and take money home for her family. It was the way of the world in countries less fortunate than others. Nash felt sorry for her and her family.

'Penny for them?' Brown said around a mouthful of banana pancake.

'I was thinking about the missing waitress and wondering if there was any news.'

'Nothing that I've heard this morning, but the countess has been playing up.'

'What's she been up to?'

'Word in the ladies' room is that she was getting very friendly with a certain waiter young enough to be her grandson last night. They were seen kissing in the corridor, and apparently, she dragged him into her room and didn't give a damn who saw her.'

'I don't know who I feel more sorry for, the poor kid who slept with her and will probably be traumatised for the rest of his life when he finds out that there's no title—and therefore no money.'

'Or? Why would you feel sorry for her?'

'I don't. I feel sorry for the family in the next room that had to listen to them cavorting all night.'

'Cavorting. You're priceless.'

'Eat up. We have a meeting with Ballas in half an hour, and I want to check a couple of things before I see him,' Nash said.

'That works for me. I've got to check over yesterday's transcripts, and then this afternoon, I'm going through a tonne of surveillance tapes.'

They left the dining room and were walking through reception when Nash pulled Brown back. He stopped at the postcard carousel, picked one up and studied it.

'What?' Brown asked.

'Shit.'

'What?'

'See that woman at the reception?'

'What about her?'

'I knew I'd seen the face before, but it took me a second to get it. Don't stare, and don't let her see you,' Nash said.

'Stop playing at being Dick Tracey and tell me who it is.'

'That's Isabel France. What's she doing here?'

'Who?'

'Alma Cullen's daughter. What the hell?'

'Jesus.'

The attractive redhead at the reception desk had no luggage except for a small carry-on bag. She wasn't staying long, then. But why had she come? Her visit could achieve nothing, and Nash wondered if she was alone or with her husband.

'She saw me during the early Barrow investigation.' They listened as the receptionist attended to Isabel France.

'Before I check in, I'd like to speak to the policeman in charge of the murders, please. It's very important that I speak to him because this monster killed my mother. I want to know what's being done about it.'

Nash grabbed Brown's hand and dragged her into the back office used for the investigation. Ballas and Katrou were preparing for their morning meeting and were startled when Nash and Brown burst in without knocking.

'Haven't got time to explain properly now,' Nash said. 'But Alma Cullen's daughter is at reception demanding to see you. Please placate her, get rid, and make an appointment for her this afternoon when we aren't here?'

Ballas sent Katrou to speak to Mrs France. He said the captain wasn't available. It bought them time to make themselves scarce after cutting their meeting short.

'This could blow our cover sky high,' Nash said. 'I only met her for a second and then handed her over to Renshaw and Bowes for questioning, but I can't take any chances on her recognising me. Thank God she never met you, Brown. We'll interview her officially later and under caution, if need be. But I don't like this. While we're still undercover, I want you to get to her and find out everything you can. I need the things she won't tell us. From what we heard, she's been impatient waiting for results at home and has come here to give the authorities grief. She might want to vent—get her while she's seething. I expect it's nothing more sinister than that.'

'Surely you don't suspect her.'

'She was one of the suspects at home.'

'But it can't be her. She's only just arrived.'

'Says who?'

'She's just checking in.'

'And this is the only hotel on the island? What have I told you? Never take anything at face value. She probably did arrive on the last flight. But what if that's what she wants us to think? It's odd that she's come all this way just to find out what's going on. She could have got an update from Barrow station. I smell a rat.'

'Anyway, she's checked in, and we've got her off our backs until two this afternoon. Should we continue?' Ballas said.

'I've spoken to the doctors. I've also checked admissions at the hospital and checked every listing on their medical records and medical appointments, but I can't find any ailments or conditions for two of our missing persons,' Brown said.

'Are you sure nothing's been overlooked?' Nash asked.

'Absolutely. I spent hours going over everything a dozen times.'

'It doesn't fit with the MO.'

'Which two guests are they?' Ballas asked.

'Edward Grantham, the father who disappeared when he went to buy nappies, and Gabby Rice, the Welsh girl. I don't get it,' Brown said.

'Could we be wrong? Maybe they haven't been taken.'

'No. There's no way they could leave the island unless they chartered a small fishing boat to get them to the Turkish mainland, and that's unlikely to happen once, never mind twice,' Ballas said. 'And even that doesn't work because they'd show up on the coastguard and shipping authorities' radar. The system is set to trigger an alarm if any unauthorised boats show up. If they'd been dumped at sea, their bodies would have washed up by now. Dead or alive, those four missing people are still somewhere on this island.'

'That's a terrifying thought,' Brown said.

'Are there any caves on the island?' Nash asked.

'Every inch of coastline has been thoroughly searched more than once.'

'It's as though they have literally vanished into thin air,' Brown said.

'Kos isn't a large or populace area, DI Brown. As you know, four days ago, when Mervyn Gould went missing, we started a house-to-house search to see if anybody was holding or harbouring him.'

'Nothing's shown up?'

'Not a sausage.'

Nash smiled at the word sausage coming from the cultured, but nonetheless, Greek accent of Captain Ballas. 'And nobody has seen anything?'

'No. We completed the search this morning. Every house, hotel, farm, business, residence—and cave—on the island has been searched, and the occupants questioned. That's over six hundred families, from Ammoudia, our northernmost outpost, to Marshal Bay in the south. And, of course, we concentrated the greatest effort on a radiating circumference around Kardamena and Kos Town. We've scoured every second of airport CCTV since Mr Gould went missing, and we've seen every person entering or leaving the airport, harbours and fishing ports.'

'Fantastic job, Vasil, you've been very thorough,' Nash said.

'For all the good it's done,' Vasil Ballas said.

'I think there's something in the fact that two of them don't have underlying conditions.' Brown had a theory and wasn't about to let it go.

'I agree,' Nash said. 'It's unusual for a perp to veer from his MO. When he does, there's always a reason for it. Good work, Brown. Keep on it.'

'Don't forget, Rice is still our primary suspect, at least in the attack on Connie Pearson, in the absence of anybody else. Don't rule her out at this stage. It's fitting that she's the one that isn't already dying of something else. And that would only leave Ed Grantham,' Ballas said.

'I want every detail rechecked, Brown. Find me something.' They were going around in circles and getting nowhere. They needed a break in the case.

'Sir.'

'Good work.'

'There's one thing,' Brown said. 'It might be nothing. And if it means something, it could go for Rice either being a vic or a perp.'

'What?'

'Physically, Grantham and Rice are both clean. Fit as they come, and nothing wrong with either of them.'

'But?'

'There's a history of mental health issues with Rice. She's had a couple of semi-serious suicide attempts. Booze and pills.'

'That's interesting,' Nash said.

'And that's not all. She's had eating disorders and periods of self-abuse. And she's had two committal-order stints in a mental health facility after violent episodes.'

'I want everything you can dig up on her. Make it a priority.'

'I'm on it.'

Chapter Thirty

C onnie had five minutes to give her guard the slip. Although she'd eaten earlier, it wasn't unheard of for guests to go back to the restaurant after letting their first meal settle. All-inclusive mentality. Connie was at the serving stations closest to the kitchens. She watched, waiting for that second when her bodyguard was distracted, and she slipped through the kitchen door.

The staff stopped what they were doing and stared in confusion as a mad English woman ran through their kitchen. One of the chefs raised his meat cleaver and held it in front of him in defence. Everyone on the island was jumpy, and nobody could blame them. The chef ran after Connie. He chased her out of the back door shouting in Greek.

She legged it past the obstacles into the fresh air and away from the waste disposal skip where the disabled child's body had been dumped. There was a plastic shrine on the ground. Connie jumped over it to avoid any damage.

Ray had the car running and was waiting for her outside. She was laughing as he sped down the hill. 'Too easy,' she said, flinging her straw hat onto the backseat. 'Where are we going?'

'Wait and see.'

'Tell me.'

'No.'

'They're going to be looking for me, you know?'

'I hope you don't get into trouble, and I'd like to advise you to stay in your room under guard, but I don't think you're safe there.'

'Don't. It terrifies me. Will there be lots of alcohol where we're going?'

'Not a drop. I'm taking you somewhere quiet where we can get away from the world.'

Connie wasn't sure if the thrill of anticipation was excitement or fear. She was angry as hell, feeling the effects of the drink, and to hell with Jeff—Jeff who? On the other hand, the churning feeling in the pit of her stomach could have been apprehension. Three people had been murdered, and another four were missing—presumed dead. Nobody said it out loud, but everybody thought it. And here she was leaving one mountain, to take a dirt track to another one. She might have to defend herself. They were heading away from the town, and this man was a stranger. She didn't know him.

'Maybe this isn't a good idea.'

'You're right, it's an awful idea. My marriage is on the rocks. You're up to your eyes in tension with your man, and we're off on a magical mystery tour.' He interpreted what was going through her mind. 'And let's face it—either one of us could be the killer.'

She turned around sharply and Ray laughed at her stricken expression.

'Have you brought anything to defend yourself against me? I think the best I can do is a leaky biro. If you can trump that, I'm stopping the car and running.'

She relaxed. It was only Ray. He was all right and she was sure she could handle him if he tried anything. She wondered if any of the victims thought they could take on their killer and win.

'Come on. Where are we going? Do you even know?'

'I certainly do. I thought we'd have a look at the Castle of Antimachia. This late in the season, I doubt many people will be there, if at all. It's only a ruin and there's not much to see.'

She felt a pang of guilt. She was supposed to go to the castle ruins with Jeff. They'd been looking forward to it. But here she was visiting it with another attractive man who made her question her fidelity. Ray grinned at her, and she felt the tension float away. She breathed a sigh of relief but didn't know why. Ray could hack her into little pieces as easily as she could plunge his leaky biro into him.

'You're deep in thought. Not far now. I planned to do this on my own today, but you clearly needed the fortification of a good friend and decided to hijack my day.'

'I did nothing of the sort. I was working on my plan to get hammered and minding my own business when you kidnapped me.'

'There's pink fluffy handcuffs in the glovebox if you wouldn't mind cuffing yourself to the backseat,' he laughed.

'In your little wet dreams, Casanova.'

'I didn't know what to do with myself today, and I was in a funk after some ugly texts from Lisa. I figured I could sink into my misery in an old ruin and watch an impressive sunset. The kitchen made me a hamper, but I haven't a clue what's in it.'

'You can bet there'll be bread, tzatziki and olives, for a start—that's standard. Aren't things any better with Lisa?'

'No. She's filing for divorce.'

'I'm sorry to hear that, Ray. Are you okay?'

'No, I'm not. But it's been coming for a while, we both knew it. Here we are. Come on, grab your sunglasses.'

He pulled up in front of a giant grey stone castle wall with turrets and grabbed the picnic hamper. The ruins were on the top of a mountain in a dusty dessert-like terrain, in the middle of nowhere. The carpark was empty. There was no barrier and just an open square gateway in the castle wall. The iron portcullis was long gone. Connie looked at the beautiful crest above the entrance.

'I read loads about this and could impress you with my profound knowledge about the place,' Ray said.

'Go on then.'

'I said I could and would even—but I've forgotten most of it. A castle built for protection in the Middle Ages and rebuilt by the Knights Hospitaller later. That's who the crest commemorates.'

The old fortress was impressive and imposing, with high stone walls creating a visible square. They walked through the gateway and stopped.

'Oh.'

Ray laughed at her and spread his hands at the wilderness.

'Well, that's a swindle. Talk about bigging yourself up to be something you're not. "I'm a mighty castle. Look how impressive I am." No, mate, you're just a wall.'

They'd stood outside a castle, but there was nothing to see inside. A couple of square concrete buildings that looked like cattle sheds hunkered to the left, and that was it. They'd stepped through the gate onto the mountain. It had the same dusty shale and tiny pebbles as everywhere else on the island.

They laughed at the anti-climax and found a rock to sit on.

'Before I sit down, you're sure this isn't some ancient artefact from three million years ago, and an angry deity won't smite me into dust?'

Ray looked at the rock. He put his ear down and listened to it, and then he knocked on it. 'No, you're good. It's just a bog-standard rock. probably still a million years old, but not one blessed by the Gods. It's the kind found in any backyard halfway up a Greek mountain.'

'That's okay, then.' They looked down the valley. There wasn't a road, a car, a person or even an animal large enough to see. It was as though the universe and everybody in it had died. 'It's stark and peaceful.'

'It's beautiful. Like you,' he said.

He looked at her, and she turned away from him. It was awkward. 'Come on then. Let's see what goodies you've got.'

The mood was broken, but the intention in his stare had been clear.

Ray opened the hamper to an impressive display of food and well-packed crockery. They had bread, a selection of meats and cheeses, dip and olives, a fruit salad, and some baklava. There was a bottle of white wine, two bottles of water and two glasses. Ray was going to open the wine, but Connie stopped him.

'Just water for me.'

'An hour ago, you wanted to drink the island dry of every drop of alcohol on it.'

'That was earlier when I was fuming with Jeff.' In truth, she didn't trust herself with half a bottle of tepid white wine. Ray would have kissed her if she hadn't stopped him, and it took everything she had to do it. She wanted that kiss and everything that followed more than she needed water. There was no denying the attraction. She'd smashed the romantic mood once and didn't know if she could do it again.

'Okay, water for now, but we will drink the wine, and I'll feed you strawberries as the sun goes down.'

There it was—the gauntlet. He'd thrown it on the ground by their feet. The time was now, right this second. She had to tell him that she loved Jeff and wasn't interested in him, not in the slightest, and she only saw him as a friend. But she didn't. She changed the subject instead.

'Do you think we've seen the murderer or maybe even spoken to him?'

'Or her? I would say it's certain that we have, even if it's just a good morning murmur in passing at the hotel.'

'It's a terrifying thought that we may have sat with the killer.'

'You don't still think it's Gobby, then?'

'Damn right I do. I know it's her, but the police said I have to keep an open mind and not trust anybody.'

'And yet here we are.'

'Indeed.'

'Do you trust me, Connie?'

She laughed, 'Ask me again when you feed me strawberries at sunset.'

'I will. What about Jeff? Do you trust him?'

She turned to him so fast that she cricked her neck and cried out in pain. 'Of course I do. Look what you've done. I'll start ticking now.' Her hand went up to massage her neck and into her scalp.

'Here, let me.' His movement was deft and sudden, and she didn't have time to protest. He turned her back to him and leaned her against his chest as he put both of his hands up to her throat.

She panicked and tried to struggle from his grasp. She was miles from the nearest town. There was a killer on the loose, and this man had his hands around her neck.

'Hey, it's okay. It's me. Bloody hell, you're tense. I'm not surprised your neck jarred. It's okay. I've got you. Relax. I can feel the knot.' He manipulated her neck muscles and let his hands glide across the back of her shoulders. He took her hat off and put it on the rock beside her as his fingers rose and lost themselves in her hair. He massaged her scalp, and the tension lifted like a weight. Damn, it was good. Too good. She had to stop him. She moved forward a couple of inches to pull away, but he eased her back into him and straightened his legs on either side of her to make a chair of his body for her to lean against.

As they sat, the sun went from being a dazzling jewel in the sky to a muted golden orb. It cast red, orange and pink hues through its rays, and everything felt too perfect. She clamped her mouth shut to stop a traitorous moan of pleasure from escaping her lips. Her body wouldn't betray her. She couldn't do that to Jeff. This was a line already crossed that should never have been stamped. She knew how Jeff felt about Ray.

Which precise second that afternoon defined the word infidelity? When had it become a thing? It was the moment she saw Ray at the airport and found it hard to take her eyes off him. The second she acknowledged her attraction to him and didn't tell Jeff she had a problem that needed nipping in the bud. That was infidelity. It built and grew in every secret smile between them and every cosy giggle. It was when his hands brushed against hers and when she caught him smelling her hair.

This.

Today was the inevitability Jeff had brought about with his childish storming off for over twenty-four hours. What did he expect?

Connie knew. He expected the same thing that she wanted from him—that he would be loyal and faithful to her. She was guilty. Then she was mad, and then she was guilty again. She hated Ray for what he made her feel.

But she didn't move away.

'What do you mean? Of course I trust Jeff. With my life.'

'He could have done it, you know. Take the first murder, that old girl in England. He could have killed her. And as for all the dead and missing people here, he's a big bloke. I wouldn't want to take him on.'

'That's ridiculous. It isn't Jeff. He's been beside me all week, I'd know.'

'All I'm saying is, do we really know anybody? I'm concerned for you, Connie. You've had death threats and several serious attacks against you. That's why I wanted to get you here with me today. I can't do much while Jeff's with you, but at least while he's gone, I can protect you from anybody else. The police are useless. How many times have you given them the slip?'

'Several. Thanks, Ray. But you're wrong about Jeff. It's not him.'

'He's controlling.'

'Yes, he is, but I can hold my own.'

'Can you?'

'Yes.'

'Can you really? I'm going to lay it on the line, Connie. When Gabby and that Rich bloke left, Ray went out straight after them. He said he was going outside for a smoke—but he'd been smoking at the table all night. It looked as though he'd waited for you to go to the ladies to follow them.'

'No. They'd been gone ages before I was attacked.'

Connie was irritated and jerked her neck away from his hands. He dropped them to rest on her thighs, and she frowned but didn't stop him.

'Jeff was outside for nearly ten minutes. That's why nobody came while you were being attacked. He didn't realise how long you were gone until he came back and saw you weren't at the table.'

'You're talking rubbish. Stop it.'

'Don't you get it? I was chatting to that couple from London, that's why I didn't notice—but it isn't my job to. The police say they were only feet away in the next bar. Who's to say he didn't attack Gabby and then come back for you? He said he was drunk and needed a smoke and some air, but his excuse was feeble.'

'Listen to what you're saying. It's madness. If Jeff said he needed air, that's what he was doing.'

'You must admit he was looking at Gabby all night and went out of his way to impress her with his singing.'

'She was a bloody spectacle. The whole room was watching her, me as much as any of you. And as for his singing, I admit, it was for her benefit—but he was showing that he was better than her, not trying to impress her. He didn't murder her or attack me.'

'You said you didn't see anything.'

At last, she pulled away from him and stood up. This was crazy talk, and she'd got herself into a stupid situation. She walked away and stood with her back to him, looking at the setting sun. It was sinking fast.

She heard him stand. Felt him behind her. And there was that second of panic again. Not sexual attraction—fear of being attacked by a madman and thrown off the precipice. Jeff had never made her feel like that. He was safe, like a childhood home.

Ray put his hands on her shoulders but didn't try to pull her into him. Instead, he put his mouth to her ear. She willed a tic attack, but when she needed one, it wasn't happening. There was no point in having a brain condition if you couldn't call on it like a genie. She felt his breath against her skin, and the fear left her. It was replaced by heat. She didn't want it.

'Listen to me, Connie. I'm terrified for your safety. I've been watching him. I've seen things.'

'What things?'

'Nothing specific.'

'Nothing at all, then.'

'You have to take me seriously. Do you know that spouses commit eighty per cent of all murders? I couldn't bear it if anything happened to you.'

'I didn't know that. But you obviously do. How would you know something like that?'

'It doesn't matter. I've been reading, trying to find ways to protect you. This person is out to get you, be it Gabby, Jeff, or somebody else. I need to keep you safe.'

'No. Jeff needs to keep me safe, and me him.'

'Where is he?' He looked around at the mountains, the valley, and the nothingness around them. 'Where is he when you need him, Connie?'

'We had a fight. He'll be worried now, but he's stuck on a bloody boat.'

'He knows you're under threat. Or, think about this. What if he knows the killer is nowhere near you for the next twenty-four hours?'

The sun was a semi-circle sitting on the ridge of a distant mountain.

'Look at the light. It's fading. I'm allowed to ask now. Do you trust me, Connie?'

He turned her to face him. His look was intense, and she didn't know if she should be terrified or amazed by the longing in his eyes. They were too close. She wanted to move away but had her back to the edge of the mountain, and there was nowhere to go. She put her hands on his shoulders and tried to move him away from the ridge.

His eyes closed as his head came forward. She turned her face away from him and pushed him harder. His kiss missed.

'What the hell are you doing?' she said.

'I have feelings for you. This isn't just a holiday thing. I want to be with you, and I think the feeling's mutual.'

'I'm with Jeff.'

'But you don't love him.'

'How dare you make assumptions you know nothing about. He's my partner. I love him.'

'He won't let you breathe.'

'I breathe just fine.'

'We can leave tonight. There's a flight at ten. Have you got your passport in your bag? We don't even have to go back. All you have to do is say yes.'

'No.'

'Tell me you don't want me.'

'You've gone mad. We can't be together. You're a married man.'

'I'm getting divorced. Lisa's seen to that.' There was a tinge of bitterness in his voice.

'And you want to go back home on the rebound and turn up with a booby prize to rub her face in it?'

'No. I want to spend the rest of my life with you. You told me Jeff would never marry you, and he makes you feel as though you're not good enough.'

'I'd had too much to drink. It was a drunken ramble meaning nothing.'

'I'll marry you, Connie. Just as soon as I'm free. I'll marry you in a heartbeat. Lisa saw it. Why do you think she left me?'

'This is madness.'

'I'm a businessman. I have several companies and enough money to sort us out until you're established and we can find a proper place together. We'll get you somewhere for now, and I'll follow you.'

'You have enough money to sort me out? Have you heard yourself?'

'That came out wrong. I was trying not to say that I'd fund us until you found a new job if that's what you want to do. Lisa will do very well, and we'll be fine too. Come home with me.'

He put his arms around her and tried to kiss her again. 'I need you, Lisa.'

It wasn't even what he said. The ridiculous situation made her jerk her head back.

'You called me Lisa.'

'Shit. Honey, I am so sorry. We've been together for a long time. It's familiar. I'm sorry, it slipped out. It'll never happen again.'

'No. It won't. Look at this,' she spread her hands. 'The setting and romance of it all. We both got carried away on a stupid attraction that means nothing.'

'No, you're wrong. I love you.'

He was pathetic. And Connie saw it. She couldn't be with a man who said he loved her when they'd never kissed, or danced, or fought over the remote. She wished Jeff was here on the mountain. With a radio, so they could dance in a castle ruin with the last mottles of sun nodes falling around them.

'You don't know the first thing about me, Ray.'

But he did. She saw in his face that he knew they were done.

Their moment had been and was gone. He looked like a lost six-year-old, and she touched his cheek. 'You have a marriage to save. And I have a man to welcome home tomorrow. Let's go.'

They packed up the picnic, and he stopped her before they left. 'I meant what I said about the threats. They're real, and I'd hate anything to happen to you. Hell, I might be wrong about Jeff. I probably am, and I let my stupid imagination run away with me. But somebody is out to get you. If you don't watch yourself, they're going to strike, and there's nothing any of us will be able to do about it. Promise me you'll be careful.'

'I will.'

'And if you need me, any time, any time at all, you have my number. Here, in England, anywhere. I'll protect you.'

'Thank you, Ray.'

'You say I don't know you. In all the time we've been together today, your condition hasn't played up once. Doesn't that tell you something?'

'Don't. I've made my decision.'

'I know.'

'You're a friend, and it's good to know you've got my back.'

But he wasn't a friend. They wouldn't even keep in touch once they left the island. It was like that on holiday.

They were done.

Chapter Thirty-One

Nash adjusted the laptop screen and grimaced when he saw his own face as well as Conrad Snow's on Zoom.

'How's it going, Conrad? You sounded hyped. What have you got for me?'

'I've seen a white coat. You need to talk to a medical professional. A doctor, maybe?'

'Which doctor? What about?'

'I don't know. Are you ill?'

'No, I'm fine.'

'I can see you with him. He can answer your questions. It's okay, don't panic. I don't think it's about you. It's the sick people.'

'Is the killer a doctor?'

'I don't think so. Witness, I believe. Victim, even. I'm getting that you must talk to him, but they're telling me it might not be a doctor—somebody in the medical field, though. It's coming on a loop. It's to do with the case. Oh shit.'

'What. Stop gazing into space like an idiot, and tell me what you see.'

'You need to get DI Brown out of the way. I'm trying to formulate my thoughts and get something definitive for you, but it's bombarding me in a rush. What I'm getting loud and clear is that you're both in danger.'

'Brown won't like being side-shifted.'

'If you don't keep her close tonight and get her out of there in the morning, she won't be alive by lunchtime.'

'You sure?'

'No. But are you willing to take the risk?'

'I'll keep her with me tonight and send her on a Jeep trip with a couple of police guards in the morning. She'll love that like a hole in the head. Thanks. Anything else?'

'Your hippie friend is driving me mad. He's a restless spirit and won't shut the hell up.'

'Max is okay, though? He's not suffering in some kind of hellish purgatory?'

'Not likely. He's having a ball. He told me he slipped into the dressing room of a strip club last night.'

Nash laughed. Remembering Max was a good feeling. 'Here or there, he's the same old Max.'

'He heard his name and popped in to say, "You'd better believe it." He's gone again now. I'm seeing a clock. That always means a passage of time. The hands are moving fast, once, twice.'

'We have several suspects. Which one is it? Do you have a name? Anything? What can you give me? I need more.'

'Molly's in danger, but she's collateral damage. Nash, it's you the killer wants. My guides are saying, "One more and then the detective." I can see one revolution of the clock. It's going down tonight, Nash.'

'Male or female?'

'I don't know.'

'You heard the perpetrator's voice. Think, man.'

'It's not like a human voice, not the way we hear people. It might be Brown first, after all. Maybe it's this doctor. But then it's you. I don't know. But I am sure they're going to kill again tonight.'

'I won't let Brown out of my sight. Is that all you've got for me?'

'No, but it's delicate.'

'What?'

'I don't know how to broach this, but Max is twittering around me again. He says to tell you your new lady wingman is useless. Tell Brown to step down because Max is on the case and will get you hooked up with a real badass.'

Nash squirmed. 'I don't know what you mean.'

'He's saying Brown's got great breasts, but she's crap when it comes to finding you a man. I have to say this exactly. "You've got a thorn in your side, and he's really bad news." He says to tell you to get rid. Does that make sense?'

'None whatsoever. Thanks, Conrad. We'll speak tomorrow—one way or another.'

'Let's hope it's by earthly means. I've got enough hassle with your fool friend.'

They laughed and said goodbye. He closed the laptop and picked up his phone. He'd pleaded ignorance to Snow, but he knew exactly what the message meant. Nash opened the dating app.

The man he was messaging was called Dave Thorn. They'd chatted twice since his initial conversation when Brown was with him. He was disappointed by the warning. Dave seemed like a nice guy, and they had some things in common— not many, admittedly—but some. Perhaps the message was wrong. But if he disregarded something from Max that warned him off a future date in England, he was back to square one in his beliefs. It made everything a load of rubbish, and he might as well disregard the warning that the killer was coming for him.

It was a risk he couldn't take.

He had several messages waiting from Thorn, and whereas five minutes earlier he'd have had a feeling of excitement, now he opened them with a heavy heart.

The night before, Dave suggested meeting in person when Nash got home. That was way too fast. He wanted to talk an ocean of words before he even thought about meeting somebody. His insecurities and worries about his job made it hard to think beyond endless dating app messages. Thorn had already asked him for an email address, but Nash wasn't ready for that. A precaution he was glad about now. He could block him from the site and never have to speak to him again.

The messages from him all day while Nash worked were lovely. Thorn said he wanted to have some words waiting for Nash after work. He came across as a genuine and warm man. He'd taken the time to write chatty messages about his life and work in the countryside.

Nash was drawn to him and hated cutting him loose. But almost everything Snow told him from Maxwell Jones and his other sources had proven to be correct. He was and always would be a man of science, but he was at the point where if Snow told him something, he was listening. He didn't have to understand it. He opened a message box on the dating site to reply.

Dear Dave,

It is with regret that, on reflection, I don't feel we would be a compatible match. I am severing our connection, but I wish you every success going forward.

Sincerely

George Shan

He read it through and hit send. Brown would have killed him. He could hear her saying that it read as though he was cancelling a broadband service. It was too formal, but it was done. He couldn't change it now, even if he wanted to. He deleted the contact to take away any compulsion to check for replies.

The dating game wasn't for him. He was too old and sensible. He felt better for having ended something before it began, and he'd have a clearer head going into his first meeting the next morning. Thorn was a brief but severe distraction he didn't need.

Nash insisted that Brown spent the night in his suite. It didn't go down well. She yelled at him because she hated the idea of sharing the space. A guard was posted outside the room, with another at Connie Pearson's room and a third undercover to keep an eye on Isabel France.

Nash couldn't sleep and didn't want to. He waited for something to happen and nodded off in his chair sometime before dawn. They'd had a quiet night, and Molly was still alive.

It was only nine AM, and he'd already had Brown screaming at him.

'I told you nothing would happen. Snow's a fraud.'

'Has it occurred to you that nothing happened because you were with me, and I kept you safe?'

'I don't see why I should have to sit on a bouncing Jeep all day getting piles. You wouldn't treat Renshaw this way.'

She carried on moaning as Nash placated her by making coffee. Blah, blah. Sexist piggery. Blah blah. He'd heard it all before.

It was better after he'd waved her away. Nash concentrated on the case and didn't have to maximise his effort to keep her ungrateful arse alive. He was talking to Isabel France first, and Nash sat at a corner table in the card room. Some large boxes of supplies had been left on the tables closest to him, partially shielding him from view and discouraging people from sitting there. The card room was rarely used throughout the day, and he was unhindered with an excellent cup of rich-blend coffee beside him.

The waiters were instructed to keep people away. He'd play it by ear over whether to use the cover story or come clean about his role.

He watched Anast go up to Isabel France and touch her elbow. He spoke to her, and judging by the wagging of her head, she wasn't impressed at being accosted. Anast escorted her over and took her drink order.

Isabel took the outstretched hand as Nash stood to greet her. He waited for recognition dawning, and if it was a game changer, he'd ditch the cover. After a fast assessment, he realised she wasn't the type to gossip about her mother's death with a nosey old man. She'd see through any subterfuge.

'Hello. Nice to meet you. May I ask what this is about?'

'Please, sit, Mrs France. I won't keep you long.'

'Are you a policeman?'

He waited for her to settle and make herself comfortable.

'Guilty as charged. But we'd be grateful if you could keep that to yourself for now. We met briefly in Barrow, if you remember. It was when you spoke to us regarding your mother. Again, please accept my condolences.'

'I knew I'd seen you somewhere. It makes me feel better knowing that somebody from Mum's case is here working the new lines of investigation. It was as though she was forgotten in the bigger picture.'

'I can assure you, that was never the case. We've been working tirelessly to catch the person who did this to your mum.'

'I'm glad to hear it. I didn't get your name.'

'Nash. DCI Nash. Though to everybody else, I am a retired shopkeeper called George Shan on holiday with my daughter.'

She laughed, 'Shan, I see what you did there.'

After a frosty start, she warmed. Her intelligence and keen observations were apparent. But as disarming as she appeared to be, she and her sister had the most to gain from Cullen's death, which put them up with the top suspects. 'Mrs France, why are you here, jumping into the middle of our investigation?'

'Call me Isabel. I was concerned that he's still out there. Nothing was being done, and I wanted to see for myself what was going on.'

'I get it.'

'And I have something that may be of use, though I was going to take the information into Barrow when I got back.'

Nash leaned forward. 'Seeing as we're here?'

She smiled, and he saw her relax. She was a smart woman in her thirties. She looked after herself, and her hair and nails were done professionally with just the right number of highlights in an otherwise natural head of curls. He noticed that her nail varnish was dark red, crossing the border into purple—not a pastel hue. He knew from Alma Cullen's case that she was a wife and mother of two who worked in sales for a local print company. You can tell a lot about a woman from the bag she carries. Nash knew a thing or two about design. While it wasn't a bargain basement brand, Isabell's bag hit the mid-range well. It didn't matter a jot to him, but he was pleased about that. A woman who spends a month's wage on a bag is frivolous.

'Tell me anything you have. At this stage, we're having an informal chat, and you can talk to me in the strictest confidence.'

'Are you saying our next talk may be formal, Detective?'

'Only insomuch as it might be taped for official records and may be used as evidence in a court case when the perpetrator is caught.' He didn't want her to know she was on the suspect list or have her clam up. He was ruling nothing out.

'I thought I was still a suspect for a moment. I'm good at most things I do, but I don't believe I could murder somebody from across an ocean.' She laughed. Nash didn't. But he tilted his head in a gesture for her to continue.

'The police in Barrow were interested in Mum's whereabouts. It seems that Margery, her neighbour, spouted some guff about her going on an outing every fourth Saturday.'

'We've been looking into that, but unless something has come to light while I'm here, it's drawn a blank,' Nash said.

'I can help you. I thought it was sour grapes on Margery's part that Mum had a tiny moment of her life that didn't include her. She's a busybody, and sometimes it's difficult to know what's true and what she fabricates for the sake of a good story.'

'I take it you don't like her?'

'Not particularly. She's all right, I suppose, but I wouldn't tell her too much of my business—unlike my mother did. Anyway, I asked her about these days out, and nothing came of it. I forgot about it until I met June Alder by chance in Morrisons. You'll remember her as a cleaner at Barrow's railway station, but she's been promoted and works in the ticket office.'

'I do remember her. She found one of the missing kids alive and well in The Florist case. I remember she was very sweet to him. Good for her on getting a promotion. Go on.'

'She did the cursory "Sorry to hear about your mum," but then she went on to say she missed their chats on Mum's Blackpool days. I didn't know what she was talking about and pressed her for more details. She said that Mum was always taking the train to Blackpool. I told her she was mistaken. I think we went for a day trip once when we were kids, but it might have been Morecambe. Everything's bigger when you're a child. But Mum doesn't know anybody in Blackpool and would have no reason to visit.'

She stopped talking, drew a breath and reached for her drink. Nash didn't prompt and gave her time to formulate her thoughts and tell the story in her way without interruption. It's something else he tried to promote in Brown. You get more out of a witness if you let them ramble.

'June was adamant. She sold her the tickets, and she went on the nine-thirty train every few weeks and didn't come back until after tea. Of course, I asked if she knew why Mum went, and she couldn't tell me much, but Mum told her she met up with an old friend that she worked with before she moved here. They met at Blackpool, halfway between their homes, went for lunch and then did some shopping together.'

'And she didn't catch the friend's name?'

'No such luck.'

'Male or female?'

'I don't know that either, but from the way the conversation went, I think it was a woman.'

'And your mum moved to Barrow from Cheshire?'

'Yes. Frodsham.'

'Can you remember where she worked when she was there?'

'She was a receptionist at Rose Cottage health centre for many years. Then, she was made redundant about a year before she moved to Barrow, but she didn't really settle to anything. She was worried about getting work and took a part-time job at The Rigger pub in Elton, that's the next village along, and after that, she worked as a care assistant until she left the area, but I can't remember who for.'

Nash was making notes, and Isabel had given him a lot for Brown to follow up. 'Thank you, Isabel. We are close to an arrest. I just need one piece of information from England in the morning, and once we have that, we'll know the name of our killer.'

'Give me a shout if I can help with anything else, Inspector.'

He stood and shook her hand.

After Mrs France left, he asked Anast to find Jefferey Pearson. 'No, on second thoughts, I'll do the spare wheel first. Get Raymond Farrell for me, please, Anast.'

Brown came to him ten minutes later. She was back from her trip, and her air was casual, but Nash knew her well enough to know she was brimming with news.

'Hi, Dad. What are you doing up here by yourself? The pool's lovely.' It amazed Nash that women share the amazing ability to swim without getting a hair on their heads wet. Brown lowered her voice to a whisper. 'Ray Farrell's gone missing.'

'Hm.'

'Hm, what? He's been gone all night. Security opened his room, and his bed hasn't been slept in, but his clothes are still hanging in the wardrobe.'

'I suspected as much.'

'He's been taken?'

'There you go again, jumping to conclusions. Not necessarily.'

'What? You think he's the murderer?'

'I didn't say that either, but it does fill in another missing piece.'

'You are the most infuriating man. Which is it? Is he the victim or the perp?'

'Or a freethinking holidaymaker whose wife has left him, and he can do what he likes.'

'Do you think he's run off with a new woman? And if he has, would it be another guest or a local?'

'Time will tell the whereabouts of Mr Farrell. Do we have news of Mr Pearson?'

'Anast is giving him a knock. He should be here in a minute, if he wants to talk to some nosey old bloke, that is.'

'He'll talk to me. Anast has been instructed to tell him I've found something belonging to him.'

'Sly old fox.'

Nash knew something was wrong when Anast ran across the tiled floor, waving his hands. He'd been asked to be the soul of discretion, but that wasn't working so well. 'Sir,' he shouted from one side of the communal space to the other, and Nash had to make a point of not acknowledging him until he was level with the table.

'Lower your voice, Anast. Remember, we are being very quiet. Yes?'

'Mr Pearson has gone missing as well. And Mrs Pearson.'

'I see.'

'Three more missing peoples is a bad omen. The spirits of our ancestors are not being happy. They call us the Necropolis Hotel. I go tell Inspector Ballas.'

'Thank you, Anast. That will be all.'

He scuttled off to find Ballas as though hell's legions were chasing him.

'The Hotel of Death. You have to admit, Brown, it's got a ring to it,' Nash said. 'I didn't see that coming. All three of them. Interesting.'

'Aren't you going to see Ballas?'

'Not yet. I'm thinking. It doesn't fit. Not all of them. Where are you?'

'Who?'

'Pearson.'

Anast flapped over to them with a smile on his face, and Mrs Pearson trailed behind him.

'Look. I find her. She's not hacking into tiny pieces and feed to the pigses.'

'There you are. Now, all is well and as expected. Thank you, Anast.' He waited for the porter to leave. 'Mrs Pearson, welcome. I was hoping to speak to you. Please join me. Would you like some tea?',

'No, thank you.' She sat opposite Nash and Brown. 'I believe you have something belonging to my husband?'

'All in good time. To ensure I give this to the correct person, would you mind telling me the number of your room?'

'I really don't see the need. The reception staff can vouch for us.' Nash raised an eyebrow. 'Very well. It's room one hundred and four-teen, but I don't feel comfortable giving you our personal information.'

Look out for room 114. Snow had struck gold again.

'And yet you did anyway. Be careful who you trust. Thank you, Mrs Pearson. Where is your husband?'

Nash knew Connie Pearson wasn't married to Jeff, and her real name was Swift. She looked uncomfortable. 'What's all this about?'

'I'll explain myself in a second, but we're worried about your husband. Is he okay? The porter thought he might have gone missing along with several other people this week.'

Connie laughed. 'That's all it is?' she waved a hand in dismissal. 'He's fine. It's a misunderstanding. He's gone on a sailing trip and will be back tonight. And I was in the spa having a massage this afternoon if you must know.'

'That's good news. And Mr Farrell? What about him?' Nash asked.

'What is this? What do you want, asking me all these questions? I must tell you, I've spoken to the police about you and your daughter. You ask a lot, considering I don't know you.'

'I'm afraid I've perpetrated a slight deception. We don't have your husband's wallet or anything else. Like you, I use more than one name. Forgive me, Mrs Pearson, but my name is DCI Nash, and this is DI Brown. We are officers from Barrow-in-Furness, in Cumbria.'

'Where? That place where they build the submarines? God-forsaken hole, by all accounts.'

'Then you have clearly never been. It's very beautiful and a good place to raise a family. Let me get to the point, Mrs Pearson.'

'I wish you would.'

'As you know, there's been some trouble on the island during your stay. We've been brought in to join forces with the Greek police to investigate.' He showed her his badge. 'We want to find out who is making these terrible attacks on you and would appreciate your cooperation. We believe you're a retired psychotherapist?'

Talk to the medical professional.

'I am, but I don't see what help I can be.'

'You're too modest, Mrs Pearson. There is a medical element to this case that hasn't been openly released. I think you're being targeted because you may have seen something that you, as a former practitioner in the field, would know was wrong. Perhaps you've heard something in conversation that meant nothing to you at the time but which could incriminate the killer. We feel you are invaluable to us with your specialised knowledge.'

'Hence the reason we've been asked personal questions about our health and lifestyle?'

'Exactly. Before we go any further, can we be assured of your confidence in this matter?'

'Of course, Inspector, and it goes without saying that I'll do anything I can to help.'

'Thank you. We are liaising with Greek clinicians and their coroner, but there's a language barrier, especially when it comes to translating certain medical conditions and procedures. I'm not sure they're releasing everything they should to us, and you're the only practitioner in your field in the complex.'

'Retired.'

'That's of no consequence. We need your knowledge and expertise, and we think you can greatly help us. You'll have to sign an NDA, of course, because we'll be asking you to look at confidential casefiles.' He watched the woman grow in stature as he played to her ego.

'You'll be privy to things that nobody else has seen. And you may discover something from a medical perspective that we've missed.'

'I'll do everything I can.'

'Thank you, Mrs Pearson. We'll be in touch later this evening. We are close to an arrest. I need some information from England in the morning, and once we have that. we will know the name of our killer.'

'Gosh, what is it?'

'I can't say at this stage.'

'I understand, and it goes without saying that I'll be honoured to help catch this vile person. I'm walking around with a target above my head, and I don't know which step will be my last. It's terrifying,

Inspector, but I'm not going to hide away and let this disgusting animal beat me.'

'Rest assured, Mrs Pearson. We need one vital piece of information, and then we'll make an arrest and get you to safety very soon.'

'I might be dead later this evening.'

Chapter Thirty-Two

A nast was on standby for Jeff Pearson to get back from his sailing trip. Nash wanted him forestalled before he went up to their room and spoke to Connie Pearson. He didn't want to give him prior warning or time to think about what he'd say. Anast used the same ruse to speak to him as he had with Connie. The first five minutes of the conversation ran along similar lines of Jeff asking what Nash had of his and Nash explaining that he was the police.

Pearson was sunburnt and exhausted. He'd been in the heat too long. Nash knew sailing was a gruelling business on unaccustomed muscles.

'What's this about? I'm not impressed at the subterfuge to bring me here.'

'I apologise, Mr Pearson, but we have an investigation to pursue, and discretion is paramount.'

'I haven't even seen my wife yet. Can't this wait until I've been to my room and had something to eat?'

'I won't keep you long. But Mrs Pearson isn't, in fact, your wife, is she?'

'No. But she's as good as. How's that relevant?'

'And her name isn't Pearson, is it?'

'What are you getting at, Inspector?'

'We're ascertaining the facts about our guests, so we have a clear picture. Do you understand?'

'Not really, but let's get this over with so I can eat. What else do you need to know? Is that it? I'm starving.'

'Not quite, Mr Pearson.'

During Nash's investigations, several witnesses, including two staff members, reported seeing Connie leaving the hotel with Raymond Farrell the previous day. Farrell was driving, which was odd as the car was on hire to Ms Swift—the name used on her official documentation. Nash had an officer checking the hire arrangement, whether Pearson did embark on his sailing adventure, what time Connie returned, and if she was with Farrell when she got back. She may have dropped him off in town instead of returning to the hotel with him. Until they had the reports back, Nash probably wouldn't get much further. Everybody's whereabouts were being checked against other timelines covering the duration of their stay. And now Farrell was missing. It was time-consuming and frustrating, but the research wheels moved slowly.

Pearson kept rubbing his head as though he had a headache. When he moved to massage his forehead, Nash saw a distinct change from normal skin to the lobster-red burn that would be sore in a couple of hours. Wherever he'd been, it included hours in the sun.

'Do you know where Raymond Farrell is? Have you seen him today?'

'Pain in the arse. Sniffing around my woman all the time. The bloke wants to sort his own missus out before starting on mine.'

'Care to elaborate?'

'It's just me being possessive. Rutting stags. He's all right in small doses, I suppose. All I've seen for twenty-four hours is a lot of ocean and the contents of my stomach every ten minutes. Why? What's he been up to?

'Can you just answer the question?'

'Is he a suspect? Is Connie okay? Have you corralled me away from everybody to tell me she's dead? I should never have left her alone. As soon as I got on that God-forsaken boat, I regretted leaving. But there was no escape.' He looked stricken.

'Given the circumstances and the threats she has received, we wondered why you'd leave her here alone.'

'We had a stupid argument. I left in a temper and shouldn't have gone. You haven't answered my question.' He stood up. 'Has he got Connie?'

'Sit down, Mr Pearson. Your partner is fine. However, it appears Mr Farrell may have gone missing, which is of concern.'

'Ray, too?'

Nash watched the cogs turning. The man could be a good actor. He'd seen plenty of them across interview tables in his time.

Pearson came to a conclusion. Sat up straight and laughed. 'The sly old devil. It's obvious, isn't it?'

'Is it?'

'Yeah. He's run off with that bird?'

'What bird?'

'The so-called singer. That Gabby with tickets on herself. I saw them making eyes at each other the other night. I thought there was something fishy when she went missing. They've done a bunk, the pair of them. I bet you.'

'And in your opinion, their disappearance, twenty-four hours apart, is unrelated to the other deaths and people going missing on the island?'

'I don't know, Inspector. That's your job to find out. But I reckon they'll be together. And why would I know where Farrell is? I'm not his bloody keeper, hardly know the bloke. Now, if you don't mind?'

'Certainly, Mr Pearson, you've been very helpful. We are close to an arrest. I just need some information from England in the morning, and once we have that, we will know the name of our killer.'

'You lot couldn't catch a cold, never mind a killer.'

'The net is closing in. We know who it is. We're just waiting for confirmation to make an arrest.'

They shook hands, and Pearson walked away, rubbing his head.

'What do you make of him,' Nash said.

'Cocky git. I don't like him,' Brown pulled a face.

'Nor me.'

Nash waited for him to be out of sight and called for his next interviewee. He spoke to another four potential suspects and ended the interview with the same line about arresting on evidence from England. The dye was cast.

By the time he went to his room to dress for dinner, He knew who the killer was.

Brown glared at him. 'I want to sleep in my own room.'

'Not a chance,' Nash said.

'We would prefer you go along with the arrangements put in place for you, Detective Brown,' Ballas told her.

She was suffering her second night away from her hotel bedroom with a balcony and hot tub, and she wasn't happy about it. This time she wasn't sharing Nash's room. She was being moved to one of the villas and had two guards assigned to watch over her.

'I'm a big girl, Nash. I can assemble a Glock faster than you can—blindfolded.'

'I want to know you're safe and well-guarded.'

'It's a waste of time. Snow's rubbish, nothing happened last night, and it's not going to tonight.'

'I'm not so sure.'

She was sitting on Nash's bed and grabbed her overnight bag. 'Okay, I'll see you in the morning if we're both alive. Have you checked your balcony doors?'

'No, leave them.'

'Don't be daft. I'm not leaving here until I know your windows and doors are locked behind me.' She closed the shutters and the French doors and ensured they were locked. 'See you, loser. Make sure the murderers and ghosts don't get you.'

'Night, Brown. See you in the morning. You too, Ballas.'

He waited for them to leave and gave it another few minutes while he made a cup of instant coffee, then unlocked the doors. He flung the shutters wide and left the French doors ajar. Not an open invitation, but no deterrent either. The scene was set.

It was eight fifteen, and he settled down with some paperwork. He'd moved his armchair into the far corner behind the French doors, and as the light faded, so did his ability to work. He couldn't turn any lights on.

He contented himself with going through things in his head. After making endless mental lists, he cross-referenced them against other information in his head. He saw each one as a typed sheet with names scored out as they'd been eliminated.

At one thirty, he had trouble staying awake and longed for a cup of strong coffee, but he couldn't risk moving. Perhaps Brown was right, and Snow was delusional. Maybe nothing was going to happen—but he doubted it.

When it came, it was sudden and made Nash jump, but his training taught him to suppress his fight-or-flight reflex. He sat without movement and watched the figure glide through the French doors. They did Nash a favour by leaving the door open, and there was plenty of moonlight. Nash had the advantage. He was accustomed to the darkness and could see in the gloom.

The murderer crept into the pitch-black room and didn't have much light from the moon behind them. They crept to the side of the bed and raised an arm. Nash saw the stainless-steel glint of the kitchen knife. The one reported stolen from the kitchen. The knife came down hard and with such rage.

They stabbed the bed in a frenzy, moving the position of attack across the duvet until it was clear there was nobody in it.

Nash spoke from the darkened corner of the room. 'Ruby Vang, I presume.'

The woman spun around with a look of horror and surprise on her face. She screamed the full-throated cry of a warrior and charged at Nash as the door opened, and four officers charged across the room to restrain her. They were a writhing mass of arms and legs as the police held the killer to the floor, cuffed her, and dragged her to her feet.

Nash read her rights and arrested Ruby Vang.

Chapter Thirty-Three

N ash had been too wired to sleep after the arrest. He'd never seen anybody so filled with that level of insane rage. He took a breath and opened the door to the interview room at Kos police station. It wasn't an interrogation he was looking forward to, and the night had been a long one. He still had a stinging cut on his hand from where Vang had attacked him during her takedown.

'Ms Pearson, or should we call you Ruby Vang? I trust you have been looked after in the custody suite overnight. Forgive my delay in getting to you, but we had to cross the Is and dot the Ts to ensure you don't wriggle out from under us. I'm sure you'll understand.'

'Go to hell.'

'Talk. Where would you like to start?' Nash said.

'No comment.'

'Really?'

'No comment.'

'We're going to play that game?'

'No comment.'

'Interview suspended at 07:08.' Nash pressed the stop button on the video recorder and buzzed an officer to guard the prisoner and the recording device while he was out of the room.

He'd arrived at Kos police station before seven o'clock, and it was going to be a hot day. Ballas had given him an odd look when he requested that Interview Room Three be available. It was like Lionel Messi wearing his lucky socks for a game. Yet Nash told everybody he was a man of science. However, it threw them off-guard, which is why he did it. He couldn't give a damn which room he was allocated, but he liked people thinking he had idiosyncrasies. It didn't do to let people get the true measure of you, and if Ballas thought he was odd, that suited Nash's cause.

The room was stifling.

He wasn't playing fifty rounds of No Comment. Not in this dungeon.

'Okay, Pearson, you win for now. But let me tell you something. I don't know how much you know about Greek law—we're only allowed to interview you for two hours in England. Here? I'm not as current on my Grecian interview procedures as I should be. I don't think they had much in the way of human rights forty years ago, and that's when I last studied European law. As I'm working on Greek rules, I must get myself a more up-to-date rule book at some point. 'And what's that I hear?' He cupped his ear. 'I think the air conditioning unit's gone on the blink. I keep telling them to kick it.' Nash raised his hand to the two-way, and on cue, the whirring of the fans stopped, and a humid silence fell over the room. 'Damn, that's unfortunate. I'll see you at some point later today, Mrs Pearson. I have other things I can be getting on with while you think about your belligerence.'

'You can't leave me here.'

'But I can. You see, you're under arrest, and I'm not. I can get the hell out of here. It'll be like a pressure cooker in half an hour. I'm going for some breakfast and fresh air. We'll see if you're more talkative when I get back.'

'Screw you.'

He spoke to the guard. 'Don't engage in conversation, Deppas, and make sure you change guards every thirty minutes. I don't want you overheating.'

'You don't want me to take her to a cell?'

'No. She's good.'

Nash took his time over breakfast with a copy of *The Independent on Sunday*, even though it was Monday. Everything happened late on the island. Ballas had offered him pastries at the station, but he fancied a walk and called Brown for an update. She'd been dealing with the media and arranging the press conferences. She said it had gone well, and she'd catch up with him when he got back.

He ate at one of the pavement cafés and strolled into the station an hour and a half later. Ballas wasn't happy.

'Nash. I've been told to give you full authority now that an arrest has been made on a British National. However, I don't know how you do things in England, but we don't treat our guests this way. How can you leave her like that when you made such a fuss about the last suspect?'

'Needs must, Ballas, I don't enjoy it. However, I knew that lady was innocent. This one is somebody virtually sub-human. If we don't make

334

her talk and she gets out of here, we'll all have a lot of blood on your hands.'

'Would you turn the air conditioning off at home?'

'Moot point, my friend. If we turn the air-con on back home, we'd have the backsides sued off us. Have you been to England recently? It's freezing ninety per cent of the time.'

'I don't want anybody getting into trouble.'

'And therein lies the beauty of the situation. We aren't allowed to torture people. More's the pity. And I guess you aren't either.'

'Certainly not.'

'Shame. Anyway, somebody jumps on me, and I plead ignorance of your laws. "I didn't know we couldn't do that, Your Excellency." Then, when they pound your door with a lawsuit—you just blame me. It's a perpetrator-less crime.'

Ballas cracked a smile and sounded almost British. 'You're evil. You do know that?'

'It has been said, but I can't get those dead children out of my head. She has to talk otherwise, we haven't got enough on her and she walks. I'll go as far as I can to get her to confess.'

'Within reason, Nash.'

'Of course.'

He took his jacket off before going back into the interview room, and when he sat, he was faced with a barrage of abuse from Ms Pearson. He let her rant and used the time to roll up his shirt sleeves. He was meticulous, and it took time to put three precise turn-ups on each. 'Marvellous place. They cook your breakfast in front of you. Mouth-watering. Speaking of cooking, how are you?'

'Bastard.'

She was a wet mess. Her hair clung to her face, and she was beet-root red with droplets of sweat forming over her cheeks and neck. 'Petorokopf, get Ms Pearson a glass of water, please. I anticipate us being here a while.'

He turned on the tape, announced the time and date and had everybody speak their names for the record. Ballas said, 'For the benefit of the tape, Ms Pearson, I ask you again, would you like us to provide legal representation?'

'I'm innocent. I do not need a brief.'

The interview consisted of Ballas, Nash and the accused.

'Constance Pearson, let's get this over with.' Nash didn't waste any time with conjuring tricks. He laid evidence bags and damning photographs on the desk in front of her. The worst was something that only came to light the morning before. He lied when he told the suspects he was waiting for vital evidence from England—he already had it.

A holidaymaker went home earlier in the week. Two days later, they went to their local police station in Hull when one of their scenic videos showed a previously unseen image of a middle-aged woman dragging a little girl around the back of the hotel. A second blow-up shot showed the knife against her throat. It was Connie Pearson. Nash picked up one of the stills from the video and threw it on the table.

'You vile creature.'

Under normal circumstances, he'd hold the most incriminating evidence back to use as a trump card when it was needed. But he was going to break this bitch and take her down hard.

'That could be anybody. It's not me.'

Nash pointed to another photograph that showed her face. He indicated the blouse she was wearing—the same one as in the photograph. 'I rest my case.'

She slumped back in her chair and looked defeated before he started. Nash had expected a better opponent. She was late middle-aged after a hard life and looked tired. They had the knife she'd tried to murder Nash with. Thirty-eight other pieces of hard evidence and 114 photographs of the crime scenes had been accumulated during the case. She was done.

Yesterday morning, a man driving to work was the first to see the hand sticking out of the fishpond like Excalibur in its stone. There they were—the bodies—between Kardamena and Kos Town. They were at the side of the road in the town's pond, which was smaller than a park boating lake. Gasses had accumulated in Mervyn Gould's body, and he'd risen to the water's surface. The rest of him followed, and five minutes later, he was bobbing on top of the water like a jolly helium-filled balloon. Police put up cordons, closed the road, and sent a diver into the pond, though it wasn't very deep. They were all there—the wretched missing people.

'Let's start with Raymond Farrell. Where is he?'

'I don't know.'

He pointed to a photograph of Ray and Connie going through a speed camera and being zapped. 'Tell me about yesterday.'

'I made a terrible mistake. But I haven't seen Jeff since I was arrested. Please let me see him.'

'We think you made more than one mistake, Pearson. Where did you and Farrell go?'

'I was upset. Jeff and I had a row, and Ray was there when I needed somebody. We went to the castle on the hill.'

'Which one of you was Ed?'

'Excuse me?'

'Forget it. Give me the details. What time did you go? What happened? What time did you get back? Was Farrell with you?' Nash sounded bored. He wanted her to know she was beneath his contempt and his time.

'Of course he was still with me. He couldn't walk all the way back, could he?'

'Bare-faced lie.' Nash flicked through a few images and found the one of Connie returning to the hotel. She was in the driver's seat, and the passenger side was empty. She had the window rolled down and was smiling.

'Oh.'

'Yes. Oh. Why did you kill him?'

'I didn't touch him.'

He'd held back the photographs of the bodies fished from the pond. It would've been disrespectful to throw them on the table with the other evidence like rubbish. He had them in a manila envelope. Nash found one of Ray Farrell and put it down.

Her hands covered her face, and she made screaming noises behind them. 'I didn't do it. I didn't.'

'We think you did. What did he do to make you so mad?'

'Nothing. He was sweet. He said he'd look after me. He wanted to take me away and offered me a new life. Ray asked me to run away with

338

him—but it made me realise how much I love Jeff. You can see that, can't you?'

'Why did you stab Raymond Farrell? We have the knife, which has your fingerprints all over it.'

'I love Jeff, and when all this silly business is cleared up, I'll spend the rest of my life proving it to him. I got out of prison once before and will do it again.'

Nash ignored the obvious new thread. 'Raymond Farrell.'

'Him again. Why do you keep talking about him? He's not important.'

'You didn't have to kill Farrell. He didn't deserve that.'

'Of course he did. I did do it. Didn't I? I think I remember now.'

'Why?' Nash asked.

'He wanted me to cheat on Jeff. It was his fault. Though, I could have killed him for having bad taste. His wife was awful. I despised her. I was going to get rid of her, but Lady Muck left before I got the chance. She was top of my list, and I had a silk scarf ready with her name on it.'

Nash glanced at the tape to ensure the confession had been recorded.

'You admit to killing all those people?'

'I can't deny it, can I? Though I can plead insanity. Have you got that? Insanity.'

'And again, for the tape. Constance Swift, AKA Ruby Vang, AKA Constance Pearson, did you kill these eight people?'

She sighed. 'No, Inspector. I didn't.'

'We know you did.'

'You think you're so clever, don't you? I haven't killed eight people, you fool. I think I lost count at twenty-eight.'

Nash didn't react. 'Let's start at the beginning. Why the boy?'

'Mercy killing.'

'How so?'

This was too easy. Now that she'd been caught, she wanted to brag.

'He was an obnoxious little prick who would grow into an obnoxious big prick. It was a mercy for society. Did you see his size? He was a dead man walking.'

'You said mercy killing?'

'Not merciful for him. In recompense to every passenger on that plane. The little bastard and his low-grade family held it up for fifteen minutes. They were heinous.'

Nash had to work through them fast while she was talking. He wanted justice for every one of her victims. If he missed any, it'd be one less life sentence for which she'd serve time.

'What about Joy Neal?'

'She was like a bloody screech owl. Never stopped screaming the place down.'

'She was dying and in terrible pain. Don't you have any compassion?'

'When I was sleep-deprived by its constant noise? It was a brat. Do I heck. It was a blessing for the awful girl. And for me. I slept that night after teaching her how to be quiet. Children should be seen and not heard.'

'I'm going to run through the bodies in the water, keep going. You're doing very well.'

'Don't patronise me.'

'I apologise. Mervyn Gould?'

'Sweaty Legs. He dripped like a tap. I was soaked on that plane. They were drunks, so annoying, both of them, but she didn't press up against me in a perspiring mound of disgusting flesh for three hours. He did, so he was the one to go.'

'How did you kill him?'

'The same as all of them. An injection of air into the axillary vein.'

Pearson's tone was cold. There was no inflection or emotion to her words, and she made Nash fear the prospect of nightmares for months to come.

'But that's not all you did, is it?'

'No. I had my own party with them. Dunking the fat boy like a doughnut in tea was the most fun. And Ray, darling Ray. The look on his face when he realised that I'd stabbed him. He was nice, and I killed him anyway. That proves insanity, doesn't it?'

'Not if I can help it.'

'I'm a therapist. I've seen enough schizophrenia. I was even diagnosed with it years ago. And do you know why? Because it's invisible, and there isn't a white coat in this land that can prove I don't have it.'

'We were talking about Raymond Farrell, not you.'

'But you have to admit. I'm far more interesting. I remember it all now. I stabbed him and pushed him off the mountain. He couldn't hold on by the ends of his fingers for long. The hardest part was driving to the bottom and hauling him into the car.'

'I bet. He was a well-made man.'

'And in that heat too.'

He could have drawn her attention to the photos of tyre tracks at the mountain's base or the plaster cast moulds of them from various sites, including the pond. And the trails in the shingle where she'd dragged Ray Farrell's dead body by his feet. But he didn't bother. There was no need.

'What about Ed Grantham?'

'Who?'

'The young man with a wife and child.'

'That wet weekend. Would you believe it? We'd been held up for fifteen minutes. We were finally taxiing and about to take off when the bloody moron pings his bell for the attendant. Guess what he wanted?'

'I've no idea.'

She laughed. 'You're not going to believe this. Bold as brass, he holds up his kid's bottle and says, "Have you got a microwave? Can you heat this up for me?" I've seen it all. The kid wasn't even crying. Jeff had it on his knee.'

'You killed him over a bottle of milk?'

'Wouldn't you under those circumstances? There's no point crying over spilt milk, Inspector. Let it go.'

'Killing the father wouldn't be the first pastime on my mind. Moving on. Maria Karali?'

All he had to do was give the victim's name, and she was off with her story. Two words and she confessed without any prompting. He worried it might be inadmissible in court due to her mental state. But she seemed as sane as any middle-aged woman he'd ever met. Until you consider the fact that this seemingly nice lady had killed all those people in horrendous circumstances.

'The waitress?'

'Yes.'

'Resting Bitchface. If there was one I could go back and undo, it'd be her. She had some spunk, you know. I liked that. I'd even go so far as to say I liked her. But she leaned over to put my glass down and breathed on my food. I couldn't have that. It was disgusting.'

Nothing the woman said surprised Nash. 'She had a terminal heart condition and still had to come to work for twelve hours a day to support her family.'

'Boo-hoo. It isn't my fault she was born in this God-forsaken hell-hole.'

Nash had to move. He needed a break and to stand or pace. He wanted to get out of there and sit by the ocean, breathing in its cleanliness. But he didn't dare move. If he broke momentum now, she could clam up. His greatest fear was that she'd retract her statement before he'd got it all down.

'Gabrielle Rice.'

She laughed again, but this time it was filled with rage. 'Gobby Gabby. She was like nails on a blackboard. And that was before she started wailing and prancing about like an overweight pony. Trust me, if Bitchface was the one I'd go back and save, Gobby is the one I'd love to do again. Slower next time. I made her say she was a shit singer.'

Connie laughed, and it carried genuine mirth and a barrel of bitterness. 'That hurt her more than the crack over the head. It took two taps with a rock and some broken facial bones to get her to say it. She was stubborn. I'll give her that. She urinated, the dirty trollop. I forced her to sing *Dancing Queen* with me but hit her again to shut her up after two lines because she ruined it. See, I'm a public servant. I've saved many brides from a miserable wedding day. They might even give me a medal.'

'Raymond Farrel to wrap this up. I know we touched on him earlier, but can you please confirm for the record that you killed him.'

'I did. And then, when he screwed his little face up trying to hold onto the ridge, I pried his fingers off. This little piggy went to market. This little piggy stayed at home.'

'And you disposed of him in the ornamental pond?'

'We're surrounded by the sodding ocean, but have you any idea how hard it is finding a body of still water on this blasted island?'

'Thank you, Ms Pearson, that's enough for now.'

'You missed some.'

'I don't doubt that for a second.'

'I mean this week. The man with emphysema was a local guy in one of the bars. He was coughing and spluttering all over the place. And his wife had diabetes. I know because she was next to me at the sink in the ladies. I smelt it on her breath, that horrible, sweet, pear drops smell of ketoacidosis. Horrible. I couldn't decide which of them to do, so I did an *Ip dip. My blue ship*—and COPD guy lost. As I said, there were others.'

'I can't stand to hear another word out of your insidious mouth for now. Even if you stop and refuse to give us more, we've got enough on you to put you away for nine lifetimes. You're never going to see daylight again.'

'Never say never, Inspector. May I go and powder my nose now, please?'

He had to get out. He was suffocating while she seemed to be enjoying herself. He wasn't going to feed her depravity for another second.

He'd have to continue the interview later, but he was sick to his stomach for now.

'Interview suspended at 13:18.'

Chapter Thirty-Four

On Thursday, 6th September 1973, in the early hours of the morning, Marcia Vance gave birth to a baby girl. She resented Brian because he was preparing for his pool night in the Cross Keys pub when she went into labour twelve hours earlier. It wasn't done in those days for men to be in the delivery suite, but they'd wear a hole in the family room carpet, waiting for their bundles of joy to arrive.

Brian stopped the van in the Rosedale maternity hospital carpark on Abbey Road. The van was an old Ford he used for work, and he helped her into the back of it. She was lying on dust sheets next to cans of paint, with the awful smell of turpentine making her ill. When they got there, Marcia was surprised that he didn't get a foot behind her to help shove her out. But he was good enough to open the back doors. He helped her down the step, grabbed her suitcase—packed for ten days—and dropped it on the tarmac beside her.

'See you later then, love. Ring me when it's over, won't you?'

And that was it. He jumped in the van and was gone in a puff of acrid black smoke.

It was the worst night of Marcia's life—and although she didn't know how bad it would be then, she was terrified. She hated her husband that night.

He'd knocked her about in the past, and there was no love in the marriage, but she'd never hated him until that minute when he blew her off in a cloud of fumes. The love never came back. It grew into a physical hatred over the years, and she could pinpoint that minute as the one that officially ended their relationship.

They gave her an enema and shaved her private area. All things that, ten years later, they realised were unnecessary, along with the ten-day post-partum stay in hospital. That was compulsory, and every woman across the country packed their bags for a ten-day stay when their time came. Women who already had children loved it—it was the most sleep they'd had in years. Babies were taken away from their mothers and put in the nursery for hours on end.

It was a different time.

Brian and Marcia called their little gem Ruby because of her rosy cheeks, and she was the apple of their eye. She grew up spoilt, playing one parent off against the other. As she practised her role in the world, she knew such entitlement and wrapped her parents around her finger until they were spitting balls of rage. But Ruby always got what she wanted.

She was eleven in February of 1984, and *99 Red Balloons* was number one in the charts. Ruby sang along but didn't care for it much. She might be able to hear it better if her mother would stop nagging.

'I've told you I'm not going to school, and that's final.'

'Yes, you are, madam, if I have to drag you there myself.'

'It's cross country this afternoon. I won't go.'

'PE kit. Now.'

Her mother had picked up two towels from the bathroom floor. She'd been in Ruby's room and had folded all the clothes that littered the carpet around her bed, and she had the blue washing basket perched on her hip.

She'd already stepped off the top stair when Ruby pushed her. There was a lot of noise. The dog was terrified and ran into the kitchen to hide.

Ruby was fascinated. She stood on the landing and watched her mother bouncing off the walls like a ball spat from a pinball flipper. Marcia turned a somersault and landed on her back. One of her legs made an S-bend, and the other was twisted behind her. She was conscious but had a lot of blood coming from her mouth. She made a gurgling sound.

Ruby walked down the stairs counting each one. Having her all twisted up like that didn't take many stairs.

'Get up.'

Her mother stared at her in terror and gurgled.

She was closer, and Ruby saw her head was twisted funny and fell at an unnatural angle. She thought her mother had broken her neck. And then she was unconscious, and Ruby didn't know what to do. She shook her, but her mother wouldn't wake up. She slapped her face, and her head moved. Ruby liked slapping her.

So she did it again.

Now what? She could ring an ambulance. She weighed the pros and cons of whether Dad would come home if she did and make her go to school. It wasn't worth the risk. Her mother was a bitch.

More blood was in her mouth now, and it was going down her throat and choking her. Ruby thought her mum would die, but maybe choking on the blood wasn't enough. She made a cup of coffee with some cold water so it wouldn't burn her throat. They might see that. Marcia hadn't moved when she got back, but Lily, the golden retriever, was beside her, crying and licking her face. Lily knew Mum was in trouble.

'Get away, Lily.' Ruby kicked her, and she yelped and ran into the living room. She poured the coffee into her mother's open mouth and listened to Marcia's gurgling.

'Hi, Mummy.'

Marcia's eyes opened, and she looked startled. Ruby poured the last dregs of the coffee, and the white bits of her mother's eyes went red. She was choking and trying to say a hundred words through her broken mouth—she didn't move.

And Ruby watched her die.

'How did you feel?' Nash asked her fifty years later as she sat across the interview table with hatred for the world in her eyes.

'It was too easy.'

In May of 1985, when she was twelve, Phyllis Nelson's *Move Closer* was number one in the charts. What a load of rubbish that was.

Her dad brought her up on his own for a while. He played the hero single father, and she played her part. 'That poor little girl.' They were a good team. She'd waited to get into trouble over what happened to her mother, but it never came. Her death was a terrible accident. She played her dad like a violin. Like her mother, he rarely refused her anything, but when he did, she didn't like it.

'I need a tenner.'

'What for?'

'The pictures.'

'No.'

It worked for her before, so she saw no reason to change it. However, Dad was bigger, so this time, she helped him down with a bar of Pears soap on the second step from the top. She put a roller skate two steps down from that for good measure.

He saw the skate, and maybe he knew about Marcia at that second. But it was too late. The slippy wet soap had been used and had a snotty viscous slime on the top particular to the brand, but it went unnoticed. He'd twisted to shout at her, and her father was falling.

Ruby ran behind him and pushed him the rest of the way. He went with a bang and a clatter, screaming to the bottom, and then he didn't stop yelling. He wasn't like Mum, who behaved herself and lay still. His head was bleeding, and he had trouble getting his feet underneath him, but he struggled to get upright.

'You monster. Have you gone mad?' he said.

He was using the wall to help him stand.

She hit him with her hockey stick that was by the front door. She hated hockey, and it took an awful lot of hits before he lay still and stopped crying.

'What happened?' Nash barely had to say a word. The story poured out of Pearson like a catharsis.

'I was sent to a foster family first.'

'You didn't go to a young offender's unit?'

'We called them borstal then, Inspector. Yes, I did. but that was later. They knew what I'd done by this point, but I could be very sweet, so they wanted to try and rehabilitate me first. That's what they said, but it was a fat lie. Do you know the only reason they put me with the foster piggies first?'

'No.'

'Because every borstal in the country was full.'

'What happened at the foster home?'

'I huffed, and I puffed, and I blew the house down.'

Pearson sneezed and went into a tic attack. It was alarming, and she jerked around on the chair as though she was a puppet on strings. Nash wondered if she was faking it but stood to catch her if she fell. She came out of the attack, and she looked tired. Ballas coughed and pretended he wasn't there, and Nash asked if she needed a break. Pearson shook her head.

'Answer for the tape, please, Ms Pearson.'

'No. Thank you. I'm fine.'

She drifted into her story. The Bradshaw family could cope. They specialised in troubled kids and knew the score. However, the judge said she was unique and shouldn't be put with other children. It was okay because the Bradshaws didn't have any other care kids at that time.

But that was before Ruby Vance. And in a time before smoke alarms were compulsory.

The couple knew the only way to deal with their special kids was with a strong dose of tough love. Firm but fair. Kind but strong. Never give the little bastards an inch. Nobody had gone up against Ruby before.

They couldn't tell her what to do. Who the hell did they think they were?

It was Christmas week, and Shakin' Stevens was number one.

On Christmas Eve, they had a crisis call from a social worker. There was an abused boy, and they had nowhere to place him. Concerns were expressed about putting him in a house with Connie, but there was nowhere else for him. The inn was full.

The Bradshaws brought the new brat into the house. They joked that Ruby would have to share her Christmas presents. Ruby hadn't developed her sense of humour. She'd spent too much time working on her manipulation powers, and it left other areas of her psyche neglected. Another kid in the house. He was older, fourteen and a moody bastard. Cuckoo in her comfy nest. She couldn't believe it.

She burned the house down that night. The Bradshaws escaped with smoke inhalation, but the teenager died. They lost their house and all their possessions. The hamsters were found curled together in a corner of their cage. The boy died trying to save them, and Connie took time out to be sad that the pets didn't survive. She didn't care about Jamie.

Maybe they threw another kid out of borstal to make way for her, but overloaded or not, the placement in a secure unit was soon found for her that night.

Ruby Vance spent the next five years there. She underwent therapy, and the first lesson she learned was that the sun didn't rise from or set in her backside. She wasn't the centre of anybody's universe. And that little bitch was going to toe the line. Ruby was smart, and she learned fast that she had to behave to get out.

She was so good and excelled at everything—therapy, lessons, and being kind. Ruby Vance was a success story and definitive proof that the system worked. They put her in a halfway house, where she was as good as gold. Never missed a curfew and always did as she was asked.

Her case went back to court on appeal, and after five years, two months and two days, Ruby Vance was free.

She was seventeen. They took her out of town, gave her a new identity and left her with foster parents in Liverpool. Constance Cross—they chose her new name for her, but she didn't mind it—was the perfect foster child, and she spent her last year as a Ward of the State there. Ruby Vance didn't exist, but there was a terrible mix-up with her records. She should never have been allowed into medical school. The name wasn't cross-referenced, and Connie Cross not only got a master's degree but qualified as a therapist in her field. She was good, too.

She dated but didn't kill anybody. And in the course of time, when she was twenty-two, she married Rowan Swift, a thoracic consultant. A year later, they had a little girl, Crystal, who was sick and didn't survive.

Crystal died from leukaemia when she was two years old. And that was unfair because Constance had been good for years. It sent her over the edge. She was angry with Rowan, and they had bitter arguments. The marriage didn't survive either. She was left with nothing but a big empty house and a hole where her emotions should be. She didn't kill Swift, but she planned it in minute detail. It was thwarted because he beat her to the crunch by hanging himself in the garage on their daughter's third birthday.

'You must have been angry,' Nash said.

'Angry? Darling, I was furious.'

'I think that's enough for now. Let's take a break, and we'll reconvene after lunch.'

When they returned to the interview, Ballas had business to attend to elsewhere, and Brown, who was finished with the press, took his place.

Constance was living in Frodsham by this time. She worked in the Rose Cottage Medical Centre, and that's where she met Alma Cullen, one of the receptionists. They were friends, and Connie found somebody she could trust and depend on in Alma.

But for a stupid oversight, the connection would have been made after Dale Butcher was found in the swimming pool when all the guest's records were checked. They pulled Constance Swift's history along with everybody else, and it recorded her living at Frodsham. Alma Cullen's dim-witted neighbour said she'd lived at Chester, several miles from Frodsham, where Swift also lived. That would have been flagged as a match if Marjorie Hodges hadn't given them the wrong place. That tiny error caused another seven deaths.

Connie hadn't killed anybody since she was a kid. Her next murder was when she was thirty-six. Through her work, she visited many nursing homes. They were all dying anyway, and giving them eternal light pleased her. It was a good thing and helped them. She was a kind person. There were lots of them. She overdosed the first one on morphine. She forged one of the nurse's signatures and palmed the blame onto her. But that was too risky.

That's when she practised and perfected her air embolism technique. She did the system a favour and helped many elderly people living their last years in pain and misery. She crossed them over. But she had to leave therapy and Frodsham behind when she went too far and killed a staff member. She got away with it because they never found the needle mark at autopsy. But it made her sphincter twitch, and she realised she was sailing too close to the wind. Alma Cullen had walked in as she was injecting the nurse.

She nearly killed Alma Cullen that day twelve years earlier too, but the imbecile was too stupid to understand what she'd seen. Connie spared her, but only because it was too risky to get rid of her. Alma left the area around that time too.

Connie had to get away. Everything was closing in. She forced her wealthy aunt Hilda to change her will, making Connie her beneficiary. She enjoyed Hilda's agony at losing her only sister after Connie killed her mother. Hilda called her psycho-child and refused to have anything to do with her when the authorities tried to make her take the damaged child. With no other family to leave it to, it would have gone to her by default, anyway. That murder was so unnecessary—but it was enjoyable. Connie took early retirement on the proceeds and moved to Urmston, near Manchester.

And Alma Cullen moved to Barrow-in-Furness to be close to her daughter.

'But I still don't understand why you had to kill Alma Cullen after all that time,' Nash said.

'Bloody *House*.'

'House?'

'House.'

'Bingo?'

'No. The television programme. *House*.'

'I don't understand.'

'Neither did Cullen. She walked in on me as I injected the nurse at that nursing home. Alma didn't know what she was seeing until she watched an episode of *House*. The killer was leaning over somebody with a pillow, about to smother them, and a nurse walked in. The killer turned around in shock. I can tell you. It was definitely a shock when she walked in on me. Apparently, the killer on a stupid programme had the same look on her face as I did twelve years ago. Anyway, it took her a while, but the silly cow put two and two together. She blackmailed me mercilessly for those two years.'

And there they had it—that tiny last piece of the puzzle. The jigsaw piece with somebody's left eye that always goes missing.

Sweet little Alma Cullen, loved by everybody and as vanilla as they come, was a blackmailer.

There was no correspondence between them. Alma turned up on Connie's doorstep out of the blue. For her protection, she'd sent a letter to her solicitor with chapter and verse that she later picked up in person and unopened. She probably got that from a television programme too.

The arrangements were made in person that day. Every first Saturday of the month, they met in Blackpool, halfway between their homes. Alma wasn't an avaricious person, one thousand pounds a month supplemented her pension, and she didn't need more than that.

Connie could afford it and didn't even mind. She admired Cullen's fortitude. They met as blackmailer and victim. But, after Pearson handed her envelope across the café table to Cullen, they'd look at the menu and have lunch together when their business was done. They often went shopping in Primark. They both looked forward to their days out, and Pearson had no desire to kill Cullen because it suited her not to.

Until Alma Cullen did get greedy.

'Oh, Connie, darling. Just a head's up. My daughter's getting married soon. Next month it'll be five thousand, dear.'

She had to go.

'So, you came to Barrow, killed her and booked yourself on a flight to Greece to escape any fallout,' Nash said.

'Yes.'

'What happened, Connie? Why all those unnecessary deaths?'

'Because I loved killing my dear friend Alma. It was exciting. I felt alive for the first time in years. You know what it's like getting old, Inspector Nash. You know how it feels to be unimportant.'

'And that triggered you into a killing frenzy.'

'Yes.'

'Simple as that.'

'Yes.'

'I don't understand how you could inflict those terrible injuries on yourself. How did you find the nerve to bite broken glass and ram your head onto a sharp windowsill?'

'It was hard. Alcohol helped. But it was imperative. Those injuries were the one thing that made you believe my innocence. You believed me when I wrote a few fake notes and said I would be the next victim. But after that and the dead mice, I needed more. As difficult as it was, I had to do it. Otherwise, you'd have caught me.'

'And yet here you are. Caught.'

'Aren't you a clever policeman? Maybe you'll get a medal to hang on your puffed-up chest and your picture in the paper.'

Nash didn't rise to her taunt. 'That hire car came in handy for transporting the bodies.'

'Yes. Bill me for any extra cleaning.'

'Extra cleaning? You transported a load of horribly battered bodies in the boot. In one case, you left Ray Farrell in there for over twenty hours until you could dispose of him. It goes beyond an extra cleaning bill. The car has been impounded.'

Nash had what they needed. A full confession for every one of the murders. He asked a few more questions to tie up the straggling loose ends, but it was over. He was irritated when she was the one to bring the interview to a close. He was going to say he'd decide when they were done. But what was the point?

'I'm tired, Inspector. Is there anything else?'

'No. I think that's everything. Thank you, Ms Pearson. You've been very thorough.'

'Do let me know if I can help you with anything else, won't you?'

'Of course, you'll be the first person I come to.'

'Now then. Is my Jeff waiting for me? Can I see him before you cart me away?'

Nash could have been kind. He didn't have to bite her, but he saw the faces of the victims and wanted to hurt Constance Pearson.

'Jeff? You honestly think he's here?'

'Of course, he's here. He loves me and will stand by me no matter what.'

'You stupid, deluded woman. He's long gone.'

'Gone?'

'Back to England. He never wants to set eyes on you again as long as he lives.'

Pearson had been jolly and animated as she told her story. Nash watched her crumple into herself. He saw somebody who may just pass for a human being turn into nothing in front of his eyes. And he felt the thrill of winning.

'And Ray's gone?'

'You killed him.'

'I didn't think I had. Yes. I remember. It's sad. I liked him, but I couldn't have him coming between us. Jeff will come back for me.'

'Goodbye, Pearson.'

Chapter Thirty-Five

'**L**isten up, team.'

They groaned.

'You look tanned, sir. Been anywhere nice?' Renshaw said.

They all laughed.

It was good to be home.

'Sir,' Bowes said. 'Help a guy out. I lost a lot of money on the betting.'

'Yeah, a whole twenty quid,' Renshaw said.

'All right, Mr Higher Pay Grade.'

'Come on, Bowes. Spit it out. We haven't got all day,' Nash said.

'So, they were running a book.'

'Got that.'

'So, when that Isabel, Cullen's daughter, went out to Greece?' Bowes asked.

'Yes.' They all laughed at Nash's long-suffering expression.

'They reopened the book with 50/50 odds against it being her. Had to be, didn't it?'

'Apparently not.'

'Didn't she have anything to do with it? Two quid's worth, even?'

'Not a thing. She came to see what was going on. Stayed two days and got a flight back.'

'Bummer.'

'Tell you what I don't understand,' Patel said.

'What?'

'The whole illness thing. The man who went out to buy nappies, what was his deal?'

'Ah. Now that's a sensible question. You see, Patel, we wasted days focussing on sick people and those with a disability or hidden ailments. It was fate playing her joker.'

'I don't get you, sir.'

'It had nothing to do with the illnesses. The first half dozen had something wrong with them, so off course, we took that basket and ran with it.'

'It wasn't premeditated that all those people had to be there?'

'No. It was the flight that triggered her. The moment flight BX842 was delayed, Connie Pearson's in-flight experience came down to sticking big red arrows above the passengers' heads.'

'Psychotic old women on the plane. That's another factor to consider next time I book my week in Ibiza.' They all laughed.

'You can't make up the facts, lad.'

Constance Swift was on remand in HMP Bronzefield, awaiting trial. They expected her to receive many concurrent life sentences. The world was safe from her, but hundreds of bad guys would still come. All with their set of secrets and lies.

Nash had got in from Kos at teatime two nights earlier. He was exhausted, and although he was due back at work the next morning at nine, he rang Bronwyn to ask how desperately they needed him. She insisted he took another day off and included Brown in the order. Nash was grateful.

He'd walked in the door with his suitcases, and Lola greeted him and was indignant about being left, even though Hayley Mooney, the station cleaner, had been in to look after her and spoil her every day. He felt tears spring to his eyes when he saw the goodness in a world that often seemed bleak. Hayley had freshened the house from top to bottom for his coming home. There were flowers, with yellow roses, his favourite, in a vase by the front door and more in the lounge. She'd left him a cryptic message on the kitchen table saying *Nanna's stew. Gas mark 4. Forty minutes.* That was so incredibly kind.

His bath had never felt so wonderful, or the food tasted so good. And as for his bed—he bathed, ate, and slept solidly for twelve hours. His traitorous bladder that had him up every four hours had passed out too.

He woke up feeling great. Living on Walney Island, he was minutes from the sea and walked briskly along the headland to his favourite bench. It was at the furthest point, a mile along the path and perched on the end of the land. All that was in front of him was the Irish Sea.

It was different from the one in Greece. That was clear blue. This distant cousin was storm-cloud grey. That was delicate and fragrant. This was furious and turbulent. This one was Nash's arm of the Atlantic Ocean.

In the afternoon, he watched television and did some gardening. He had the rest of the stew from last night and a nice piece of brie that he bought on his way home with a slice of nutty brown bread. He preferred cheese to a sweet dessert.

When there was a knock at the door, he was trying to decide what to do with the rest of his night. People didn't knock at eight in the evening. He had a worried expression on his face as he answered it.

Molly Brown stood on the doorstep in a fluffy brown jacket that stopped above her midriff. She held up a bottle of red.

'Are you going to invite me in? It's bloody Irish Sea out here.'

He laughed and opened the door wide. 'Molly. What on earth are you doing here? How delightful to see you.'

'All right, Dad. You can stop with the creepy old man's voice now. Actually, I came to thank you. Corkscrew?'

'Nice wine. The good stuff that gets you drunk, eh? What are you thanking me for?' He handed her the bottle opener.

'For scoring us, and especially me, an extra day off work. Have you any idea how knackered I was last night?'

'I was the same. I slept the clock around.'

Nash poured wine and led her to the lounge. She grabbed the bottle on her way.

'Don't think you'll get lucky because a girl buys you French wine.'

'Lady, you haven't got the equipment.'

They settled into Nash's comfy armchairs and discussed anything but the case. It was nice to have company, and it made Nash realise how much he wanted to meet somebody. His was often a lonely life. He commented as much to Molly.

'Right, maudlin arse. Give me your phone.'

'I'm done with dating apps.'

'You are not.'

'I can't.'

'Why not?'

'Because of Dave Thorn.'

'What about him?'

'What if he's messaged me?'

'He can't. You said you'd blocked him.'

'I have. But I hate the thought of him messaging me and getting no reply. It was a horrible thing to do. What if he can see that I'm online and I'm not talking to him when he did nothing wrong? I feel bad.'

'Toughen up, sister. You're playing the dating game now. Move on. He will have. I promise you,' Molly said. She passed the phone to Nash to open the app.

They looked and swiped and pulled faces, good and bad.

'People your age are far too old for you.'

'I think that's a compliment.'

'It is. You're not old. Work keeps you young.'

'You keep me young.'

'This one. Kelvin. Forty-nine. Own hair and teeth—it's sad when people get to the point where they say that instead of own house and car, but he's got both of those too. I'm liking him. Tall, handsome, and black.'

'He's gorgeous. He'd never be interested in me. What does he do?'

'He's a solicitor.'

'Do you think he'd reply?'

'Maybe. You're going to the shop before work tomorrow, though.'

'What for?'

'To buy yourself an ego.'

They messaged Kelvin, but he hadn't replied when Molly left. Nash checked his messages five times before he plugged his phone in for the night and went to bed.

The next morning before meeting with his team for an early debrief, Nash had scheduled a fifteen-minute meeting with Conrad Snow to thank him for his help on the case. Nash had bought him a bottle of fine cognac from duty-free and felt that it spoke quality because of all the straw used as decoration around the bottle.

They shook hands. 'You shouldn't have. After all, I'm on a retainer now.'

'They've agreed to payment for you? That's fabulous and went through faster than I expected.'

Nash brought him up to speed on the case. He wasn't Max, but it was like talking to a friend. Any reluctance to listen and be advised on his part was long gone, and while he still didn't believe in what this guy did, he was on board with him doing it.

'Max is pissed with you.'

'Why? What have I done?'

'He says you should have got laid in Greece, but apart from that, you never told him his cat had died.'

It was true. When Max was on his deathbed, Dexter was run over outside his house, and Nash kept it from him.

'Tell him I'm sorry. I thought it was for the best. Are they together now?'

'No. He knew you'd ask. But it doesn't work like that, and he says you're a dickhead for thinking it does.'

'What is it like?'

'He says he'll have to kill you if he tells you that. But they don't walk around with physical forms and sit on clouds playing the harp all day. They are a form of consciousness. They are energy.'

'That's disappointing.'

'Isn't it? I agree. He says you're going to be busy. A new case. He said don't believe anything. Everything in this one is false. Whatever you're told. Turn it on its head and reverse it. Now he's rambling. 35mm film negative. Hall of mirrors. Sleight of hand. Back to front and inside out. He's just spouting phrases at me. Lies and deceit. Faces underwater, and somebody you thought was gone is coming back. That's it. He's left us.'

'I'd like to say that was helpful, but it isn't.'

'Have faith. It will be.'

He went to work that morning with a spring in his step.

'Listen up, everybody. We have a new case.'

Printed in Great Britain
by Amazon

19665708R00214